IMPERIAL WIZARD

ARCANE AWAKENING
BOOK ONE

J. PARSONS

ROYAL GUARD

CHAPTER
ONE

VERDAN'S EYES flew open as he inhaled sharply and instinctively cringed from the expected pain. Pain that had haunted his every waking moment for what seemed like untold ages. Bracing his mind, Verdan began to formulate the spell that would put him back under, but this time, something was different. There was no pain.

Every time Verdan woke from his self-imposed slumber, he recast his spell, sending him back into the long-term stasis he'd devised. He couldn't even remember how many times he'd cast the spell, how many years he'd slept away here in his hideaway.

Still, there was no pain, and that made it all worth it. The sheer bliss of being pain-free was enough to make tears well in his eyes.

A smile crept across his face as Verdan dared to breathe once more, the stale air making him cough and splutter.

"*Aer*," Verdan croaked as he made a soft throwing motion with his right hand and focused on the concept of a fresh breeze.

Overcharging the spell a little, Verdan made sure to freshen the air, not just move it.

Immediately, he felt a slight drain on his energy reserves, as a soft breeze filled the chamber he was in, ruffling his hair and disturbing the dust around him. It was a minor spell, one that used only a single word of power and a straightforward concept, but it was still the first spell he'd been able to cast without being in agonizing pain for a long, long time.

Verdan sat up and simply breathed in the air for a few minutes, recasting the air spell every so often. For the moment, he was content to sit and enjoy his freedom from the curse that had driven him to this extreme solution. In truth, he hadn't known this would work.

The stasis spell he used was one he had created himself, but even so, it was inaccurate enough that he didn't know how long each casting lasted. He'd cast it the first time not knowing if it would be minutes, months, or years that he would sleep.

For an average person, such an open-ended spell would be worthless. For a man suffering under a death curse from a powerful hex witch, a curse that was designed to torture the recipient until they killed themselves, open-ended oblivion had been quite appealing, really.

Ironically, it was only due to the sadistic nature of the curse that he'd survived. If it had started at full strength, he would have never been able to finish creating the spell. Instead, it had started weak, gaining in power each day and causing more and more pain until he couldn't take it any more.

The whole thing had been a race against time, one that Verdan had barely won.

Still, he'd survived. That was what mattered. The first thing to check was how long Verdan had been asleep. The war had been in full swing when he'd been cursed, and he couldn't help but wonder what he would find when he emerged once more.

It didn't really matter to him which side won. It wasn't like there was much difference between the two sides. One was led by a self-named Wizard-King, and the other by the latest in a line of Wizard-Emperors. One was new and different, the other as old as recorded memory. It was more a matter of siding with friends and family than the political aspect for someone at his power level.

Feeling a little more in control of himself, Verdan pulled himself up into a sitting position, groaning as his protesting muscles exerted themselves. A quick check of himself was enough to ensure that everything was working, just weak.

Sighing and leaning back against the wall for a moment, Verdan simply enjoyed the lack of pain, enjoyed feeling like his mind was his own once more.

Verdan was a simple researcher, a Wizard of moderate power. He wanted to do his own thing and not be beholden to any larger powers. Hopefully, the war was over, and he could finally get a chance to claim some land somewhere and kick back for a while. The thought of relaxing and retiring from everything for a few years was an enticing one, but first, he needed to get up off the floor.

"Okay, enough woolgathering, up we go. *Disir*," Verdan muttered to himself, bracing himself on the nearby wall and getting to his feet as he conjured a pale orb of light in the palm of his hand.

The soft illumination revealed the room well enough that he could look over the area in which he'd slept so many years away. It was an emergency bolt-hole he'd made a few years earlier that was fifteen foot square, with a hidden entrance and some basic supplies.

Well, a few years before his first cast of the stasis spell, anyway.

The storage box containing the supplies was actually the original recipient of the stasis spell that Verdan had used on himself. He'd been working on a way to store perishable materials in the long term. Little did he know at the time that he'd be using an unstable variant of the spell on himself.

Shaking his head, Verdan examined the box and smiled in satisfaction. The Aether construct that had been regulating the spell was still functioning. Breaching the seal of the box, Verdan reabsorbed the Aether of the construct absently as he rummaged through its contents.

The first things Verdan took was a clean set of clothing and his staff. Picking up the six-foot length of ebon wood, he put the soft orb of light he'd conjured atop its end, fixing it in place with an exertion of his will.

With the room lit up nicely, he started to get changed, shedding the loose robe he'd slept in. The new clothing wasn't anything special, just a tunic, loose trousers and a dark green cloak with a series of pockets on the interior. His favorite cloak had been ruined by a nasty acid attack just a few days before he'd been cursed. Hardly enough time to replace it before he'd had to seal himself away.

While it wasn't a huge inconvenience for him, this new cloak didn't have any sigils on the interior, leaving him without one of his primary defenses. It would also be a hard one to replace. He'd have to find the same enchanter if he wanted the same effects, and even then, that wasn't guaranteed.

Still, the war should have ended by now. He doubted anyone would remember him. Verdan was a capable researcher and a decent Wizard, but he was hardly an archmage or a prodigy.

Unfortunately, it was a similar situation with the staff. Verdan had broken the original one when he defeated the husband of the Witch who'd cursed him. The man had been a powerful Wizard himself, and though Verdan had won, it had been a closer call than he would have liked.

He'd been cursed not long after that battle, and a new staff had been the last thing on his mind. All of which meant that Verdan had only been able to store his backup staff. An annoying issue, but not a huge problem.

This equipment was only to get him to a town or a city. Once he was back in civilization, he could buy proper replacements.

He had a small pouch of coins and gems in his cloak, enough to cover such an expense. It was all that was left of his life's savings. Verdan had done a lot of theoretical research on stasis spells, but getting the time and assistance needed to create a new ritual from scratch had been expensive.

A good mage was never out of work for long, though, so he had no concerns about getting more.

"*Agora*," Verdan gestured to the wall with his staff, visualizing a door opening as he cast the spell.

A part of the wall that looked identical to the rest swung out and away from him, letting in both blinding sunlight and a very welcome breeze of crisp air. The light made Verdan blink blearily, and he stopped supplying the small gray orb at the top of his staff with magic, the magelight disappearing a moment later.

Walking forward with a touch of anticipation, Verdan emerged from his chamber and found himself standing on a stone ledge halfway up the side of a cliff overlooking the endless blue of the ocean.

Squawking birds and the crash of waves against rock gave the whole sight a rather relaxing ambience, one only highlighted by the salty tang of the sea air.

It was almost a picturesque location, beautiful and pristine. The problem was that it wasn't the landscape he'd left behind.

He'd picked a nice cliff near a small village that he'd been to before, but the closest water had been a small lake. There should have been miles of landscape between this cliff and the ocean. Just how much had changed while he was asleep?

"*Hefan raf*," Verdan intoned, using one of his favorite spells as he stepped off the edge of the cliff.

Small bands of compressed air wrapped around his body as he slowly descended through the air, holding him aloft as he directed himself down to the narrow strip of land at the base of the cliff. The water lapped gently at the shore as his feet touched the ground, and despite the general anxiety he was feeling at the change, he couldn't help but smile at the pleasant scene before him.

The steady thump of the end of his staff hitting the rocky ground measured out his pace as he walked along the narrow shoreline and took the nearest path inland.

He didn't recognise anything around here; nothing looked the same at all, but the path he'd found seemed well-trodden. Hopefully, it would lead somewhere. The best result would be civilization of some description, but only time would tell.

Setting off down the path, Verdan eyed his surroundings, taking in as much as he could as he looked for any sort of landmark or similarity to what he remembered of the area. Nothing seemed quite right, though.

Verdan was starting to wonder just how long he had slept for. Every time he'd awoken, he'd cast the stasis spell again with every iota of magic he could command, but Verdan wasn't even certain how many times he'd done that. The whole experience was a blur.

A pulse of dark energy from somewhere to the north pulled him out of his musings on how long his spell may have lasted.

Dropping into a fighting stance and raising his staff defensively on instinct, Verdan extended his awareness out into his surroundings, catching a second pulse as it rippled past him. North-east.

"Damn it all," Verdan cursed as he set off at a jog toward the source of energy.

Despite the time that may have passed, he was still a representative of the Grym Imperium.

His oaths as an Imperial Wizard bound him to investigate immediately. Dark magic was a temptress that seduced even petty dabblers further into depravity than they could possibly imagine. There weren't many duties that a Wizard had to the empire, but dealing with dark magic was in the top few.

"*Hast*," Verdan barked out as he started to pick up the pace, air whipping past him as his spell gave him more speed.

Thankfully he'd not cast much since awakening. He could afford a small enhancement spell like this, and still be able to throw some battle magic around if need be. There were benefits to being a generalist like Verdan; the main one, in this case, being that he had a wide range of spells and effects to draw on without forcing something to work.

Two more pulses of energy washed over him as he honed in on their source, each one making his hair stand on end and unsettling him a little bit more. There was no reason to be projecting energy like this; any Wizard worth his salt would do exactly as Verdan was now.

It only invited destruction.

The implication that they could do something like this with impunity scared Verdan. Perhaps the Imperium had long since moved away from the area, though—that would explain it. Regardless, it didn't change his duty right now.

Rocky cliffs and bracken gave way to a light woodland as he closed in on the source of the magic, slowing his pace to a light jog while keeping his enhancement spell active. The main focus of the spell was his speed and endurance, but there was some carry-over to reaction time as well, a useful bonus when going into a potentially hostile situation alone.

The dark magic was like a lodestone, drawing him in as the woods thickened, and he began to hear guttural chanting. The words were unknown, but the language was one he recognised as a variant on the Infernal tongue. Abyssal speech mixed with dark magic usually meant ritual summoning or sacrifice, for power or favor, sometimes both.

Slowing down to move as stealthily as he could through the undergrowth, Verdan soon found himself at the edge of a clearing filled with a vision straight out of one of his nightmares.

Several buildings were haphazardly constructed in the clearing, their odd angles and strange geometry marking them as something no human would build. Among the buildings were several dozen humanoid figures dancing around a central altar dominated by a blood-stained stone slab.

Verdan didn't need to see the fine details to know what he would find.

This was a ritual sacrifice set-up, one that he remembered well from the last time he encountered the Cyth. He'd been an apprentice then, only able to fetch help to exterminate the creatures and rescue their captives.

Not now, though—now he had the power to save anyone caught by these disgusting things.

The Cyth were creatures twisted and corrupted by the foul magics they practiced, the unholy creatures they worshiped granting their blessings while leaving their mark on both their soul and flesh. There were countless types of Cyth, with new variants constantly developing.

What a Cyth worshiped and what they practiced would shape the creature's form, granting them more power over time as their form was suffused with abyssal energy.

Thankfully, it looked like all the creatures were Cyth Lai, with only one Cyth Bayne leading the ritual. A Bayne was a higher-order monstrosity capable of wielding the dark energies that filled it.

Usually, any Bayne would hide its presence for fear of being located by anyone searching for dark magic. It would never conduct a ritual like this without at least a dozen more like it backing it up.

A Cyth Bayne had the same magical prowess as a Wizard who was finishing their apprenticeship at the Imperial Academy. While that was nothing to sneeze at, it was also easy prey for a squad of guardsmen with proper backup.

Focusing on the current problem, Verdan took a moment to survey the clearing in more detail, noting the apparent age of the buildings, and that only one of them had guards outside it.

The guards were stationed off to one side, next to a dark patch of ground that could easily be an underground cell to keep prisoners. No doubt they were keeping their captives below-ground and bringing them up one-by-one to be sacrificed.

Given the fresh blood on the ground around the altar, and the eagerness of the surrounding Cyth Lai, Verdan knew he couldn't wait any longer.

It was time to act.

CHAPTER
TWO

CIRCLING the Cyth clearing took several precious minutes, each one bringing the moment that the Bayne would sacrifice the next victim that much closer.

Thankfully, Verdan knew that this type of ritual would take some time, so he had a few moments to prepare. Still, he didn't know how fresh those bloodstains were. Those few moments might expire at any moment.

It also didn't help that some Cyth were wandering in and out of the clearing, making it that much harder to get to the other side without being noticed.

A rustling from up ahead made Verdan freeze mid-step. A pair of Cyth were emerging from behind a small thicket of trees, dragging a dead deer.

Both Cyth were humanoid, with long curling horns sweeping up from their foreheads and exaggerated bestial features, like goats. Likely they had once been human, but they could also have been animals corrupted by the energies given off by a ritual like this. It was hard to tell, and it also didn't make much difference at this point.

There was no going back once they were like this. Abyssal energy was tenacious once it had a hold of someone.

Waiting for them to drag the deer well past him, Verdan crept through the undergrowth until he was at the rear of the building with the two guards. He could see now that there was a definite passage leading underground, right where those two guards he'd seen before were posted.

The entrance was built into the side of the building, and looked to be little more than a packed earth tunnel. The guards were bestial humanoids, just like the first two he'd seen, but these had filed down their claws and were holding spears that were tipped with a jagged blade meant to draw as much blood as possible.

"*Aer*," Verdan whispered, visualizing a gust thumping the door on the front of the building so that it shook in its frame. The spell hit with an echoing bang and a loud rattle of wood.

The abrupt noise cut through the air, and Verdan smiled to himself as he saw it had caught the attention of the two Cyth.

The guards looked at each other before turning and heading that way. The two Cyth spread out slightly, leveling their spears as they looked around the front of the building, trying to find the source of the sound.

With both guards gone, Verdan edged out of his hiding place, holding his breath and treading softly as he kept low and made his way to the tunnel. With a final look around, he headed down into the darkness.

"*Disir*," Verdan conjured the softest magelight he could, affixing it to his staff as he held it before him as both a makeshift lantern and a ward against danger.

The soft gray light drove back the darkness, revealing a fifteen- to twenty-foot long tunnel that led to a wooden door.

As he came closer, Verdan saw that a heavy iron bolt was on his side of the door, sealing it closed. The bolt mechanism was covered in rust and looked poorly-maintained. Any attempt to open it would be dangerous without precautions being taken.

The last thing he wanted was to draw the guards down here with a squealing door bolt. Not when he was voluntarily putting himself in their prison.

"*Tawel*." Verdan split his attention further, portioning off a part of it, as he'd been trained to back when he'd been in the academy.

It was a difficult mental juggling act to maintain multiple spells, but it was essential for any Wizard who wanted to survive a battle. His latest spell formed a bubble of sound suppression around his staff, dampening any sound in the local area.

Reaching out and pulling the bolt across, Verdan heard a faint squeak, little more than a murmur. The resistance from the handle as he pulled it across let him guess just how loud it would have been otherwise. It was definitely a good job he cast that particular spell.

Keeping both spells active, Verdan gripped the handle and heaved back on the door, slowly dragging it back across the floor to let the light from his staff enter the room beyond.

A number of muffled moans and groans greeted his ears as he stepped inside, the suppression spell making them into soft whispers of pain. A dozen or so people were bound and laying wearily on the floor. His entrance woke them, but they were unable to do anything other than recoil from the sudden light in the room.

"Help, please, help us," one of the people closest to him cried out, the spell muffling it down to a hoarse whisper.

To Verdan's relief, they were speaking Imperial Common, just with a strange accent that he didn't recognise. It looked like they had won the war after all, not that it really mattered.

Putting his finger to his lips to silence them, Verdan leaned his staff against the wall next to the door. Binding the suppression spell to the staff as well, Verdan walked to the other side of the room, where he was outside the area of effect.

 Kneeling at the first person he came to, Verdan saw a young man with a bruised face and a pale, unhealthy look. Giving him a quick once-over, Verdan saw no obvious injuries that would explain his weakness.

Verdan's gaze settled on the ropes binding the man, and he examined them more closely. Using his Aether sense, Verdan could feel that they were made from what looked to be threaded Cyth hair and imbued with a healthy dose of Abyssal energy.

The presence of such a concentration of corruptive energy against the skin would cause discomfort, pain, and illness over time. Not to mention how it would interfere with Aether manipulation and spellcasting.

The Imperial Academy used a similar situation to teach Wizards how to cast when being afflicted with outside energy. Verdan would be able to cast when restrained like this, but it would be an intensely unpleasant experience.

"Thank you, Lord Sorcerer, gods bless you," the young man whispered in an odd accent as Verdan undid the knot on the ropes and threw them to one side, absently wiping his hand on his cloak as he did.

"You can thank me by freeing the others. You should regain your strength now that you're away from the corruption." Verdan gave the man a gentle push to one of the others as he moved to the next person himself. The man had given him a strange look in return as Verdan had spoken, likely finding his accent just as odd.

One by one, all of the bound people were freed from their restraints. It was only as Verdan started to walk back to his staff that he saw a final form curled in the corner, covered in filth.

Each of the men and women he'd freed so far had blonde hair. The shades varied, but the basic coloring was the same. From what he could see, this last person seemed to have darker hair, though that could well be due to the filth that was caking them.

Still, the difference piqued his interest, as did the fact that none of the others was moving to their aid.

"No, Master Sorcerer," one of the liberated men stepped in front of him with a worried expression, as Verdan started towards the corner. "She's a Witch; if she's released in this situation, her powers could get us all killed."

The apprehension in the man's whispered words stunned Verdan. He'd fought against Witches in the past, but by and large, they were beloved by the common folk, being far more in touch with the land and nature than the average Wizard.

He also had no idea what a 'Sorcerer' was, and this was the second person to use the term, but now wasn't the time to argue semantics.

Fixing the man with a stern gaze, Verdan waited until he was out of the way before walking over to the Witch. She was beaten and bloody, had clearly been tortured by the Cyth, and was damaged in mind and body.

Checking her over as gently as he could, Verdan scowled in distaste as he found three different bindings of Cyth hair—one around her neck, one around her wrists, and the final one around her ankles.

Concerned for her health, Verdan moved her hair to check and cursed softly. Faint black lines could be seen around her neck, a visible mark of the corruption eating away at her from the inside.

She was at the borderline of what he could save. Anything more, and he'd have been forced to kill her himself.

Burning the bindings free with a slight application of fire-aspected Aether, Verdan took a deep breath and centered himself. He needed to act now if he wanted to save her.

"*Iacha*," Verdan spoke softly, holding a hand to her face as he envisioned a flow of healing and soothing Aether passing into her from his hand, isolating and purging the corruption.

Thankfully, the corruption had just begun taking hold, so he could destroy it before it became permanent. With that dealt with, Verdan used a second spell to clean off the worst of the filth and the dried blood, which would hopefully stop infection from setting in.

A wave of exhaustion hit Verdan as the spell took hold. The drain on his magic from this one spell was equal to everything else he'd cast since he'd woken up. He knew why, of course; it was his poor visualization, mixed with a broad effect against hostile magic. Thankfully, Verdan had the Aether to brute-force the situation like this. Otherwise, the witch would be dead.

Even so, the drain he felt was much higher than he'd expected. Turning his focus inward, to where his Aether was concentrated, Verdan realized that he hadn't circulated his Aether at all since he'd awoken.

Even worse, his gathering spiral had decayed and broken down without his oversight, putting his Aether draw-rate at that of a non-Wizard.

The gathering spiral was an essential thing that all Wizards were trained to do, to draw in Aether. After a time, it became second nature; he could only blame the confusion he'd felt at waking for not starting it again.

The problem was that, over time, the spiral would decay and lose its coherence, so it needed to be maintained at all times for the best efficiency.

Turning his mind's eye inward, Verdan started to push and pull on the ambient Aether in his body, sending it moving throughout him in a very loose spiral that culminated in the core of his being.

By pulling the magic from his extremities into the center, he would create a gradient that would help draw fresh Aether in from the environment more quickly, while also focusing more Aether in his core for use.

With the spiral created, it was a simple matter to partition another part of his mind to keep it running. When he had more time, he would work to compress and tighten the circle, which would speed the flow of magical energy and improve the benefits he received.

He was in no danger of running out of stored Aether, but it would be foolish to go any further without setting up at least the basic form of the spiral.

"Thank you," a soft voice whispered, drawing him back to the world around him as he looked down into the blue eyes of the Witch, his hand still on her cheek as she blinked blearily.

"Not at all. Rest for a few minutes and recover," Verdan said kindly, helping her sit up before moving back toward the huddle of people at the center of the room. "Now, who here knows how to fight?"

"I do," one of the men stepped forward, his face and arms bearing a multitude of scars, fresh and old alike. "I don't have the skills you do, but I am a fire enhancer."

"I can fight as well," a woman said from the back of the group before Verdan could answer. "I am an air and water manipulator."

"Frankly, I don't understand what any of that means. Please explain." Verdan said, confused in the extreme by their statements. There were lots of ways to manipulate magical energy, but the terms they were using were foreign to him.

"It means we can channel the elemental forces of the world through Essence, like you," the first man said with a frown that was mirrored on the faces of everyone else present.

"Okay. Well, you two do what you can do when we head up. Try to coordinate with each other to be as effective as possible," Verdan said with a shrug, noting that their confused looks only got more pronounced at his instructions.

Suppressing a building headache, Verdan turned to the remainder of the group. "Right—do any of you know how to wield a weapon at all?"

"We are traveling guards. We've got some training and can brawl a bit," Two men stepped forward, their faces alike enough that they had to be brothers. Verdan could see the muscles on their arms and the strength in their builds. They'd do for what he had planned.

"Why didn't you announce yourselves when I asked for fighters?" These people weren't making his life easy. There was no time for him to be repeating himself to get the information he needed.

"We're not Sorcerers. We have no Essential Essence," one of the brothers said with an embarrassed expression. The way he said it was almost as though he was ashamed, which made no sense to Verdan at all. He'd known these people for mere minutes, and he already wanted to pull his hair out.

"Right, moving on—what are your names?"

"Tim and Tom, Lord Sorcerer."

"Of course, what else would they be? Great. Okay, you two stay behind me when we head up, I'll get you a weapon each, and then you guard the rest of them while we three forge a path out of here." He gestured to the two self-proclaimed Sorcerers as he did. Noting how everyone but those two seemed relieved, while the two Sorcerers looked more confused than ever.

Before he could start to work out what issue they had with his plan, the door to the room swung open, and one of the Cyth guards walked in. Its eyes went wide, and it shouted something that was, thankfully, muffled by the suppression spell on the staff.

The Cyth's moment of shock was enough for Verdan to throw an arc of compressed air at it with a slash of his hand, "*Aer!*"

A crescent of shaped air flew across the room like a chill wind, slicing the Cyth Lai's throat with a spray of black blood. His spell-enhanced reactions had let him act before it could call for aid.

There was a tense pause that hung for a few moments before the fire Sorcerer rushed forward and claimed the spear that the Cyth had been holding, picking it up and grasping it with the easy competence of a veteran fighter.

Verdan had intended to equip the two brothers with the first weapons they came across, but he wasn't going to argue at this point.

"Grab the body, drag it in, keep it out of sight," Verdan ordered the brothers, who quickly scurried over to grab the body and pull it into the room.

As soon as they were clear, Verdan shut the door once more and motioned everyone back. There was an opportunity here.

The captives inched forward anxiously, but obeyed Verdan's command and didn't come too close. He couldn't blame them, really; he could only imagine how desperate they were to get out.

Clearing his mind, Verdan waited patiently by the door with another spell primed and ready to go. His patience was rewarded when the door opened a minute later, and the second guard angrily stomped in. A point-blank blast of pressurized air ripped most of its throat out and sent it to join its comrade on the floor.

Snatching up the spear it had carried, and throwing it to Tim, Verdan turned to the others. "Tom, you get the next spear. Everyone else, it's time to go, but I want at least two of you carrying the Witch, understood?" He glowered at them until two people moved to gather up the Witch's limp form.

She'd lapsed back into unconsciousness almost immediately after Verdan had healed her. Not surprising, given how much corruption had been forcibly pushed into her body. Hopefully, she'd recover quickly.

Leading the group out of the room and starting up the tunnel to the surface, Verdan kept a watch for any more Cyth that might appear, the two Sorcerers a step behind him as he advanced.

They almost made it to the surface without issue. Verdan was all of ten feet from the entrance when two Cyth stepped inside, their forms framed by the daylight behind them.

The speed spell from earlier was still enhancing Verdan's reactions, so he snapped off a quick air spell at them before they could respond. A spike of compressed air hit the Cyth on the right, drilling straight through its chest.

A moment later, a spear flew past him to catch the second Cyth in the chest, cutting it off before it could call for help.

The fire Sorcerer dashed forward to retrieve his weapon, moving with the kind of speed that only magic could provide.

A small voice in the back of Verdan's mind noted that he hadn't heard the man utter any Words of Power to cast a spell, but now wasn't the time to ponder such things.

A few hurried steps brought him to the lip of the tunnel, letting him see that the surrounding Cyth had started to realize what was happening and raised the alarm.

"*Niwlla*," Verdan spoke, letting the sound suppression and mage-light effects fade away as he held a hand out and released a vast plume of fog into the area.

The heavy fog swirled about as it flowed out to cover the exposed area between the buildings. It rose a good fifteen feet in the air before Verdan released the spell. Once he did, it started to settle, dropping down and spreading out beyond the initial area.

Spells like this had a high cost initially, but now that it was in place, he was free to move his attention elsewhere. For now, he would just keep his personal speed effect active. Verdan wanted to conserve Aether where he could.

"*Aer torr*," Verdan used a slight variant on the spell for the arc of compressed air. This one was sharper and packed more of an edge to it.

He always felt odd saying that there was an edge to air, but it was true nonetheless.

The arc of air rippled out through the fog, sending a surge of billowing mist out as it went. It formed whirling vortices in a frankly beautiful effect. Interactions between spells were always fascinating, but unfortunately, now wasn't the time.

The dark outline of the horned Cyth Lai he'd aimed at crumpled as the projectile struck it, other nearby Cyth crying out in alarm as they saw it fall.

"Now, move!" Verdan urged the others, motioning in the opposite direction that he'd sent the spell. The treeline was directly behind the tunnel entrance. If they could reach it, they would have a better chance of getting away.

The two Sorcerers were already on the move. The man was heading forward at a more-normal speed than before. His eyes were always on the move, however, and he moved to engage a pair of Cyth that came charging around the side of the building.

The woman, meanwhile, was moving forward in a more studied and careful manner as she made a series of gestures, and Verdan felt a foreign power cut him off from a section of the fog he'd conjured.

Before he could do anything, a fifteen-foot diameter area of fog around her condensed into a tight sphere, obscuring her completely but leaving a hole in their cover. Several Cyth caught sight of them and started charging their way, braying hunting calls as they came.

The area around them was thinner now, making it easier to see them and increasing the rate at which the whole fog cloud would decay. She had effectively ruined Verdan's plan to get away without a big fight.

The dense cloud of fog that represented the woman started to steadily move away from them, seemingly abandoning them without a second thought.

Verdan cursed her mentally but had no attention to spare right now. More and more Cyth were responding to the hunting calls from the few that had seen them. The male Sorcerer was still locked in combat, leaving just Verdan and the brothers to protect the rest.

"*Tyn!*" Verdan made a grasping motion toward a nearby Cyth, yanking it forward and across the ground to him. "*Aer!*" A blast of pressurized air sent it crashing down as it tried to rise, clawed hands grasping at its throat as it dropped the spiked club it had held.

Cracking the creature across the temple with his staff to knock it out, Verdan kicked the club over to Tom, motioning for the brothers to start taking people toward the trees. At least both of the brothers were armed now.

A flash of darkness out the corner of his eye made Verdan whirl and pull his staff up in front of him, "*Ast!*"

A blue half-dome appeared in front of him, rippling in place as a lance of dark energy slammed into it and exploded in a cloud of inky darkness.

The Cyth Bayne had joined the fray.

Holding the shield up, Verdan kept himself between the civilians and the rapidly-organizing Cyth. A few more streaks of darkness came out from the thinning fog, but they lacked any real degree of accuracy.

Two of the attacks struck Verdan's shield, while the rest flew off too far to one side to pose a threat. He could only hope that one hit the fleeing Sorcerer in the back. It would serve her right for abandoning them.

Verdan kept in between the Cyth and the captives as they moved further back, but his attack spells and all of the movement had banished the majority of the fog. He could see the Bayne's slightly-taller and more muscular form now. Its every step was announced by the rattle of bone charms that hung from its horns.

Half-a-dozen Cyth came charging from one side just as the last of the group was entering the treeline. Verdan turned to attack them, but was forced back in position as the Bayne unleashed a series of faint, sickly green projectiles at the people he could see.

Each projectile had only a small amount of power behind it and would do little to Verdan's shield, but it could badly injure or cripple one of the people he guarded.

The group of ex-hostages realized that Verdan couldn't protect them from the oncoming creatures and immediately panicked. The two holding the Witch threw her to the ground and ran, almost all of the others doing likewise as they scattered from the oncoming Cyth like rabbits before a fox.

The only two to hold their ground were Tim and Tom, their faces pale but their expressions determined as they stood their ground. Verdan wished that he could help further, but the Bayne was still releasing a seemingly endless series of weak lance attacks, keeping Verdan's attention entirely on him.

CHAPTER
THREE

EVERYTHING WAS FALLING APART. The brothers were about to be overrun by a pack of Cyth if Verdan didn't do anything. The captives had scattered to the winds, and Verdan was too busy blocking the attacks from the Bayne to do much else.

He couldn't even use a static shield to block the Bayne's attacks. The Cyth was sending arcing and looping bolts of Abyssal energy that came in from multiple angles, requiring Verdan to continuously move and adjust his shield.

Part of him wanted to stop shielding the captives, to let them suffer for abandoning him so easily, especially the two who had thrown the Witch to the ground. He knew it was just their fear, though, and he couldn't blame them for that. Not like he could with the female Sorcerer who'd fled immediately.

"Ha!" A wordless exclamation came from behind him.

Verdan risked a glance back to see the fire Sorcerer hurl his spear with enough strength to impale one of the Cyth and send it flying backwards.

Barely pausing to make sure it was dead, the man charged into the remainder of the pack and delivered a flurry of blows to a second creature, finishing with a right hook to its face.

Verdan was certain that the final punch had been enhanced by magic. It certainly seemed too powerful a hit not to be. The Cyth reeled back from the hit, shaking its head in disorientation.

Taking advantage of its weakness, the Sorcerer swiftly darted in and delivered an elbow to its gut as he wrested its spear free from its grasp. Dancing back and away from its pitiful attempt to catch him, he cut the Cyth Lai down with its own weapon.

Two Cyth stopped their charge when they heard the cries of their brethren and doubled back to attack the Sorcerer. The remaining two, however, continued to close in and exchange blows with the brothers.

Thankfully, both the men had clearly fought monstrous foes before, as they held firm and met the Cyth with weapons raised and ready.

The powerfully-built Cyth were physically stronger than the two humans, knocking them back with the strength of their impacts before swinging wildly at them.

Tim and Tom were doing their best, but it was only a matter of time before they were struck, and their lack of armor would make that a deadly proposition.

Feeling the urgency of the situation, Verdan tried to judge how far the captives had fled and whether he could afford to shift his focus from pure defense to fighting back. He needed to deal with the Bayne so he could help the others.

It was a risk, as he couldn't be entirely sure that the captives were far enough away, but he was burning through his reserves steadily, and his gathering spiral was nascent as best; he would need to spend hours in meditation to build it up further before it would be useful.

There were two parts to casting spells: the Words of Power and the visualization. Words of Power drained magic as they were spoken, but in turn, reduced the visualization requirement as they carried their own concept with them.

A two-word spell was stronger than a single word, and a three-word spell was stronger again, but it had to be the correct three words, with the correct visualization, to make the concepts work.

Wizard duels were usually lost due to mental fatigue more than running out of magic.

As if to punctuate his thoughts, the Cyth Bayne sent out a curling spread of Abyssal darts that required Verdan to rapidly move his shield in order to catch them all. It was a strain to do, and it reinforced that he had to change tactics.

Verdan had spent the last few years fighting in a civil war that had torn the entirety of civilization apart. He'd survived battles that had left more-powerful Wizards dead and buried.

It wasn't a ridiculous capacity for magic or a vast knowledge of words of power that had kept him alive. No, he'd survived through sheer stubbornness and knowing when to use powerful spells and when not to. This was one of those moments.

The fog had all but dissipated now, lingering only a few inches on the ground and adding an eerie atmosphere to the battle as whorls of fog followed each spell projectile.

Verdan had a clear vision of the Cyth Bayne as it marshaled the remaining Cyth Lai and started towards him. With each step, it reached out and made a throwing motion, vile Abyssal energy coalescing in its claw before streaking out towards Verdan.

The first two strikes shattered against his shield with faint hissing sounds, the other two going straight past him in the direction of the fleeing captives. Verdan's eye twitched, but he deliberately made no move to stop them.

The Bayne cocked its head in surprise at Verdan's abrupt inaction. Confusion played across its face before its eyes widened in horror as Verdan dropped his shield and raised a palm towards them.

"*Grym thanr bel*!" Verdan barked each word as clearly as he could, feeling the strain on his magic as each word drained more of his reserves.

Mortals were not meant to speak the words of power.

Doing so was uncomfortable at best, and downright agony at worst. A three-word spell wasn't the worst he'd ever experienced, but it made his throat feel like he'd swallowed tiny shards of glass.

The last word of power left his lips as a final thrum of energy concentrated in Verdan's palm, and a small bead of blue flame formed before shooting out toward the Bayne and its minions. The bead swelled as it traveled, becoming an orb that expanded out to around three feet across.

The Bayne clapped its hand in front of it with a panicked expression, a thin dome of inky black magic forming in front of it a moment before the orb of fire impacted it.

First, there was the crack of the explosion, then the roar of flames as the ball smashed through the Bayne's shield and exploded in a huge ball of crimson flame, sweeping out past the Cyth to scorch the ground all around them.

A wave of heat and flame rushed toward Verdan as he conjured his shield once more to protect him from the worst of it. A small amount of hot air and flame wrapped around the shield to hit him, but he was at the very edge of the explosion, so it was minimal at best.

Verdan would normally want to be further away for an empowered spell like that, but he was having a bad day, and the Bayne had truly pissed him off.

The Cyth hadn't fared so well. They had taken the full force of the blast, and only charred corpses remained. The slight protection of its shield meant that the Bayne was only mildly charred but still very dead.

Still, Verdan took a moment to put the reinforced butt of his staff through the head of each of the Cyth, just in case. Once burnt, twice shy.

The sounds of fighting from behind him had fallen off as the others defeated the remaining Cyth Lai.

Verdan turned in time to see Tim plunging his spear into the chest of the last one standing, driving it up against a tree to hold it still while Tom crushed its skull with a heavy blow.

"Everyone okay?" Verdan called out as he took a look around for any more Cyth.

"Yes," the fire Sorcerer called back as he stalked amongst the corpses, occasionally stabbing down to ensure that the Cyth were truly dead. A sensible precaution in Verdan's eyes; likely the Sorcerer was a veteran of some conflict as well.

The brothers were slow to respond at first, making Verdan look back to see them standing guard over the unconscious Witch. Neither of them seemed in bad shape, they had a few cuts and swiftly darkening bruises, but that was it.

Considering the poor start to their escape, they'd done quite well for themselves.

Everyone else was long gone by this point, which left Verdan with mixed feelings. He was happy not to be responsible for a large group of people, but he felt at fault for not making their rescue smoother and less dangerous.

Maybe if he'd attacked the Cyth immediately, things would have been different. Sighing heavily, he stopped himself from going too far into what he could have done and walked back to the others.

"Do any of you know where we are?" Verdan asked, glancing around at the unfamiliar land as they all gathered together next to the unconscious Witch.

From the change in the landscape around his resting place, Verdan had a sinking feeling that any places he was familiar with had most likely changed completely.

"Aye, Lord Sorcerer," Tim said hesitantly. Both brothers were around six feet tall with brown hair and eyes, Tim running to a more lithe build while Tom was more muscular by far.

"We're south of Hobson's Point, one of the old enclaves that got hit pretty heavily in the last Rising. We were raised there as kids, so we recognise the area. I can get us there without too much of an issue. We just have to head toward the mountains." Tim pointed to a distant white peak above the treeline, its surface marred by multiple giant craters.

"Damn, so far away," the Sorcerer cursed, rubbing his face and wincing as he touched a fresh gash across his cheek.

"Are we close enough to get there for nightfall and find some shelter?" Verdan asked, glossing over the Sorcerer part for now. Too much had changed from his time. He was feeling a little lost and out of his depth.

Verdan knew his spells were out of the ordinary from the looks they were giving him, but he didn't want to add to that by also showing his ignorance and questioning things.

He'd already concluded that something had drastically changed while he had been in stasis, or he'd been locked away for a lot longer than he'd expected. Perhaps both.

"Yes, if we move quickly," Tim said after a pause, his eyes flicking to the Witch as he spoke.

"We're not leaving her behind," Verdan said firmly. He didn't know how much things might have changed, but Witches weren't their enemies, as far as he was concerned.

Besides, it would be nice to have another magic user to hand if she woke up, and at least he knew how Witches worked, unlike Sorcerers.

"I'll carry her. We'll not fall behind," the fire Sorcerer spoke up, as he stepped forward and gathered her up with ease.

His movements had a casual strength that seemed beyond what Verdan expected for him, even with his muscular frame. Just one more thing to add to his list of discrepancies.

"Okay then, lead the way, Tim," Verdan motioned roughly north with his staff.

He didn't want to be out in these woods after dark if creatures like the Cyth could have settlements. That thought alone made him want to scream in frustration.

If there was a city less than a day away, why had they allowed such corruptive filth to establish themselves so close by?

_**_

The next few hours of travel were somewhat tense. They didn't know the landscape particularly well, and there was always the fear that there would be something just around the corner.

If Verdan could have been certain that they were in a peaceful area, he would have meditated and worked on compressing his Aether-gathering spiral as they went, but right now, he just couldn't take the chance.

Not that a few hours of quick work on it would make much of a difference, but anything was better than nothing.

Thankfully, the fire Sorcerer carried the Witch without complaint, barely speaking as they trekked on through the thick forest. What-ever magics were at play within this 'Sorcerer', they seemed to grant an improvement to his physicality.

. . .

When they paused for a break after a few hours, Verdan made sure to check on the Witch and the progress of the corruption she'd absorbed. He should have gotten all of it earlier, but it was worth checking as his visualization was always poor for healing spells.

"How is she?" The Sorcerer asked, his gravelly voice tinged with concern.

"She's fine. Her body is reacting well, and fighting off the effects of the corruption from the bindings they used on her. If we make it by sundown, I will heal her further."

Verdan wished he had the spare magic to heal her now, but until he had the time to attend to his spiral, he was going to husband what he had left like a miser.

"Good," the Sorcerer said with a grunt. Something in his voice made Verdan linger for a second, and after a brief pause, the Sorcerer continued. "What do you intend to do when we reach Hobson's Point?"

"Rest, find somewhere to stay, and figure out what's going on. Anything more than that, I'll work out when I get there," Verdan said with an expansive shrug. He didn't know enough to be making decisions right now. He needed some natural sleep and a hot meal.

"I was captured when I tried to defend a farm that was being raided. There were only a few dozen people in danger, but there were many Cyth, so the others abandoned me when I tried to help." The Sorcerer shuddered at the words, his gaze turning momentarily distant. "I owe you for my freedom, and I respect you for caring enough to defend those weaker than you. You are no Sorcerer—in truth, I do not know what you are—but it does not matter. I offer you my service for a month as your retainer to pay this debt."

Verdan met the man's fierce gaze, sensing the determination and passion that was bound within him. He had never liked those that refused to help others, and his oath still bound him to protect and guide the common folk of the Grym Empire, regardless of how much things had changed.

The thought that those with the power to fight back were picking and choosing their battles sat poorly with him. He was no crusader. That was a path for fools and heroes, neither of which he aspired to be.

That being said, Verdan would also not back down from the darkness if it came calling. "Very well, I accept. I require a guide and someone to guard my back."

"You will not regret it. My name is Kai, and my spear is yours for as long as our paths are united." Kai gave him a short bow, before seating himself next to the unconscious Witch in a classic meditative pose.

The thought made Verdan pause for a second, and he looked at Kai again. Yes, the pose he was in was a traditional meditative pose. A meditative pose was such an odd thing to remain the same when it seemed that everything else had changed.

Verdan was unsure what to think about the fact that he'd acquired a sworn retainer for the next month. On the one hand, it would be incredibly useful, but he didn't want to get dragged into any political issues.

Kai's statement that he had no idea what Verdan was worried him. No matter how much things had changed, the empire's Wizards should still be known.

Frustrated, and hating how little he knew for sure, Verdan went on a patrol of the area. The forest was healthy enough here. No lingering dark taint from the Cyth seemed to be corrupting it, a good sign.

The problem was that a settlement like the one they'd just left would indicate a heavy Cyth presence in the area, one far greater than those they'd killed. In time, this healthy woodland would become twisted and corrupted beyond recognition.

"Ready to go?" Tim called out as Verdan came back in toward them, nudging his brother and getting up as the Wizard nodded in reply.

Gathering up their meager possessions, the group started off north once more, hoping to reach the enclave by dark.

CHAPTER
FOUR

THE SUN WAS HALFWAY toward the horizon when they reached the first landmark that the brothers recognised.

With a better understanding of where they were, the group's pace picked up despite the dimming light, and after only another hour of travel, they reached their destination.

Hobson's Point was a walled city that sat atop a natural plateau at the base of the mountains. A single clear road wound up to the top, with rocky terrain preventing a more direct route to the city.

The gates for Hobson's Point sat across the road near the top of the incline, giving them a good view of the area and making it a defensible point.

Considering the surroundings, Verdan hazily remembered a fishing village being the closest settlement when he went to sleep, and even that was further west, toward where the ocean was at the time.

To see a weathered city that looked twice as old as him sent a shiver down Verdan's spine. Looking closer, Verdan saw that the masonry of the city walls was old and scarred, with some battle damage lingering in the form of chipped battlements and scorch marks.

"Hobson's Point is one of the oldest Enclaves, and one of the few that isn't run by a sect. Old and battered, but still going," Tim announced with a touch of pride, as they started up the trail to the open gates of the city.

The brothers had become steadily more relaxed around Verdan as the day wore on, no longer fearing a bad reaction for speaking out of turn. Which was a relief for Verdan.

"Sect?" Verdan queried in an absent tone as he took in the city. Realizing he'd spoken out loud, Verdan grimaced and glanced over to see that Kai was giving him a searching look, his head cocked slightly to one side as he considered Verdan.

"You know, one of the Sorcerer sects. They rule over most of the Enclaves these days, from what I've heard," Tim said, too caught up in his joy of being back to pick up on anything odd.

Sighing a little, Verdan realized that he would have to explain things a bit more to Kai. The warrior might have sworn himself to Verdan for now, but they barely knew each other.

The gates to the city were guarded by four men wearing leather armor that had small metal pieces protecting key areas. Each guard was armed with a long spear and had easy access to a small iron basket with javelins in, ready for throwing if needed.

The guards nodded to them as they approached, their gaze lingering on the unconscious Witch before flicking to Verdan's staff and Kai's scowl.

"Our companion was injured. She is healing but needs rest," Verdan said, getting ahead of any problematic questions.

"Of course, Lord Sorcerer, let us know if we can be of assistance. Please bear in mind that Hobson's Point is a neutral Enclave run by the City Council. We ask that you abide by our laws when within our walls."

"That won't be a problem," Verdan said, his smile a little strained.

"Very good. Welcome to Hobson's Point," the guard said, stepping out of the way with a relieved expression as he waved their group inside.

The city's interior was a letdown for Verdan. He'd seen the old, tall walls that protected Hobson's Point and had been expecting something similar to what he was used to.

Instead, he found an odd blend of old-looking stone buildings and newer wooden ones. Cobbled paths wove off from a central paved causeway, and disappeared into the somewhat disorderly nest of buildings.

The basics were there, but the buildings were small and quite plain. The most interesting things he could see were some glass windows with a slight bluish tint to them.

To say he was disappointed was somewhat of an understatement, but the group had paused while he looked over the city and now looked expectantly at him for direction.

"Are there any taverns or inns we can stay at?" He asked the brothers, guessing from their awkward shuffling that they were waiting to follow his lead.

"Yes, but we don't have any money, you see," Tim said, cheeks flushing red as he trailed off. Everything made a bit more sense to Verdan then.

They assumed that he would have the funds to buy them all some-where to stay as he'd not been captured. A great idea, if not for the possible issue with his currency.

"The coins I have may be a problem. They're not local currency. What do you think you can get for them?" He pulled out two impe-rial marks and handed them over, the silver coins glinting in the soft light as the brothers took them.

"These are solid silver. I bet we could get five silver darn for each of them," Tim whispered, eyes wide as he looked at the coins. "We'll need to find a money-changer. Hopefully, there's one around here."

"Wait," Kai said, holding up a hand before turning and walking back to the gate guards to speak with them. The guard closest to them listened to Kai's request and pointed off to the center of the city, giving directions.

Coming back to them, Kai nodded down the main causeway and motioned for them to follow, setting off at a brisk walk as he took the lead.

The walk through the city was illuminating for Verdan. He saw a wide range of people in various situations, everything from poor and bedraggled to armed and armored in polished, gleaming steel.

Sadly, there were more of the former than Verdan would have liked, with many people lingering aimlessly, the blank look in their eyes showing how they had lost hope that they could improve their situations.

The money-changer's building was a solid-looking, two-story business with thick walls and a pair of guards out front, their scowls keeping the majority of the locals well away.

"Kai, could you come in with me?" Verdan asked, sighing in silent relief as the Sorcerer nodded. He wasn't functioning at top form right now, and he had no idea of the local worth of his items, so some advice would be good.

The Witch was a concern, so Verdan waved for the brothers to wait outside as he headed into the building with Kai.

"Welcome, Sirs. Do you have an appointment, or if not, how can I help?" The first room was a reception of sorts, with a young man manning the desk, his manner warm but his eyes calculating as he eyed the two of them.

"I have coins and a few gems that need converting," Verdan said, pulling out an emerald and flashing it at the man, trusting greed to get the right reaction.

"Of course, please take a seat. I will fetch the owner at once." The man said, already out of his chair and moving by the time Verdan put the emerald away.

Verdan nodded, but the receptionist was already gone, heading through a door in the rear and leaving them alone.

Verdan took the opportunity to examine the room a little further, noting the quality of the decorations and furniture. Clearly, a lot of business passed through here, which was a good sign.

"Gentlemen, a pleasure to meet you both. My name is Gregory Devro, owner of this establishment and local money-changer." A well-dressed man came out from the rear with the receptionist, walking forward to shake their hands with a wide smile. "Please, follow me."

Verdan smiled internally at how little things like this changed. He'd never really been to places like this that often, but so far, this was all the same.

"Now, I believe you have some items that need converting. Could you display them and give me some context to their acquisition?"

Gregory said as he led them into a small room with a large table, taking a seat on one side and gesturing to the other.

"Yes, I have both coins and gems. I found them in an old tomb south of here," Verdan said, keeping his explanation short and sweet. Fewer details meant less chance of him slipping up later.

As he spoke, Verdan pulled out what he had—thirty imperial marks and a small assortment of gems that ranged in size and clarity.

"Oh, very interesting indeed. Was there anything further, or did you search the whole place?" Gregory asked as he took a close look at the goods on display, picking up one of the coins to examine it further.

"It was only small. This was everything that was of value."

"Such a shame. They're very interesting, you see. Given my business here, I deal with many local adventurers and the loot they find, but I've not seen coins like this before. They almost look like the coins of the Third Empire, but they're not quite the same, and they certainly don't look thousands of years old!" He chuckled at his own words, not noticing that Verdan had gone pale at his words.

"Thousands?" The word tore itself from Verdan's mouth before he could stop himself, the implications making his veins run with ice-water.

"Oh yes," Gregory said without looking up from the coin. "The Third Empire is the oldest civilisation that we have records of at two thousand years old. We know that there were others preceding it, but not what they were called or any real details outside of some fantastical stories."

Gregory turned the coin in his hand and peered at the imperial stamp on it. "Their society still shapes life today, though. It's such a shame that a particularly bad Rising destroyed them. Still, life goes on, and we struggle forward."

Verdan said nothing, simply taking in the information and keeping his expression as neutral as possible. He doubted he'd ever know exactly how long he'd been asleep, but he knew now that it was measured in thousands of years, not hundreds.

It sounded like that 'Third Empire' had been a distant successor to the one he'd lived in, though long enough apart that Wizards were only tall tales.

If that was true, it also meant that whatever had happened to abolish Wizardry had happened in between him going to sleep and that empire.

"More to the point, I can offer five gold darns for everything here," Gregory said with an expectant smile, holding a hand out for Verdan to shake.

"Seven. Those coins are older than the Third Empire. A collector would pay through the nose for them," Kai said, leaning forward to negotiate when he saw that Verdan wasn't responding.

Verdan tuned out their arguing as he processed it all, eventually pushing it all to one side as Gregory and Kai shook hands, and the money-changer went to fetch their coins.

Kai gave him an odd look, but Verdan shook his head before he could speak. This wasn't the time or place to discuss things.

"Here we are, six gold and fifty silver darns, as agreed. Please, do come back if you have any further items like this," Gregory handed the pouch of coins over to Verdan, who thanked him before rising and heading outside.

The two brothers and the Witch were where he left them, the Witch still unconscious but looking far more healthy than earlier.

As they walked out, both of the brothers turned to Verdan with an expectant expression once more.

Having the others immediately rely on him to judge what to do next was an extra weight on Verdan's shoulders, but nowhere near the heaviest. After all, Verdan had to decide what to do with his life after finding out that everyone and everything he knew was gone.

Even the very land itself had changed from what he remembered. A maddening thought in itself.

"There's a tavern we've stayed at before when visiting. Nothing fancy, but it would do while we get our bearings. Do you have enough for us all?" Tim asked hesitantly, seeing the clouded expression on Verdan's face.

"Yes, it'll be fine. Please, lead on," Verdan said shortly. He needed to sleep on all this and get something to eat. He'd figure it out tomorrow.

Exchanging a look, the brothers led the way through the streets of Hobson's Point, a little uncertain at first, but gaining in confidence the further they went.

The tavern they came to was a somber place, mostly empty, with a half-abandoned look that didn't inspire any confidence. Tim seemed certain this was the place, however, and led them inside.

The interior was in far better shape than the outside suggested, a warm fire in the corner giving it a homely feel. The innkeeper was a middle-aged man with short hair and a warm smile, a smile that only grew as Tim spoke to him.

"My friend here tells me you need rooms?" The innkeeper said as Verdan walked over to join them.

"Yes, please. Four in total, with food, for at least two nights," Verdan said. He doubted the prices would be high here, given the state of the place.

"Very good. That will be fifteen copper darns per room per night plus ten copper darns per meal. That's a total of two hundred and fifty copper for two nights and two meals each for five people. I'd settle for two silver, though and forget about the last half-darn. If you want to stay longer, we can call it four silver and make it four nights."

The innkeeper rattled off the prices with practiced ease. As he spoke, Verdan watched Tim from the corner of his eye, using his reaction to judge the prices.

They seemed very low to his mind, from what he'd picked up; a hundred copper darns was one silver, and one gold darn was one hundred silvers in turn. A half-darn was a fifty copper piece, so it was well within his budget.

"Here, four silver darn for four nights. Which rooms should we take?" Verdan produced some of the new coins he'd received and passing them over.

"Thank you kindly, and welcome to the Plucky Wanderer." The innkeeper said with a beaming smile as he passed them some keys. "The stairs on the right lead to four rooms. I'll mark them down as yours. I'm Bob Davenport. If you need anything, just holler. Oh, and dinner is in about an hour."

"Thank you, we'll get settled in as soon as possible," Verdan said with a nod, motioning everyone upstairs so that they could divide rooms accordingly. Tim and Tom could share one, Verdan got the second, Kai the third, and the Witch was given the fourth.

Verdan expected the Witch to wake up either this evening or overnight. Obviously, she would be disoriented at first, so he left her on the bed with the door unlocked; no need to make her feel like she was being kept in there against her will.

Dinner was a meager affair, but Bob promised that much better fare would be provided tomorrow. Given the day's events, Verdan didn't even notice, simply eating the last of the slightly-stale bread he'd been given and turning in for the evening.

He had a lot to think about.

CHAPTER

FIVE

THE MORNING BROUGHT a measure of peace to Verdan. He'd always found sleeping on an issue helped him to process it, and this time was no different.

Seating himself on the bed, Verdan settled into a comfortable position and quietened his mind before getting to work. First of all, he was going to focus on compressing his gathering spiral.

The tighter the spiral, the stronger the pull on the ambient energy, and the faster rate at which he would recover expended Aether.

It was a long and slow process, both to recover Aether and tighten the spiral, but every bit of progress he made on his spiral would pay dividends in the future.

Partitioning his mind, Verdan tasked a portion of his attention to what he was doing, while the rest considered what to do going forward. Being able to manage some mental gymnastics was key for a Wizard, and with a spiral this small, it was easy enough to do.

Verdan's most-pressing decision right now was whether he wanted to try and change the world or just focus on what he wanted. He could already see that a lot of magical knowledge had been lost, and he could work to bring it back.

The sheer scale of the task was daunting, and even considering it made Verdan think of what he'd lost, of what he'd done.

No, Verdan couldn't bring himself to commit to such a task. He'd already spent years fighting to change the world, only to find out that it was all for nought; no one even remembered the Grym Imperium, let alone what they'd done to advance civilization.

There was nothing for him down that path. Instead, he was going to establish himself here and spend some time on his research. He'd always planned to do just that when the war ended anyway.

Verdan rose from where he sat and moved to look out at the city through the single window in the room. He felt all the more out of place looking at the unfamiliar architecture in the morning light.

Sighing to himself, Verdan turned away and rubbed his face with shaking hands. So much had changed, and so much was lost.

Forcing his mind back to the safer thoughts of reviving Wizardry, Verdan realized that any students he taught would only know what he himself knew. He had none of his more esoteric arcane devices to expand their knowledge.

Of course, you could manage without external aids, as the first Wizards had done, but it was a much longer and slower process.

Maybe it would be different if he had an Arcane Lexicon, but the chances of one of them surviving this long were slim to none, and he doubted any current Enchanters knew how to make them.

Mind calmed and a decision made, Verdan headed downstairs to find the brothers, Kai and the Witch sitting eating their breakfast.

"Morning," Bob called out cheerfully as he saw him come down the stair., "Breakfast?"

"Please," Verdan nodded gratefully to the innkeeper as he took a seat with the others. Kai and the brothers seemed ill at ease but were trying to hide it.

The Witch looked distinctly uncomfortable as well. Her gaze was locked apprehensively on Verdan as though waiting for the other shoe to drop.

Verdan knew that the locals had some strange thoughts about Witches, which likely explained her apprehension. "I'm glad to see you're awake. Any lingering after-effects?"

"No, none so far," she said hesitantly. "The whole thing is a haze, if I'm honest. I remember a fire starting in my house and running outside, but not much from there on." She looked down at the table and wrung her hands nervously.

"You were bound with Cyth hair. It was corrupting the natural energy in your body to weaken you enough for them to corrupt you further. It's no surprise that your memories were compromised."

Verdan didn't disguise the disgust in his voice as he explained the Cyth's techniques. "If things went as I would expect, then you would have been left there until you were too far gone for it to be reversed. It's one of the more horrific ways they create a new Cyth Bayne."

"Ancestors preserve me," the Witch said in a whisper, her eyes wide and skin pale. The real implications of her situation were sinking in now, though Verdan regretted being quite so blunt with her.

It was easy to forget how horrible the world could seem to those who hadn't experienced it to the same degree.

Verdan had seen enough terror and horror in the war to be able to process it, but the same wasn't true for everyone else. In some ways, he was happy that she was reacting so poorly to what he described. It gave him hope for the general standard of this current age.

"Will I recover fully?" Her tone was soft as she stared down at her hands, clearly fearing the worst.

"Yes. I was able to aid your body in purging the worst of the corruption. The rest will simply take some time, but as a Witch, you should have no problem at all," Verdan explained with his best attempt at a warm smile.

Everyone knew that Witches were naturally skilled at removing corruption, after all. Whatever the odd relation between Witches and the locals, some things would still be true.

"Thank you," the Witch said, falling quiet as she stared down at the marks on her wrists where she'd been bound.

"So what do you all have planned now that we're back in the city?" Verdan asked, moving the conversation along to give her time to adjust.

"Well, we wanted to talk to you about that," Tim said with an awkward shift in his chair. "Kai said that he's staying with you for a month. We're hoping you'd be willing to hire us on as well."

Tim's smile grew uneasy and faded as Verdan didn't immediately respond. "We'd guard anything you needed looking after, maybe do some errands and stuff for you as well. We owe you for the rescue and want to help."

"I see," Verdan said, sitting back in his chair and giving it some thought as he looked over the earnest guards. "I do need some local guides and advisers. I'll take you on for a month, paying room and board only, and then we will review. Acceptable?"

Verdan held his hand out to Tim. He was happy enough to keep the two of them on, for now, anyway. Verdan couldn't help but feel a little responsible for them, and leaving them without work felt like a poor ending.

"Yes, Boss!" Tim reached over to shake his hand with enthusiasm, his brother doing the same a moment later.

"Fantastic, then finish up your breakfast and let's go for a walk to recap on a few things," Verdan said, starting to mentally prepare himself for the extended question-and-answer session that was coming.

He wanted to be at least somewhat honest with them and see how they reacted. He'd use that as a measure for what to do in the future. He wasn't looking forward to it, though.

"I'm sorry to be rude, but could you tell me your name? I don't like owing a debt to someone I don't know," the Witch spoke up, catching Verdan's attention once more.

There was a hint of resolve in her voice now, one that had been absent earlier. Verdan could tell that she was already recovering from the corruption that had built up in her body.

"I'm sorry, that was my fault. My name is Verdan," he said with a shake of his head, admonishing himself for being so lax with his manners.

"I'm Gwen. I owe you so much for rescuing me, I wish I had anything to repay you with, but I'm almost certain that the Cyth destroyed everything I owned when they captured me." Her eyes fell to her hands once more as she spoke, her voice filled with a thick layer of longing and despair, one that resonated with Verdan's current feelings.

"Well, it seems to be the done thing for those I've saved to work for me. Why don't you join us for a month and see what happens?"

Verdan hated himself for offering, but he felt guilty about her lack of options.

"Truly? But I have no alchemy equipment, nor am I the best at using such things, if I'm being honest." The hope that had flared in her eyes lasted only a brief moment before fading as she grimaced and looked away.

"Of course, a Witch such as yourself has plenty to offer besides alchemy," Verdan said with a reassuring smile.

She wouldn't be as powerful as some of the older Witches he'd faced, but any Witch was a dangerous foe in the right conditions. He'd find out what type she was another time.

"I see. Well, you did save me," Gwen muttered, somewhat reluctant to accept the offer, though she did shake his hand in the end.

Kai looked distinctly displeased by what Verdan had said as well, but Verdan chalked it all down to their odd attitude to Witches. After all, some of the other captives had wanted to abandon her.

Exactly why they felt this way about Witches baffled him. It was just one more mystery for him to figure out, though they did seem to be racking up rather quickly.

His breakfast arrived a few moments later, Bob putting a nicely-coloured omelet and some fresh bread down for him. Nothing extravagant, but simple and filling, which was what Verdan wanted right now.

Everyone had finished their food by the time he was done, so Verdan headed straight back to his room to grab his staff. Once he was ready, he made his way back down and beckoned for the others to follow as he left the Plucky Wanderer.

Chill air blew past as he opened the door to the outside, sending a shiver down his spine. It would take Verdan some time to get used to this cool mountain air.

"So, where to, Boss?" Tim asked as they came out.

"Well, I have my first task for each of you. Tim, Tom, Gwen, I want the three of you to ask around and see if you find out some of the recent events here. I also want to know if there is a library and if there is somewhere we could set up on a more-permanent basis."

Verdan could see a nervous look in Tim's eyes, so he explained further "That could be anything from a house for sale to an abandoned warehouse. I don't care. I just need as much space as possible. Meet us back here at mid-day with what you've found, and I'll decide what to do from there."

Verdan looked to each of them in turn as he gave out the orders. To his surprise, they nodded and headed off without questioning anything.

The brothers were more enthusiastic than Gwen, but he'd still expected them to question him a little.

"What about me?" Kai asked as the others disappeared off into the city.

"We're going to buy you a weapon. It's entirely backwards that I've got something, and you haven't," Verdan tapped the end of his staff onto the cobbled road in emphasis.

Kai had left his weapon behind to carry Gwen back to Hobson's Point, but he still looked every inch the capable warrior, and Verdan intended to equip him accordingly.

"I can't argue with that," Kai gave a small half-smile and inclined his head for Verdan to lead the way. "I will pay you back once I earn some funds of my own."

"No need, consider it a gift," Verdan said, waving away his offer of repayment. Kai didn't look pleased but nodded and left it at that. "Besides, we have more important matters to discuss. You said yesterday that you knew I wasn't a Sorcerer. How?"

Verdan kept his voice low as they walked towards an area they'd passed the day before that had featured a sprawling market of temporary stalls and permanent shops.

He was taking a chance by discussing all of this with Kai, but he needed information, and the Sorcerer struck him as trustworthy.

"You speak words in a strange tongue when you channel your magic. You also don't seem to be restricted in what element you use from what I've seen. You created fog and fire, as well as whatever those shields were. I've not seen anything like them before." Kai paused and shrugged with a glance at Verdan. "That doesn't even cover your accent and strange knowledge."

"I see," Verdan said before going quiet for a moment as his mind raced. If he were recognised as different for a simple shield, this would be more difficult than he thought.

He had no choice but to place his trust in Kai and see how things played out. Going for the most dangerous part straight away, Verdan took a deep breath and spoke carefully, "I'm a Wizard."

"A what?" Kai turned to give him a quizzical look, raising one eyebrow in question.

"A Wizard? A manipulator of energy that casts spells using the language of reality itself?" Verdan's voice started to climb as he saw the lack of reaction on Kai's face.

Stopping and taking a breath, Verdan made himself keep his voice low. He'd known that Wizards were gone from everyone's reactions, but for someone not to even recognise the word was painful.

"I'm sorry, I've never heard of whatever that is. Is it like sorcery?" Kai asked, a little confused but trying to engage on the subject.

"Okay, let me explain from the top," Verdan rubbed his face in exasperation. He was just going to have to tell him everything, well, almost everything.

"The easiest way to explain this is that I'm from somewhere where there are no Sorcerers, and life is very different to this. It's not a place I can get back to, so I want to make the best of my life here. I need to know where to put down roots, what Sorcerers are, and what a Rising is."

Verdan kept it to the main questions he had. He didn't want to overload Kai right now.

"That would explain a lot," Kai said slowly, clearly trying to wrap his head around it.

"I can't picture how any civilization could survive without Sorcerers, but you're proof that other methods exist, I suppose." He nodded to himself, reaching some sort of internal conclusion about the place that Verdan came from. "So you don't know how Sorcerers work at all?"

"From what you've said, I know it involves elements, but I use the ambient energy of the world and shape it to have the effect I need. The actual energy itself isn't dependent on any singular element." Verdan said, navigating them down a street that was basically empty.

He didn't want people listening in on this.

"I don't understand how that's possible, but I can see the power it gives you," Kai said, looking at him with fresh respect in his eyes. "Sorcerers are those who have meditated on an element and have been blessed with Elemental Essence by it. By meditating on the element further, we are able to draw in energy relating to it and rebuild our Essence, which we use to power ourselves and the abilities we have gained from it." Kai gestured to himself "I am a Fire Enhancer, so I use Essence to give myself the attributes of fire, such as short bursts of speed and power. I can use it for other purposes, but Enhancing is my speciality."

"Fascinating," Verdan said, his frustration falling away as Kai spoke. His first love had always been studying the arcane, and the things Kai described made no sense using his current frame of reference. That meant that either the nature of magic had fundamentally changed, or they were applying a veil of mysticism to magic and not understanding the base processes.

Given that his magic worked without issue, he could only assume that Kai's ancestors had stumbled into a whole new way to manipulate the energy of the world.

For the first time since he'd awoken, Verdan felt a stirring of enthusiasm in his chest. A mystery like this would be so satisfying to solve.

"Okay, so we'll discuss that more later. What about the Rising?" Verdan made himself move on from sorcery for the moment. There would be time enough for that later.

"You may know it by a different name. It's the term we use for when the monsters rapidly increase in numbers and attack every area of civilization they can. Cyth, creatures from the depths of the world, foul things from the mountains, everything."

"The look you have says you don't recognise this. Just what sort of a place are you from?" Kai had stopped and was looking at Verdan with undisguised curiosity now.

"Somewhere very different, that's all that's worth saying on it. Just work on the assumption that I don't know anything about how things work around here," Verdan said uncomfortably, not liking having to hold things back from Kai.

It was a necessary evil, but one he still disliked.

"Very well, then the first thing I should mention is that we should stay here in Hobson's Point," Kai said as they started walking once more, heading toward the market stalls that were now in sight.

"Oh, why?"

"Many Sorcerers are competitive and prideful. They would not like a powerful new way of wielding magic to emerge. The old days where Sorcerers were only concerned with defending humanity are long gone. Power and pride are the new ideals that they aspire to."

"Ah, I see. I remember you saying that Hobson's Point is one of the few cities not run by Sorcerers. A fortuitous place for us to end up then," Verdan said as they approached the market.

"Indeed it is. How much should I spend on my weapon?" Kai nodded toward a nearby stall that was a permanent addition to a blacksmith.

Several weapons, tools, and implements were on display, each with crude wooden signs that had prices carved into them. The spoken language was surprisingly similar to what he was used to, and the written language seemed the same.

Everything was slightly off, but it was close enough for him to recognise what it meant. Most of the prices were in half-darns, the fifty copper coin, but a few nicer pieces were priced in silver.

Given that Kai would be keeping him alive, Verdan didn't mind spending a bit more on his weapon. He had plenty left from what was converted after all.

"No more than three silver," he told the Sorcerer, picking an arbitrary number that he thought would let Kai have his pick of what was there.

"Very well," Kai said with a nod, stepping forward to look over the items in greater detail.

There were a few weapons available, ranging from poorly-made to a few worthy pieces, but Verdan was pleased to see that Kai went through them with a careful examination.

Eventually, his new retainer settled on a dark wooden spear with a flat, leaf-shaped head and an iron-capped base with a spike. The whole thing was around six feet long and was the most expensive item there at two-and-a-half silver.

Even Verdan, an admitted novice when it came to most weaponry, saw that it was a step above everything else on display. Kai also took a belt with a long knife for a half-darn, likely for emergencies and utility.

"Anything else?" Verdan double-checked, paying the blacksmith when Kai shook his head, taking out the three silver and getting a half-darn in change.

As he was about to walk away, Verdan considered the brothers and the Cyth weapons they had. He should probably take care of that as well.

Going back to the blacksmith, he bought a sword for Tim and a flanged mace for Tom. Kai checked both weapons to make sure they were of acceptable quality and seemed satisfied, so Verdan gave the blacksmith the half-darn back and added another silver.

Taking the weaponry back to the Plucky Wanderer, Verdan got more information from Kai on Sorcery and the Rising.

He didn't like what he heard.

It seemed that humanity was on the back foot, living in walled cities and relying on Sorcerers to keep local monsters, beasts, and cults from becoming a problem.

Every Rising saw at least one city lost, whether to starvation from a lack of farmland or from having their walls breached by one of the more-organized groups of enemies.

"The Rising, does it come with a period of higher magical density?" Verdan asked, a sinking feeling growing in his stomach.

"Yes, usually it's a time of fast cultivation for Sorcerers, which at least helps deal with the problems it brings," Kai said, keeping his voice low as they passed by a group of locals.

"Damn," Verdan muttered, realizing that a Rising was what he knew as an Aether Dawn, a time when the ambient Aether rose to exceptionally high levels.

Increased monster activity had been noted for an Aether Dawn, but that was never an issue. In the days of the Grym Imperium, dedicated teams of Wizards and Imperial Guards subjugated known areas where monsters congregated.

From what Kai had said, such teams were a thing of the past, so an Aether Dawn would bring about a much greater response from the creatures, causing a Rising.

Verdan knew that delicate magi-tech had existed to extrapolate the next Aether Dawn, allowing for a culling to be undertaken. Without that, it was no wonder things had gone badly.

To make matters worse, humanity stood alone.

Gone were the Neisar and the Vesperai, the two other founding races of the Imperium. Even the minor races like the Fwyn no longer lived alongside them.

Perhaps they still remained elsewhere, but the days of working together were long gone.

CHAPTER
SIX

THE OTHER THREE members of their impromptu group arrived back around midday with news from their explorations. Verdan immediately sent the two brothers upstairs to get their new weapons and drop the poorly-made Cyth ones off.

They would do for emergency weapons in the future, but they had better options right now.

While the two brothers upgraded their armament, Verdan waved Gwen over to join him and Kai at one of the larger tables.

He'd given Bob a half-darn earlier for lunch, so Gwen was swiftly supplied with a mug of foamy beer and a bowl of hearty soup.

Bob had really followed through with his promise for better fare, providing a ham hock and smoked sausage soup with a big chunk of fresh bread. Verdan's portion had been delicious, and it looked like Gwen was entirely on board with that view.

"So, what did you find?" Verdan asked once everyone was assembled and had their lunches served.

"No library," Tom said, taking a long sip of beer with a satisfied expression.

"The library was burnt down in a fire a few years ago. No one bothered to rebuild it," Tim added, giving his brother an exasperated look. "It seems that the city has been in hard times since the last Rising. A lot of folks left for better options elsewhere. Not that there are many around here; Hobson's Point is one of the most-northern cities still standing. The Sorcerers tend to stay further south where all the food-producing cities are."

"So what does Hobson's Point provide?" Verdan asked, wondering what kept people here if there was a general movement south.

"Well, it's traditionally been the source of metal. There are lots of mines in these mountains. With more and more responsibility going to Sorcerers, there's less call for large numbers of weapons and less need for metal. The few mines still active are the main source of revenue for the city now. Without the miners and the foundry workers, this place would be deserted." Tim seemed to take the poor situation of the city quite personally, looking glumly down at his beer as he explained.

"Interesting—so the city is all about production," Verdan murmured to himself. That meant there would be trained workers for hire if needed. He doubted everyone would have abandoned the city after all. Depending on what he did to make himself some money here, that could be particularly useful. "What about a place for me to work in?"

"I spoke with a few men in the city's eastern district, where the warehouses and foundries are based. They said a few empty warehouses would be up for sale and gave me directions to the owner to speak with him directly," Gwen said, taking over from the brothers.

"Did you look at the warehouses? What were they like?" Verdan sat up attentively. He was keen to get somewhere as a more permanent base of operations.

"All of the same type, really—basic and large, with no purpose beyond keeping out the worst of the weather," she shrugged awkwardly, not meeting his gaze as she answered. She still seemed out of sorts from their conversation this morning.

It was likely just the last remnants of corruption in her system, though.

"Very well, what's the name of the owner of the properties?" Verdan wanted something a bit more than a basic warehouse, but many a worthy endeavor began from humble beginnings.

"Tobias Brock. He owns most of the warehouses in Hobson's Point, from what people say. He has a shipping business that runs goods out to other cities, so he's been buying up the warehouses for storage. He has a house in the center of the city. We can head over this afternoon if you want?"

"Yes, let's see what he says," Verdan said, nodding to himself as he rose from the table. "Enjoy your lunch and relax for a bit. I'm going to meditate for a while before we visit Mr. Brock." He got the same confused look from everyone at the table, but they didn't say anything further as he headed up to his room.

His gathering spiral was working steadily away, but it was barely adequate for a novice. His old instructor from the academy would have burnt his eyebrows off for such a loose spiral.

There was so much to do and so little time to do it in, but he knew he needed to take the time to rebuild his foundations properly. He either did it right the first time, or he'd be paying for it for years to come.

Seating himself on the floor, Verdan settled into a relaxed position and turned his mind inward. Taking the time to follow the technique properly, he built up the mental image piece by piece.

First came the framework, the most vital part of what he was doing. He had to picture his and the gentle movement of energy within him.

Once ready, he focused on the energy flowing into him. It came in two ways, a passive flow from where it soaked in through his skin and an active one from the air he breathed.

Each breath drew in fresh energy, allowing it to circle within his lungs and pass into his blood.

The energy inside him ran in a loose spiral that led to the very core of his being. Its lazy loops did little to encourage the energy being passively drawn in through his skin, relying instead on the energy he breathed in.

That wouldn't do, not at all.

Mentally seizing the spiral, he started to compress it, making the existing loops take up less space within him.

He'd worked on it a little yesterday, but now he was going to settle for nothing less than perfection.

Sweat started to bead on Verdan's forehead as he pushed all of his willpower into the effort.

The three-loop spiral he'd had already started to slowly compress in on itself, shrinking down to be a fraction of the size that it had been earlier.

With a half-smile, Verdan layered new loops into the spiral. This early in the process, he was able to make it straight to twelve before running out of space.

He was still within novice territory, but a jump from three layers to twelve would take a novice weeks of work. Verdan's experience and tempered mental strength were proving their worth already.

Releasing the mental image, Verdan breathed out fully before inhaling deeply. The fresh Aether was pulled immediately into the spiral, moving much more quickly down into his core, where it would be refined into energy for him to use.

The passive draw from the surrounding energy was slightly increased as well, the movement of the Aether within him drawing it in like a whirlpool.

As with all parts of dealing with Aether, the concept was the key part and taking the time to focus and create the mental image properly allowed for so much more to be done.

-**-

Verdan returned to the common room a few hours later, satisfied with his newly-expanded spiral and the steady trickle of energy it provided.

"Ready to go meet Tobias?" Verdan asked as he walked over to where the others waited.

Tom had fallen asleep and had to be nudged awake, but in short order, they were out the door and following Gwen's lead toward the center of the city.

The general state of the city improved as they headed closer to the center, the buildings looked in better repair, and the citizens had more purpose to their movements. It seemed this was the area least-impacted by the lack of work, but Verdan knew that it was only a matter of time before the rot set in here as well.

"Here, it's just down this road, I believe," Gwen said, turning down a side road that led past several gated compounds, each with a several-story tall house.

One, in particular, had what looked like a seating area outside its gates. Several wooden benches framed with wrought iron lined the wall on either side of the way in.

Stopping at the entrance, Gwen tested the gate and shrugged in Verdan's direction as it swung open.

"Take a seat. I'll head in with just Kai," Verdan said, nodding toward the benches before stepping past Gwen and onto the paved interior of the compound.

It wasn't a huge area, but it was nicely laid out, with enough greenery to make it feel organic. Verdan's staff rapped on the stone pavement that led to the building with each step he took, the sound echoing around the quiet compound.

The door opened when they were a short distance away, an imposing man in plain clothes stepping out to regard them. Bald, with a tailored beard and hard eyes, the man's cold gaze sent a shiver down Verdan's spine.

Running his eyes over them both, the man stood at ease and spoke in a deep but clear voice. "Can I help you, gentlemen?"

"I'm seeking a meeting with Tobias Brock regarding some property he owns," Verdan replied evenly.

This man reeked of danger, but that was nothing new for Verdan; besides, between Kai and him, they could likely deal with most dangers they would come across.

"Which property would that be?" The cold gaze came back to rest on him. Verdan could almost feel it measuring and judging him, making his hand reflexively curl around his staff.

"I'm looking to purchase a warehouse to base my operations in," Verdan said, shoulders square and not flinching from the weight of the man's gaze.

"Very well, please wait here while I see if he is available to meet with you," the man stepped back inside and closed the door, audibly sliding a bolt home as he did.

"That was a dangerous man," Kai said softly, stepping up beside Verdan. The Sorcerer carried his spear in one hand, resting it on his shoulder with a relaxed stance.

"Yes, which makes me wonder just who this Tobias is," Verdan replied just as softly.

It was unusual for a property owner to have such an obviously-dangerous man answering his door.

Maybe this would be an interesting meeting, after all.

A few minutes passed as they waited outside, the walls of the small compound sheltering them from the wind and letting the soft sunlight bring a touch of warmth to them. All in all, it was as pleasant a waiting experience as Verdan could ask for.

"Mr. Brock will take an audience with you now," the door had silently opened to reveal the intimidating man from earlier, who waved them forward and held a hand out to Kai. "Your spear, please, and your staff."

"Of course," Kai passed over his weapon as they stepped inside the large building, Verdan following suit a moment later.

"This way, please," the man said as he laid the staff and the spear on a table. "Your weapons will be returned when you leave."

Gesturing for them to follow, the man led them down the long hallway and further into the house. A few paintings hung on the walls, but there was little decoration beyond that, giving the hall a practical feeling that Verdan approved of.

They passed several doors as they walked along, but they were all closed and gave no indication of what may be within. Verdan couldn't help but wonder if the lack of decorations was a theme or if it was just this corridor.

Either way, it spoke to the character of the man they were going to meet.

The end of the hall brought them to another closed door, their guide rapping three times on it and pausing for a moment before swinging it open.

The room beyond was less opulent than Verdan had been expecting, though by no means did it look cheap. Several well-padded chairs and a dark wood table stood upon a matching dark wood flooring.

The far side of the room was dominated by an oversized window through which Verdan could see an extensive portion of the garden at the rear of the building.

The only occupied chair was to the right of the table, angled toward the window, and three more sat to the table's left. A slight scent of mint filled the room, drawing Verdan's eyes to a steaming mug that sat on a coaster atop the table.

The man in the occupied chair was facing the window, with his legs crossed at the knee as he gazed out at the garden. Even sitting down, he was obviously a big man, with broad shoulders and long legs. Despite his build, however, the man was gaunt and had a sallow complexion.

Reaching out to pick up the steaming mug, the man, who Verdan assumed was Tobias, carefully took a sip before placing it down once more and waving to the other chairs.

"Please, take a seat," the gaunt man's voice was deep but felt lacking in some way, making him sound almost disinterested.

"Thank you," Verdan said as he entered and took a seat, Kai doing likewise. Their guide closed the door behind them before standing against the wall behind his employer.

"So, Brent tells me that you're looking to buy a warehouse of mine," The gaunt man said, sipping his tea once more before turning in his chair to meet Verdan's gaze.

Tobias's face had a striking paleness to it, his overall complexion seeming sallow and unhealthy. Verdan was no healer, but even he could tell that there was something wrong.

"Yes, I'm new to the area and need a space to set up my operations. It was recommended that we speak to you for something along those lines," Verdan said, noting the lack of interest in Tobias's gaze as he listened to what he was saying.

"I see. What operation would that be, restarting one of the mines?" Tobias asked, turning back to the window once more.

"Alchemy and research, actually. I need the space for storage and equipment," Verdan said evenly, noting with an inner smile as Tobias stilled and then turned back to him, his eyes seeming to come alive for the first time.

Verdan had so much to do that it was difficult to settle on just one thing, which is why he'd gone with calling it alchemy and research. That sort of title covered almost anything he'd want to do, which was probably for the best.

That being said, he did intend to start with some alchemy, particularly as Kai had mentioned that there were several alchemical concoctions that Sorcerers used to help regenerate their powers. Sadly, Kai didn't know how to make them, but it seemed the perfect place to start his investigation of this elemental sorcery they used.

"Are you a trained alchemist, then?" Tobias asked, sipping his drink almost absently.

"Not in the way that most are. I know how to make a few things, but I'm interested in learning more," Verdan said with a smile. He'd had some general training at the academy, but nothing beyond the basics.

He could see that his odd answer was intriguing Tobias even more, enough that the gaunt man moved his chair so that he was facing them straight on.

"That accent, I can't place it. Where did you say you were from?" Tobias took a measured sip of his drink. His pale blue eyes fixed on Verdan over the lip of the mug.

"I didn't," Verdan said with a small smile. "Suffice it to say, it is somewhere far away from here, and I doubt you'll ever meet anyone else from there. I want to compare our alchemy with your own. I have funds but no equipment, ingredients, or space to work in. I'm sure you see the issue I face," Verdan reached into his robe and produced a single gold coin, placing it on the table with a metallic click.

"Wine or tea?" Tobias asked as he finished his drink.

"Tea, please," Verdan said, intrigued by whatever it was that Tobias was drinking. Kai echoed his request a moment later, his stoic expression revealing nothing to anyone in the room.

"Excellent—three teas and some food, please, Brent," the pale man said to his looming guard, who nodded and left without a sound. "Now, let's discuss what requirements you have in specific."

"Glassware, reagents, storage, workspace, and books," Verdan rattled off without hesitation. "I don't know what you might have access to, but any of that would be welcome."

"Before the slow decay of our city, I was responsible for the lion's share of the movement of goods into and out of Hobson's Point. It's why I own the majority of the warehouses you were looking at. I may have lost a good portion of my workforce, but I still have the infrastructure and the contacts to get you whatever you need, for a price." Tobias's gaze bore into him almost hungrily, like Verdan was meat on display at a butcher's window.

"I have money....."

"No," Tobias interrupted, leaning forward in his chair with an intense look in his eye. "You're one of the more-interesting things to happen around here in quite a while, you see. A man of mysterious origin, with ready gold and an interest in alchemy. I want to be part of what you're doing. What I want is for you to come to me for your materials and your requests. I always trust my instincts, and they're telling me that working with you will be an interesting experience."

"I see," Verdan said shortly, keeping his face impassive as he considered the businessman's words.

Having someone with skill and expertise to acquire goods on his behalf would be advantageous, very much so. The problem was that it was another person with more information on him.

Even if Verdan didn't tell Tobias everything, he seemed like an intelligent man and would no doubt discover more than Verdan intended.

Still, there were some very clear positives to working with him, ones that he couldn't exactly ignore, much as he might want to. He just wasn't in a position to make all this work on his own.

"Very well, I agree in principle, but I need you to show that you can come through for me with the equipment," Verdan said, feeling a weight settle onto him as he bound himself to yet another person.

His plan of isolated research was feeling further and further away each day that passed.

"Of course, I would expect nothing less." Tobias said with a broad grin, rising from his chair to properly turn it to face the table as Brent reentered the room. When standing, Tobias was easily six-and-a-half-feet tall, his gaunt frame looking almost skeletal. "Ah, Brent, please serve and then send someone to start rounding up a convoy team. I want them to leave the day after tomorrow at the latest."

"Yes, sir, of course. Their destination?" Brent asked, as he set down a wooden tray and passed each of them a steaming mug and a small plate with a selection of cold cuts.

"Dresk, directly as well. If we can get anything to take to sell, do it. Otherwise, they're just going with a shopping list."

"Yes, sir," Brent said as he withdrew from the room, leaving them alone once more.

"Ah, it feels so good to have a purpose once more," Tobias said with a satisfied smile as he tucked into the selection of meat with clear hunger. "So, I can arrange for all the equipment and some basic ingredients, but it will cost you that gold piece you flaunted. I'm willing to let you use a warehouse as a temporary measure as well, but I have an idea for something that would be even better, as long as you don't mind living next to where you work?"

"Not at all," Verdan said, as he took a sip of the pale green liquid in the mug. Watered-down wine had been the drink of choice in the Imperium, but this mint tea was quite pleasing in its own way.

Verdan placed the mug back down as he reached forward to slide the gold coin across the table to Tobias, doing his best not to sigh at spending such a large amount.

"Excellent, excellent. Meet me back here tomorrow morning, and I'll show you what I think would suit you. In the meantime, please do think of anything else you need as well. It will take a minimum of two weeks' hard ride for the convoy to get there and back. That's with them moving light and fast as well."

"I'll think about it, and we'll return in the morning. Thank you for your hospitality, and I look forward to working with you," Verdan reached out to shake the other man's hand as they rose and left the room.

Verdan knew a dismissal when he heard one, and besides, he wanted to take a walk around the city while it was still light.

Brent was waiting outside and conducted them from the house with smooth efficiency, returning Kai's spear and Verdan's staff to them as he opened the front door for them.

"Well. That was interesting," Verdan muttered as they retraced their steps to the gates.

That hadn't at all been what he'd expected going in, but it did solve a number of issues he'd been concerned about. Still, only time would tell if he'd made the right choice to partner with Tobias.

CHAPTER

SEVEN

VERDAN MADE sure to give the three who'd remained outside a summary of what they'd discussed with Tobias. He wanted to ensure that if they were staying to work with him, they were kept in the loop.

Once he was satisfied, Verdan glanced up and judged the sun's position in the sky. They had enough time for further exploration, but there was no need to bring everyone with them for that.

"I'm going to explore the city a bit. Your time is your own until tomorrow morning. I want us all to visit Tobias as a group again. In the meantime, I don't want you all to be without money. Take these," Verdan pulled out a silver coin for each of his followers.

By local standards, that would be enough to keep them going and offer a bit of security for them. He still had just short of five and a half gold, so he had money to spare for the moment and wanted to make sure the others could get anything they needed.

They each thanked him before heading back towards the outer city, except Kai, who waited for the others to get a distance away before turning to Verdan. "There's somewhere else we should visit if you can spare some time?"

"I should think so. Where do you have in mind?" Verdan cocked his head in interest, wondering what Kai intended. He'd wanted to wander and familiarize himself with the city, so there was no harm in giving Kai some time.

"The Adventurer's Guild. They will be the only way to gain the reagents you need for creating potions that restore Essence." Kai said, absently tapping one finger on his chest as he spoke.

"That's the term you use for your internal energy, correct?" Verdan asked, consulting his mental list of Kai's terms, which were different from his own.

"Yes, it refers to the well of power that fuels our abilities. Though it refills over time, potions to quicken its restoration are both highly-sought-after and expensive." Kai said, starting back down the street as they spoke, Verdan pacing him with a thoughtful expression.

"Are they quite rare, then?" Verdan asked, considering the potential financial implications of his delve into alchemy.

"Yes, though it varies by what type of potion. The main ingredient of a replenishment potion is a heart from a creature that has wielded energy. Those Cyth we fought, for instance, their hearts would fetch a good price. The stronger the creature, the better the end result, as well." Kai led them towards the area where the nicer buildings transitioned into the outer city.

"That sounds like it would include other Sorcerers," Verdan said softly, thinking of some of the more-reprehensible things he'd seen done in the name of power.

He'd helped in a few raids on dark magic cults, and he still had the occasional nightmare about the things he'd seen.

"Yes. Anyone caught doing it is hunted down and killed, but it makes the end result both powerful and more effective, so many still do it," Kai said, his expression cold but an underlying tone of rage filling his voice.

Verdan had heard enough hostility in his life to recognise a personal hatred when he heard one, and didn't say any more on the matter.

They walked on in silence for a few minutes before Kai gestured to a large building that sat at a crossroads. It was three stories tall and took up as much room as the entirety of Tobias's compound, with an intermittent trickle of people coming in and out as they approached.

Watching the people carefully, Verdan noted that the vast majority of them seemed to be armed and armored, with the look of professional fighters and monster-hunters.

It was odd to see how mismatched they were, with varied weaponry and armor even within the same party. In truth, Verdan was still getting used to the fact that most people weren't part of the army in one form or another. In the Imperium, monster-hunting groups were formed from all the military branches, but they were far more standardized than what he could see here.

"This is the Adventurer's Guild. There's one in every city, and it's the hub from where mortals and Sorcerers alike can take jobs relating to the trade," Kai explained, gesturing to where a battered-looking group approached a freight entrance with a cart in tow.

Verdan couldn't see the interior, but he could guess that it was stacked with harvested materials from monsters and nature alike. Verdan didn't look too closely, however, as he registered one of the words that Kai had used.

"Mortals?" Verdan stopped walking and turned to eye Kai with a raised eyebrow.

The use of that term to refer to those without magic implied the very height of arrogance as far as Verdan was concerned, especially considering how limited their sorcery seemed to be. Powerful, absolutely, but so limited in scope.

"Yes—apologies, I hate that term, but it just slipped out," Kai said with a grimace and an expression of distaste. "It has become common parlance in the southern cities, where Sorcerers are treated more like nobility than anything."

"I see. Please don't use that term around me. I dislike such arrogant posturing. You've mentioned the southern cities a few times. We should sit down and go over the geography of the world at some point. I would like to know where we stand."

In Verdan's time, the Imperium had stretched close to two thousand miles, from the northernmost tip of the continent down to the islands of the south. He'd come from the northern end himself, so he knew that there had been a dozen or more cities further north than Hobson's Point.

Thinking about the old Imperium made him crave a map. He longed to see how everything looked now. The coastline alone must be hugely different to what he remembered. The fact it had advanced so close to his hidden chamber told him that much alone.

"I'm sorry, it won't happen again. When we have a chance, I will find something to show you. The main thing you need to know is that things are more fractured now than they've ever been. Alliances and pacts are now between clans of Sorcerers, not between cities or nations. It's part of why I came north, to get away from what they're making us into."

"I see," Verdan said again, not liking Kai's description of the south at all. It sounded like one of humanity's biggest enemies was itself right now. "We'll discuss that more later. Show me around the Guild first."

Kai nodded jerkily and led the way into the huge building. The exterior was practical, durable and without frills, giving a utilitarian look to the building. The interior was even more so at first, bare stone flooring giving the whole place a cold feel. The entrance led them to a large room with several exits and a central kiosk-like setup where two severe-looking men dealt with a short queue of people.

Several guards were posted around the room, and though it was mostly empty, there was a general flow of traffic throughout the chamber as people moved from one area to another.

"This is where jobs can be posted for Sorcerers and adventurers alike to complete. Once posted with the guild, the jobs are separated and displayed in one of three areas," Kai said, with a nod to the central structure before pointing out three of the exits from the large chamber. "Subjugation, harvesting, and tasked."

"Two questions—what are adventurers and what would come under 'tasked'?" Verdan asked as they stepped to one side to stay out of the flow of people coming in and out of the building.

"Adventurers are those without magic that still do jobs for the Guild. They usually form small groups that cover shortcomings and take on the smaller jobs. 'Tasked' is the area where all the more-particular requests go. For example, killing one specific monster, rescuing someone, or anything with a sensitive time frame."

"Interesting, so what's the going rate for harvesting monster hearts?" Verdan had to admire the setup; it was the most-organized part of the city he'd seen yet, and it sounded like it might be one of the few things keeping money moving through the area.

What little he knew of alchemy lead him to believe the hearts would be useful at some point, so it was a good measure of the costs involved.

"Right now, quite low, as there aren't any established alchemists in the city. Most of the jobs on display are for subjugation or gathering materials. With so much unclaimed land around Hobson's Point, there is no shortage of monsters to be found."

"Interesting, let's post a job then. I'd like to see how this works," Verdan said, rubbing his jaw thoughtfully as they approached the kiosk.

The short queue had been dealt with by the time they arrived. One of the men had left towards a nearby exit that had the most traffic. Sending a questioning look at Kai's way, Verdan wasn't surprised when he was told it was the built-in tavern and eatery.

Running his eyes over the people present once more, Verdan realized that only a few were actively looking for work. A lot seemed to be relaxing and talking or lingering in corners.

"Welcome to the Guild. How can I help?" The man at the kiosk asked as they reached him, pulling Verdan back to the job at hand.

"We're looking to post a bounty on hearts," Kai replied, taking the lead initially.

"Any specifics in type, strength, or element?" The man pulled a piece of paper from under the desk, along with an inkpot and quill. Arranging his equipment, the man dipped the trimmed feather into the ink before waiting for Verdan's answer.

"Fire element, type and strength irrelevant," Verdan said, not really caring about the specifics at all, but also certain that most requests would have at least one addendum if they asked upfront like that.

"Very well. How many are you requiring?" The scratch of the quill on the paper continued as the man wrote down their requirements.

"A dozen," Verdan picked a number out of the air that would probably do. Twelve would be enough to give him material for experimenting with a few different methods, all being well.

"Very good. Total bounty? We recommend a half-darn per heart."

"Seven silver," Verdan worked out the quoted rate to be six silver, so with a slight incentive there, they would hopefully get a swift fulfillment.

"Excellent. Please deposit the coins here. What name should I put on the request?" The man pulled out a small box that he placed on the desk.

"Verdan Blacke," he dropped the coins into the box and watched as the lid was shut and locked, the assistant putting a marker on the lid and tucking it away once more.

"And where will you be staying?"

"The Plucky Wanderer, for now," Verdan's lips twitched in a small smile as he saw the look in the assistant's eyes at the tavern's name. Clearly, it wasn't associated with people who put bounty requests out on a regular basis.

"Very well, all complete. Please let us know if you change residence; we will send a runner in the meantime when your job is complete."

"Thank you," Verdan nodded to the man and moved away towards one of the exits that Kai had pointed out earlier. There was a stylised, snarling face over an open entrance to a short corridor, which led to a room about half the size of the main chamber.

There was a similar kiosk to the previous area and numerous boards around the room, each with a few scattered pieces of paper showing. Under each paper was a code, and Verdan watched with interest as a group went to the kiosk and quoted a code before leaving.

The assistant operating the kiosk made a note of some form and then updated the job that was on display. Walking over to take a closer look, Verdan saw that there was now a red marker below the code.

"Each group attempting a job gets a set amount of time to complete it. Red means that someone is currently attempting it. If the time lapses, a second green dot will be added, showing that it's open once again but that someone has already tried it once. The original group could still turn it in, but they'll have competition now."

"I see," Verdan said thoughtfully, listening as Kai went on to explain more about how the whole process worked. He wasn't that interested in the details. He'd likely be posting requests more often than completing them for other people if he had his way. "I think I've seen enough. Unless there is something else while we are here?"

"No, this covers the majority of it. The alchemists I've met all put jobs here for resources to be harvested. I didn't know if you have something similar where you're from."

"Yes and no," Verdan said with a shrug. They'd had request boards like this, but nothing as organized as what he could see here. "Thank you for showing me."

Kai simply nodded in response and led the way back out of the Guild and towards the Plucky Wanderer.

_**_

The rest of the afternoon and evening passed quickly, Verdan's new companions providing easy conversation as they all tucked into roasted chicken and potatoes. Bob had continued to spend Verdan's money well, and the few other patrons in the tavern looked surprised by the quality of the food they were able to buy.

"Well, I think I'm going to turn in for the evening, Gwen. Could I have a word with you, please?" Verdan said, rising from the table and motioning to the stairs up to their rooms.

"Oh," Gwen said, her face falling for a moment before she took a deep breath. "I did agree, didn't I?" Gwen stood up, her expression resolute as she followed him to the stairs. Verdan turned to face her once they were out of earshot, but her eyes were on the floor, and the look on her face gave him pause. "Your room?"

"Yes, I suppose that would be best," Verdan said, a little confused by her behavior but happy to oblige. He wanted to see what she knew about alchemy. A little privacy would no doubt be best for the discussion.

Heading up to his room, Verdan opened the door and waved her inside. Following her in, Verdan closed the door before leaning his staff on the wall. "Right, so as you may know, I'm going to be doing a lot of research into alchemy. You said you aren't the best, but what do you know how to do if you have access to the right..... huh?" Verdan started talking before he turned around, so he was more than a little surprised when he found that Gwen was in the process of removing her tunic.

"Wait, what?" Gwen said, clearly just as surprised as he was. Her tunic was in the process of falling down her shoulders, but she'd paused as his words registered.

"Please, get dressed," Verdan turned away once more. He wasn't sure what was going through her head, but she was clearly not interested in him that way, and he wasn't going to take advantage of her.

"Thank you," Gwen said softly a few moments later, fully dressed once more.

"Do you want to explain what that was all about?"

"I thought it was the price you demanded for saving me from the Cyth," Gwen said, clearly embarrassed and confused by the whole situation.

"What? How did you get that impression?" Verdan sighed and rubbed his face. Her actions made a lot more sense now that she thought he was demanding sex.

"When you said that I could earn my keep through "other means," if not this, then what did you mean?" Gwen folded her arms, her posture a little defensive as she got her composure back.

"Well, ritual magic, of course—that and some much needed support in battle. Do you value your power so little that this was the first thing you thought of?" Verdan threw his arms up in exasperation.

He was getting increasingly frustrated with how hard-headed everyone seemed to be here. It was like he was speaking a different language sometimes.

"What power? I'm just a Weather Witch with some minor alchemy knowledge, not some all-powerful Sorcerer," Gwen snapped back, an unseen breeze ruffling her long dark hair as she squared up to him, blue eyes flashing angrily.

"You ask me what power, and you're a Weather Witch?" Verdan asked incredulously. Weather Witches were the most directly dangerous of all the Witches, even when caught unprepared.

"Oh, like that means anything," Gwen rolled her eyes and faced off against him, hands on her hips now as the tempestuous nature of weather Witches reared its head. "Witches are little better than regular folk when compared to Sorcerers like you or Kai. At best, our magic is unreliable. At worst, it's downright dangerous."

"Explain," Verdan said, cocking his head to one side with interest, his frustration fading away.

He realized he was letting his own experiences color his perception of what she was saying. There were some clear misconceptions at play here.

"Well, everyone knows that Witches have wild, untamed magic. It reacts to emotions first of all, but only strong emotions and not always how you'd expect."

"I see, but what about your Familiar?" Verdan knew from the confused look in her eyes that he'd found the cause of the misunderstanding.

"What's a Familiar?" Gwen asked, in a far more relaxed posture now that they'd found the issue.

"Witches channel the Aether, the natural energy, of the world directly, rather than draw it in and shape it like Wiz..," Verdan caught himself with a cough before he finished the word. He'd almost got too carried away with his explanation there. "Like with Sorcerers, is what I mean. The Aether responds to you, but you can't communicate with it properly without a Familiar, a divine creature that will allow you to control your magic consciously."

Verdan left out the part where their magic became a blend of arcane and divine through the use of a Familiar. No need to confuse her.

"How do you know this?" Gwen whispered, eyes wide as she listened with rapt attention.

"It's common knowledge where I am from. Sadly, I don't know the specifics of how to obtain a Familiar. That will be down to you. All I can say is that it's possible and that it will give you control, though of course, I will help where I can," Verdan said, genuinely regretting not ever finding out how the process occurred.

"My grandmother was said to have had great control over her magic, far beyond the rest of the family. Maybe there will be something in her journals I can find," Gwen mused, all anger forgotten as she considered the new information.

"We will study it together if you like, but for now, I need to complete my meditation, if you don't mind?" Verdan nodded toward the door, and Gwen flushed before apologizing and leaving.

That hadn't been quite the conversation he'd been expecting, and he still didn't know what she knew about alchemy, but he supposed it had been rewarding, nonetheless.

Seating himself on the floor with a sigh, Verdan cleared his mind and started the process of soothing his consciousness into a relaxed state. He needed a few minutes to find his bearings after that.

Once he was in the right frame of mind, Verdan got to work and continued building his gathering spiral.

CHAPTER
EIGHT

VERDAN ROSE EARLY the next day for some more meditation, managing to make it to a total of eighteen layers for his gathering spiral before he needed to head down to meet the others.

Eighteen was the last of the 'novice' layers. Each one from this point would be harder to do for an apprentice Wizard, as they now needed to compress the overall spiral. Given that Verdan had been compressing his spiral from the moment he started rebuilding it, he wasn't so worried about that.

They all gathered downstairs over the course of the next hour, Bob providing a thick porridge with a generous dollop of honey for breakfast. Verdan noticed that there was a growing number of patrons now. It seemed that the better fare was drawing in business for Bob.

Once they'd eaten, Verdan led the way back to Tobias's home. The chill mountain wind was biting and cold, but that seemed to be usual for Hobson's Point. Still, Verdan was relieved when they arrived at Tobias's estate. He was looking forward to getting out of the chill.

Of course, Verdan could create a warming effect to banish the cold, but it seemed wasteful. He had more important things to save his Aether for.

"Ah good, exactly on time," Tobias called out, opening the door as they approached. Brent stood behind him with a pleased expression, or at least, what passed as pleased for Brent.

Tobias was wearing a heavy jacket that seemed to swallow his gaunt figure, the outfit complete with a wide-brimmed hat and thick leather gloves. Brent was in a far-less-bulky outfit, but the slight jingle as he walked and the sword at his hip told Verdan that he was no less prepared.

"So, we're going to see something?" Verdan asked with a leading tone, quirking one eyebrow at the pale man.

"Yes, a location that I think will be perfect for you. If you are willing to take on the slight burden that comes with it, of course," Tobias said, his eyes glinting mischievously as he stepped past Verdan to greet the others.

Clearly, Tobias wanted it to be a surprise of some sort, an easy enough thing to play along with for now. After all, it cost Verdan nothing, but bought him some goodwill with Tobias, and perhaps gave a bit of insight into how the merchant thought.

Sighing softly to himself, Verdan followed along as Tobias led them to the northern part of the city. Much like the rest, this part of the city was run-down and lacking in care and attention. That being said, it seemed more aimed toward production and industry than the areas they'd seen so far.

Few people lingered around, and fewer still looked to be in good health, but there was an odd area of activity here and there. Ore was still being brought into the city and worked into ingots, then sent on in their raw form, or processed further into the day-to-day goods that people needed.

One particular area caught Verdan's eye as they passed by. It was a series of large buildings which each seemed to contain several furnaces. The buildings were arrayed around a sizable storage area for logs, which was currently empty of the necessary fuel.

To Verdan's eye, they looked like variants of the glasshouses he remembered from the great industrial sites of the Imperium. Efficiency usually demanded they be built within deep forests, their hunger for wood insatiable when providing glass to an entire continent.

Now, the glasshouses were cold and quiet, their lumber stores empty and long disused, just another sad sight in a city full of fading memories.

"Ah, here we are, though please do forgive the state of the area. It's unavoidable with the current problems." Tobias led them toward a set of black iron gates that acted as the entrance to some sort of walled compound. "The gates should be unlocked; there isn't really much call for them anymore."

"What were they for?" Verdan asked, pushing one of the gates open as they stepped into the compound.

The interior was dominated by a large, angular building which was longer than it was wide. There was something about it that gave the impression of solidity, and Verdan knew it had been built to last.

"Well, this was the heart of the Crea family's work. They were a family of skilled alchemists, one of the founding families, in fact. All manner of alchemical agents were made and stored here, hence the security."

"I see, and how much of that is left?" Verdan asked, intrigued as to what equipment might be remaining that he could use.

"Sadly, very little," Tobias said regretfully, a complicated expression on his face as he regarded the workshop. "The Crea family is all but gone now; their youngest was killed during a harvesting expedition, and the parents wasted away through grief. The last member, Natalia, lives here still, in what were the servants quarters. I sold all the equipment and assets on her behalf to help pay for the conversion, as well as ongoing costs. She was injured in an alchemical accident, you see, and has some health issues."

"So, she still lives here?" Verdan asked, tapping his chin in thought as he processed the sad story of the previous owners. He wasn't sure how he felt about that, but he sympathized with her problems.

"Yes, and I should mention that one of the conditions of sale was that the buyer must allow her to remain and that her basic needs are provided for. That's from me, though, not from her," Tobias said with an oddly-protective tone to his voice.

"I can do that, but what would all this cost me?" Verdan liked this place the more he looked at it, but the cost was definitely a concern when he had no current income.

"Three gold, which is a steal for a place like this. I'd normally say around ten gold at least, even with the low cost of property in the city. I'm only offering it so cheaply because of the extra parts to the deal and our partnership. What do you think?" Tobias gestured expansively to the whole compound as he spoke, smiling at Verdan as he did. He was clearly confident in his pitch, and there was no reason he shouldn't be. It was definitely a good one.

Considering Tobias's words, Verdan took in the rest of the estate, noting a few storage buildings off to one side, as well as a large mansion to the left.

While the workshop was the largest building, the mansion had an understated elegance to it. There were few decorations and embellishments, and what was there wasn't ostentatious. He liked it.

"So far, so good. Let's meet the current resident before we go any further. Her word is final, after all," Verdan kept his expression as neutral as he could, but a flicker of victory on Tobias's face told him he'd probably failed there.

"Of course, I sent her word that we were coming, so she will no doubt be waiting in the main house," Tobias set off at a fast walk, Brent shadowing him a few feet back and keeping an eye on the area as they went.

As they neared the mansion, Verdan noted that all the windows had a slight bluish tint to them, which he'd seen a few times in the city now.

"The local glass production uses a specific recipe that produces this lovely blue glass. A lot of local buildings use it as a mark of pride, but the family that lived here were among the first to settle Hobson's Point and were proud of their heritage. The blue windows are just a display of that." Tobias said, noting where Verdan was looking.

"I see," Verdan said absently. The more he saw of this city, the more he saw how prosperous it had once been, and the more he wondered how the rest of the continent fared.

Things hadn't been perfect in the Imperium, not by any stretch, but at least life had been stable for the common people. The war had mainly been fought outside the cities, where damage was manageable, and there was less chance of a reckless attack causing a high death toll.

He knew he couldn't turn around a whole continent, but he could at least do something with this city. Bringing this workshop back up to speed would have a knock-on effect in the local area.

After all, alchemy was always hungry for glass vials, bottles, and containers. He had everything he needed for a supply chain to support his work.

"Here we are," Tobias said cheerfully as they arrived at the door to the house, Brent opening it and leading the way inside. "Please, go on in."

Verdan followed in after Tobias's bodyguard, taking note of the dust that had gathered on much of the house's interior. Given what Tobias had told them, it wasn't surprising, but it was good to see some supporting evidence for what he'd been told.

The first room on the interior was a foyer with stairs leading up and several doors that led further inside. One of the doors stood open, and Verdan could hear the crackle of flames from further inside.

"Brent, good to see you again. How's the wife?" A woman called out as Brent went through the door at the other end of the foyer. Her voice was low and husky but with a strained tone, as though she had to struggle to speak.

"She's well, thank you, Miss. She asked after you recently. She wanted to make sure you were looking after yourself." Brent stayed in the doorway but smiled at the unseen woman as he waited for the rest of them.

"Be sure to thank her on my behalf," the woman said as Verdan walked past Brent and into what looked like a reception room of sorts.

Several large sofas and armchairs were situated around the room, along with a long table in the center and a large fireplace at the rear, in which a fire was burning brightly.

The furniture had a mixed quality to it, as though it was more of a random selection of pieces than ones belonging to any theme. Then again, from Tobias's comment on selling assets, that might well be the case.

The woman speaking to Brent was sitting near the fire, a wise choice on a day like this. Strangely, she was wearing a thick black lace veil that almost completely obscured her face.

Dark blue elbow-length gloves and a long black dress completed the outfit. The dress was clearly of quality make, with its scooped neckline showing off her impressive curves while remaining modest enough for daily wear.

As far as Verdan could see, she was an elegant and beautiful woman, which made him wonder why she was wearing the veil and what injury she had suffered that stopped her from working. He hadn't seen any other veil-wearing women around the city, so he doubted it was a cultural thing.

"Good morning," she inclined her head in his direction and gestured toward one of the nearby three-seat sofas.

"Good morning. My name is Verdan. It's a pleasure to meet you," he said as he took the seat she'd gestured to, the rest of the group filtering in and taking seats themselves.

"A pleasure. I'm Natalia, previous owner and last member of the Crea family." Natalia said, inclining her head slightly.

"Well, as you may imagine, my dear, this is the man I wish to sell the estate to. Alchemist, man of mystery and, hopefully, a good business partner," Tobias said, his eyes glittering with humor as he reclined back in his armchair.

"Alchemist?" She repeated the word in an almost-loving way, a touch of longing in her voice.

"A dabbler, but I aim to learn and discover. I'm from somewhere very different, and I intend to study the differences with interest," Verdan flashed her a smile, but the veil concealed whatever reaction she might have had.

"To make yourself a fortune and retire at an early age?" Natalia's voice was neutral, any small nuances somewhat obscured by what he assumed was damage to her throat.

Her voice had become steadily huskier as she spoke, and she coughed heavily after she finished, almost hunching over in her chair from the force of the cough.

Verdan gave Tobias a concerned look, but the merchant made a subtle gesture that everything was okay.

"Money will be made, but it's secondary to the research itself. Knowledge is power, after all," Verdain said, noting how Tobias softly sighed to himself as he dismissed the money-making aspect of it all.

While what Verdan said was true, he was too practical to dismiss his finances altogether. He intended to focus on production at first and then slowly transition over to pure research in time.

"What do you think, Natalia?" Tobias prompted after a few moments of silence.

"Well, he says all the right things, so if you're willing to trust him, then I will too." She rose to her feet and looked over at Verdan, "Please, don't disappoint me." Turning away, she started towards the door without saying anything further.

"I won't," Verdan said as he rose to his feet as well, Natalia pausing for a second before leaving through the door they'd only recently come through.

"Well, in all honesty, that went better than expected," Tobias said once they heard the front door of the house close. Brent nodded in agreement, despite a pained expression on his face, which he quickly banished when he saw Verdan looking his way.

"So, what now?" Verdan asked, seating himself once more as he realized that the merchant wasn't getting up.

"Well, I'll have the place cleaned up tomorrow for you, so if you like, you can move in any time after that, providing you agree to our deal, of course. I've sent a fast caravan to Dresk already. You should have all the fundamental requirements of alchemy before too long. So the real question is, do we have a deal?"

Verdan thought about it for a moment. It was a big investment of his remaining capital, but the potential benefits were high. It was secluded, to an extent, designed for alchemy, and built with plenty of room for expansion.

Verdan had a feeling this was as good a place to use as a base of operations as he was going to find around here. "We have a deal. We have two more nights at the Plucky Wanderer. We'll move in here after that. Here's your fee." Verdan passed Tobias the gold, satisfied that it was money well spent.

"Excellent. I'll arrange for my people to spruce the place up and make it ready for your arrival. Stop by on the morning that you want to take possession, and Brent will sort out your keys for you."

"Thank you, please let me know once the equipment has arrived as well," Verdan shook the gaunt man's hand and gave Brent a nod before heading back out.

_**_

Verdan spent the rest of the day in quiet meditation, slowly working to increase the density of his spiral.

Now that he had somewhere to work from and goods on order, he wanted to increase the amount of energy he had to work with. The more he had, the more he could do, and the more he could learn.

Half-a-day of concentrated work left him exhausted but took him from eighteen layers through to twenty-eight, a considerable jump in number.

Verdan was solidly in what was commonly known as the Journeyman stages now, where students were still forming their first complete spiral and expanding their vocabulary.

He had a long way to go, and it would only get more challenging, but there was something satisfying about seeing how quickly he was moving through these initial stages.

With some hard work and dedication, he would get through both the Journeyman and the Adept stages by the time his equipment arrived. He wasn't sure how much Aether would be needed to work on his alchemy projects, but better safe than sorry.

_**_

With a goal in mind, Verdan spent the next two days exploring the city and meditating whenever he had spare time, pushing himself all the way to forty layers on his spiral by the end of their stay at the Plucky Wanderer.

Everything from thirty-six up to a complete spiral was the early stages of being an Adept. Verdan smiled faintly as he remembered the long nights of wrestling with his gathering spiral when he was a true Adept.

Adept's were senior apprentices, tasked with maintenance and support, expected to watch everything their masters did and absorb it all like a sponge. His own master had encouraged questions, lighting a fire in Verdan that gave him a never-ending thirst for knowledge.

A knock at the door drew him out of his reverie. Verdan blinked in surprise at the late hour of the visit. "Excuse me, Mr. Verdan, there's a package here for you," Bob's voice came from outside his room.

It was their last night at the Wanderer, and Verdan had already retired for his evening meditation, so he wasn't expecting any deliveries or visitors.

Rising to his feet, Verdan opened the door to find the innkeeper holding a reasonably-sized box.

"What is it?" Verdan frowned at the box in confusion. Nothing should have been arriving from Dresk for quite a while yet.

"No idea, sorry. A runner dropped it off just now," Bob said with a shrug, putting the box down next to the door when he saw that Verdan wasn't going to take it. "Have a nice night."

"Thanks, you too," Verdan gave Bob a half-wave as he pulled the box into his room and carefully opened it up.

Nestled inside the box and carefully packaged were a dozen fleshy masses, which he assumed must be the hearts that he'd ordered through the Guild, though with some extra flesh in a few cases.

Unfortunately, he'd not been expecting such a quick delivery from the Guild, so he had nothing to work on them with. Well, nothing alchemical, anyway.

Biology had been a much-neglected aspect of science within the Imperium. Wizards had tended to ignore it, grouping it with potion-making and leaving it to the Witches.

Verdan only knew the little he did from some research he'd done on the human body when creating his stasis spell.

Tapping into his magic, Verdan extended his senses outward, examining the hearts for any magical residue that might be getting drawn out as the 'Essential Essence' the Sorcerers needed.

Nothing. Not even a hint of active magic to them. They were inert flesh with no magic to be drawn from them, as far as he could tell.

The Guild wouldn't have cheated him on his first-ever bounty; it was just bad business. Which meant that he must not be understanding just what the process was to extract the Essence.

The few alchemical techniques that he knew were based on using naturally-beneficial ingredients and then improving them by infusing energy into the mix.

It might be a similar situation here, with the hearts being used directly as ingredients rather than a source of power to be drawn from.

Whatever the reason, it definitely warranted further investigation. The real question was how he was going to do that investigation. He needed help, and those textbooks were still in Dresk right now.

Putting the lid back on and placing the crate in a corner, Verdan pulled together an Aether construct and bound it to the box, intoning "*hoer*" under his breath as he did so.

Releasing the construct, Verdan felt a slight chill brush past his fingers as the spell took hold. He'd added enough power to the spell to last overnight, keeping the hearts cold and, hopefully, preserving them.

Tired, and with more questions to ponder, Verdan climbed into bed and let his musings on how to go about his research lull him to sleep.

_**_

The next morning was a busy one as they said goodbye and moved their belongings from the Plucky Wanderer over to the Crea estate.

Verdan made sure to take the hearts himself, recharging the construct he'd attached to the box as he did.

Brent was ready with the key when Verdan arrived at Tobias's home, passing it over with a few comments on what had been done to the house and the workshop.

Apparently, anything left over had been stored in a basement room in the workshop for safety. That would likely include a few pieces of equipment and random things that had been missed previously.

Intrigued, Verdan resolved to head over and investigate as soon as feasible. First, though, Verdan gathered the group together and headed over to their new residence.

The area surrounding the old Crea residence was as decrepit as the last time they'd been here. Verdan could see hungry faces in windows, young and old alike, as they passed through.

Old oaths of responsibility tugged at Verdan's heart, reminding him of his recent good fortune and the money in his purse.

"Tim, Tom, I've got a job for you," Verdan said, the brothers picking up their pace to come alongside him.

"Yes, Boss?" Tim asked, waiting for their task expectantly.

"Here's ten silver each. I want one of you to buy bread and the other off-cuts of meat. Split it into as many portions as you can and then hand it out in the local area," Verdan said, passing each of them a handful of silver.

Watching the two guardsmen jog back toward the center of the city, Verdan tried to tell himself he was buying goodwill, and it was all a logical use of the funds he had.

The truth, however, was that he couldn't bear to see starving children, not while he could do something about it. Silver went a long way in the most basic of foodstuffs. Hopefully, it would be enough to take the edge off and help a few of those suffering the most.

Gwen was too wrapped up in her own thoughts to really pay much attention, but Kai gave him an approving nod when Verdan glanced his way.

It was good to know that they shared some of the same values.

Verdan didn't know quite how to treat Kai at the moment. The Sorcerer acted like a sworn retainer, but Verdan had little need of a warrior in his preferred line of work.

Time would tell, he supposed.

The Crea mansion was three stories tall despite its practical design. Six different bedrooms were spread across the top two floors, Verdan quickly claiming the master bedroom for himself.

Surprisingly, even in the overly-large bedroom he picked, there was little in the way of decorations or anything ostentatious. It all felt very practical and straightforward.

Perfect for his tastes.

Kai and Gwen took rooms on the top floor with him, leaving the brothers to take those on the next floor down along with the empty room. At this rate, no doubt he'd find someone else to live there in short order.

Verdan did consider asking Natalia if she wanted to move in with them, but he wouldn't want to live in his family home with a group of strangers if he was in her situation. She had come out to speak with them briefly when they arrived, but no doubt watching strangers moving into her old home was quite painful for her.

Putting the few possessions he had in his new room, Verdan made his way back out of the residence and across to the workshop, admiring it as he went. The building was the size of a medium warehouse, with at least two floors to it and thick reinforced doors at the entrance.

It was the sturdiest of any building he'd worked in, but that was perhaps necessary when dealing with alchemy.

Unlocking the doors, Verdan stepped inside the main area of the workshop, which was a surprisingly-filled storage area. It seemed to run two-thirds of the length of the building and a good half or more of its width. Dividers were evenly spaced along the edges for organizing goods in and out.

Crates, barrels, and storage racks sat empty and ready for use in each small zone, their contents long removed and most likely sold off.

Stairs up sat on each side of the storage area, with matching stairs down and a number of doors that led into the ground-floor rooms.

Picking the closest one to the entrance, Verdan was somewhat disappointed to find a bare stone room. Everything had been taken, right down to the furniture and workstations.

He'd thought that might be the case, but it was still disheartening to see that he was starting from scratch. However, it also meant he could design all of these rooms to do what he wanted from the ground up.

Once he worked out what that would be, of course.

Rubbing his face, Verdan did a lap around the whole building, mentally cataloging what was available. There were six workrooms on the ground floor, along with the central storage area.

Four larger rooms were upstairs, alongside two smaller storage areas, and three large storage areas filled the basement of the building.

It was a lot of space, with a lot of room for materials and products. Tobias hasn't been exaggerating when he said there was enough room for truly industrial output.

One of the storage areas in the basement was filled with the leftover parts that hadn't been sold off. It was a motley collection of items, a few crates of implements in less-than-pristine condition, and a couple of serviceable pieces of furniture.

Several burn marks marred the furniture, likely why it hadn't been sold on, but if he hauled all this back upstairs, he could at least have several bookcases and a chair to start things off with.

Leaving it all, for now, Verdan headed back to the residence to check in with everyone else and give some thought to how he'd want everything set out.

Perhaps he would equip one room while he waited for the delivery from Tobias. At the very least, he would have an idea of how everything came together then.

Tom and Tim were standing outside the residence when Verdan exited the workshop. The brothers were speaking to an older man with short gray hair and a powerful build, Tim beckoning him over when they saw him emerge.

"This is Samuel, a local foreman for one of the logging parties. He came to thank you for the food we gave out earlier," Tim said as Verdan reached them.

Samuel had a close-cut beard that was streaked with gray, warm brown eyes, and a kind face. Verdan wasn't a great people person, but he took an almost immediate liking to the man.

"Pleasure to meet you, glad to see someone moving into the old Crea place," Samuel said, his deep voice heavily accented but clear enough for Verdan to understand.

"You too, I hope to be doing a lot around here, and I will make sure part of it feeds back to the local workforce." Verdan said with a respectful nod to the other man.

"Is that so? Well, I reckon you'll be quite the popular man," Samuel said with a hearty laugh. "I know most of the folk around here. If you need anyone or anything, just give me a shout."

"Well, as you're here, I do have a few questions," Verdan said, thinking of the empty rooms in the workshop.

"I'm all ears."

"I need glassware suitable for alchemy, I've got some on order, but more is always welcome. I also need a few carpenters to make storage, chairs, and tables for the workshop. I'm willing to pay a little extra for it to be done in a good time frame." Verdan could see the mixture of hope and interest in Samuel's eyes, but something seemed to stop him from getting too excited.

"Well, there's a small problem with that. The logging grounds are closed right now. They have been for a few weeks, actually, which is why things are getting grim here. Something nasty moved into the area, you see. We went from being relatively safe to having attacks every day." Samuel said, grimacing and rubbing his left shoulder as he shook his head.

"We had to abandon the place or die, which meant no lumber for glass-making, forges, or carpenters. The southern woods are filled with Cyth these days, so they're no good either, not for a proper logging operation, that is." Samuel's shoulders slumped as he described the issues they'd been having, an understandable reaction in Verdan's eyes.

"Have you put a bounty out?" His first thought was the adventurers in the guild. They would be a good initial response to something like this.

"Aye, a team of three went in after it and never came back, so none of the rest will take it without more money in the bounty. No lumber means no work, which means no money to increase the bounty with. A vicious cycle."

"I see, and if the creature was driven off and the area made safe?"

"Why, I'd have the boys down there the same day, a few have risked going back on their own already. That's how eager they are to get going."

"Hmm, let Tim know where to find you. I'll most likely want to speak to you in the morning if that's okay?" Verdan tapped his chin in thought.

He wanted that operation going once again. It would give him access to a lot more without needing to pay through the nose for it. The goodwill of the locals would have its own benefits as well.

That being said, he wasn't making any decisions without more information.

"Of course! Drop by anytime. These two already know where to find me when you want a chat," Samuel bobbed his head and gave the brothers a wave before heading back out of the estate.

"What're you think, Boss? Are we hunting it down?" Tim asked, a little hesitant but willing to commit to the task.

"Maybe. Is Kai inside?" Verdan wanted to speak to the Sorcerer first of all, and when Tim nodded, he headed inside to track Kai down.

The Sorcerer was standing in the kitchen, feeding wood into the stove, when Verdan found him. A large pot sat on the stove, filled to the brim with vegetables and water, slowly heating up while Kai closed the stove and started preparing a chicken.

"Taking over dinner?" Verdan asked with a smile. The image of the scarred and imposing Kai cooking for them all amused him no end.

"Would you rather take over?" Kai paused to give him a look over his shoulder, his lips twitching into a smile as Verdan threw a hand up in defeat.

Sitting down at the table, Verdan passed on the information from Samuel as he watched Kai work. The chicken soon turned into portions that were added to the stew, Kai covering it over before joining Verdan at the table with a thoughtful expression.

"So, what do you think?" Verdan prompted after a few moments of silence from Kai.

"It's a dangerous job. If we're going to put a bounty out, it needs to be either for eradication or for a subjugation bounty. Eradication would be to kill everything dangerous in the area around the logging site, and subjugation would be to deal with the root cause. Whatever moved into the area must be dangerous enough to drive out so many other creatures; that or it's a group of creatures taking over a large tract of territory. Regardless, it's not something to be attempted with just a three-man group. Larger groups will only be looking for higher bounties, I'd say fifty silver for the eradication, minimum, and more like a whole gold for the subjugation."

Verdan instinctively winced at the thought of parting with one of his two remaining gold coins. The time when he could spend gold like water was far, far in the future.

Fifty silver was doable, but it would only be a temporary fix at best, meaning that at some point, the loggers would be attacked once more.

Arranging for an eradication to clear the area to send them back with the knowledge that they would be attacked again felt like a betrayal of trust to Verdan. If he was going to do that, he would also instigate some form of protection for the site to manage future issues.

However, adding protection to the site brought him straight back to the cost concern. That meant that the eradication was off the list, and that didn't leave much in the way of choice.

"What about if we did it ourselves?" Verdan asked somewhat reluctantly.

"That depends. How many of those strong fire conjurations could you do?" Kai made a rough gesture to reference the fireball that Verdan had used on the Cyth Bayne.

"I could do one more with the reserves I have, but my recovery rate is still abysmal, and it would take some time before I could do another. I have enough saved up for an extended fight with smaller effects, and hopefully, a bit more if I put some work in." Verdan said, sighing at the sorry state of his Aether reserves.

"The four of us could do it, then; you'd provide ranged support while I occupy the strongest, and the brothers hold the rest off you," Kai said with a slow nod, his eyes distant as he pictured how it would play out.

"Oh, and what about me?" Gwen said from the doorway, arms folded and eyes flashing with indignation as she stared them down.

"Well, do you have control over your magic?" Verdan raised an eyebrow in her direction, noting how quickly her anger shifted into frustration as she muttered something under her breath. "Exactly.

This will be a dangerous job. I couldn't in good conscience take you unless you can defend yourself."

"Did you say you were going to the northern woods?" Gwen asked after a few moments of thought, flashing them both a brilliant smile when Verdan nodded. "That's where my family home is, where my mother's books and my grandmother's journal is. Now you definitely have to take me."

"Gaining a familiar isn't an overnight process. You will need time to properly commune with nature," Verdan said with a frown, automatically disapproving of any rushed magical processes.

"And you will need time to properly survey and hunt in the area, time best spent from a base camp like the cottage I grew up in. Besides, one of my ancestors warded it to keep away most monsters and things of ill intent." Gwen's smile took on a smug quality as she spoke, turning the argument around on him.

"She does have a point," Kai said softly, making Gwen crow in victory and clap her hands together.

"Very well," Verdan said with a sigh, not able to argue with both of them. "We head to your home first and then organize our hunting from there. We'll spend the night here first and head out tomorrow. Tell me in the morning if you need any additional supplies. I've got some more meditating to do." Verdan rose and quickly left before they could get any more concessions from him.

The whole issue echoed in his mind as he climbed the stairs. He just didn't get it. Why wasn't the city doing anything about it?

That was a problem for another day, however. Right now, they were going into a dangerous area with little information and little preparation. In a situation like that, any extra Aether he brought could save a life.

He had a hard night of meditation ahead of him.

CHAPTER

NINE

VERDAN GOT LITTLE SLEEP OVERNIGHT. Instead, he spent most of the time he had focusing on pushing his spiral construction as much as he could.

When first learning, novice Wizards were specifically told not to do this, mainly to stop them from overreaching or doing it wrong.

Still, given the situation, Verdan felt confident in flouting the rules like this. After all, it wasn't like there was anyone left to gainsay him.

Staying up until the early hours of the morning, Verdan managed to add twelve more layers to his spiral, making it a total of fifty-two out of sixty.

He was so close to finishing the spiral he could almost taste it. Another day or two of work, and it would be finished.

After the few hours of sleep that he did get, Verdan headed down to the kitchen to see if there was any food left. He'd skipped the evening meal for more meditation time, and his stomach was definitely telling him about it.

"Morning, Boss," Tim greeted him as he walked in, the ex-guard munching happily on an apple. "I hear we're heading out to help the loggers today and visit Gwen's home to boot."

"Morning, Tim. Yes, the first will help with what we're doing here, and the second should help Gwen control her powers," Verdan said, before gesturing toward one of the two extra apples Tim had with a questioning look.

"That'll be good. I've never had a bad experience with a Witch myself, so I never put much stock in the stories you hear, but a lot of folks do. A bit of control might well go a long way to helping folks stop fearing them," Tim said, shrugging and tossing Verdan an apple.

"I hope so. Where I'm from, Witches are respected and all but revered by the common folk. They're seen as guardians of nature and the first line of defense against a lot of things that might slip by more traditional methods." Verdan bit into the apple eagerly as he spoke, explaining it all around mouthfuls.

"So, they must have some better way of control where you're from then. Is there not a way to send a courier or someone to get a book on what to do for Gwen?" Tim asked, frowning slightly as he considered the issue at hand.

"Sadly not; there's no way back now. The best path forward for her is to read her grandmother's journal. I'll try to do what I can to help her along as well," Verdan said, quickly moving the conversation away from where he was from.

"Sounds good to me. Tom and I don't know a lot about the whole magic thing. We'll leave that to you three." Tim shrugged and went to grab the last apple before pausing, eyeing Verdan, and tossing it his way.

"Ahh, thanks," Verdan said, biting into the new apple eagerly. "So, do you need any supplies for a trip out into the woods?"

"Food, some general equipment maybe. Nothing too much though, maybe a few silvers each to be fully prepared and with food enough for everyone."

"Here, there's Tom's amount as well." Verdan passed him a handful of silver without hesitation. "Let me know if you need anything else." If there was ever a time to spend his money, this was it.

"Will do. We'll go get it sorted now. Thanks, Boss," Tim threw him a lazy salute and headed upstairs to fetch his brother.

"Tim," Verdan called after him, "make sure to stop by Samuel's house on the way and let him know that we're taking care of it. If he could get someone to keep a watch on things here for me, I'd appreciate it." Tim waved a hand in acknowledgement, carrying on up the stairs.

_**_

Several hours passed, with both Kai and Gwen taking some silver themselves and going to get things they thought were essential for the expedition.

The drain on Verdan's funds was already high for this. He was down to just under two gold darns.

While that was a considerable amount in itself, from how quickly he'd burnt through the rest of his funds, he was getting a little concerned.

Still, they had everything together by lunchtime and split it, mostly evenly, between five packs. Verdan saw that the brothers had brought everything from food, flint, bedrolls, and whetstones through to replacement clothing, bandages, and herbal remedies.

Everything they could think of was in those packs. They didn't know what would be needed, so it was all in an effort to try and give them an option for any eventuality.

Verdan doubted that a lot of it would be needed, but it was better to be prepared and not needed than the other way around.

The only thing missing was alchemical support, antidotes, toxin neutralisers, healing potions, anything like that.

Apparently, such items were like gold dust currently, mostly bought up in advance by the Sorcerers who still remained in the area.

That would change once Verdan was set up, but for the moment, it limited them to more mundane equipment.

"Everyone ready?" Verdan asked, looking over the small group as they donned their packs and the equipment they'd bought. He got a slew of nods from the others, so wasting no more time, he led the way out.

The main entrance to Hobson's Point was on the eastern side, where they'd entered not so long ago, but there was a second entrance on the north-western side. This entrance led straight into a narrow pass through the mountain range and to the forests beyond. Fortified and guarded to a much higher degree, the second entrance was a gateway to the more-dangerous lands north of the mountains.

Tim and Tom had spent some time with Samuel, discussing the logging operation and the area in general. From what they told him, normally, the area closest to the pass was actually safer than that to the south.

To the east of Hobson's Point, a city had been destroyed in the last Rising. A powerful Cyth force overwhelmed them before scattering into the area. No doubt that event was the cause of the Cyth settlement that Verdan had come across, the impact of such a loss for humanity causing problems even years later.

In contrast, the northern territories were stable and more predictable in where the dangers would lie. The exception was when something new moved into the area like they were seeing now.

There were a large number of guards at the gateway to the pass, as well as two looming towers with ballista in case something large came through, but they did little more than nod in the group's direction as they passed through.

It made sense, really. The guards were only there to protect the city, not the people who wanted to head north.

A certain weight settled onto the group as they passed through, mainly due to the knowledge that they were leaving the implied safety of the city behind. Anything could happen now.

Everything Verdan had heard so far told him that the wilderness to the north was nothing like the area he'd known in the past.

_**_

It took a whole afternoon of walking to make it through the pass, the rocky terrain worn away by countless previous travelers to provide a passable trail they could follow.

The land before them was slowly revealed as they reached the end of the pass, a large forest covering it for as far as he could see. A series of switchbacks brought them down a short way to the level of the forest and a large clearing that sat at the base of the path to Hobson's Point.

The clearing would have once been completely void of plant life. That much was easy to tell. Despite that, there were shoots of green appearing here and there throughout it now that spoke to its disuse.

A permanent fire pit laid claim to the center of the area. A check over it determined that it was cold and waterlogged, but still serviceable enough.

A path had been carved through the undergrowth at the far side of the clearing. From what they'd been told, following that path would bring them to the trail to the logging camp in short order.

Their first destination was Gwen's family home, but thankfully, it was in the same direction as the camp, initially at least.

"Do we stop here?" Verdan asked Gwen, gesturing to the fading light as the sun started to dip below the horizon.

"We can, but the cottage is just a few hours from here. If we hurry, we can be there before dark and sleep with the wards in between us and any monsters," Gwen said with a shrug, leaving the decision to him.

Verdan thought about the options for a moment before nodding and gesturing to the trail, "Let's push on now. The possibility of the wards is worth the risk of traveling so late. Gwen, you take the lead with Kai."

"No problem, let's get going," Gwen set off immediately, her excitement showing with the extra spring in her step as she started down the trail. Kai followed a few steps behind her, spear ready for any creatures they might encounter.

"You go next, Boss. We'll take the rear and make sure nothing sneaks up on you," Tim said with a firm nod, his smile strained as he looked around them at the fading light and the looming trees.

"Shout if you see anything," Verdan told them as he followed after the other two. Splitting his attention, he focused on the concept of a bright bolt of fire, one that would illuminate as well as burn.

It wasn't his normal spell, but one that would be worth the extra drain on his reserves to cast.

Carefully constructing the concept of what he wanted, Verdan took a second to commit it to his short-term memory before letting it fade away.

Making new and unfamiliar spells on the go was a complicated matter, but the less familiar with the spell he was, the more he needed to compensate with either raw power or more specific wording, which in turn was mentally fatiguing.

The complexity of the process caused a tendency for Wizards to rely on a set group of spells with which they were most familiar, a dangerous habit in Verdan's opinion. Though, perhaps he was guilty of that to a certain extent as well.

Keeping an eye on the shadowy undergrowth to either side of the path, Verdan quickened his walking to match the two ahead of him.

With every other step, his staff would thud into the ground, measuring out their pace. The steady rhythm of the impacts were somewhat soothing in the tense situation.

The dim light cast eerie shadows that shifted and changed as they moved past. Each and every shadow could, and probably did, conceal something that would kill them if given a chance.

Minutes passed uncomfortably slowly at first, the threat of the unknown keeping them on edge and dragging out the travel. They passed the split in the path for the logging camp early on, Gwen taking the right-hand fork to take them toward her old home instead.

A few more turn-offs came and went as they hiked on, the disused path growing more and more dilapidated as they traveled on.

CHAPTER
TEN

Kai rubbed his thumb down the smooth grain of his spear, appreciating its fine make once more as he walked a few paces behind Gwen. It had been more than he'd expected from Verdan to get him such a weapon, but then again, what had Verdan done that wasn't more than he expected?

Everything the man did, from the way he conjured his Essence through to the way he spoke, was different and subtly foreign. One of the southern sects might be tempted to beat his secrets free, but Kai held himself to the old code of conduct and respected the other man's privacy.

No matter how frustrating it was.

Things had moved so quickly since Kai had awoken in the Cyth dungeon, weaponless and certain that he would face impending death with no salvation.

His whole worldview had been turned on its head by Verdan's explanations, not the least of which was the 'Aether' the Wizard had mentioned a few times.

At first, Kai had thought it was Essential Essence. However, he soon realized that wasn't the case, as no mere Sorcerer would be able to use so many different elements with ease, nor need to speak aloud in that strange language.

The very air had seemed to reverberate, resonating with something inside Kai when Verdan had conjured his fireball at the Cyth settlement, a terrifying and awe-inspiring sight.

Gwen sidestepped a pothole, drawing his eyes to her and his mind to another of Verdan's revelations.

Witches were dangerous, chaotic, and the source of many small evils—that was the general opinion of the Sorcerer Sects, anyway. To say that Witches were something else entirely was disturbing at best, and downright dangerous at worst.

Some of the more fractious among their number might take offense to Witches being viewed as equals to Sorcerers.

Personally, Kai had always wondered about Witches, but he'd trusted in what he'd been taught. Now, with Verdan arriving and bringing such strange knowledge with him, Kai wasn't so sure.

Part of him wanted to doubt Verdan, but with everything else he said being demonstrated to be accurate, what was Kai meant to think?

It didn't help that Gwen had an admirable passion in her soul, a passion that had been ignited by Verdan's comments on how she might control her magic. Kai found himself looking at her in the same light as he would an inadequately-trained Sorcerer, not as a potential disaster.

"Kai," Verdan called to him, his voice soft but carrying an undercurrent of concern that set Kai on guard immediately.

Gripping his spear a little tighter, Kai slowed down so that Verdan caught up with him, watching their surroundings carefully as he did.

"What's wrong?" Kai kept his voice soft and didn't turn to face Verdan, wary of giving away anything. Keeping his focus on their surroundings, he looked for what might have caused Verdan to speak up.

"Something is stalking us. I'm not sure what, or for how long. I caught a flicker of Aether a few minutes ago, and when I started searching for more of it, I sensed at least three sources." Verdan told him equally softly, not sounding worried, just wary.

"I've not seen anything," Kai said, frowning in concentration as he recalled their journey so far. He'd not noticed anything particularly worrying or indicative of anything too bad, which was now quite a bad sign in itself.

Years of hunting monsters meant that Kai had a strong awareness of his surroundings; not just anything could hide from him.

"Trust me. It's there. Whatever it is used Aether, or Essence as you would call it, with a darkened aspect to it. Whatever they are, they're difficult to pin down and locate. They're likely some form of shadow creature, one that naturally hides by using Aether. That would explain it evading my detection."

"Can you give me any more specifics?" Kai was becoming increasingly more worried. Shadow creatures were known to be dangerous, not necessarily for their fighting ability but for their skill in ambush. That Verdan was able to sense them at all was impressive. Of course, that was assuming this actually was a group of shadow creatures.

"They feel coordinated and fast. I can't get anything more specific than that, with the way they fade in and out of my senses," Verdan said with a frown of displeasure.

"That's not good. How close are they?" Kai kept a lid on his emotions, not letting anything show that might give anything away. Body language could be sensed by even brutish creatures, after all.

"Thirty feet out into the undergrowth, sometimes further away, sometimes a little up ahead. I get the feeling they're waiting for something."

Kai stopped himself from grimacing. That sounded like they were walking into an ambush. Exactly what he'd expect from something that was infused with the Essence of shadow.

The only question now was what to do—push on and stay aware, try to change direction or try to fight their stalkers?

A hard choice, but thankfully one that rested with Verdan, not with him. Glancing up at the tall Wizard, Kai could see that he was also considering their options.

"I could try to chase one of them down and see what's out there," Kai offered with an open palm. He disliked being on the defensive like this. He'd rather take the fight to them.

"No, it's getting too dark for that. It would be too easy for them to evade you and ruin our chances. We'll stick to the path for now. Stay up at the front with Gwen and keep your eyes peeled."

"Alright, send me a signal if you see anything. They might just be waiting to catch one of us off guard after all," Kai said before quickening his pace once more.

"Everything okay?" Gwen asked as he caught up with her once more.

"There might be trouble. Just carry on as normal for now, and let me know if you see anything suspicious." Kai considered not telling her at all, but that would bring its own risks, and he didn't feel comfortable lying to her.

_**_

Despite the tension in the air, nothing immediately happened. Each minute spent traveling brought them closer to safety, and yet it also added to the ball of tension that was nestled in Kai's gut.

He could almost feel the hungry gaze of whatever was out there on them.

Gwen had been a little unnerved at first, but she'd settled down now and was focusing on getting them back to her home. It helped somewhat that the moon had come out and was giving them some light to see by.

Kai knew better than to relax, however. They were walking in the light gray of dusk now, and pools of shadow were all around them, pools that could hide anything.

"Here, just past these rocks, and we're at the glade," Gwen said, relief evident in her voice as she pointed out a rock arch that was positioned over a faint trail that led off from the main path.

Kai began to relax but noticed a slight glint in the air just in front of Gwen. He tried to stop her, but the Witch stepped forward just before he could reach her and pull her away.

Gwen cried out in surprise as she walked straight into something; the air across the entirety of the path seemed to shimmer and shake as she hit the glint he'd seen.

Webbing.

The whole path was covered in shimmering webbing, all but invisible when still but easily spotted when disturbed like this.

Gwen was cursing and trying to pull free, but both her hands and the left side of her body were stuck fast. "Kai! Help me out of this!"

"*Thanr disir!*" Verdan's voice cracked the dark evening air from behind them, a flash of light illuminating everything as an incandescent bolt of fire sped past Kai to envelop a dog-sized patch of darkness on a nearby tree.

The bright light of the fire banished the surrounding darkness for a brief moment, bringing everything into stark contrast. The patch that Verdan had struck hissed in pain and became slightly visible, revealing long segmented legs and a furry body with far too many eyes.

Two further patches of darkness had been highlighted by the light, though their stygian depths untouched by the illumination Verdan had provided. A distant part of Kai's mind appreciated the irony of their own stealth magic providing their location.

Gwen seemed to be making progress in getting herself free, so Kai raced towards the creature that Verdan had hit with his initial shot. It was still smoldering with dimly glowing embers, giving him somewhere to aim.

The creature realized its ambush had been foiled and released the obfuscating darkness that surrounded it, revealing a black spider the size of a hunting dog, its fangs exposed as it reared back threateningly. Even without the darkness shrouding it, the creature was difficult to see, giving Kai little to aim at as he closed in and thrust out with his spear.

The spider jumped to one side with explosive speed, the tip of Kai's spear catching the edge of one leg as it went. Swift-moving steel cut deep into its chitin and flesh, coating his weapon with shimmering blue-black blood.

Kai had expected to remove its limb with such a strike, not simply bleed it; the chitinous exterior of the creature must be particularly strong.

The spider hissed in pain, abruptly changing direction as it scuttled towards him and leapt again, this time toward Kai's neck.

Igniting the Essence in his core, Kai felt the speed and unrestrained energy of fire flood his body.

The spider was quick, far too quick for an ordinary soldier to keep up with, but with the fire racing through his body, Kai was more than its match.

Swinging his spear around, Kai planted a heel and thrust up at the leaping spider a bare moment before it struck him.

The hooked spikes that were the spider's fangs were barely inches from his throat, glistening with venom as it tried to drive them home. Kai's spear impaled it through its thorax and held it in place.

Twisting and pushing, Kai grunted with effort as he brought the creature up into the air before slamming it down and driving his spear all the way through with a visceral crunch. The spider spasmed and flailed for a brief moment before curling in on itself, its blueish lifeblood staining the dry ground beneath it.

"Disgusting," Kai muttered with distaste as he pushed down with a booted foot, pulling his spear clear and spinning it around, flicking off the blood and gore that stained it.

His fight with the spider had lasted only seconds, but he could see another spider's corpse on the far side of the group, a small trail of smoke coming from it, marking it as Verdan's work.

"Yes!" Gwen shouted from behind him, as a slight breeze brought Kai an astringent smell that made him grimace in distaste.

Turning to look, Kai saw miniature bolts of lightning jump from Gwen's hand to burn away the spiderweb she was stuck to, releasing more of the foul smell.

Unlike Verdan, who was completely in control of his magic, Kai could see Gwen flinching as the lightning flashed once more, burning away yet more of the web.

This was why people turned away from Witches. Kai knew that Gwen wouldn't hurt him on purpose, but if she was flinching from her own magic, just how much control could she really have?

Every horror story Kai had ever heard about Witches ran through his mind. Tales of Witches killing someone who had tried to help them, their magic turning against their would-be rescuers.

However, after his conversations with Verdan, Kai wasn't quite as bothered as he had been before. True, it was disconcerting, but if the Witches where Verdan was from could control it, then so could Gwen.

With some of the fear taken away from the situation, Kai couldn't help but wonder what Gwen would be able to do when she had full control of her powers.

Ignorant of his thoughts, Gwen was finally able to free herself with a larger blast of lightning from her hand that was accompanied by a gust of wind from the other.

Gwen stopped and stared at her hands with an unreadable expression for a few moments. Visibly shaking it off, she turned to meet Kai's gaze, giving him a nod before moving toward Verdan and the two brothers.

Seeing Gwen free, Tim and Tom turned toward her and moved to meet her halfway, turning their backs on the nearby shadows.

A flicker of movement from the treeline caught Kai's eye as another of the giant spiders came scurrying forth and leapt at Tim.

Kai was still filled with the Essence of fire, its primal energy speeding his reactions to the point that he was already moving before the creature was halfway to Tim.

It wasn't going to be enough, though. The eight-legged monster was just too quick for him to intercept over such a short distance.

"*Ast!*" Verdan barked, throwing a hand out towards Tim and conjuring a pale blue dome in between the guard and the leaping spider, which impacted with a dull thud and fell heavily to the ground.

Tom lunged forwards to strike the creature before it could recover, bringing his mace down on it with a heavy two-handed blow. The steel ridges of the weapon smashed through the spider's carapace with ease, pulping the flesh beneath and leaving behind a vicious wound.

Kai arrived a split second later, all of his speed going into a powerful thrust that sent his spear powering through one side of the creature and straight out the other. It was hard to tell if Kai's strike had been needed to finish the creature off; all that mattered was that it was dead.

"That's all of them," Verdan called out a moment later, moving to crouch over one of the dead spiders and examine it a little closer. "What are these called, do you know?"

"No idea, not something I've fought before. Definitely shadow Essence, from how fast they were and their tricks with darkness, though," Kai said, pulling out a rag to clean the ichor off his spear.

He'd fought shadow Essence creatures in the past and had it much worse than this. Verdan was almost the equivalent of several caster Sorcerers by himself.

"Yes, we're lucky that the illumination from my spell seemed to damage the Aether constructs they were using for the webbing and for their camouflage. An interesting weakness; perhaps they don't encounter many things that can produce bright light." Verdan said, tapping a finger on his lips as he walked over to examine the remaining webbing.

Kai's internal translation of that explanation was that the bright light had disrupted their shadow Essence, which did make sense after all.

Waiting a few more moments to make sure the fight was over, Kai took a deep, calming breath and quietened his Essence, letting the energy that was coursing through him fade away once more.

Every time he used his Essence, the world felt sluggish afterwards. Thankfully, though, the effect never lasted for long.

Kai approached the section of spiderweb that Gwen had burnt herself free from, which was still smoking and giving off a horrific smell. Grimacing in distaste, he used his spear to cut through the strands in the center.

The unburnt strands were remarkably tough and resistant to being cut, but after a bit of effort, he was able to cut down the center and split the whole web in two, making it droop to either side and open up the pathway.

"Nicely done. Now, let's get moving, and get behind those wards before anything else happens," Verdan said, heading straight through the gap and on towards the rocks that Gwen had pointed out.

Kai waited for everyone else to pass through before following at the rear, staying wary for any more hidden creatures, just in case Verdan had missed one.

He gave the corpses of the spiders one last look as he walked away. It was a shame that it was so late and so dark. He would have loved to harvest them for anything usable. Shadow Essence was relatively rare after all, so anything that could be taken might have been useful. It just wasn't worth the risk right now.

In Kai's opinion, greed and overconfidence killed Sorcerers more than anything else.

He'd seen it so many times.

They would stay too long, go too far, or take too little backup, and then not make it back. He had no intention of making the same mistake himself.

CHAPTER
ELEVEN

VERDAN WAS BARELY a step into the glade that Gwen's family had called home when he felt the distinct touch of an Aether probe assessing him.

Bringing a defensive concept to mind, Verdan swept his gaze across the clearing as his heart pounded in his chest. The Aether used had been strong enough to belong to something powerful.

His eyes saw nothing, but his Aether senses picked up more magic as his companions were likewise tested.

Thankfully, the Aether was withdrawn once all of them had been assessed, and Verdan was able to follow the flow back to its source: to a towering oak tree across the glade from him.

The tree was central to the area, in a way that seemed deliberate more than accidental. Thinking of where he was, Verdan realized that the tree must house the nature spirit that maintained the wards on the glade.

Thankfully, that meant it was no threat to any of them, for so long as they remained guests, anyway.

Relaxing slightly, Verdan breathed a subtle sigh of relief that he hadn't overreacted. He'd been anticipating some form of spirit from Gwen's description, but he hadn't imagined that it would be such an old one.

No young spirit could manage that level of strength and such a deft application of it. That meant that the tree Verdan was looking at was old, very old. He'd guess a thousand years, at least.

It raised his estimation of Gwen's family line. Not just any Witch could claim a home that such a fierce guardian protected.

Happy that things were in order, and a little more reassured now that he knew the strength of the spirit that was maintaining the ward, Verdan took the time to look over the glade properly.

The area was around a hundred feet across, with a large cottage in the center and the towering oak looming protectively over it. No other trees, or any plants larger than a bush for that matter, were growing within the clearing, giving it a secure and enclosed feeling.

Soft moonlight played across a fair-sized pond on the far side of the cottage, and a bench had been set up to overlook the water so that the cottage would be to their back. It was a welcoming scene, one that Verdan appreciated after recent events.

"It's good to be back here," Gwen said softly, smiling slightly as she looked around at the glade. An invisible weight seemed to drop away from her, letting her finally relax and look at peace in a way that she hadn't since she first woke up in Hobson's Point. "It doesn't look like it's changed at all."

It wasn't surprising that she hadn't been truly relaxed, but hopefully, being here would help her make a full recovery. The damage done by the Cyth corruption was extensive, and it would take time for it to heal.

The presence of a powerful nature spirit would help, though, as would her being in a place that resonated in a positive way with her. Verdan would need to examine her again for an accurate time-line, but he estimated a full recovery in the next few days.

"I can imagine, the spirit powering these wards is a strong one indeed," Verdan said carefully, noting how her expression flickered to sadness and then back to hope at the mention of the spirit. So, she was aware of the source of the protection.

Interesting.

"Verdan," Gwen said, hesitating for a moment and biting her lip before turning to face him and continuing, "do you really think I'll be able to learn control? The idea of dealing with spirits and controlling my magic is like a dream, but you make it sound so normal."

"That's because it is. Where I'm from, every Witch has a familiar and can deal with nature spirits as easily as I do the flows of Aether. I don't know if your grandmother's journals can provide any insight, but I promise that it's possible," Verdan said solemnly, looking her straight in the eyes as he spoke.

It was a shame she wouldn't be able to learn Wizardry. Verdan was sure that Gwen would have made a fine apprentice.

"I suppose that's all I can ask for, thank you." Gwen said before taking a deep breath and motioning to the cottage. "Now, let's get you all inside where it's warm and dry."

"Is there anyone else here?" Tom asked as they headed toward the entrance.

"Not anymore, my mother died a few years ago. I'd been meaning to move back, but the area had become a bit dangerous. I guess I don't have much choice anymore," Gwen said with a shrug and a grimace. "But, that's enough of that. With the ward in place, everything should be in good condition." Putting action to words, she headed inside, leaving the door open behind her as she went.

The interior was dark and cool initially, but Gwen soon had a fire going using some dried logs that had been piled to one side. The growing fire illuminated the room and gave off a pleasant wave of heat, giving the cottage a homely feel.

"Cozy," Tim said, his brother grunting his agreement as they set their packs down by the door.

"Help me get these candles lit, and I'll give you a quick tour," Gwen started towards a box in the corner, but Verdan waved her to stop and focused on the concept of a warm, soft light that was bright enough to fill the room.

"*Disir*," Verdan spoke the word gently, causing a glowing orb to swell in his left hand, its gentle radiance filling the room and banishing all but a few shadows. Picking up a chamberstick with a burnt-out candle, he fixed the globe to its top, slightly altering the spell as he did. "Here, use this for now."

"Damn, now that was impressive. Just what sort of Sorcerer are you?" Tim said with a low whistle, his sentiment echoed on the other three's faces. Kai looked particularly impressed as Verdan handed the chamberstick to Gwen.

It was a strange reaction. Why pick that, out of all the things he'd done, to be so impressed about?

"I'm not. I'm a Wizard, which is something else entirely, and apparently something that isn't in these lands anymore," Verdan said simply, having already covered this with Kai previously and confident that they'd have no idea what a Wizard was.

Still, he knew he'd need to have this conversation sooner or later, so he wanted to get it out of the way. It gave him time to speak with them about what he needed to do from their perspective to not stand out.

"Stronger than a Sorcerer?" Gwen asked, eyeing the glowing orb atop the chamberstick warily as she spoke.

"I don't know yet. How would you rate me, Kai?" Verdan asked, genuinely interested in what the Sorcerer would say.

"Middling to strong, but with unparalleled versatility. I've seen two of the four pillars of sorcery from you, Projection and Manipulation, but not Enhancement or Augmentation." Kai said, shrugging slightly as he spoke.

"What constitutes those last two pillars?" Verdan asked, intrigued by further insight into the types of sorcery.

"Enhancement is using Essence to empower your own physicality. Augmentation uses the same Essence to empower objects or people. I awakened as an Enhancer. It's how I kept up with those spiders; I ignited my Essence to fuel my body the entire time." Kai explained with a tap on his sternum.

"I see. That's something that I can replicate with spells, but not as directly as you, it would seem. What interests me, though, is that the way you describe it is so different from the way I work," Verdan mused aloud, rubbing his jaw thoughtfully as he spoke. He should have expected that the Sorcerers would have some form of doctrine, but it was so contrary to his own magic. Why break things apart into four categories?

"Well, at least we know why you use those words when you do stuff now. That was a bit confusing for us," Tim said with a laugh, Tom grunting with a nod of his own.

"Yes, though please keep my origin and my difference to yourselves. While I only want to help, no doubt some would feel threatened by me and seek to control me or cast me out because of that." Verdan wished he didn't have to worry about such things, but human nature was fickle and wary of change at the best of times, only becoming more so as money and power became involved.

"Don't worry about us, Boss. We've got your back," Tim piped up immediately, his earnest tone making Verdan smile despite himself. He'd been quite lucky finding people such as this to help him.

"If even part of what you have said is true, I'll owe you a debt greater than I can express. You needn't worry about me." Gwen was still holding the chamberstick with his light spell attached, her posture a lot more relaxed than when he'd first passed it to her.

"Thank you, all of you. Your support means a lot to me," Verdan said with a smile. He hoped that he would earn the loyalty of those present and keep them with him. This was an essential step in reaching that goal.

"Well, follow me and let me show you the rest of the cottage," Gwen said after a moment, motioning for them all to follow as she led the way.

The cottage was even larger than he first thought. The ground floor had a large living room, a kitchen, and a dining area, while the upstairs held three decent-sized bedrooms. The really interesting part was what had been dug out below ground.

There was a stairwell in between the living room and dining room, with stairs leading both upstairs to the next floor and down to a cellar. Gwen was already heading down toward the cellar with her candlestick in hand.

The expected cellar was present on their right when they left the stairs, though there was far more than Verdan had expected. Not the least of which was an extensive library that seemed to dominate the underground portion of the home.

The floor was worked stone, but several rugs lay around a reading area that held a long, low table and a few chairs. The air was cold, but Verdan could fix that easily enough.

"Not what I was expecting down here," Tim said, looking at the book-filled shelves in surprise.

"This is the stored knowledge of my family for hundreds of years, everything from journals to books on herbal remedies and potion-making. My grandmother's journals will be here. I just need to find them and see what happened to give her control." Gwen gestured to the array of books, pointing out a few examples as she spoke.

In some ways, this was a treasure trove for Verdan as well. He'd have to see if she would let him read up on some of the alchemy notes her family had compiled.

"That's everything though, let me take you upstairs, and you can sort out where you want to stay," Gwen said as she started back up the stairs, the rest of them following along behind her with Verdan lagging along at the end, reluctant as he was to leave the books.

Gwen took her own room, leaving two rooms between the four of them. The expected pairing of the brothers in one room, while he and Kai shared the other, seemed reasonable enough, so Verdan didn't raise any objections. Kai immediately volunteered to take the floor, pulling out his bedroll and making himself comfortable, despite Verdan's offers to do the same.

He did consider whether he should spend some time meditating and working on his gathering spiral, but in the end, Verdan decided that he was better off getting his sleep and tackling their first true day of hunting fresh and ready for action. The Aether consumed for a pair of firebolts and a shield would be just about recovered overnight.

Still, he would have to be careful with his casting until his recovery speed was increased to match.

Banishing his worries and thoughts, Verdan took off his boots and settled in for the evening, enjoying the reasonably soft mattress and the security of sleeping in a warded glade.

CHAPTER
TWELVE

THEY HAD no fresh food for breakfast the following morning, though thankfully they could supplement the rations they'd brought with some dried goods from Gwen's cellar.

A section of the glade cultivated fruit and vegetables, but they'd had no chance to harvest anything the day before, leaving it as something to look forward to when they returned.

They were all refreshed after a surprisingly good night's sleep, and in short order, they were armed and ready for a day of hunting and exploration.

Gwen was staying behind at the cottage; she intended to find as many of her grandmother's writings as possible and start working through them, so it would just be the four of them heading back out.

"Ready?" Verdan asked, a little regretful that he wasn't able to stay behind for a good day of studying himself.

"Ready," Kai said with a nod, Tim and Tom chiming in a second later.

"Then let's go. Kai, then Tom, me and Tim at the back, happy with that?" Verdan pointed to each of them as he called out the marching order, everyone nodding that they were happy with that arrangement.

"Where are we going first?" Kai asked as he grabbed his spear from where it was leant against the cottage.

"The logging camp first. I want to see what we find and then search that area. Those spiders give us a good idea of what sort of creature is being pushed into this area, but we have no idea what's causing that yet."

"Okay, let's go then," Kai shouldered his weapon and led the way out of the glade, the rest of them following behind as they left the safety of the wards.

The woods were a completely different experience in daylight. Threatening shadows and ominous pools of darkness had been replaced by pleasant greenery and gentle birdsong. Verdan might even have thought that they were in a completely different place if it weren't for the damaged spiderweb they came across as they retraced their steps.

There was no sign of the spider corpses. The local scavengers had been quick to take advantage of the free meal that had been left for them.

The spiderweb was a good reminder, though, no matter how nice these woods looked right now, they were here because of how dangerous they'd become.

The birdsong was a positive sign, but they hadn't seen any other wildlife as of yet, which might be happenstance, or it might be a symptom of the larger issue in the area.

_**_

They reached the turn-off for the logging camp around mid-morning. They'd made good time so far, having not encountered anything dangerous on the way, but Verdan could feel a certain tension in the air now.

He wasn't sure what it was or what was causing it, but it felt like the calm before the storm. It could be something he was picking up on from the Aether subconsciously. It could also be an expression of how unsettled he'd felt since he'd woken up in this new world.

Glancing at the others, Verdan saw no sign of the same tension on their faces. Perhaps it was just in his mind after all.

Still, just to be safe, he partitioned a section of his focus and formed a concept for a protective shield, something fast and easy to create. If danger did strike, Verdan wanted to be ready at a moment's notice.

_**_

The logging camp was a small clearing with a few rudimentary structures for shelter and storage, nothing too expensive to set up or maintain. It was all overgrown and covered in weeds now, the first steps in nature reclaiming the area already well underway.

"Nothing here I can see," Kai said with a frown, looking around the still clearing as he moved further in. A flicker of motion drew their attention, but it was just a flutter of wings as a few birds flew away.

Verdan paused for a moment and reached out with his Aether senses before nodding. He couldn't sense anything either. "Seems clear to me. Let's look for tracks and see what might be stalking the area."

Spreading out but staying close enough to watch over each other, they searched through the abandoned camp, finding precious little to help them on their mission. There were claw marks on the walls of the storage building, their size and depth telling him they came from something large with powerful claws.

"I've found some tracks over here," Tim called out from the northern side of the camp. Moving closer, Verdan saw that he stood beside a pile of rubble that might have once been a structure of some sort. The former guard was peering intently down at the ground between the ruins and the woods.

Verdan watched with interest as Kai joined him, and the two conferred for a moment. Verdan had no real skill in tracking, but he found it absorbing enough to watch.

"He's right. Something big came this way, likely looking for food it could scavenge from the camp. Should we follow it?" Kai said, slowly following the first few feet of the tracks back towards the woods.

"We may as well. We've not seen anything else out here so far," Verdan said with a shrug. The lack of monsters they'd encountered so far was worrying in itself. For an area that had been abandoned, Verdan had expected there to be far more creatures.

"Okay, I'll go first. Be careful and stay aware," Kai said, keeping low to the ground, his spear at the ready, as he followed the tracks into the dense woods.

The tracks led them steadily deeper into the woods, staying on a mostly northern path as they went. The woods were thick and obscuring, with Kai being forced to pause and backtrack a few times to make sure they were still following the tracks.

"Wait, do you hear that?" Tim muttered as they clambered across a particularly overgrown area.

"Yes—what is that?" Verdan paused and listened more closely, hearing a distant low sound from somewhere up ahead.

"Rapids," Tom said gruffly, pulling himself up and over a large rock to carry on after Kai.

Sharing a look with Tim, Verdan followed suit and carried on along their path. The sounds grew as they came closer, turning into the dull roar of fast-moving water, which soon revealed itself as a long section of rapids that began shortly after a natural ford.

Kai and Tom were a short distance ahead and were waiting at the treeline for Verdan and Tim to catch up.

"The tracks head in there," Kai pointed across the rapids to a barely-visible cave mouth. The cave was set into the side of a large hill overlooking the rapids. "No sign of any movement. It could be out, or it could be asleep."

"Are we going in?" Tim asked, looking a little worried at the idea of heading into an unknown cave.

"Yes, but don't worry. I'll light the way and be ready with a shield," Verdan said, giving Tim's shoulder a comforting squeeze as he stepped past and led the way across the ford.

The water ran quickly but was fairly shallow and easy to traverse, letting them all get across and take up positions on one side of the cave in only a few minutes.

"*Disir.*" Verdan cupped a hand on the top of his staff as he created an orb of bright light and poked it around the corner of the cave. His other hand was up and ready to cast a shielding spell if needed. The light from his staff illuminated a good distance into the cave mouth, showing nothing but a few bones and bare stone. "Looks empty enough."

"Looks can be deceiving," Kai said, his expression grim as he grabbed a smooth rock from the river and threw it into the darkness at the rear of the cave. The stone skipped and skittered out of sight, its movement echoing back to them as a clatter of noise.

Several moments of tense silence passed with no reaction from anything in the cave, which was either a good sign, or a really bad one.

"I'm going to head in with Kai; you two stay out here and keep watch," Verdan said, gesturing for the brothers to take up a vantage point.

"Got it, Boss," Tim said, sharing a relieved look with his brother before moving closer to the rapids to survey the area.

Glancing once at Kai, Verdan started slowly advancing, the Sorcerer trailing along behind, staff high to let the light fill the area.

The cave was perhaps fifty feet deep with a slight curve towards the end, a reasonable size for some sort of den or nest.

Looking around as they made their way in, Verdan saw clear signs of recent habitation from something fairly large. To top it off, there were a number of bones scattered around the rear of the cave, some of which looked quite fresh.

"Nothing, but it was here recently," Kai said, poking at a few of the bones as he looked around.

"Let's look around the area, and see if there are any more tracks," Verdan suggested, leading the way back out to where the brothers were waiting for them.

Glancing around, Verdan saw that Tim had climbed atop the small hill the cave was set into and was surveying the area from the higher ground. Once he'd seen that they had emerged, he hurried down toward them, skidding down a section of loose ground and almost falling in his haste.

"There's something down there in the woods. It almost looks like a campsite of some kind," Tim said as soon as he came close enough that he didn't have to shout, pointing down the hill in the direction the water was flowing. "It doesn't look occupied right now. I couldn't see anyone moving around anyway."

"A camp?" Verdan echoed with a cock of his head. "Who would be camping out here?" The question was only partly rhetorical. After all, he knew the least about the area out of all of them.

"I need to see the camp," Kai said, his expression wooden and tone neutral as he turned to look off in the direction Tim had pointed. "We might have found the cause of the disturbance in the area."

"What do you mean?" Verdan asked, but Kai had already set off down the slope towards the trees, either ignoring Verdan or too caught up in his thoughts to hear him. "Right. Well, let's go see then, shall we?"

Verdan followed Kai's trail down the slope, moving a little quicker than normal to keep up with the Sorcerer, who was already a short distance ahead of them.

They carried on in tense silence for a time, Kai eventually slowing down so Tim could catch up and lead the way to the camp he'd seen. Verdan was a little concerned by how worried Kai seemed.

The normally unflappable Sorcerer was visibly uneasy about something. Kai was also clearly not in the mood to talk about it, so Verdan contented himself with watching carefully and waiting to see what secrets this camp might have.

"Here, this is it," Tim said softly, pointing to a point up ahead that Verdan couldn't quite see.

"Give me thirty seconds, then follow," Kai whispered back, waiting to make sure that they heard and understood before heading forwards at a slow pace.

The Sorcerer kept to the densest parts of the undergrowth and moved with surprising stealth, reaching the edge of the campsite just as Verdan started forward to follow him.

The clearing revealed itself as Verdan came closer. It featured a rudimentary firepit, several crude structures made from local materials, and a large pit of some sort. There was no sign of movement throughout the area, and Kai motioned for them to wait before stepping out of concealment.

The Sorcerer was still visibly tense and moved carefully through the camp, examining everything intently before moving over to look into the pit.

"We're clear, come on out," Kai called out, his tense posture somewhat relaxing as he stepped away from the pit. "This is an old camp from the look of it, though not that old."

"How can you be sure?" Verdan asked, moving into the camp to take a look around as well. These grounds could house a dozen or more people by human standards, but something was telling him that this wasn't a camp for humans.

"The bones in the pit have been gnawed clean but don't look too old. The firepit hasn't been used in a long time either," Kai said, his tone somewhat absent as he stared off into the distance in thought.

Taking a look in the pit, Verdan saw that it was filled with bones of all shapes and sizes, everything from a skull big enough for a large bear down to small bones that would belong to rabbits and the like.

Exactly why whoever had built this camp would have such a range of bones to dispose of baffled Verdan. He could understand the rabbits from hunting, but if they had to fight a bear, why bring its body back to their camp?

The brothers had matching worried expressions as they looked over the camp, both of them keeping one hand on their weapon at all times. They didn't seem to recognise the camp the way that Kai did, but they'd seen enough to know it was bad news.

"Talk to me. What are we looking at here?" Verdan asked quietly, coming over to stand next to Kai as he spoke.

"I've been north of Hobson's Point a few times. The land around here hasn't been in human hands for a long time, and it shows with the creatures that have taken over. One of the expeditions was exploring and looting an old fortress that's a fair distance northeast of where we are now. When we got to the fortress, we found signs of habitation and someone using it as a resting spot. The leader of the group posted guards and made camp, setting us all to clearing the ruin and finding what we could." Kai's voice was equally soft as he spoke, his gaze remaining fixed on a point in the distance only he could see.

"It was a trap?" Verdan asked, but Kai shook his head with a grimace.

"They came back on the third day of our camping there—fifty of them, in a large hunting party. They were returning with the bodies of some poor things they'd been hunting. I found out later that their whole culture is based around hunting and skinning other creatures. The more powerful, the better, though they prize sapient creatures over all else."

"That's horrifying," Verdan whispered, trying to imagine what sort of twisted culture would be built around that.

"It was," Kai said grimly. "Cyth are vile creatures, but they're predictable, and the lesser Cyth are almost mindless in some ways. These things, though, they were different. You could tell they were smart and that they enjoyed fighting us. We lost more than a few people, but we chased them down and avenged them, burning their camp to the ground in the process."

"You think it's them again?" Verdan asked, feeling a shiver run down his spine at the description Kai gave. He didn't recognise the creatures that Kai was referencing; they were either something new since his time, or they were rare enough that they'd never come up.

"I do. The camp looks similar in style and layout. Not to mention, it fits perfectly with their patterns and what I've since learnt about their culture. They prize the skins and furs of powerful creatures, so it's no wonder that their moving into the region drove all sorts of monsters further south."

"That would explain the issues, and why there have been so few monsters for us to encounter," Verdan said with a nod, not liking the answer but not able to deny that it fit with what they'd seen so far. "What do you call these creatures?"

"Darjee," Kai all but spat the name out, gripping his spear tight in reflex. "After our encounter with them, I went out of my way to learn about them from other Sorcerers. None of what I learned was good."

"Undoubtedly," Verdan murmured to himself. It sounded like the Darjee would have dealt with the majority of the local monsters, leaving themselves as the sole issue for Verdan and the others to deal with. "Tell me more; any detail could be important."

_**_

They lingered at the old Darjee camp for another hour, as Kai explained what he knew about the aggressive species and all the knowledge he had gained since his first fateful encounter with them.

Unsurprisingly, Kai knew a lot about them, enough that Verdan was able to get more of an idea of who they were.

Apparently, the whole impetus of their culture was based on hunting and domestication. Where humans might hunt deer and raise herds of cattle, the Darjee instead hunted sentient creatures almost exclusively.

The powerful and those without practical benefit were killed and harvested, while the rest were taken as slaves.

Skins and pelts were in high demand in Darjee society. Kai had seen enough to know that they were symbols of wealth and importance for them.

According to some reports Kai had read by those who had led raids into Darjee land, slaves were raised for both labor and food alike.

Verdan couldn't help but walk over to the pit of bones in the camp and stare down into its dark depths, disgusted and enraged in equal measure.

"You say these camps are normal?" Verdan asked, turning away from the pit and focusing on what Kai was saying.

"Yes, they establish them around the border of their lands as hunting outposts and then cycle through them, giving locals time to recover before they return."

"That means they'll be back," Verdan said, looking at the remnants of the firepit in the middle of the camp and trying to judge how old it was.

"Yes, they cycle through several in an area a few times, and then change areas. The camp isn't rundown enough for them to have left the area yet, so chances are, they'll be back."

"I see," Verdan said, taking a steadying breath as he pushed aside his desire to punish the Darjee and considered the long-term implications.

Verdan couldn't tell the workers to return to the camp, not knowing that they would be attacked at some point. Equally, simply killing this hunting party would be only a temporary solution.

He'd have to consider their next moves carefully.

"So, should we head back to the cottage now?" Tim asked, gesturing at the sun with a wave of his hand and a questioning expression.

Between all the searching and traveling, it was after midday now, and given that they didn't know a direct route back, it was an excellent question.

"Yes, let's head back and see what success Gwen has had today. I need to think about what we're going to do next," Verdan said, putting his considerations to one side for the moment.

"If we head east from here, we should cut across the trail leading north. We can follow that back to the cottage," Kai said, pointing in the opposite direction to how they arrived.

"If you say so. Lead on, Kai," Verdan said, happy to let someone else lead the way.

The Wizard knew his sense of direction wasn't always the best, so it was a relief that Kai was willing to lead the way back. He needed to get used to having minimal Aether and no Aether constructs to assist in travel. He was far too reliant on the others for direction at the moment.

"This way," Kai said, moving off towards the east without any more delay.

As usual, the Sorcerer moved at a quick pace, forcing the other three to jog and catch up to him before he could go too far.

_**_

It took almost an hour for them to find their way back to the path that led north. It turned out they'd gone further west than any of them had anticipated while tracking the trail they'd found at the logging camp. Thankfully their pace was much quicker once they were back on the trail, and they made good time back to the cottage.

There was a palpable feeling of relief once they were within the wards of the cottage again, a sense of security that wasn't there when traveling through the potentially monster-infested woodland.

"You're back. How did it go?" Gwen rose from where she was sitting at the front of the cottage, waving them over as she put the book she was holding down onto a small pile next to her.

"Mixed results, really," Verdan said with a grimace. "We think we know what's caused the issue in general, but we can't do anything about it right now."

"What do you mean?" Gwen asked, looking between them with concern.

"Darjee," Kai said sharply, making it into a curse word.

"Damn, that's not good at all," Gwen said, paling and looking more than a little worried. "It does explain everything, though."

"Yes, so Kai has told me. We need to work out a way to deal with the group that comes through here. That's the only way to really secure the logging camp."

"But how will we know when they're here? My mother always said they frequently roam between places," Gwen asked, sitting back down at the entrance to the cottage with a worried expression.

"Well, I'm still working on that part," Verdan admitted, rubbing his jaw thoughtfully as his mind drifted away for a moment. He had a few ideas, but he was limited by the amount of Aether he had.

He'd meditate on it tomorrow.

"We found a camp. It may come down to checking in every few days for a while. Eventually, they'll be back," Kai said with a shrug.

"That sounds like you might want to stay here a lot longer than you initially planned?" Gwen turned back to Verdan with a raised brow.

"Yes, potentially anyway. I'm not willing to head back before we've done what we came to do, and if today is anything to go by, the true threat is the Darjee group that's roaming the area."

"Well, that gives me more time to read, so it's not a problem with me," Gwen patted the books next to her with a smile.

"And you two?" Verdan turned to the brothers, who were waiting patiently behind him.

"You're the boss, Boss," Tim said with a grin. Tom grunted and nodded a moment later.

"Well, let's get settled in then. We can head back tomorrow or the day after, once I've had a chance to think of something," Verdan said, giving the others a nod before heading down to the pond behind the cottage.

Perhaps some meditation would help make the solution clear to him.

_-**-_

Verdan was able to make some progress on his gathering spiral over the next few hours, but that was it. There was no miraculous way to get by the Aether requirements that any of the solutions he could think of.

If he had his usual Aether generation and reserves, it would be a simple thing to do. A temporary Aether construct mixed with a warding spell could send him a pulse of Aether when its preset criteria occurred, which would be the presence of the Darjee.

The problem was that the Aether drain for such a spell would undoubtedly be higher than what he was currently drawing in.

With no better option available, Verdan considered how to change his normal approach and make it feasible. The construct would need a reservoir of Aether to power the ward and keep it coherent without access to him.

Verdan paused mid-thought and smiled slightly, realizing that he didn't need the ward to be active all the time; if it activated every morning for a short time, he could dramatically reduce the Aether costs.

He would still need to provide the construct with a large amount upfront, though, and then top it up every few days.

Hopefully, his progress in compressing and expanding his gathering spiral in-between times would be enough to balance the equation with little impact.

If not, the whole endeavor would eat into his reserves, which was exactly what he didn't want when there was a fight on the horizon.

Anything that hunted sentient creatures for fun was going to be a dangerous enemy, after all.

It would do for now, but he'd sleep on it and see what he thought tomorrow. Rising from the bench, Verdan glanced up at the shining moon amid the darkened sky and wondered just what other nasty surprises were waiting for him in this twisted version of the world he knew.

_**_

Verdan rose early the next morning and snacked on some of the dried rations they had before returning to his spot by the pond, where he could watch the water once more. The gentle movement of the pond water and the occasional ripple from the fish was quite soothing and helped him think.

Dropping into a meditative state, he began to work on his gathering spiral, condensing it down and adding new layers. Each new layer required him to manually take control of the spiral once more.

Once Verdan had made the changes he wanted, he could pass it to the part of his consciousness that kept it running, releasing it from his waking mind.

It was tiring and straining work, with Verdan pushing to do as much as he could each session, which in turn meant a larger change to his mental concept of the spiral, which made it harder to update.

The meditative state helped, but it was hard work no matter how you came to it. Only his years of experience in dealing with Aether allowed the process to be this quick.

The others left him to his work for the morning, so when he withdrew from his meditation around midday, he'd managed to complete the fifty-fifth layer of his spiral.

There were only five more layers to go before he finished it, at which point he would be on par with a freshly-graduated Wizard from the academy.

Once the first spiral was established, it would be time to work on a new one, building it around the framework of the first spiral to increase the pull on the Aether.

More spirals meant faster gathering and larger reserves, with an established Wizard having up to six spirals, a senior Wizard up to thirty-six and an Archmage over two hundred.

After a certain point, there were diminishing returns when adding new spirals into the framework, but there was still a vast gulf between even a senior Wizard and an Archmage.

Supposedly, there was more to becoming an Archmage than simply more spirals, but Verdan had no idea what it would be.

"You seem satisfied with your meditation today," Gwen's voice jarred Verdan from his thoughts. Blinking in surprise, Verdan saw that Gwen was sitting next to him with a plate of food in her lap."Here, you missed our lunch, so I saved you some."

"My thanks," Verdan said with a nod, taking the offered plate and digging in with vigor. It was easy to push aside his hunger when he was meditating, but it all came back once he was done. "I'm making good progress on restoring my strength. How goes your study of your family journals?"

"Frustratingly," Gwen said with a grimace that settled into a frown. "My grandmother clearly had far more control over her power than anyone else in the family, but no one could figure out why."

"I see. Did your grandmother perchance have an animal that followed her around or appeared near her frequently?"

"Yes. I was only young at the time, but I remember she always had a hawk that rode on her shoulder. Its feathers would almost shimmer in the light, changing between dark blue and black." Gwen spoke softly, her gaze on distant memories that only she could see.

"That would be her familiar, an unusual-looking animal that accompanied her around. It fits the bill perfectly. Did the journals say when she first showed up with the bird?" Verdan spoke in between bites of fruit, the salted jerky having already been devoured.

"No, I'll have to look at some of her earliest journals and see if she wrote about it at all," Gwen glanced back at the cottage and shifted uncomfortably.

"Please, don't feel the need to stay. The sooner you find out more about this process, the better for all of us," Verdan said with a chuckle, laughing all the harder as Gwen thanked him and swiftly headed back inside without further ado.

Verdan rose with a wince from the bench, putting his empty plate to one side. Sitting in one place all morning had done him no favors at all. Familiar with such issues, Verdan knew it would do him some good to stretch his legs, so he started off on a lap around the warded glade.

Along his path, Verdan saw that Kai was outside of the cottage, the Sorcerer running through a series of set movements that seemed to be part combat practice and part stretching routine. The concentration on Kai's face deterred Verdan from interrupting him, and he moved on with his lap around the area.

The brothers were sparring up in the northern part of the glade, their movements a little slow at first as they worked through some new techniques and got further accustomed to their weapons. They were too engrossed in their fight to notice Verdan approach, so he carried on his way after watching for a moment. He didn't want to disturb their training any more than he did Kai's.

The warm sun was pleasant, and before he knew it, Verdan was back on the bench watching the pond. He'd allow himself a bit of time to relax. Then he would work on his spiral once more.

It looked like the Aether construct to warn him of the Darjee arriving was their best bet, so he would need as strong a foundation as he could to keep up with the demands of such a complicated construct.

Closing his eyes, he basked in the warmth of the sun for a little longer. The work could wait for now.

CHAPTER
THIRTEEN

THE NEXT MORNING rolled around with surprising speed. They all spent most of the previous day on their individual projects, only coming together at the end to put a meal together and recap their work during the day.

Verdan had made decent progress. He'd finally finished his first gathering spiral and was feeling a bit more confident about making an Aether construct to monitor the Darjee camp. It would be Aether-intensive, but that wouldn't be an issue if he kept progressing at this rate.

Each successive spiral was slightly more complex than the last, requiring more concentration, more time spent on compression, and a better grasp of splitting the mind to work on different tasks. Thankfully, it was still all things that Verdan had done in the past, so he was confident of progressing at a reasonable speed.

"So, I've given it some thought, and I'm going to go ahead with using a spell to monitor the Darjee camp, though that does mean that we'll need to go back every other day to recharge it," Verdan announced his decision after finishing the fresh fruit they had for their breakfast.

"That's no issue. It will give us a chance to explore the area as well. There may be other threats that we haven't encountered yet," Kai said with a firm nod of approval.

"I'm making good progress with my reading, but there's still a long way to go. Perhaps you could join me tomorrow?" Gwen added, looking over at Verdan with a raised brow.

"Of course, if we head down today so I can position the spell, I can spend tomorrow going through what you've found so far," Verdan said with a smile. He was already looking forward to sinking his teeth into those journals.

Verdan had plenty of alchemy equipment on the way, but he wanted to get his knowledge to the point that he'd have something to do with it all once it arrived.

The others all agreed with his plan, and split up to start getting everything packed up for their journey back to the Darjee camp. Now that they'd been there once, it would be an easier trip, but they were still going through unsecured land to get there.

"Good luck," Gwen called out as she sat on the steps of the college and watched them go, a book already in hand. Verdan envied her; he'd much rather not do this, but he'd promised that he'd take care of the problem, and this was part of doing that.

Kai lingered for a moment more before turning away and leading them out across the wards and into the forest proper. The safe feeling from the ward faded as soon as they left the glade, the morning light bathing the dense undergrowth as they retraced their steps once more.

The place they'd fought the spiders looked no different from anywhere else now, which begged the question of how many fights might have happened here; the land was quick to reclaim the bodies and grow over the scars, hiding it from new travelers. Verdan could see a similar thought on the faces of his companions as they pushed onward. The sooner they got to the Darjee camp, and he could enact the spell, the better.

Despite their misgivings, they made good time to the camp, finding it just as abandoned as previously, though the refuse pit showed some wear and tear from scavengers.

"So what now?" Kai asked, his posture tense and his eyes watchful despite the lack of Darjee.

"Well, now I create an Aether construct with two integral components, one for detection and one for messaging me. This may take some time, so don't let anything interrupt me," Verdan said, taking a seat on the floor in the center of the camp, his staff across his legs, and taking a few deep breaths as he closed his eyes.

Like with any spell, visualization was vital in creating a construct, perhaps even more so than usual. With that in mind, Verdan started from the basics of what he wanted and worked his way up.

The first step was to visualize a contained well of Aether that would power the construct. Verdan's personal choice for this was a sealed box that contained a few ports for connecting external spells to the Aether within.

Of course, it didn't really matter what form the well took. The key was that there was a clear barrier between the Aether inside the well and the ambient Aether in the outside world. Verdan chose a sealed box, as he also visualized that the connections for the Aether were one-way only, which helped limit Aether loss.

With that done, Verdan visualized two spells attaching to the connectors. The first would detect nearby creatures and categorize them as either humanoid or non-humanoid. It would repeat this effect every four hours.

The second spell would send a direct message to Verdan with the information from the first spell. Thankfully, he would be staying nearby, so the Aether cost wasn't too exorbitant.

The mental strain of holding everything together had been building as Verdan worked. This was a complicated construct to make, one that was straining his ability to keep it all together. He had to act quickly.

"*Gward canfo dyn neges,*" Verdan intoned, each word taking exponentially more effort to speak, with the fourth word seeming to burn his throat on the way out. Despite the pain, the spell took shape as power poured out of him like water and hung in the air like a drop of water, invisible but detectable to his Aether attuned senses.

A pulse of Aether rippled out over the clearing from the droplet, a tight packet of Aether flowing to him from it a moment later as it registered the presence of five humanoids in the local area.

Verdan rose to his feet, his mind not quite catching the problem with the feedback from the spell until he was already turning to speak to Kai. His eyes went wide as he looked at his three companions. It registered five humanoids, not four. There was something, or someone, else here with them.

"What, what's wrong?" Kai asked, eyes narrowing as he saw Verdan's reaction.

"*Canfo dyn,*" Verdan said, throwing out a quick and dirty spell that was a cut-down version of the construct he'd just created.

A ripple of unseen Aether swept out from him, but this time he was able to get detail on where each of those five readings came from.

Kai and the brothers caused disturbances in that wave, but there was another disturbance out in the woods.

Narrowing in on it with the spell, Verdan was able to work out that it was around fifteen feet into the woods. He felt its presence for the briefest of moments before the spell faded, but it wasn't enough to gather any more details.

Verdan had spent far too much Aether already between the construct and that rough spell. He dared not cast anything else right now, just in case they found themselves in a fight.

Verdan's gaze must have automatically turned and followed his attention to the fifth person, as Kai frowned and glanced over to see what he was looking at.

With both of them looking their way, the hidden watcher realized it was exposed and bolted. There was a barely visible flash of gray fur as something small jumped to its feet and ran away, moving nimbly through the dense foliage.

Kai growled something and took off after the creature with blistering speed, his legs almost a blur as he went into a dead sprint. It was the first time that Verdan was able to see Kai use his powers without any distractions, but sadly there wasn't time to do a proper study of them right now. All he could do was watch as Kai streaked off into the forest, only to plow into a wall of soil that thrust itself up out of the ground in his path. The power behind Kai's charge was enough for him to smash through the wall with little difficulty, but it slowed him down and disoriented him for a moment.

Verdan frowned as he hurried along in Kai's wake. Kai had said that the Darjee never fought with magic, which meant this was likely something else entirely. Keeping his focus on the world around them, Verdan watched for any further signs of magic while Kai raced off into the undergrowth at speed. Tim and Tom were running to them now as well, their weapons in hand and expressions grim.

Verdan felt a few flickers of Aether further into the woods, but the distance meant that there was little he could do without seeing what was happening or who they belonged to. Pushing on into the woods as fast as he could, Verdan arrived just as a disheveled Kai smashed through another wall of soil and thrust his spear down at the creature he was pursuing.

The creature heaved up a smaller, much more compact wall at the last moment, catching the strike and stopping it mere inches away from its target. The momentary pause in the creature's flight gave Verdan the time to see it clearly.

Five feet tall, with long and thick claws, gray fur, and large dark eyes, the creature was something Verdan was familiar with—a Fwyn.

Fwyn were one of the main non-human members of the Grym Imperium. They were exceptional builders and diggers, even without their inherent magic. More importantly, that meant that their descendants were included in his oath of service.

Kai had smashed his spear free of the wall while Verdan was recovering from his surprise at seeing a Fwyn. The Sorcerer closed the distance to the smaller creature before it could react and thrust his spear towards its chest.

"*Ast*!" Verdan barked, conjuring a hasty shield in between the two combatants, stopping Kai's blow but shattering under the impact. "Kai, stop!"

"What are you doing, Verdan? It might be working with the Darjee!" Kai shouted in surprise, his eyes flicking to Verdan for a brief moment.

"Stand down, I want to talk with him first," Verdan said, waving for the oncoming brothers to wait where they were as he slowly moved towards the Fwyn, not wanting to antagonize it with any quick motions. "Do you speak Common?" He saw its eyes flick to him for a moment before going back to Kai. It clearly realized something was happening but wasn't sure what to do.

"Monsters don't talk, do they?" Kai asked as he backed up a few steps, some of the tension draining away as he watched them both.

"Some of them do. I'll see if I know the language he speaks," Verdan said as he came to within half a dozen steps of the Fwyn, capturing its gaze with his own. He wasn't surprised it didn't speak Common. That was rare even back in the height of the empire. "High Imperial? Trader's Tongue? Low Imperial?" He listed each of the other languages of the empire, in its own words. The Fywn reacted to the final question, and Verdan smiled in satisfaction—Low Imperial it was.

"A human speaks the tongue of our ancestors?" The Fwyn replied in the same language, its voice surprisingly low and gravelly for its short stature.

"I do. My name is Verdan."

"I am Gruthka. Why do you squat in the camp of the Darjee, sachka?" Gruthka used the same word for the Darjee as the others had, causing Kai to visibly tense. The last word he used wasn't one Verdan recognised, though, and he'd been raised speaking Low Imperial.

"Sachka?" Verdan let the word hang as a vague prompt.

"Yes, one like him," Gruthka pointed at Kai, who immediately bristled at the action. "I saw you use magic."

"Ah," Verdan paused, weighing his options, before deciding that honesty was always the best policy. "I'm no Sorcerer," he decided that Sorcerer was the best translation, "I am a Wizard."

"A Wizard? They all died with the empire. The tales of our forefathers tell us as much," Gruthka's eyes were wide as he stared at Verdan, his voice full of disbelief.

"Not all of them. I slept under a spell and awoke only recently," Verdan said, giving Gruthka the full story in the knowledge that he couldn't spread it to humans and cause a problem. Gruthka clearly understood what a Wizard actually was, which somehow made proving it more important. "I'm surprised that you know what a Wizard is. The humans I've met so far have no records that go that far back."

"We Fwyn live longer than humans and pass on our ancestral memories with pride. We've watched your kind burn their own civilisation down many times in the pursuit of strength. The Empire was a different time, though that would explain why you chose to talk rather than to kill. Why are you here then, Wizard?"

"I was placing a ward on the area to alert me if any Darjee return," Verdan said, keeping it simple to see what information the Fwyn would offer them.

"They will. They've been hunting this area for some time. Things have been different recently, though. They're capturing sentients, not just hunting them. Have they taken one of yours?"

"No, we haven't encountered them yet, but I was told how much of a threat they could be. Do you have any idea of when they'll return?" Verdan asked, trying to prompt the Fwyn further.

"Our forefathers passed down stories of Wizards who fought to hold together what they could while the world crumbled around them. Wizards who held to their oaths, even when no one else did.

Are you one of them?" Gruthka's gaze was intent as he watched Verdan, giving his words a weight that resonated with him.

It was a difficult question. It cut deep to Verdan's worries about his new life in this changed world. He was no hero. He'd seen true heroes fighting in the war. He wasn't going to start a crusade to rebuild the empire in his own image or make the world a better place. That didn't mean he could just let it go, though. He'd sworn an oath, and he couldn't just walk away from that. He knew that it would make his life difficult and would bring trouble down on him, but he couldn't live with himself if he abandoned the principles that his friends had fought and died for.

"Yes," Verdan said, the single word breaking the pregnant pause that had built while he wrestled with the idea. "My oath still stands."

"Then I ask for your help. The Darjee have ravaged my clan. They have been hunting us for the last few months. Each time they come, they capture a few more of us, taking the captives to their main camp. We suspect they are trying to breed slaves or, worse, livestock," Gruthka said, ending on a whisper that was filled with dread.

"Gods below, that is a horrid thought," Verdan said, repulsed by even the idea of what the Darjee may be trying to accomplish. "I will do what I can, but I am no war Wizard, able to destroy regiments of enemies single-handedly."

"No, I understand that, but if we kill this hunting party when they next arrive, we will have destroyed a third of their strength. Enough to risk a raid on their camp to free my people and drive off the Darjee." Gruthka's large eyes all but sparkled with excitement and hope, drawing Verdan even deeper into his plan.

"How many of you would join in this raid?"

"I could convince a dozen to follow me if you were coming. Wizards are still a large part of our ancestral stories and would give them hope," Gruthka grew more excited with each word, no doubt envisioning them driving the Darjee before them like rats.

"A dozen? How many would we be facing, both here and then in the main camp?"

"Twenty now, with a total of sixty, so forty more at the camp." Gruthka's energy was waning now as he considered the odds that were stacked against them.

"I will help, but let me speak with my companions," Verdan said, giving Gruthka a nod before stepping aside and gesturing the others over so he could translate and explain most of what Gruthka had told him. The part about the empire would stay out. He'd simply say that the Fwyn had come across people like him in the past.

"This is a dangerous mission indeed, though from what you've said, the area will not truly be safe until the Darjee are dealt with. I'm in favor of it," Kai said, still keeping one eye on Gruthka while they had their meeting.

"We agree. Besides, it'll be a good chance to earn our keep," Tim said with a hefty grin and a wink.

"My companions agree," Verdan said, switching back to low imperial for Gruthka, "we will aid you in this fight. Tell me what you know."

_**_

Unfortunately, Gruthka knew very little beyond the location of the Darjee camp and a rough estimate of their numbers. This particular band of Darjee had been plaguing the Fwyn for some time, whittling down their numbers slowly but steadily. The dozen Fwyn that Gruthka could call upon for a raid were actually all of the remaining adults in the clan that could fight. There were other clans in the area, but Gruthka had no authority to summon them. They could only hope that some would come anyway.

One thing that Gruthka did know was the Darjee schedule. He estimated two, maybe three, days at most before the Darjee would return to this camp. That gave them a window of opportunity to prepare and a chance to take out a good portion of the Darjee in a surprise attack.

"How many of your people could join us in an attack in three days time?" Verdan asked, considering the options they had before them.

"Three, maybe four. The others are too far away or out of contact right now. I can summon them to a nearby burrow, but we would need to know when to strike," Gruthka said, gesturing off to the west.

"What if you came with us?" Verdan mused, more to himself than anything, tapping his fingers on his staff in thought. "My construct will warn me when they return, we can all come back, and you can liaise with the others so that we attack at the same time."

"That will work," Gruthka said slowly, clearly thinking it over to see what could go wrong. "Yes, that will work. I will return to the burrow now and send word. Are you able to wait here for a few hours?"

Verdan simply nodded, and the Fwyn inclined his head in response before turning and heading into the woods. Kai and the brothers tensed slightly at the movement but made no move to stop Gruthka as he ran off, the shadows of the woods allowing the gray-furred creature to vanish from sight with ease.

"I hope he was meant to do that," Kai said, a slight edge to his voice as he stared off in the direction Gruthka had left with a hooded gaze and a tight grip on his spear.

"Yes, he'll come back and then return to the cottage with us. Then, when I'm alerted that the Darjee are returning, we will all come back here so he can fetch the others," Verdan said, looking round to find a comfy spot to rest while they waited.

"It feels wrong to work with a non-human. Are you sure he's trust-worthy?" Kai asked, shifting his weight as he glanced from Verdan back to the woods.

"As sure as I can be; his hate of the Darjee seems real enough. The rest we can work on," Verdan said, seating himself against a large tree with a sigh.

"Hmm, we'll see," Kai muttered, walking off into the woods.

"Don't worry, we're behind you all the way," Tim said, leaning in and speaking in a low tone to keep it between them. "Anyone else, and we'd be worried, but we believe in you, Boss."

Verdan smiled back at the guard, touched by their faith in him despite their lack of knowledge about the Fwyn. "Thanks, it's appreciated."

Tim gave him a wide grin before heading over to join his brother, who was busy munching some jerky from his pack. Seeing the brothers settle in, Verdan took the opportunity to head back to the Darjee camp and infuse the construct he'd created with enough Aether to ensure it would last for a full three days. He doubted he'd have a chance to come back and refill it at this rate.

-**-

The wait for Gruthka, and the following journey back to the cottage, was filled with silence. Kai was uncomfortable with

Gruthka's presence, and the Fwyn quickly picked up on his body language, giving the whole thing a tense atmosphere.

There was a brief moment of worry when they entered the glade with Gruthka. The spirit powering the wards turned its attention to them, giving Gruthka significantly more scrutiny than the rest of them. The small Fwyn froze in fear at the initial scan and almost fled in a panic before Verdan could calm him down.

Still, once they were inside and Verdan explained the situation, things calmed down nicely. Gruthka was intrigued by how different the atmosphere was in the warded glade and almost immediately wandered off to look around on his own.

Gwen came from behind the cottage to greet them, stumbling a little as she saw the Fwyn walking calmly with them. Verdan quickly explained the basics of what had happened; he didn't want the ward to pick up on her feelings and drive the Fwyn out. He doubted the ward had sufficient complexity to pick up on something like that, but it was better safe than sorry.

"So, how long do you have?" Gwen asked one he'd finished explaining, walking alongside him as they made their way back around the cottage to Verdan's favored spot on the bench by the pond.

"Two, maybe three, days; not long, but it will have to do," Verdan said, noting the small pile of journals and books next to the bench as they approached. Gwen had clearly been busy while they were away. "How goes your research?"

"Mixed results," Gwen said with a heavy sigh. Sitting down at the other side of the bench, she grabbed the top journal off the pile and rapped a knuckle against it. "This is the journal she was keeping when she gained control, but the whole thing is filled with religious nonsense. She talks a lot about becoming closer to the goddess and how her belief helped open her eyes. Nothing helpful at all."

"Nothing helpful!" Verdan spluttered, going into a coughing fit for a moment before fixing Gwen with an incredulous gaze. "Have you forgotten that Witches have a patron goddess?"

"Well, no, but why does that matter? It isn't like we pray to her or anything," Gwen said with a shrug, casually showing a level of disrespect to her patron that would horrify the Witches he'd known.

"I think this is one of those situations where I can provide some key information again," Verdan said, pausing to take a drink from his water flask and gather his thoughts. "What do you know about the goddess of Witches?"

"Ceravwen, goddess of rebirth, women and Witchcraft. Patroness of Witches and linked to the first Witch according to legend. Lots of ties to nature and a few other gods," Gwen rattled off, clearly knowing the basics at least.

"All correct, but missing a few key bits. The biggest is that she wasn't just linked to the first Witch. Ceravwen personally granted the first generation of Witches their powers. The first Hearth Witch, the first Hex Witch, the first Herbal Witch—you get the idea. She is your patron, as all Witchcraft uses her power inter-mixed with Aether, power that is replenished through prayer, cere-mony, and worship. More importantly for our current needs, she is the one who sends familiars to provide her followers with control of their powers." He paused to shake his head in disbelief once more at this new world in which he'd found himself. "I thought this was a matter of finding the right ritual, not that you didn't even worship your own benefactor. No wonder you have no control. You're trying to wield divine power without the proper tools."

"But, that makes no sense. Why would we stop worshiping Ceravwen if she held so much power?" Gwen protested.

"These things don't happen straight away; I imagine it was a slow, quiet death of worship until so few were true believers that she was blamed for the lack of control as well," Verdan said, tapping a finger on his chin as he considered how it could all have played out.

"Could it be so simple?" Gwen said, more to herself than anything. "We only needed to believe in her to gain control?"

"It could be. I'm no Witch, though. My advice is to read the books and learn about her. It takes more than lip service for this to work; you need to truly believe. Perhaps you could try and perform some form of communion during a storm. All the Aether will be stirred up and active to begin with, and it will be when your magic is most linked to nature. If that doesn't work, I'm all out of ideas," Verdan gave her a slight shrug, not having anything else to offer.

"Yes, okay, I need to think about all this," Gwen said absently, gathering her things up in a daze and turning to go back to the cottage. "Thanks, Verdan."

Verdan contemplated Gwen's problems for a few moments before shaking his head. He had no more information to give, and the time he had before the Darjee arrived was going to be spent expanding his gathering spiral and building his reserve of Aether. He had a feeling that some larger spells would be called for soon, and anything with a large area of effect was Aether-intensive by its very nature.

Slipping into his meditative state, Verdan took control of his second spiral and began to compress it, ready for expansion. He had a few days to work with, and every minute would count.

FOURTEEN

GWEN SAT in her mother's chair in the downstairs library, absently reading from a journal while considering Verdan's words. The idea that Ceravwen was the missing link to control her powers was ridiculous at first glance. Everyone knew that Ceravwen didn't care for her title as patron of Witches. Though, maybe everyone was wrong. Time and again, Verdan was shaking her view of the world. She didn't know what to believe anymore.

The men had returned yesterday afternoon, and she'd spent all her time since then reading about Ceravwen and her domain. Gwen hadn't learned much about Ceravwen growing up. It was time to remedy that.

Gwen already knew some of the basics from common knowledge, but she focused more on learning about Ceravwen's domain. Women, rebirth and Witchcraft, it was an interesting domain. It was even more interesting how it all meshed with Ceravwen's husband, Dassdarth.

Dassdarth was the patron god of Nature and Hunting, a wild god by any standard. There was a lot of overlap between his nature aspect and Ceravwen's domain; Gwen's weather magic was a perfect example.

Verdan had said that Ceravwen was the source of the original weather Witches, but Gwen couldn't help but wonder how much Dassdarth had to do with it.

A distant rumble of thunder brought her back to her plans for this evening. There was a storm coming in, and if she wanted to try to connect with Ceravwen, now was the time. A storm was the perfect representation of her weather magic. From her grandmother's notes, it would be the time to commune with her patron and try to connect with her.

The only question was whether she wanted to do it, to link her fortunes to some unknowable deity that her ancestors had turned their backs on. She had so little information on what worshiping Ceravwen really meant. For all she knew, it could mean blood sacrifices every new moon.

Sighing softly, she closed the journal and set it to one side. She was being ridiculous. She knew full well that Ceravwen was a positive force in the pantheon of gods, so there was no chance that she would ask for any foul rituals to demonstrate obedience. Dassdarth was more of a neutral figure but still on the positive side of things.

If she was honest with herself, she was just afraid, afraid of committing to something bigger than herself. It was bad enough spending so much time with people she barely knew and having them live in her childhood home, but at least this was a temporary thing. Committing to Ceravwen was a bit more permanent than that.

"I guess it comes down to what I want more," Gwen muttered to herself, glancing back over to the book she'd set down. Her grandmother had spoken a lot about Ceravwen, saying that it was more important to be genuine in what you did than to follow set rules. To Gwen, that sounded like a chaotic way to worship someone, but it appealed to her all the same.

Thunder rolled again, closer this time. The moment of decision was drawing ever closer.

Gwen sat in her chair, indecisive and unsure.

Thunder boomed, echoed by several smaller echoes, each loud enough for Gwen to almost feel the thunder. It sounded like a massive storm. The far-off lightning strikes were pounding out a steady beat, like a distant drum urging her onward.

A flicker of energy sparked around her hands, reacting to the strength of the storm above. Arcing lightning jumping harmlessly between her fingers, each arc a brilliant white that both hurt her eyes and mesmerized her while leaving behind a bit of warmth. She rarely got to see her magic in a quiet setting like this. It was a bittersweet pleasure to watch it. She knew that once the storm passed, it would end, and she would be unable to bring it back.

It was that thought that made her rise to her feet. She'd seen the others use their magic so often that it physically hurt her to think of living any longer with no control. Between Verdan's strange, surprisingly versatile magic and the impressively controlled power Kai had demonstrated, she had more than enough examples of how things could be.

With her decision made, she blew out the candle and raced upstairs, her feet finding the steps in the dark with an ease born from years of usage.

Lightning split the sky, illuminating the whole cottage for a moment as she emerged into the living room. Heavy raindrops already coated the windows, the steady patter of rain a comforting sound as she stripped down to little more than her underwear. There was no point in getting everything wet.

Heart racing and suddenly out of breath, Gwen shivered as she opened the door to the cottage and a chill wind whipped through, bringing no small amount of water with it.

After a deep breath and a single step, she was outside, pulling the door shut behind her, the cold rain hitting her directly as she stared up at the voluminous clouds that filled the sky. Searing bolts of crackling light arced between them, her magic providing a faint echo as it jumped between her hands, warming them and warding off a small portion of the biting wind.

There was only one place that would do for this—the ancient tree that Verdan said powered the wards that protected the glade. The tree had watched countless members of her family come and go. It was only right that she was near it when she tried to connect to Ceravwen. Kneeling before it, she looked up at the swaying branches, then up at the looming darkness beyond it, pushing away the cold, the thunder and the rain as she focused on what she wanted.

"Ceravwen. I know my family has long since turned from you, but I wish to repair that bond. I wish to learn and become a Witch like my ancestors were, in control and able to do good for nature and man alike." Gwen spoke aloud, the wind stealing her words the moment they left her mouth.

Verdan had told her of how he gathered Aether and shaped it to his will, a carefully-monitored and mentally-intensive process. She'd imagined the link to the goddess to be similar, and searched in vain for it as she whispered her request for control once more.

Lightning flashed, and the roar of thunder broke her from her concentration. The sheer volume of the thunderclap made it feel like the ground beneath her had been split in half. A shiver ran down her spine as she thought of the destructive power of the storm raging around her, and just how fragile and defenseless she was right now.

Pushing away her awe, Gwen started to focus down and block it all out once more but paused with a grimace. This was Verdan's way of doing it. This wasn't her; this wasn't Witchcraft. Her grandmother spoke in metaphors and strange flowery language, but she always focused on how they were all one part of the larger design of nature.

For better or worse, Gwen was a weather Witch, a storm Witch by any other name, and this was her natural environment. She could feel her magic racing around her, active and surging in a way she'd never really experienced before, but she'd never stood out in a storm like this either.

Throwing away the rational approach, she followed her instincts and opened up her senses, drinking it all in. The freezing cold, the biting touch of the wind, the pounding rain, the bright lightning, and the deafening thunder. Accepting it all, reveling in it all, she found what she was looking for: a glimmer of understanding, a notion of the true nature of weather, of storms, of what she could be.

For the briefest of moments, Gwen understood it all. At that moment, she made the connection she sought, her goddess welcoming her open heart with equally open arms. Something touched the very core of who she was, drawing out a thread and spinning it into a cord that was pulled away and into the sky.

A caw broke Gwen out of her reverie, her eyes flicking up as she saw something large and dark descend down towards her. Lightning flashed, its brief illumination revealing a large raven, its feathers a shimmering blue-black that captured the eye.

Lifting her hand without thought, Gwen stared in surprise as the raven gently settled onto her wrist before hopping onto her shoulder, providing a strangely familiar and comforting weight. The raven cocked its head and stared at her expectantly. Gwen simply returned the stare with a confused expression for a few moments. It was only when the lightning split the sky once more that she realized that things had changed.

The magic all around her was as chaotic and unresponsive as always, but now she could feel it in a more tangible way through the cord that had been pulled from her. No, it was a bond, a bond that led right to the raven on her shoulder.

From that bond, a trickle of energy ran down to her. It was magic that was unlike everything around her. It was calm, welcoming, and soothing in a way that she hadn't expected at all.

Drawing on it eagerly, Gwen felt some of it flow from the raven into her and with it, the chaotic magic all around her became tangible. It was only the slightest use of her intent to send a gust of wind out from one hand, its passage creating a vortex in the rainwater that was beautiful in itself. The cold of the rain was somehow muted now as well, as was the wind. She could feel it, just not to the same degree as before. Truly, her magic had awoken now.

"Thank you. Thank you, Ceravwen," Gwen whispered, tears mixing with rain as she wept, her joy only slightly tainted by the knowledge that her family would never know this feeling.

The magic from the raven was consumed by use, but only slightly. The majority of the energy was taken from what was around her. She instinctively knew she could do the same effect several times more with what she had left.

This must be the power of Ceravwen. This was the key to every-thing. She could feel a slight trickle feed down the bond, forming a pool of magic in her core. It was such an odd sensation; she could manipulate it as though it was a third hand that she'd never known she had. It was clumsy and awkward for now, but even that was a huge step forward compared to before.

The storm above was passing by, its lightning withdrawing as its fury was wasted on the indomitable mountain range that sat between them and Hobson's Point. Gwen watched it go with a hint of sadness, as the feeling of being connected to all of nature was receding with it, leaving her tired, cold, and wet.

"Here, put this on," Kai said from next to her, making Gwen start in surprise and flush a little. Kai was holding out a voluminous cloak to her, his gaze studiously off to one side. Suddenly highly aware of her limited, soaking wet clothing and how revealing it all was, Gwen took the cloak and settled it around her shoulders, pulling it tight around her. She wasn't as cold as she thought she'd be, standing out here in the rain, but the cloak was still more than welcome.

"Thank you," she said softly, blushing even more as Kai turned back to her and gave a slight bow.

"It was my pleasure." Kai gave her a small smile as he turned to let her lead the way back to the cottage. It looked good on him.

"I'm sorry if I woke you," Gwen said, pulling open the door to the cottage and stepping inside.

"Not at all. It was the thunder that woke me. I simply happened to see you out there and thought you'd get cold," Kai said, shutting the door behind them and gesturing for her to lead the way into the kitchen. "Tea?"

"Please," Gwen took a seat at the kitchen table, pulling the cloak tight and enjoying its warmth as Kai lit the stove and set a kettle atop it.

Watching the usually stern and stoic Sorcerer set himself to make her a cup of hot tea was an unusual experience for Gwen. She'd been unsure of what to think of him at first. He'd seemed cold and distant when they first met. However, she was beginning to think he actually cared a great deal more than he liked to show.

"I saw what you did—was your communing a success?" Kai turned to look at her, showing none of the fear or loathing she was used to when people saw her powers.

"Yes, or at least, I think so. I seem to have made a new friend at least," she nodded to the raven that was still sitting on her shoulder, watching them both with interest.

"So I see. What was the term Verdan used, a familiar?" Kai cocked his head. The bird copied his motion, and he smiled before looking over to Gwen.

"Yes, I don't really know how to explain it, but he calms my magic, makes it usable. The goddess herself sent him to me. Verdan was right about that, at the very least."

"He does have a habit of being right about these things," Kai muttered, shaking his head slightly as he poured out two mugs of the mint tea that Gwen kept on hand. Coming over to the table, he sat opposite her and passed across one of the mugs.

"Thank you."

They sipped their tea in comfortable silence, letting the warmth do its work and banish the lingering cold of the outdoors.

CHAPTER
FIFTEEN

VERDAN WAS deep into his morning meditation on the morning of the third day since they'd left the camp when he felt a flicker of Aether approaching him in the form of a message spell.

Accepting the message, Verdan tried to keep the majority of his focus on the work he was doing on his second spiral. Once the latest layer was locked in place and his visualization was secure, Verdan turned his attention to the message.

The construct left behind at the Darjee camp had sent him a message stating that fourteen humanoids were within its detection range. Interesting. It looked like their quarry had finally arrived.

Of course, it could be a wandering group of other random humanoids, but the chances of that were slim. Maybe once this was dealt with, Verdan would spend some time examining the Darjee and see if they had any identifying Aether signatures. If they truly had no magic of their own, then he doubted they would, but it would be worth a look.

Verdan had already questioned Gruthka on what else was in the area and whether they were humanoid in form, but the Fwyn was evasive about the matter.

Given that Verdan was likely the first human that the Fwyn had met in a long time that wasn't trying to kill him, that was under-standable. With the state of the relationship between the Fwyn and the humans being what it was, Verdan could only imagine what had happened to other members of the Imperium.

One of the perks of formal training as a Wizard was the mental discipline and self-control that was taught from day one. Despite years of practice, Verdan had to struggle to get his thoughts under control before they could spiral down into darker subjects. He could do nothing about what had happened. He was thousands of years too late.

Repeating that it was out of his control to himself like a mantra, Verdan got himself calm and his mind back in order. He was clearly overtired.

Taking a moment to gather himself, Verdan rose to his feet and winced at a flare of pain in his back. He'd not slept for the last two nights, instead spending the time in complete focus as he built his second spiral. The gains he'd made had been impressive, but there was a physical price to be paid.

"*Hyn*," Verdan channeled his Aether into a spell of refreshment, sending the power through his body to revitalize him. He had to be careful not to get reliant on measures like this. They were highly addictive and exceedingly dangerous; an infusion of Aether couldn't replace everything the body needed. Still, it was enough to get him back into top form, and Verdan had walked the line with spells like this before. He knew what he was doing.

Feeling more awake now, Verdan started to collect his things before heading downstairs to find where everyone was.

Stepping outside, Verdan spotted Tim and Tom working together to spar with Kai. The brothers were losing, but not as badly as they would have been a few days ago. That was encouraging progress.

Moving around to the side of the cottage, Verdan saw Gwen and Gruthka were sitting together in the vegetable garden. Satisfied that he knew where they all were, Verdan headed over to the sparring trio.

"I've had a pulse from the camp. Fourteen humanoid creatures have arrived." Verdan's words cut through the general noise from their fighting, making all three of them turn to face him with mixed expressions. "We have time to get to them tonight if we leave straight away. What do you think?"

"The sooner, the better; we need to attack before they realize things have changed," Kai answered immediately, Tom enthusiastically nodding along with him.

"Tim?" Verdan turned to the third man with a questioning look.

"I'm concerned about camping out in the forest or trying to travel back here during the night, for that matter. It feels like we're committing to an all-or-nothing attack. Wouldn't it be better to wait for the morning?"

"If we wait until morning some of them might head out hunting. That means trying to ambush two different groups, with a much higher chance of us being spotted and some of them escaping. If they've only arrived today, this is the best time to catch them all together," Kai pointed out, gesturing in the rough direction of the camp.

"Yeah, I suppose that's true," Tim said, nodding his grudging agreement.

"All agreed?" Verdan waited a moment before nodding. "Right, let's do this then. I'll go get Gruthka." He turned to head towards

Gwen and Gruthka, hearing the other three rush back to the cottage to grab everything they needed.

To his surprise, Gruthka was manipulating some of the soil with his magic, forming it into different shapes and naming it in Low Imperial. Gwen was then repeating the words back to him, with Gruthka correcting any mistakes. Her accent was understandably atrocious, but she seemed to be slowly picking up a few important words.

Low Imperial wasn't a complicated language. It had been the most-common language in the Imperium and was used primarily for informal conversations. With so many different species living alongside each other, it was a strange mix of words but was easy for everyone to speak.

"Gruthka, the Darjee are here," Verdan called out, naturally dropping into Low Imperial so the Fwyn could understand him as he approached. Seeing Gruthka nod, Verdan waited as the Fwyn nodded to Gwen and got to his feet.

As Verdan turned to leave, a large raven flew down to sit on Gwen's shoulder, its black eyes staring at him with a surprising weight to its gaze. Frowning, Verdan reached out with his Aether senses and felt the reservoir of energy that sat, calm and controlled, within the bird. A slight connection ran between the raven and the Witch, making a smile spread across Verdan's face. He'd hoped she'd be able to do it.

"Congratulations, Gwen," he said, his smile turning into a grin as she realized what he was talking about and flashed him a huge grin of her own. There was an energy to her, a spark in her eyes that hadn't been there before. It would be interesting to see if she now started to develop some of the more physical properties of her magic. It was a shame he'd not been there when she made that connection. He'd likely just been too caught up in his own progression.

"Thank you. It turned out that it was the lack of connection to the goddess that was holding me back." Gwen told him, her grin faltering as she saw Gruthka stand up. Rising to her feet as well, Gwen looked between the Fwyn and Verdan with a worried expression. "What's happening?"

"The Darjee have arrived, or so I believe. I originally intended to leave you here, but if your magic is under control, you're welcome to come with us," Verdan said with a gesture to the raven on her shoulder, drawing her eyes to her new familiar.

In any sort of normal circumstance, he would never take a novice spellcaster into a fight, but this was Gwen's home. She deserved the opportunity to defend it. Besides, Witches were some of the most natural spellcasters out there. Now she had her familiar, Gwen would get everything under control in no time at all.

"I don't..." Gwen stopped mid-word, her gaze rising to the clear sky above as though searching for an answer. A few moments passed before she nodded, her expression firming as she looked back down to Verdan. "Yes, I will come. I'll get my things now." Nodding to herself, the Witch ran back toward the cottage, leaving Verdan to finish explaining the situation to Gruthka.

_**_

They all gathered at the edge of the glade a few minutes later, armed and armored as best they could be. Kai was impassive, his quiet confidence doing a lot to reassure the others. Tim and Tom looked apprehensive but had an element of resolve in their posture of which Verdan approved. He had high hopes for the brothers in the future.

Gruthka was difficult to read. Verdan hadn't known many Fwyn, and the few he had known were only acquaintances at best. That being said, Gruthka's already large eyes seemed to be even wider than usual as he observed them all, giving off an air of eagerness and excitement.

"Okay, everyone ready?" Verdan gave them one last opportunity to back out or grab anything else they needed, but a tense silence was all that answered him. "Then let's move out. We'll follow Gruthka, as he's the most familiar with the local area. He knows a more-direct route to the camp than what we used before, and every minute counts." Verdan saw Kai frown unhappily, but the Sorcerer made no move to argue or contradict him. He clearly understood how important it was that they make good time.

Giving a final nod, Verdan motioned for Gruthka to lead the way and fell in behind him, the others following along as they stepped out of the safety of the glade and started towards the confrontation with the Darjee.

Memories from the war flashed through Verdan's mind, stabbing their way deep into him as he remembered other expeditions, other sorties and other friends and comrades. Smiling faces that became twisted into expressions of torment and agony. Death. So much death. Sometimes it felt like a reaper dogged his every step, lovingly running his scythe across the throats of those he cared about the moment he looked away.

"Verdan, are you okay?" Gwen asked, her worried voice dragging him out of his memories and back to the present. The others had all overtaken him. He must have fallen behind a little in his dazed state, and Gwen had slowed to check on him. "You've gone pale, and your hand is shaking."

Verdan looked down at his free hand, noticing how it trembled against his side. He felt unbalanced, as though his mind teetered on the edge of some unknowable abyss. Taking a deep, steadying breath, Verdan partitioned his mind and thrust all of the memories into the new section. His old master had taught him a method to segregate painful memories, and Verdan quickly followed his teachings. He did not need this right now.

"I'm fine, thank you," Verdan said, smiling wanly at Gwen in a pathetic attempt at reassuring her. He'd had a few nightmares and bad moments since he'd awoken, nothing that he couldn't handle. This, though, was something else entirely.

The atmosphere was similar enough to a few of the missions he'd been on to trigger his memories. He could keep it separate and out of mind for now, but his master had been very clear on the potential for long-term problems if he relied on this too much.

Keeping up the smile until Gwen seemed reassured enough to quicken her pace and catch up to the others, Verdan rubbed his face and took a few shaky breaths. He needed to keep it together right now.

Verdan strengthened the partitions in his mind using the techniques he had been taught. He couldn't afford any issues during the fight.

With the memories safely locked away, Verdan gripped his staff firmly and quickened his own pace to rejoin the group, ignoring the curious glances he got from the others.

_**_

With Grutka leading them, they made good time through the woods, the Fwyn avoiding the natural obstacles that lay in their way and taking what shortcuts they could to speed their path onward.

No matter the skill of their guide, the journey itself still took time, and from the position of the sun, they were halfway through the afternoon when Gruthka came to a halt at a small stream.

"Follow this upstream, and it will lead you to the Darjee camp," Gruthka told him, pointing a claw at the winding path of the water. "I will fetch the others and return as soon as I can. Begin your attack in one hour."

"We will, good luck," Verdan gave the Fwyn a firm nod, his composure fully restored after the hike through the woods.

The Fwyn returned the nod and scampered off into the undergrowth, swiftly fading from view as he darted between patches of heavier brush.

"Now we wait." Verdan took a seat against a tree, crossing his legs and laying his staff across his lap.

Sadly, the Aether construct in the camp had run out of power an hour or two ago. Still, the last pulse he'd had from it had confirmed the same number of creatures in the camp as before. Hopefully, that wouldn't change in the next hour.

The others chose their own spaces to rest, taking advantage of the few minutes they had, yet not relaxing enough to lower their guard. This was dangerous territory, and their surprise attack on the Darjee could easily be turned around on them if they weren't careful.

Silence stretched on between them as they waited, the sun ever so slowly making its way through the sky.

Eventually, Kai looked up at the sky and frowned before meeting Verdan's gaze and raising an eyebrow in silent question. The Wizard was confident that the hour mark was approaching as well, so he simply nodded and rose to his feet. It was time.

_**_

The group gathered together and started moving upstream, Kai going first, followed by Tim, then Verdan and Gwen, with Tom taking the rearmost position. Kai had been instructing the others as best he could on moving quietly, but even so, Verdan winced at what Tom considered stealth.

The stream continued for a short distance before showing itself to be linked to the previous body of water they'd come across. They were but a stone's throw away from the camp. Kai seemed to recognise where they were as well, leading them around until they were coming toward the edge of the treeline that surrounded the camp. Peering through the undergrowth, Verdan got his first real look at the Darjee.

Fourteen Darjee were present throughout the camp, some walking, some talking, some tending a firepit or doing other camp chores. The Darjee were dog-faced humanoids, muscular and large. They carried themselves with a slight hunch, and long, coarse black hair covered their bodies. Each Darjee was clad in leather and fur, with dangling tanned hide and bone accessories.

One particularly robust specimen wore a thick fur pelt around its shoulders and seemed to have some sort of status among the others. Verdan watched with interest as the fur-clad leader ordered the others around and took charge of the camp's operation.

There was a clear social structure at play here. Verdan was reluctant to make too many assumptions, but it seemed to be based on the quality and number of pelts, furs, and hides they wore. While that might not be the most useful information right now, it was worth noting. The sight of so much fur on display made him feel sick. Kai's words on how the Darjee only hunted sentient creatures for their pelts lingered in his mind.

"After you," Kai whispered as softly as he could, glancing in Verdan's direction from where he was crouched behind a tree.

Verdan eyed the encampment carefully, calming his mind and noting distances between the various targets. The Darjee were too spread out for him to hit them all with a single spell. Well, not unless he used something big and Aether-intensive. It was an option, but not a good one.

It was frustrating to work with such limitations, but his progress was steady, and even a fraction of his power was better than nothing. Verdan just wished that he could support his companions more.

A group of five Darjee were clustered off to one side of the camp, making a tempting target for an opening attack. Alternatively, the leader he'd spotted earlier was in plain view in the center of the camp with another Darjee. Both were good, but Verdan didn't have time to mull over the choices. Going with his gut, Verdan decided to even the numbers a little.

"*Thanr bel*!" Verdan barked out the words, packing as much emphasis into them as he could to strengthen the empowering portion of the spell concept.

A bead of red flame flew out from his hand, slowly swelling as it sailed into the camp, growing to around two feet across before impacting one of the Darjee. The sphere audibly cracked as it hit the unfortunate creature, blooming out in an expanding ball of fire that swept over the cluster of Darjee and sent out a ripple of heat across the whole camp.

The screams of the heavily-burnt Darjee rent the air as Kai raced forward. Tim and Tom tried to keep up, but almost immediately fell behind as the fire Sorcerer channeled his Aether. The Darjee reacted quickly, shaking off the shock of the abrupt attack like seasoned fighters and moving to meet the charging humans.

Low walls of packed earth reared up in front of the Darjee as they tried to converge, blocking their path and separating them from each other. More than one Darjee ran straight into a wall as it reared up in front of them, crashing and falling heavily to the ground in a shower of dirt and stone, dazed from the impact.

Stretching out his senses, Verdan could feel a concentration of Aether on the far side of the camp. It looked like the Fwyn had arrived.

The Darjee that avoided the walls were able to close in on the charging Sorcerer, flexing their hands to extend seven-inch long claws. To Verdan's surprise, their claws didn't look like the normal ones seen on predatory animals. Instead, they were black, with swirling lines of white running through them, looking more like black marble than anything else. For all that they didn't use Aether, these creatures were certainly altered by it somehow.

The Darjee had reacted quickly, and even the slowest of them moved with surprising speed given their size, but Kai was still quicker.

The first Darjee that Kai came to swiped at his face with its claws, but the Sorcerer slid to one side, his spear following him in an almost lazy arc that dragged its leaf-bladed tip across the belly of the creature. Blood sprayed out from the deep cut, and the Darjee yelped in pain, flinching away from the attack.

Skidding to a stop, Kai changed the grip on his spear and reversed its movement, skewering the Darjee before it could recover with the spike at the base of his spear.

Nearby, the other Darjee were quick to try to capitalize on Kai's spear being occupied, and redoubled their efforts to reach him through the impromptu maze forming around them.

"*Aer!*" Verdan barked out three times in quick succession, using a motion of his hands to guide the spell, He sent out blasts of pressurized air that knocked back the harging Darjee, staggering their arrival and giving Kai time to face them one or two at a time, rather than all at once. He would do more, but the empowered fireball had been a heavy drain on his reserves, and he might need another one before the end.

Two Darjee managed to make it through Verdan's interference, rushing for Kai with eager growls. The extra time that Verdan had bought the Sorcerer meant that their prey was ready for them, however, and they were forced back by the flashing steel of Kai's spear.

Tim and Tom arrived as Kai held back the two Darjee, the two brothers flanking each side of the Sorcerer as they pressured the Darjee.

Satisfied that they had matters well in hand, Verdan turned his attention to the rest of the Darjee. The earthen walls were still erupting from the ground to confound the Darjee, but now they had less of an impact. The dog-faced warriors were now moving carefully and not charging forward, slowing down but not stopping.

Still, Verdan saw at least a few Darjee had been bound by thick stone restraints where they'd fallen after hitting a wall, effectively removing them from the fight. It seemed that the Fwyn had thought up a few ways to manage the Darjee attacks.

Changing his attacks from the Darjee nearest his companions, Verdan started to work in concert with the Fwyn. Rapid blasts of pressurized air would knock over a Darjee, with the Fwyn then binding them in earth and stone once they were down. Half of the Darjee were dead or bound now; it was only a matter of time.

Verdan kept an eye on the fighting and was pleased to see that the brothers were working in harmony with Kai. Tim and Tom were fighting defensively, protecting Kai as he took down the Darjee that reached them one at a time.

With no need to deal with multiple opponents at once, Kai was reaping a bloody toll on the Darjee. The Sorcerer's spear was already glistening crimson and dripping with the blood of his fallen foes.

Despite their teamwork, any normal human would have been overrun by the Darjee. Only Kai's 'Essence' allowed him to be quick enough to outpace the Darjee so easily.

A portion of Verdan's awareness studied Kai as he slew another Darjee, watching how the Aether was drawn into him and how it behaved around him. There was something familiar about it. Verdan pushed his musing to one side—now wasn't the time.

"*Aer Tor!*" Verdan used the two-word spell in conjunction with a slice of his hand, sending out an arc of pressurized air toward a pair of Darjee that were trying to outflank Kai.

Some Wizards looked down on those who used motions to help form their spells, but Verdan's experience was that it helped shape the spell and reduced the mental effort of forming it. Plus, there was a visceral satisfaction to feeling like he'd thrown the air that ripped through the monster.

One of the two Darjee he'd targeted saw the attack coming and rolled underneath it, losing some fur and flesh in the process. The other caught the brunt of the spell, the blade of air ripping through him messily in a shower of blood and gore. The Darjee that had ducked the attack rose into a dead sprint, going straight for Verdan, aiming to reach him before he could cast again.

A crack and a flash of light seared Verdan's retinas as a bolt of blue-white lightning burst into being, striking the Darjee in the side and throwing it off its feet with explosive force. The acrid odor of burnt fur and flesh warred with the strong ozone smell of the lightning as Verdan blinked rapidly to help his vision recover. The lightning bolt, which was still slightly superimposed on his vision, had clearly come from Gwen.

Glancing over, Verdan saw the weather Witch leaning against a tree, pale and sweating as she panted and tried to catch her breath. Magic for Witches was a lot more physical than it was for Wizards. She must have used everything she had in that one strike to be in this state already.

Turning back to the fight, Verdan surveyed the others to see where he was needed, but it looked like it was all but over. Tom was pulping the brains of a Darjee with his mace, Kai was impaling his latest opponent on his spear, and the Fwyn had secured the few Darjee yet to reach the fight with stone restraints. In barely a few minutes the whole fight had been decided.

None of the Darjee that had fought Kai and the brothers had survived, and those bound in restraints were slowly swallowed by the earth, disappearing into impromptu graves. Verdan had seen such a tactic in the past, but it still sent a chill down his spine. Being buried alive was a bad way to go, but nothing the Darjee didn't deserve.

"You both did well. The training is paying off," Kai said, his voice cutting through the silence that followed the fight as he gave the brothers a slight smile. Both Tim and Tom were breathing heavily from the short but intense battle. Still, they perked up at Kai's words.

"You all did well," Verdan said, nodding approvingly first at Gwen, then at the brothers, proud of how well they'd all performed.

"Is it always this tiring?" Gwen came over to him, still breathing heavily and looking a little flushed from the sudden exertion.

"Well, what have you done with your magic prior to this?" Verdan kept half an eye on everyone else as he answered Gwen, just in case there was still a hidden threat.

"Something similar to those air blasts I saw you were doing— that's it really," Gwen said after a moment of thought.

"Consider the power of a lightning bolt compared to that," Verdan said, nodding as he saw the realization dawn in her eyes. "All that energy has to come from somewhere, and more importantly, your body has to cope with it moving through you."

"So, I should stick to air blasts for now?" Gwen asked with a frown and a slight grimace.

"No, you should push yourself where you can, both in the strength of what you are casting and the variety of effects you create. Just don't overdo it. You never know when you need to be in top shape." Verdan drew on the little Witch knowledge he had to guide her. It was very different to being a Wizard, after all.

"I think I get it," Gwen said, nodding with a thoughtful expression as he spoke. A flutter of wings heralded the arrival of her raven, the large bird gently setting down on her shoulder. Verdan hadn't seen it leave, but that wasn't surprising, given how stealthy familiars could be.

"Good, it's important to explore the breadth of what you can do with your magic. Don't simply rest on a few tricks that work, because one day, that might not be enough," Verdan said, mixing his cautionary words with a reassuring pat on the shoulder. "Now, I need to speak with Gruthka. Take a few minutes to rest."

Leaving Gwen to sit down and recover, Verdan walked around the perimeter of the Darjee camp to where the Fwyn were hidden in the trees. It was easy enough for him to locate them; all the Aether they'd been using had caused something akin to turbulence in their local area, highlighting their position to those with the ability to notice.

There were four more Fwyn with Gruthka, though the newcomers backed away as Verdan approached, watching him warily. In contrast, Gruthka stepped out of the treeline to greet Verdan, his gaze lingering on the Darjee camp.

Ignoring the four sets of large black eyes watching him from the undergrowth, Verdan nodded to Gruthka and gestured to the Darjee camp. "Thank you for the help; those stone restraints were very useful."

"It is our traditional way of dealing with the Darjee. They are too quick to dodge if we try projectiles. Fighting like this is how we've survived this long," Gruthka said with a hint of pride that twisted into bitterness at the end.

"I promised to help, and I will. We'll get your people back," Verdan said, his soft voice belying the steel in his eyes and the rage that burned within him. Seeing the furs and leathers the Darjee wore, and knowing they mainly came from sentient creatures, had filled him with a cold fury.

He was no hero. That was what he told himself; it was like a mantra that he was using to cope with this new world at this point. He'd promised Gurthka that he'd help him, and he would. Verdan's oath would be fulfilled, and in this little corner of the world, the empire's values would stand. He could do no less and still honour the fallen.

CHAPTER

SIXTEEN

GRUTHKA ALREADY KNEW where the main Darjee camp would be located and the best way to get there, so there was little need to wait now that they'd dealt with the hunting party.

Kai also stated that he advised against any sort of delay. The Sorcerer pointed out that the Darjee would know something was amiss as soon as their hunting party failed to report in. If they were going to act, they had a brief window to do so.

Despite Verdan's assurances, Gruthka seemed almost surprised when Verdan declared that they were ready to head north with the Fwyn.

Verdan might be a Wizard with a passing knowledge of Low Imperial and an awareness of who the Fwyn were, but he was still a human. In Gruthka's eyes, humans were the most untrustworthy race known. Verdan hoped that this joint venture would start to undo some of the damage done.

Once Verdan confirmed they were still heading north, the Fwyn exploded into action. Gruthka had ordered them to ready supplies already, but they'd been left in a nearby secure location, just in case.

While the Fwyn gathered their supplies, Verdan and his companions prepared themselves. There was sure to be a nasty fight at the end of this journey.

Interestingly, the Fwyn were also able to provide a pair of wooden shields for the brothers. The make of the shields seemed human to Verdan, but Gruthka didn't explain where they had come from.

Once ready, they set off as a group, making some headway into their journey using the last few hours of light that they had. Gruthka had said that the main camp was a full day's travel away, so they pushed on into the early evening before stopping. This way, they had only a half-day of travel tomorrow to look forward to.

Kai found them a nicely defensible area for their evening camp, and, at Gruthka's command, the Fwyn got to work.

Verdan watched with interest as the Fwyn created a shelter of compacted earth for them all, lining the outside with threads of stone for stability. The small creatures worked in harmony with each other, allowing them to channel large amounts of Aether into a spell and accomplish larger workings in a short span of time.

It was an interesting method, and Verdan wondered how they avoided issues with some of them having different ideas of what needed to be built. After all this was done, he'd need to sit down with Gruthka and see what he could find out.

_**_

Verdan awoke just before dawn the next day, and took the opportunity to meditate outside the shelter before everyone else was awake. For once, he didn't create more of the spiral or condense it. Instead, he grabbed hold of it with his will and began to speed the cycle, drawing in the Aether at a faster rate.

It was a will-intensive activity, and within minutes there was sweat beading on his forehead. At the same time, however, he got half again as much Aether as he would normally. Given that they were going up against a ferocious and numerically superior foe, Verdan was certain he'd need every last drop of precious Aether he had.

Verdan maintained his effort until everyone else had awoken, his face pale and his skin clammy by the time he released the spiral. Sighing deeply, Verdan hunched over and rested his elbows on his knees, his chest heaving as though he'd been sprinting around the camp. He'd recover soon enough, but there was a reason why he'd done it this early in the day.

Opening his eyes and looking around, Verdan was pleasantly surprised to see just over a dozen Fwyn were speaking quietly outside the shelter. They seemed to be deferring to Gruthka, who saw him watching and came over.

"Wizard, your fame has brought more of my people to aid us. The ancient tales give hope to those who had long since given up. It warms my heart to see them joining us, bringing us together once more. You have my thanks," Gruthka said, bowing low to Verdan, who returned the bow from his seated position.

"It's easy to let despair take hold, but today we'll show them that your people can strike back in a way they never expected. With so many Fwyn by our side, we will surely be victorious." Verdan put as much confidence as he could into his words and saw Gruthka straighten up in pride.

"We're not leaving without our clanfolk. Not a single one is going to be left behind," Gruthka declared with a firm nod, heading back to his companions to pass on Verdan's confident words.

"Encouragement?" Kai said from behind Verdan, his voice pitched low enough that the Fwyn wouldn't hear him, even with their oddly acute hearing.

"They needed it," Verdan said, equally softly. He turned to share a look with the Sorcerer. They both knew how dangerous this was going to be, even with a few more Fwyn on their side.

Stretching his back and wiping the sweat off, Verdan gathered his things and got to his feet. He'd taken off a lot of layers for his medi-tation, but he was quick to put them back on now that he could feel the cold wind biting at him.

His Aether reserves were as high as they'd been since he woke up; he was ready as he was going to be.

Kai, Gwen, and the brothers were ready not long after him. Everyone had the same determined expression as they prepared quietly for what was coming. None of them thought this was going to be easy.

Still, Verdan had a few ideas, especially with a few more Fwyn on their side. A bit of earth-craft might just be able to level the playing field a little.

_**_

Gruthka carried on leading them north, taking them on paths and trails that meandered through the pristine forests of the area. Few creatures bothered them on their journey, which wasn't surprising given the number of them passing through.

As the sun was just starting to reach its zenith, Gruthka brought their group to a halt at the base of a large tree-covered hill. Gesturing for the other Fwyn to rest, Gruthka beckoned for Verdan and Kai to follow him up the hill.

The three of them climbed to the top, with the short Fwyn picking his way easily through the thick and tangled roots of the trees as the two humans struggled to keep up with him.

When they reached the top, Verdan climbed up onto a rocky outcropping and got a good view of the area. There was a large group of ruins just beyond the hill, which looked to be where the Darjee were squatting.

In fact, there was something familiar about the layout of the ruins. If Verdan looked at it from the right angle, they almost matched what he'd expect for the remnants of an old Imperial forward base. Interesting.

The walls and buildings that had once been part of whatever this was were in absolute ruins. The least-damaged area was the shattered leftovers of the outside wall, followed by what looked like a collapsed main building in the center of the ruins. The rest was chaotic and disorganized, with some signs that other groups had built over some areas at some point. The whole thing had likely changed hands more than a few times over the years.

"This is where they base themselves. Darjee like to live in ruins like these when out hunting and raiding. What do you think?" Gruthka said, turning his wide eyes to Verdan expectantly.

"I think that they have grown sloppy, if they ever were disciplined to begin with," Verdan said, after translating the Fwyn's words for Kai.

From Verdan's point of view, he had only recently been fighting in the war, so he had the right mindset for looking at weak points in an enemy's position. To him, the Darjee were arrogant beyond belief.

A cursory look at the ruins told him that they had a few stationary guards but no roving patrols, and no magical protections that he could sense. With adequate magical support, a decent attack force would roll over this camp with ease.

Sadly, they were a ragtag group of combatants at best. Kai was a capable fighter, and Verdan was ready to provide fire support, but they were only two people. So much of this depended on the Fwyn and Verdan's other companions. Still, Verdan was quietly confident, as long as they had time to prepare.

Pushing back from the top of the hill, Verdan led the other two down to where the rest of the group waited. It was late morning now, and he wanted to strike in the early evening, so they had time to work with.

CHAPTER
SEVENTEEN

KAI WATCHED as Verdan engaged in an animated discussion with the Fwyn, as he called them, in their own tongue. It was so strange to Kai that these creatures had taken to the Wizard so calmly. Kai was almost tempted to learn their language simply to understand how that had happened.

The ease with which they'd become allies and the acceptance of the Fwyn as they traveled together cast doubts on some of Kai's previous experiences. Sleeping in a shelter created by the strange creatures was an illuminating experience for Kai. A group of earth Sorcerers couldn't put together a fortified structure like that so easily, not without being individually very powerful.

While Kai might not know much about the Fwyn, he knew that they weren't individually that powerful, so they must have some trick to doing it. The suggestion that Sorcerers could learn from non-humans would get him killed in the south, but that was what Kai saw here.

However, Kai couldn't lay all the blame at the feet of the battle-mad Sorcerers that plagued the land. He knew he'd never considered peaceful resolutions either with non-humans in the past, and he was as progressive as any Sorcerer could be.

Truly, Verdan was making Kai re-examine himself, one belief at a time.

Kai's eyes slid over to Gwen, considering that revelation as well before he cleared his mind and took a meditative pose on the ground. It looked like the conversation was over, and they were doing something fairly substantial, so Kai would use the time he had as best he could.

Seating himself on the lush grass, Kai turned his mind inward to his soul. The elemental Essence within him was slowly replenishing after the last fight, and Kai had enough to fight now if needed, but he would rather ensure he was fully prepared.

Grasping the energy flowing within him, Kai brought to mind the concept that had first allowed him to become a Sorcerer. The burning energy of flame, the speed of fire, the heat of his body as he moved faster and faster.

A bead of sweat rolled down Kai's face as he focused on that concept while holding the flow of energy. As the energy flowed inside him, it passed through the lens of his concept, changing into elemental Essence and settling into his core.

As the energy that had naturally built up within his body was diminished, Kai started to breathe deeply and with purpose. An essential skill for any Sorcerer was learning to breathe correctly. It was vital to bring in as much fresh energy as possible, to breathe deeply, but of the right things.

It was easier to grasp the surrounding energy as he breathed while in a meditative state, but it was yet another thing to focus on.

Managing his breathing while holding onto the Essence and concept at the same time was always like juggling to Kai. He lacked the skill with it that some of his peers had, but he didn't let that stop him. Every day he would cultivate the energy within him, push his boundaries, and practice splitting his focus like this.

The best method to increase a Sorcerer's strength was highly debated amongst the different clans. Some said that it was best to inflate your Essence by cultivating at the peak of potency, forcing your soul to expand to accommodate the new energy being drawn in. Others said that the opposite was true. They theorized that the soul was like any muscle and needed to be used, that it would grow in time due to usage and that cultivation should be done when you had no Essence remaining.

Kai didn't know which one was correct. His chosen approach was simple. He maintained his daily meditations around an exercise routine, strengthening his soul alongside his body. Perhaps it wasn't the most-efficient way, but there was something relaxing about settling down to meditate after a heavy training session.

Kai's struggle to balance the different things he needed to focus on to cultivate properly was interrupted by a strange sensation.

For a brief moment, Kai was able to sense energy flowing through the ground toward a small circle of Fwyn. The energy was solid and strong but equally unyielding and slow to change, nothing like the Essence he cultivated.

A blink of his eyes dispelled the vision, leaving Kai sitting on the lush grass, covered in sweat yet feeling rejuvenated. Kai felt fresh energy sweep into him and slowly spread throughout his body as he took a final, deep, cleansing breath. Maybe it was due to his conversations with Verdan about imagery, or perhaps his inspiration from their fights. Either way, he'd not had as refreshing a meditation session in a good while.

Kai had already been at a reasonable level of energy prior to meditating. Now, he was as close to peak condition as he'd been in a long time.

A slight rumble pulled him from his thoughts, and Kai watched in fascination as the Fwyn grouped together and began to raise rock from the ground to form a thick wall perpendicular to the slope of the steep hill they'd climbed earlier. The rock emerged slowly, but it rose steadily, creating a wall three times as tall as Kai and at least thirty feet long over several minutes.

Once finished, they created two more walls, each fifteen feet long and continuing from each end of the original wall at a right angle that brought them toward Kai. A final wall all but sealed the shape, leaving only a ten-foot gap directly in front of where Kai sat.

The Fwyn were noticeably tired now, but they gamely continued on, a few of them moving to the interior of the walled area while the rest began a new wall that extended out from the previous one. This new wall was half as thick and slightly shorter than Kai, but it was no less impressive.

Over the next few minutes, the Fwyn formed a smaller version of the shape they'd first created, with the gaps in the two walls lining up perfectly.

The tired-looking Fwyn then created a barrier that was ten feet out from the frontmost wall and was thigh-high on Kai.

The end result was a barrier that would slow the Darjee down, followed by two doorways that were protected by walls that would funnel the Darjee down a singular path.

Walking through the center of the first box shape that had been created, Kai admired the defensive structure that they'd put together. The walls were firm and thick, not to mention tall enough to discourage climbing.

Reaching the interior, Kai saw that the Fwyn who had broken off from the group had created steps going up the wall and a corner platform at the top. There would be no protection up there from enemy attacks, but Kai was reasonably sure that Verdan would be up there, and he doubted the Darjee would be able to touch him.

All in all, it was an impressive fortification to be created within a single hour, especially by a dozen five-foot-tall creatures. Interestingly, two of the Fwyn hadn't taken part in the building effort. Instead, they stood off to one side, speaking quietly with each other.

Satisfied with their defenses, Kai headed toward the hill. He would find a vantage point and keep an eye out for any wandering Darjee, just in case.

CHAPTER
EIGHTEEN

THE MAJORITY of the Fwyn were exhausted after creating the fortification, so they settled down to wait for a time. Even as relaxed as they were, tension was thick in the air. Everyone present knew that the Darjee were close by, and there was a chance they could find them.

Having spent some time on watch, Kai headed over to an area a little distance from the fort, searching for some seclusion. He had intended to cultivate his Essence while remaining on watch, but he had struggled to maintain his meditative state.

Part of it was the upcoming battle. Kai was worried about what would happen; his heart was unsettled, and so was his mind. There was so much that could go wrong, and for all that he couldn't understand the Fwyn, there was no denying that Gruthka and the others were far more intelligent than Kai had given them credit for.

A fierce rage at the Darjee was growing within Kai, one that would soon find an outlet. But he also found himself disturbed by the implications; if the Fwyn were sapient, who knew how many other sapient races were out there? The Fwyn were considered little more than beasts by everyone Kai knew. It was disconcerting that they were all wrong.

With such questions straining his usually adept self-control, it only took a small thing to interfere with his cultivation. That distraction came in the form of a pair of memories. Twice now, Verdan had cast that expanding ball of fire attack near Kai. The first time, Kai had been too far away to hear the chant that Verdan used, but not this time.

Grym thanr bel. The words as a whole were nonsensical to the Sorcerer, yet one of them called to him. Thanr. It rolled off of Kai's tongue with a burning sensation, as though he was speaking in flames, not with air. It was all sensation and no substance, but it was a window into something new for him.

At some point, Kai would need to meditate deeply on the word, drawing on its inspiration to improve and develop his image of Fire. After all, the stronger and more complete the image, the more powerful the Sorcerer, that was always true.

Becoming stronger was always desirable, but not when it interfered with his cultivation right on the eve of a potentially deadly battle.

A branch snapped off to the right.

Kai was on his feet, and his spear was in hand in a flash, his gaze sweeping the area for the sound. His tense muscles relaxed as he saw one of the non-builder Fwyn coming out of some bushes, baring its tiny, pointed teeth at him in a smile when it saw him.

Kai flashed it a brief smile in return and was about to sit back down when he saw a flicker of gray in the undergrowth behind the Fwyn.

At the same moment, the Fwyn glanced down at the ground with a frown before it froze and then dove forward with a cry.

The flicker that Kai had seen burst out of the undergrowth in the form of a gray-furred Darjee. The creature's seven-inch claws swiped through the space where the Fwyn had been a moment earlier.

The Fwyn shouted something in a language that Kai didn't understand as it hit the ground, twisting in place to throw up a hand at the Darjee, something flashing up from it to hit the attacking Darjee in the chest.

The dog-faced creature stumbled back with a hacking cough, staggering down to one knee as it clutched at its chest. Weakly, it tried to slash at the Fwyn, but it couldn't quite reach the small creature.

The Fwyn jumped to its feet and, to Kai's surprise, rushed forward to land a punch on the Darjee. The Fwyn's tiny fist should have barely rocked the Darjee, but instead, the creature howled in pain and collapsed to the floor.

Kai arrived before either party could fight further, driving his spear into the Darjee's chest with a swift thrust, piercing its heart. With the immediate threat dealt with, Kai realized that part of the Darjee's face had been rotted away, precisely where the Fwyn had punched it.

Glancing at the four-and-a-half-foot tall creature at his side with a bit more respect, Kai pulled his spear free, nudging the Darjee's arm aside to reveal rotten flesh where it had been clutching its chest. Impressive.

"Kai!" Tim shouted from behind them, making Kai glance back to see that the others had gathered at the front of the boxy fort. Tim was pointing at a slope to the side of the hill that sat between them and the Darjee camp. Looking over, Kai saw two figures standing atop it. No doubt they'd been drawn by the scream from their compatriot.

The Fwyn next to him wasted no time in starting to rush back to their base, eager to put walls between it and the soon-to-be-attacking Darjee.

On consideration, Kai decided that the Fwyn had the right idea. The Darjee had disappeared back over the hill, but they would be back, this time with friends.

Verdan was already ushering the Fwyn back into their building, directing them in their language while Tim, Tom, and Gwen took up their positions at the front thigh-high barrier.

The rot-wielding Fwyn started to head inside when they reached the fort but paused and instead joined their group, nodding to Kai as it did. He was happy to have the help, especially when its powers were so debilitating. Gwen, on the other hand, Kai was not so happy to see at the frontline.

"I'm staying," Gwen said firmly, seeing the look in Kai's eyes as he walked over to her.

"It's too dangerous here. You're not a trained fighter," Kai said sternly, ignoring the defiant look in her flashing blue eyes.

"I don't need to be trained; I've finally got my powers," Gwen said, her eyes narrowing dangerously as a spark jumped from one hand to the other.

"Which you haven't used in a proper fight yet. You're not ready to be at the front like this," Kai said evenly, returning her stare flatly.

"We don't have time to argue. Gwen, stay up front, but make sure you're behind the others at all times. You are a destructive force now, but you have no protection, and you're not battle-trained. Let them take the brunt of the attack while you crush the foes around them, understood?" Verdan said, coming over and ending the argument with a firm statement

"I understand," Gwen snapped, turning on her heel to stalk away.

Kai and Verdan exchanged a look, and the Wizard started to say something, but a cry from one of the brothers drew their attention to the distant slope. The Darjee were coming.

Kai took command of the front defenses as Verdan headed back inside, positioning Tim and Tom at his flanks, with Gwen and the Fwyn at their back. Hopefully, the thigh-high barrier would slow the Darjee down, but it wouldn't stop them. They were almost guaranteed to have to pull back inside the first section of the fort, but once there, the other Fwyn could give them some support.

Kai gripped his spear firmly as he looked at the group of Darjee that was pounding down the slope toward them. There was over a score of them, each snarling and baying for blood as they raced to close with the waiting defenders.

"Stay calm, keep stead, and talk to each other. We'll all make it through this if we fight smart," Kai said softly, instilling as much confidence into his words as he could.

"Don't worry, we've got your back," Tim said, rolling his shoulders as he hefted his shield and readied his sword.

"Yeah," Tom added, a distracted note to his voice making Kai give him a sharp look. The burly man was looking down at the ground with a frown like he was trying to understand something.

"Get it together, Tom. Now is not the time," Kai said, not sparing the man a second glance as he looked back at the charging Darjee. He had no time to babysit the others now. He could only hope they'd listened to him during training.

The closest Darjee were only a few dozen feet from the barricade now. Thankfully, their disorganized charge had caused them to spread out somewhat, but there were still half-a-dozen of them grouped together at the front.

"*Rew liff!*" Verdan shouted from behind them. A moment later, a wave of cold swept past them, with a blast of ice flying overhead to impact the ground in front of the barricade. Rather than stabbing into the earth, the ice seemed to spread out on impact, forming a sheet along the ground.

The closest Darjee leapt over the growing sheet of ice, clearing it without issue. The Darjee behind it were forced to either run over the ice or try and go around the outside.

The Darjee were forced to break up into several smaller groups. Some of them were able to leap across, while others ran around the exterior of the ice. One particularly unfortunate Darjee was unable to change direction in time and found itself slipping and sliding across the ice.

A grin crept across Kai's face as he ignited the Essence in his core and sprang forward, the world slowing down around him as the activated Essence swept into his body. His right foot landed on the low wall in front of him, and he pushed off hard, flying up and out to meet the Darjee.

A deafening crack followed a flash of light as a bolt of lightning shot through the space below Kai. The crackling blast of energy struck one of the Darjee, knocking it off its feet. At the same time, an orb of roiling brown and black energy flew past, hitting another Darjee in the face. The unfortunate creature sprawled to the ground as its face rotted and decayed, its screams cut off as the magic made it through to its throat.

The final Darjee to make it across the ice snarled as it saw its companions struck down, its gaze focusing on Kai as he fell toward it, spear first. The dog-faced creature was quick to dodge to one side, batting at Kai's spear with one hand while the other tried to rip across his face.

Kai kicked out with his closest foot as he twisted in the air, bringing his spear over the Darjee's claw as his foot hit it in the chest and knocked it back. The force of the impact made the Darjee stumble, off-balance and unprepared for the leaf-bladed spear that ripped through its throat a moment later.

Kai was careful to stay off the ice as he flipped his spear around and plunged the spike on its butt down into the Darjee's chest. It was always best to make sure.

The Darjee were avoiding the ice and coming around the side to reach them, but they seemed unsure whether to push for the fort or go for Kai. Their lack of cohesion split them even more, as some went for him and some went for the fort, spreading them out and giving Tim and Tom a better chance.

The last thing Kai wanted was for the brothers to be overwhelmed with multiple Darjee, so he was making himself a target. Let these savages focus on him while the others supported him from afar.

The next Darjee were racing closer, and Kai moved to meet them, his spear light in his hands as it swept through the air, drawing blood and forcing the Darjee back. Even with their long claws, Kai had a definitive reach advantage, and he used that to its utmost.

"*Garec bel!*" Verdan shouted from somewhere in the fort, a spray of something passing over Kai's head to hit several of the oncoming Darjee. Kai didn't see what exactly hit them, but it was something nasty, from the audible crack of bones being broken.

Kai's current opponent didn't realize that its reinforcements had been delayed and charged forward to try and close in with the fire Sorcerer. With his Essence ignited, Kai was more than a match for the fast-moving creature and slid to the side as he swept his spear across.

The Darjee leaned back to avoid the leaf-bladed tip of the spear, but Kai reversed his movement and stabbed down with the rear-end of the spear. The spike on his spear rammed into the side of the Darjee's knee with a crunch and a spray of blood as Kai yanked it free.

A swift slash of his spear opened the creature's throat as it howled in pain, but Kai had already moved on to his next target.

CHAPTER
NINETEEN

TOM WATCHED ANXIOUSLY as the Darjee swept over the slope and raced toward their fort. Kai and the Fwyn that the Darjee had tried to ambush had barely made it back in time, but thankfully they were here. Tim didn't even want to imagine how badly this would go without Kai helping them hold the Darjee off.

Most of the Fwyn had gone deeper into the fort for something, but the one Kai had been with had taken up position behind him, while Gwen was behind Tim.

It was odd. This new Fwyn didn't smell the same as the others. The majority of them smelled earthy, like fresh loam mixed with stone's reassuring stability and strength. This one, however, smelled sickly sweet, but with undertones of something pungent. It was almost like rotten eggs, just not quite as nasty.

Tom didn't understand why the Fwyn smelled so different, but he didn't want to ask about it either. A lot was happening, and a lot was changing at the moment; it felt stupid to ask such a little question.

It was even worse now that the Fwyn had made this fort. The stone they'd raised had kept the earthy smell of the Fwyn somehow. It was almost overpowering being among it like this.

"Don't worry, we've got your back," Tim said, his voice cutting into Tom's deliberations and making him glance over to his brother.

"Yeah," Tom said, agreeing with whatever Tim had said without hesitation. He trusted his brother to make all the decisions; Tom was just happy to go along with what he wanted most of the time.

"Get it together, Tom. Now is not the time," Kai said, his eyes fixed on the Darjee with an intensity that made Tom shiver.

"Sorry," Tom mumbled under his breath, shifting position to make sure he was ready for the Darjee. People depended on him; he could think about these strange smells later.

A wave of freezing cold blew over them as ice flew overhead, smashing into the ground and forming a sheet of ice to trip up the Darjee. Barely a moment later, Tom had a brief whiff of something burning as Kai moved forward fast enough to be little more than a blur.

Gwen said something garbled in a language that Tom didn't understand, her tone sharp and urgent. Before Kai could even hit the ground after his high jump, Gwen and the Fwyn stepped up and threw out their hands.

Ozone and the sweet, rotten egg smell filled the air, as lightning blasted from Gwen's hands and the Fwyn hurled an orb of brown and black energy. Tom felt himself watching the flight of the orb with interest. The concentrated energy felt almost familiar somehow.

Looking back to the fight between Kai and the Darjee, Tom felt a little envious as he watched Kai move with deadly grace and a level of precision that he could never emulate. Tim was more likely to be able to fight like Kai; Tom knew that he lacked the flexibility and agility to keep up with them.

Since they were boys, Tom had always been the strong one, the brute force to back up Tim's plans and ideas. Now, things were changing; Tim was picking up the lessons from Kai with a speed that Tom couldn't match.

The training and the sparring had helped Tom develop his strength, and he felt more confident in a fight than ever before. The problem was that Tim was growing faster and learning more every day.

At this rate, Tom would be left behind and no longer be needed. He'd spent his whole life protecting his brother, protecting the only family he had left. The idea that Tim wouldn't need him anymore was a terrifying one.

"*Garec bel!*" Verdan's voice echoed through the fort as a spray of fist-sized stones blasted past them. The heavy projectiles struck the Darjee with enough force to knock them off their feet, slowing them down even more.

The howls of the Darjee and their screams of pain as they pushed through the attacks to reach them were secondary to Tom. The word that Verdan had used was ringing in his mind. *Garec*. It resonated with him, just like the smell of the earthy Fwyn. Something deep inside him bestirred itself as he focused on that sensation of resonance.

"Tom!" Tim's voice was distant, but the urgency brought Tom's eyes up to see a trio of Darjee bearing down on his brother. The dog-faced monsters had bypassed Kai in search of easier prey. One of them bore a patch of scorched fur where Gwen had hit it with lightning, and another had disgustingly rotten flesh running up its

right arm. Injured as they were, they would still be too much
for Tim.

Their magic support hadn't been enough to stop the Darjee, so it
was down to Tom. Tim could fight one on his own, so it was down
to him to take the other two.

Determination swept through Tom as he moved with purpose, a
walk becoming a steadily-increasing run as he pounded past his
brother. Something was awake in him, something new that
rumbled like the boulders of an avalanche. Slow to start but
unstoppable when it got going.

That image of a rolling boulder lingered in Tom's mind as one of
the Darjee bared its teeth and raced to meet his charge. Lowering
his shield and focusing on bracing it as best he could, Tom bore
down and charged directly into the creature.

Tom kept his eyes on the Darjee as they came together, noting
absently that the brown wood of his shield had turned gray as they
covered the last few feet to each other.

Tom expected to knock the Darjee back and follow up with his
mace before it could recover. The Darjee was tall but slender, so he
knew his bigger build meant he out-massed the creature.

In reality, Tom hit the Darjee and dropped his shoulder, ramming
into it with everything he had and sending the creature flying with
a surprised cry of pain. Stomping down with his front foot, Tom
felt his boot gouge up the ground ahead of him as he came to an
abrupt stop.

The Darjee flanking the one he'd rammed was on him in the blink
of an eye, claws glinting in the sun as they raked toward his chest.
Hours of training with the fast-moving Kai was all that saved Tom
as his shield snapped into place in front of him, blocking the
attack.

The claws screeched as they skittered over the stone shield, leaving behind a long furrow where they'd struck. The Darjee's other hand grabbed onto the edge of the shield, and it tried to wrench it to one side. Hunching down slightly, Tom resisted the pull for a moment before moving with the pull and bringing his mace down at the Darjee.

His mace bore a flanged head with a pointed tip, but now it was covered in stone, and the flanged ribs around the head were dotted with small stone spikes.

Tom knew he should have been shocked or concerned about the changes to his equipment, but it all had a rightness to it that bypassed such feelings. Besides, Tom rarely focused on why things were happening; he just accepted the world for what it was and moved on.

The Darjee had managed to duck out of the way of his stony mace, but Tom was quick to press the attack, his mace moving in constant sweeping motions as he drove the Darjee back.

The creature snarled and growled at him, slashing out with its claws and trying to get around his flank, but Tom bore it all on his shield. The menacing thrum of his mace as it rushed through the air was enough to keep the Darjee from committing to something more drastic.

The Darjee that Tom had bashed with his shield had been stunned by the impact. With a few moments to recover, it had just been starting to groggily get back up when the one that Tom was pursuing backed up into it.

The impact between the two was minimal, doing little more than delaying them for half a moment as they broke apart. Unfortunately for them, that was all that Tom needed.

The Darjee had been keeping just out of reach of Tom's mace, so even a slight delay in its movement gave him the opening he'd been waiting for. Tom's mace was in motion as soon as the Darjee stumbled over its fallen companion, the weapon whistling as it came thundering down.

Realizing it was in a bad position, the Darjee made a split-second choice and tried to block the stone mace. It chose poorly.

Bone and flesh alike were broken and ruptured as the stone-enhanced mace struck the Darjee's crossed arms with all of Tom's strength behind it. Yanking the mace back from the ruined mess of the Darjee's arms, Tom finished the creature with a swift overhead strike, planting his mace directly into its face.

Burning pain rushed through Tom's right leg as the other Darjee clawed at the closest part of him it could reach, but the second swing of his mace dealt with that problem before it could strike again.

Looking around, Tom realized that the battle was all but over. There were only half a dozen Darjee still standing, and they were pulling back from the death trap that the fort had become.

Burnt, broken, and decayed bodies were scattered all around the fort, including one lying at the feet of his brother.

"Tom, are you okay!" Tim shouted, rushing toward him with a concerned expression.

"Yeah," Tom said, turning to face his brother and wincing as he put weight on his right leg. He could feel where the claws had hit him, and the burning pain of the wound wasn't fading.

"What happened to your shield?" Tim asked, looking at the stone-covered shield in Tom's left hand. "And where's your mace?"

"Oh," Tom said, glancing down at his empty right hand with a frown. Looking behind him, he saw that his mace was embedded in the chest of the second Darjee, though it had lost its stone enhancement. Reaching over and grunting at the pain from his leg, Tom retrieved his weapon and started limping back to the fort.

"You're limping. Did they get your leg?" Tim asked, sighing heavily as Tom shrugged and didn't answer. "Come on, let's go see if anyone has any bandages."

Tim moved to support his brother, but Tom glared at him and carried on limping. He'd get there under his own power; he'd had worse wounds.

Kai was methodically working through the fallen Darjee, ensuring that no survivors were hiding among them and that any wounded were finished off.

Meanwhile, Verdan was conferring with Gwen and Gruthka, gesturing first at the Fwyn gathered at the entrance to the fort, then at the dead Darjee.

Tom hadn't spent much time examining the Fwyn in any real detail, but even he could pick up how shocked the small creatures were. Verdan had told them about how the Darjee hunted the Fwyn. This might be one of the few times the Fwyn had won against the dog-faced creatures.

"Are you two okay?" Verdan asked, looking over to them with a concerned expression.

"Yeah, but Tom needs a bandage," Tim said, pointing to the wound on Tom's leg.

"I'll take care of that, and then you should speak to Kai," Verdan said, addressing Tom as he gestured to the stone-clad shield Tom was carrying.

"Yeah," Tom said, considering the shield with interest as he realized that there was a slight link between it and the rumbling motion within his core. Carefully taking hold of the link, Tom unbound the shield from him. A brief moment passed with nothing changing, and then the stone began to slough off the shield, falling to the ground as dust.

"*Iacha*," Verdan said as he crouched down in front of Tom and reached out with one hand to touch the wound on his leg. A wave of soothing energy flowed into Tom's leg, making the pain he was feeling seem distant and removed.

"Thank you, Verdan," Tim said earnestly, inclining his head to the Wizard, who waved off the thanks.

Tom glanced down at his leg and realized that the bloody gash that the Darjee had given him was now half the size. It was as though the healing had been sped up by a week or two.

"All the Darjee are dealt with," Kai said as he walked over to them, his eyes lingering on Tom.

"Excellent. They should be on the backfoot now, so we need to act quickly," Verdan said, tapping his lips in thought before nodding to Kai. "Take Tom, Gwen, and Dru and head for the left half of the ruins. I'll take Tim and the rest of the Fwyn over to the right. Our priority is to secure the prisoners, but make sure that none of the Darjee escape if we can help it."

Dru was apparently the name of the Fwyn that used the brown-black energy that Tom had sensed earlier. He gave the diminutive and large-eyed creature a nod, smiling in satisfaction as it nodded back.

"Very well—call for us if you need support," Kai said, hefting his spear and motioning for his group to follow him.

Locking eyes with his brother, Tom tried his best to communicate his faith in his skills. Tim would be safe with Verdan, and Tom would watch Kai's back. This would be fine.

Hefting his mace and shield, Tom hurried after the fire Sorcerer, Gwen and Dru falling in behind him.

TWENTY

Tim watched as Kai and his group headed off for the left side of the ruins, leaving himself, Verdan, and all the Fwyn. Well, all of them bar Dru, which was a shame. Tim had watched the small Fwyn use his magic to great effect in the fight; Tim would have liked to keep him with them.

Still, it made more sense for Dru and Gwen to go and support the others. There was no need for them in this group when they had Verdan. Tim had never met a Sorcerer that came close to matching the sheer range of abilities that Verdan demonstrated. The list was endless: fire, protection, warding, fog, light, even healing. When they had time, Tim was going to ask how to learn to be like Verdan, but he had no doubt it would involve years of training.

Tim had been on the fence about asking Verdan before, but today had changed everything. He'd always known that Tom had a love of stone and earth; he had been fascinated with the mountains when they'd been younger, and it had only grown since then. That was understandable, but what Tim saw today was on another level entirely.

Tom was a Sorcerer. It was an easy statement that was simple enough to back up. One look at the stone-covered mace he'd been using would be enough. Sadly, that didn't make it any easier for Tim to understand.

Tom was just taking it in stride like he always did, but Tim was going to need time to deal with this. He'd have to ask Verdan and Kai if it meant he could become a Sorcerer as well. Now, that was a scary question to ask.

Tim sighed and pushed it all out of his mind. He had a job to do right now. He couldn't afford to be distracted by silly hopes like that.

Verdan had been speaking to Gruthka in the Fwyn's language while Tim was deep in thought. With a final nod, Gruthka beckoned to the other Fwyn and headed off toward the ruins at a jog.

"Follow me, Tim. We'll be supporting the Fwyn while they search for their kin," Verdan said, taking off after the Fwyn at an easy pace. With their much longer legs, it wasn't hard for Verdan and Tim to outpace the short Fwyn.

"Verdan, I don't want to question your choices, but why have we split up?" Tim asked, his eyes on their surroundings as he spoke, just in case.

"I am concerned that the Darjee will realize their position is untenable and flee, taking prisoners with them. To limit this, we need to seem like less of a threat and cover more ground at the same time." Verdan explained as they crested the hill that the Darjee had come over. "It's about keeping the momentum and stopping them from reacting with any real thought."

"But, what if there are too many for us to deal with in smaller groups?" Tim asked with concern, looking out at the large area of ruins and thinking how many Darjee could be hidden inside.

"It's a risk, I'll grant you that, but a calculated one. From what Gruthka told me, that was the majority of them that we fought. Some survivors ran, and there will be more that didn't join the attack, but not enough to overwhelm us. Their lack of magic and ranged weapons gives us a distinct advantage here." Verdan told him as he started to descend to the closest area of the ruins. A thick stone wall had once surrounded this section, but Tim could see several areas where the stone had crumbled over time.

The Fwyn stayed close behind them as they approached, and Tim kept the rest of his concerns to himself. Verdan knew what he was doing, and Tim's job here was to protect him, not second-guess his decisions.

As they drew closer to the ruins, Tim began to see signs of habitation, marks that showed how long the Darjee had been squatting here. Some of it was easy to see, such as the path had been cleared through a section of crumbled wall, which was obvious even to Tim's untrained eye.

Verdan paused and focused on something for a moment as he muttered under his breath. Seemingly satisfied, the Wizard stepped forward and led the way through the closest damaged section of the wall. "Be careful; there's two of them nearby."

As if summoned by the Wizard's words, two Darjee leapt out of hiding as Tim followed Verdan inside. The closest one went straight for Verdan, while the other went for Tim, rushing forward with frightening speed.

Tim reflexively lifted his shield as the Darjee leapt on him, its claws digging deep into the wood even as Tim twisted and drove his sword up and under its ribs. Thankfully, Darjee anatomy was reasonably similar to that of a human, so Tim's strike caught several essential organs.

Twisting the blade before drawing it back out, Tim knocked the corpse to one side and looked over at Verdan. The Wizard's opponent was also dead; some sort of strike had cut away a generous portion of its neck.

"Onward," Verdan said, giving Tim a nod as he carried on into the ruins.

If the looming walls and mounds of crumbling stonework gave Verdan pause, Tim didn't see it. As far as he could tell, the Wizard was just as comfortable here as he had been in Hobson's Point.

Twice more, Verdan alerted Tim to Darjee ambushes as they continued into the ruins, and each time they dealt with the ambush quickly and without issue. The second ambush was the largest yet, with five Darjee hidden in a ruined house.

Thankfully, Verdan was able to deal with two of the Darjee on his own, and the Fwyn used their magic to obstruct and bind the others while Tim killed them. Part of him wondered if Verdan could have done it all himself, but he had no idea what purpose the Wizard would have for letting Tim fight more. Every Sorcerer Tim had met, even Kai to a certain extent, relished fighting as much as possible. They took pride in dealing with the majority of the enemy, in demonstrating their abilities.

Tim knew intellectually that Verdan was different, but those differences only seemed to be growing as time went on.

"Tim, there's something up ahead," Verdan said as they passed through a broken archway. "I'm detecting several Darjee and a variety of other creatures. I think we may have found our prisoners." A familiar expression of concentration settled onto Verdan's face as he spoke, muttering a few more words under his breath that Tim didn't catch.

"What do you want me to do?" Tim asked, holding his sword at the ready as he looked to Verdan for guidance. Part of him was remembering his own time as a prisoner of the Cyth, the fear and anticipation building every day.

Determination flowed through Tim as he vowed to protect the captives from the Darjee. He would save them as Verdan had once saved him.

"Take half the Fwyn and circle to the right. Wait for my signal, then move in and secure the captives. The Fwyn will support you from a distance, but the up-close fighting will be down to you. Understood?" Verdan said, smiling slightly as Tim nodded. "Good, I'll tell the Fwyn to follow your lead."

Tim took a steadying breath as Verdan spoke to the Fwyn in their language. He could feel the pressure of the situation bearing down on him, reminding him that he was only a guard, and not even that good of one.

Verdan finished translating his instructions and moved off to the left, half of the Fwyn following behind him like large-eyed earless ducklings.

"Right, we can do this," Tim said, forcing a confident smile as he saw the blank expressions on the Fwyn that were with him. He wished he could speak whatever language the Fwyn used; it would make this so much easier. For now, he would just have to trust that they would follow his lead, as Verdan had said.

The archway they had come through led to a two-way intersection, lined with houses in various states of ruin. Verdan had headed down the left-hand path, so Tim led his group down the right, keeping a wary eye out for more Darjee as he went.

Without Verdan to spot ambushes in advance, the ruins became a lot more menacing than when Tim had first entered them.

Shadowy corners and half-ruined walls created perfect hiding spots, and the Darjee were already faster and stronger than Tim.

Thankfully, the training with Kai was showing its worth against the Darjee. Without the practice against someone stronger and faster than him, Tim doubted he would have survived this long. Verdan might have been able to keep him alive, but he wouldn't have been able to send Tim off on his own like this.

Tim banished his worried thoughts and focused on his surroundings as they came to a ruined house on their left. At least, he assumed it had been a house at some point. The building was little more than two walls and a pile of rubble, but it let Tim see into a large plaza beyond this row of buildings.

At least a dozen Darjee were grouped up in the plaza, watching over a number of cages that contained one or more creatures. Tim had to grab the nearest Fwyn and calm them down when they saw the cage which held their brethren.

Tim understood their urgency, but the Fwyn in the cages were alive. Injured and malnourished, but alive. If they went charging in, who knew what the Darjee would do? They would do the captives the most good by following Verdan's plan.

The cages were on the right edge of the plaza, backed up against a large building that looked almost sturdy in comparison to the rest of the ruins. Tim noticed a round tower extending up from one corner of the building, or what was left of one anyway.

Motioning for the Fwyn to move back, Tim retreated to the road and looked for the distant tower, spotting its tip over the ruined buildings. That would be his guide.

Tim didn't know how long they had until Verdan would act, so he picked up the pace as they wove through the ruins. Fortunately, it seemed that the Darjee had set their ambushes at the exterior of the ruins as Tim saw no sign of any foes as they hurried along.

Using the tower as his landmark, Tim managed to get close to the large building without too much issue. He gripped his sword tightly and slowed down as he drew closer, his heart pounding in his chest.

The Darjee were just on the other side of this building, hardly any distance at all and more than close enough to swarm Tim and his companions before they could react.

Thankfully, the building they were approaching was fairly solid around the exterior. It was the interior that had crumbled away over the years. The entrance where the doors would have sat at the front was empty and open, letting Tim creep inside unopposed.

Broken walls and piles of rubble filled the ground floor of the building, with a crumbled stairway leading up to a half-destroyed area up above him. The outer walls were still mostly intact, as he'd seen from his vantage point earlier.

Motioning for the Fwyn to follow him, Tim picked his way over to the rear wall. Turning to the closest Fwyn, Tim gestured to the wall, making motions to try and communicate what he wanted them to do.

It took a minute for the Fwyn to understand what Tim was after, but once they did, they moved with purpose up to the wall and worked together to weave their magic into the old stone.

Tim couldn't see what the Fwyn did or how it worked, but the end result was precisely what he was hoping for. A hole had formed in the wall, smaller than his fist and perfectly circular.

Leaning up against the wall, Tim peered through the hole and grinned in triumph. They were right behind the cages. It took another minute of gesturing to the Fwyn to communicate the next step, but Tim was confident that they'd understood him in the end.

All that was left now was to wait for Verdan's signal.

_**_

When it came, Verdan's signal was clear and to the point. One moment Tim was watching the Darjee as they gathered near the cages, arguing amongst themselves; the next, chaos. A small orb of flame had flown right into the middle of their group, blossoming into a large ball as it traveled through the air. The ball hit the ground and exploded with a concussive blast of fire that burnt the nearby Darjee and knocked them off their feet.

Tim had seen Verdan use this attack before; it was powerful but drew heavily on the Wizard's strength. Thankfully, Tim could see several Darjee had been either killed or heavily wounded by the attack, and most of the rest were charging off where it had come from.

"Okay, now, open it up," Tim said, backing away from the hole in the wall and motioning urgently to the Fwyn as he did.

The small creatures moved closer and lifted their hands in unison, miming a pulling motion as the stone around the hole shifted and flowed away. Tim was fascinated by the magic being displayed, but he didn't have the time to focus on it right now.

He'd communicated to them as best he could that he wanted a door to get through to the cages, and it seemed they understood. The ancient stone wall shifted and groaned as a whole section of it flowed like liquid out into the surrounding area.

Tim didn't wait for them to finish, taking his chance to duck through when it was large enough for him to fit. Heading for the closest cage, Tim looked around for any nearby Darjee and to see who was being held within the large wooden cages.

Some Darjee that had been stunned by Verdan's attack were still nearby, but they were preoccupied for the moment, allowing Tim to reach the first cage without issue.

Each cage was a large wooden structure, designed with thick wooden posts at each corner and a sturdy frame. Wooden bars restrained the six Fwyn within it, though Tim doubted they were even needed.

The Fwyn inside were lethargic and ill-looking at best. Two of them stirred at Tim's approach, but they did little more than lift their heads to look at him.

"Break the bars, hurry," Tim said in a hiss, gesturing to the poles keeping them in. The Fwyn's magic would be better-suited for this task than his sword.

One of the Fwyn limply lifted a hand and pointed to the top of the cage. Following the gesture, Tim saw a series of bone charms hanging from the roof. Just looking at the things sent a shiver down his spine, one that was similar to the feeling of Cyth magic. Thankfully, it wasn't quite as bad, but it was just as repulsive. Verdan would be able to explain more when he examined these things, but for now, Tim knew what he needed to.

A stealthy exit was out of the question, so Tim went for the next best thing and started to hack at the bars with his sword. Thankfully, the wood wasn't that thick, so he could make quick work of each one.

A few solid chops of his sword and a grunt of effort broke one of the bars, but the Fwyn inside simply groaned and struggled to rise. Tim was about to commit to chopping more of the bars open when a pair of his assigned Fwyn appeared by his side, stepping past him to grab the captives and drag them out of the cage.

Even stepping inside the cage seemed to drain the two Fwyn, but they worked quickly to pull the captives free. Once outside the cage, the rescued Fwyn started to perk up slowly. Tim was tempted to wait for them to recover before moving on, but he had no idea how long it would take.

Distant sounds of explosions and screams told Tim that Verdan was still fighting with the bulk of the Darjee, but time was precious. Some of the remaining Darjee could notice their rescue attempt at any moment, and that would be a bad thing.

Having fought some of them now, Tim was confident that he could take one of them in single combat. The Darjee were fast and strong, but they were wild and without restraint. Tim could take advantage of that. More than one would be a problem, but how much of one depended on what the Fwyn could do to help.

Struck by a thought, Tim looked around at the surrounding cages once more, looking for which cages didn't have Fwyn. There were two that Tim could see, a big man with flowing red hair and a large wolf with white fur.

The big man was in one of the front-most cages, so Tim would have to fight to get to him. The wolf, however, was at the rear, just a little bit along from where Tim had exited the big building.

Taking a chance, Tim hurried over to the wolf as the Fwyn finished pulling out their brethren and started cutting into new cages with their claws. Tim doubted they would make quick progress, but it was worth doing.

The white-furred wolf lifted its head as Tim approached, its vibrant amber eyes regarding him with interest as he laid his shield down and started chopping at the wooden poles.

A shout of alarm from off to one side told Tim that the Darjee had finally started paying attention to what was happening behind them. Ignoring them for the moment, he focused on chopping through the poles with heavy blows before looking up.

Two Darjee had gone straight for the Fwyn but were being knocked around by flying clods of earth as more Fwyn boiled out of the building to join the fight. In comparison, just a single Darjee was coming after Tim, but he had no backup to rely on.

Kicking the last pole he'd been chopping free, Tim grabbed his shield and looked at the wolf with regret; it seemed just as drained as the Fwyn by the cage.

"Don't worry, I'll get you out of here," Tim said, anger thrumming through his veins as he looked at the deplorable conditions the wolf had been kept in. No creature deserved to live like this, especially not such a beautiful one.

Tim's words seemed to bestir the wolf, and his hands clenched as it struggled to get on its feet. He could see a leather collar wrapped around its neck, threaded with something that he couldn't quite make out. Maybe it was some form of owner's mark. If it was, the wolf might be trained to fight or hunt, which could be helpful right about now.

Turning his attention from the wolf, Tim readied himself as the approaching Darjee skirted the outside of the last cage between them and raced forward. The snarling creature had a vicious grin on its dog-like face as it threw itself at him, slashing down with one claw.

Ready for the attack, Tim was able to slide back and avoid the brunt of the strike. Darjee claws were sharp, however, and his opponent still left scars running down Tim's shield where his claws had caught it.

Staying light on his feet, Tim circled to the left as he kept out of arm's reach of the Darjee. There was an arrogant look in the creature's eye as it turned to follow him, as though it dismissed Tim as a threat.

Waiting for the next attack, Tim saw the Darjee tense before it leapt forward, stretching out to grab at his shield. The moment the creature tensed, Tim started rushing forward, pushing his shoulder forward as he drove his shield into the creature.

Off-balance and slightly stunned, the Darjee was able to avoid Tim's stab, but not entirely. Instead of piercing its heart, Tim caught the creature in the side, drawing blood and making the Darjee snarl in pain.

Pressing the attack, Tim cut the Darjee again and again as it stumbled back, keeping it off balance as he batted its hands away with his shield and slashed with his sword. Tim felt himself drop into a focused state as he kept up the onslaught, moving with a level of speed and precision that felt almost foreign.

The Darjee tried a last-ditch attempt to close with Tim and grapple him, but Tim read its actions in its stance, its intent in the flicker of resolve he saw in its eyes. Bringing his shield up, Tim let go of the handle as the Darjee grasped it, pulling his arm free in one smooth motion.

Seizing his blade in both hands, Tim grinned savagely at the Darjee and swept his sword through the air above his shield. The tip of his blade drew a bloody line across the Darjee's throat, and his shield fell to the ground with a thud as the Darjee collapsed.

Tim looked down at his sword in surprise; it felt like he'd touched on a higher standard of fighting for a moment there. The sword had felt more like an extension of his body than a weapon in his hand. All this training with Kai was really paying off.

A sudden weight struck Tim from behind as he was tackled to the ground, burning pain digging deep into his sides as sharp claws ripped into him. Twisting and thrashing to get away, Tim drove an elbow back into whatever was attacking him, causing it to grunt and loosen its grip for a moment.

Tearing himself free with a cry of agony, Tim got away from the grapple and tried to get his sword up between him and the Darjee that he had just elbowed in the gut. He barely got it into place before the Darjee was on him, wrestling his sword to one side and lunging forward to bite down on his shoulder.

Fresh pain ripped through Tim as the Darjee's teeth came close, far too close, to his vulnerable neck. Adrenaline coursed through his body as he fought to push the Darjee away, but it was too heavy for him to move in such an awkward position.

Terror mingled with rage as Tim wrestled with the Darjee, his right hand gripping the sword, his left gripping its wrist to keep the claws away.

A snarl came from off to one side, and Tim felt despair wash through him as the Darjee ground its teeth deeper into his shoulder. This was it. This was how he was going to die. The new Darjee would be able to just walk over and rip his throat out.

Tim stared in shock as the wolf that had been in the cage appeared in his vision, its jaws flashing down to grip the Darjee by the neck and pull it away. The Darjee relaxed its bite at the sudden pain, but Tim cried out as it still managed to rip away a chunk of flesh in the process.

The Darjee and the wolf tussled with fast movements on the floor as Tim lumbered up off his back, sword clutched in a death-grip.

A high-pitched whimper rang out as the Darjee broke free from the wolf and clawed down its side with a spray of blood. The wolf fell back for a moment, and Tim made his best attempt at a lunge. His focus was entirely on the sword's tip as he drove it into the Darjee, catching it in the chest as it turned back to finish him off.

Driving the sword deep with all his weight, Tim bore the Darjee to the ground and let go of his sword as he fell on top of it, his strength failing.

The Darjee was heavily wounded, but Tim lacked the strength to do anything more than hold it down. Thankfully, however, Tim wasn't alone.

The wolf had blood matting its fur, but it limped forward and seized the Darjee by the neck once more, worrying it back and forth. It was a brutal and messy kill, but in short order, Tim was free to roll off the body and try to catch his breath.

Tim could feel every gouge down his side and the burning pain in his shoulder where the Darjee had ripped away his flesh.

The wolf hobbled over and slumped against Tim, sniffing his face before lying down by his side, clearly spent.

Tim patted his new friend on the side, thankful for its intervention in the fight. Looking at it properly, he realized he'd been wrong. The wolf's fur wasn't white; it was silver, something he'd never seen before.

Looking up at the blue sky above them, Tim tried his best to ignore the pain wracking his body. He'd just lie down here for a little while and then go help the Fwyn. Just a little while.

CHAPTER
TWENTY-ONE

VERDAN'S FEATURES were hard as stone as he butchered the Darjee. The Fwyn behind him were restraining and pulling down the odd one here and there, but the majority of the damage being done was by Verdan's spells.

He'd chosen the site of his trap carefully, ensuring that their enemy would be funneled down a narrow stretch to reach him. He was confident that his first empowered fireball had killed a few, but it had been little more than the bait to get them over here.

"*Hoer niwlla,*" Verdan spoke with a throwing motion, causing a fresh wall of freezing mist to fill the area in front of him. It wasn't thick enough to obscure anything, but it was incredibly cold, sufficient to sap the strength of the Darjee. Releasing the old mist and focusing instead on the new one, Verdan threw a pair of lesser fire bolts at two Darjee still standing. The bolts of flame lost some strength entering the mist but were still enough to finish off the wounded Darjee.

A few moments passed without any further enemies presenting themselves, so Verdan started forward, one hand at the ready to form a shield.

It was foolish for a group with no magical support to take on a trained Wizard, especially without surprise or being able to prepare the battlefield. It seemed that no one had ever taught that to the Darjee, and Verdan was going to rectify that.

The Fwyn followed Verdan as he picked his way through the bodies, letting the mist disperse as he reached it. He'd renewed the casting in case another wave had been coming, but it looked like this was all of them.

All being well, Tim should be releasing the captives now, with the other group of Fwyn supporting him. Verdan was a little concerned with what the Darjee might have in place to stop magic-wielders from escaping, but he was sure Tim would figure it out.

Rounding the corner of the narrow street he'd chosen as a kill zone, Verdan found himself at the entrance of the plaza. In the distance, he could see large cages framed against one of the larger ruined buildings he'd seen here.

Verdan could see movement around the cages, too much for a few Darjee guards. It looked like Tim had been successful.

Hurrying over while still keeping a general eye on the surrounding area, Verdan saw the Fwyn slowly breaking into the cages by clawing through the wooden bars. It looked like most of the cages were already dealt with; there were just one or two left to break into.

Looking closer as they joined with the other group, Verdan saw the bone charms dangling from the ceiling of the cage. Sweeping it with his Aether senses, Verdan wrinkled his nose in distaste and instinctively incinerated it with a blast of flame. He knew the oily sensation of abyssal energy anywhere.

Forcing himself to examine a second charm with more restraint, Verdan could tell that the energy it held was different from that of the Cyth. It was still abyssal energy, of that he had no doubt, but it was different. Darker, somehow, less corruptive than the energy of the Cyth, but more stifling.

Even now, he could feel the presence of the charm pushing on the Aether around him, leaving a low-Aether zone around it. The charms weren't powerful enough to banish the Aether completely, but he could now understand how the Fwyn were being kept prisoner.

"*Thanr*," Verdan all but spat out the word as he incinerated the charm, unable to restrain himself any longer. He had some ideas as to the foul origin of the raw material for the charm. Thankfully, his attack only destroyed the binding and the extras to the charm. He would make sure the bones themselves were buried.

"Where is Tim?" Verdan asked a nearby Fwyn. It was time to finish regrouping.

"He was injured. We took him inside the building," the Fwyn replied, pointing out the large building that Verdan had noted earlier.

"Injured?" Verdan echoed with concern, hurrying in the direction the Fwyn had pointed. He mustn't have been able to draw off all the Darjee with his opening attack. Damn it, Verdan had considered sending all the Fwyn with Tim, not just half of them, but he hadn't wanted to make their group too large.

Cursing himself for the mistake, Verdan raced through an archway in the stone to find the makeshift medical area the Fwyn had set up.

Dirt had been gathered and formed into half-a-dozen beds, upon which lay Tim, several Darjee, and a silver-furred wolf.

"*Iacha hast!*" Verdan intoned, forming the image of an effect that both healed directly and sped up the body's inherent healing in his mind. Once ready, Verdan went down the line, tapping each injured person one after the other. Tim drained the most Aether from him, but the wolf was also oddly difficult to heal. It was as though Verdan had to push his Aether into it, not simply establish a connection.

The wounded Fwyn thankfully had little more than superficial cuts. Some were deep, but the Fwyn were hardy folk, and a little healing was all they needed to get on their feet.

Tim was in worse shape, with multiple deep lacerations up his side and a nasty bite wound on the shoulder. Thankfully, the main issue he faced in the short-term was blood loss, and Verdan's spell would directly counter that by greatly increasing the rate at which Tim's body replaced it.

Satisfied that all the wounded were on the road to recovery, Verdan went back to the wolf and examined it more closely. There must be something that was causing the issue with his Aether. Verdan had never come across a creature that was naturally resistant to Aether other than the things that dwelled in the Abyss.

Looking the creature over with both his regular and Aether senses, Verdan quickly spotted the source of the issue. The wolf was wearing a collar of some description, but it was hideous, using the same abyssal energy as the bone charms outside.

Verdan ran his fingers around the collar, searching for a buckle or some other method of release. No, nothing there, which was odd, as the collar itself was flush against the wolf's skin.

Looking closer at the collar itself, Verdan saw that the leather was threaded with small pieces of bone, and a few of them seemed to actually hold the collar onto the wolf's neck.

Standing back and wishing he could wipe the greasy feeling from his hands, Verdan contemplated what the collar represented. The bone charms it contained were to restrict Aether flow, and the ones piercing through both the collar and the wolf's flesh allowed the effect to pass through the creature. That explained the difficulty he felt healing it.

Verdan had seen many abyssal items and effects in his time, but this was truly something horrific. He could only assume that this was intended as a long-term method of controlling the creature and preventing it from accessing any Aether.

Kai had said that the Darjee were slavers, so it made sense that they would have something like this to prevent their slaves from fighting back.

The problem they faced now was how to remove it. Verdan refused to let such a vile thing continually hurt the wolf, but he was unsure of what he could do to help it. There were some similarities to what he had done with Gwen, but this was far more complex. For one, Gwen had only been suffering from prolonged exposure, not having the thing actually inside her. The second issue was the difference in energy. The energy the Cyth used was like a sickness that attacked life and drained it dry. What Verdan was facing here was a more subtle effect; it might be that prolonged healing wouldn't be enough to cure the aftereffects.

It went against the grain to leave it alone, but Verdan wanted to examine the wolf more carefully, and he needed a proper location for that. A dirt bed in a ruined building wasn't the place for magical experimentation.

"We're taking the wolf back with us. Could you get one or two of your people to watch over it?" Verdan asked Gruthka, who had arrived partway through the examination.

"Yes, of course," Gruthka said, calling out for two of his people to watch the wolf before turning back to Verdan. "I want to thank you for what you have done. We have rescued almost thirty Fwyn, far more than we ever hoped for."

"It was my duty. No one deserves this fate," Verdan said, looking down at the collar on the wolf's neck with a disgusted expression. It should have shocked him that such practices were not stamped out immediately, but it was yet more evidence of how far things had fallen.

"There were three non-Fwyn here from what my people have told me. Two humans and the wolf. One of the humans was dead when we found him, recently at that."

"Damn," Verdan swore, unable to help but wonder if they could have saved the other human by getting here a little faster. "What about the human that lives? Where is he?"

"This way," Gruthka said, heading back outside and off to the right, where the Darjee bodies were being piled. About thirty feet from the pile, a large man with red hair was sitting against a wall, drinking from a container of some sort. "We've been able to speak with him, unlike the other humans. He is no Wizard, though."

"Thanks, Gruthka," Verdan said, nodding to the Fwyn before heading over to the big man. "Greetings, my name is Verdan. I'm in charge of this expedition. Are you injured at all?" Verdan swapped to Common for the moment to ensure he was understood properly.

"Greetings. I apologize for not rising. I'm still recovering from that cage. I should be fine soon, though," the man said, nodding in greeting to Verdan. Now that he was up close, Verdan could see that the man had bright green eyes, and though he wasn't overly muscular, he gave off a powerful feeling.

"Not a problem. Do you mind if I attempt to help with that?" Verdan asked, cocking his head to one side as he spoke. "I have another that is struggling from the affliction of these charms, so seeing what helps with a healthy subject would be useful."

"Not at all, as long as I can remain seated. I owe you and your people greatly for my release." The big man said, turning slightly toward Verdan to face him.

"I'm glad we could help. We came here for the Fwyn, but no one deserves this. Do you know of any other areas where they keep captives?" Verdan asked, stepping closer as he did and laying a hand on the man's shoulder. He could feel the lingering effects of the charms' abyssal energy, though it was far weaker than in the wolf.

"No, just this area. I'm surprised that you would come to rescue the Fwyn; most humans have poor relations with the other races these days." The big man looked Verdan over and frowned in thought. "Are you a Sorcerer? You don't seem to be, but I saw the power you wielded."

"No, I'm not a Sorcerer. My name is Verdan Blacke, and I am a Wizard, perhaps the only one left, from what I can tell." Verdan gave him a short bow before whispering a word of power and injecting a small amount of Aether into him with a cleansing concept.

"Well met, Verdan. My name is Elliot. Thank you for whatever you just did. That made things much nicer," Elliot said with a sigh, some of the tension fading from his posture.

Touching Elliot's shoulder once more, Verdan sensed a reduced amount of abyssal energy within him, but it was still there. It would need either a much larger use of Aether or repeated sessions to clear it.

"So, tell me, how do you know Low Imperial?" Verdan asked, finally speaking the question that had been burning within him.

"Low Imperial?" Elliot echoed with a frown, shaking his head slightly.

"The language the Fwyn use," Verdan said, swapping languages and continuing in Low Imperial. "This language."

"This is the language of the ancients, one passed down through our people as part of our heritage. As far as I was aware, only my people and a few of the non-human races still spoke it. You cannot be a relative of mine; you are far too small. How have you learned it?" Elliot asked, surprise written across his face as he openly stared at Verdan.

"Where I am from, it is one of our main languages," Verdan said truthfully. He didn't want to go ahead and start spilling his secrets to just anyone at this point. Besides, he was a little insulted by Elliot calling him small. Verdan wasn't the tallest or strongest out there, but he'd never been considered small before.

"Fascinating, I would speak more of your homeland with you if you are willing," Elliot said with a thoughtful tone.

"Perhaps another time. For now, what do you intend to do? You are free to do as you wish, though you are welcome to journey back to Hobson's Point with us."

"Hobson's Point, is that the city to the south of here, the one that used to be known for its glass and metal?" Elliot asked, quirking one bushy red eyebrow in Verdan's direction.

"Indeed it is. You are welcome to join us there as my guest for a time," Verdan said, feeling the pull of his oath to ensure that those he rescued didn't fall immediately back into trouble.

"Very well, I accept. It has been a long while since I stayed in a city for more than a few days. Perhaps it is time to change that." Elliot nodded slowly to himself and flashed Verdan a smile. "I will be well enough to move shortly. Please, do not let me keep you from your responsibilities."

"Thank you," Verdan said, returning Elliot's smile with one of his own. He was growing to like this red-headed giant of a man already. "If you need healing again before we leave, please just ask."

Verdan left Elliot to his rest and went to go get a complete report of what had happened here. Some of what Elliot had said had seemed a little odd, but now wasn't the time to press him.

CHAPTER
TWENTY-TWO

Over the next hour, Gurthka and the Fwyn tore down a section of the ruins and formed a makeshift camp to house them while Verdan treated the wounded. They had seen no sign of any Darjee since capturing the plaza, but it was best to be prepared.

Verdan had used a significant amount of Aether between the healing and the general combat, so he used this time to meditate and regain as much as he could. Gruthka had spoken to the captured Fwyn and confirmed that this was everyone who had been taken, so they did not need to press any further.

Kai and his group arrived shortly after the Fwyn finished shaping their defenses, bringing a welcome boost to their strength. The fire Sorcerer reported engaging a dozen or so Darjee over several small skirmishes, but they had been dealt with easily enough.

Thankfully, none of Kai's group had been injured in their fights. Kai had been able to meet the Darjee and match their speed and strength, while Tom had been able to protect the casters.

It wasn't quite the same as having properly-trained backup, but it was more than Verdan had hoped for when he realized the state of civilization. Especially now that Tom had become a Sorcerer.

Verdan had been shocked when he realized that Tom was using Aether; he'd seen no signs of Tom having it until then. How exactly Tom went from not using it all to using it adeptly and in complex ways, Verdan had no idea. At this point, it was just one more piece of data for him to consider.

He'd been confident that Sorcerers were inherently different from Wizards before, but now, he was certain. What Tom demonstrated was nothing like what Verdan and his colleagues had gone through.

In some ways, Verdan was jealous of the other man. He'd spent years working his fingers to the bone in the academy, and that was just to be taught how to do it. A Wizard's potential was entirely self-dependent; no one could do the work for you.

This, however, was something else entirely. The potential of it all was astounding. Verdan had mistakenly assumed that Sorcerers had to train for their powers. That lack of training, mixed with the sudden onset, nullified a few of his favored theories on Sorcerers.

Once they were back in Hobson's Point, Verdan would have to speak with Tom and see if he would do some experiments or even just answer some questions that Verdan had.

"Verdan, Tim is waking up," Gwen called out, breaking Verdan from his meditation and bringing him back to reality.

"How is he?" Verdan asked, rising to his feet wearily to follow Gwen over to where the wounded were sheltered.

"Drained, but alive. Will you be able to do more?" Gwen asked, giving Verdan a worried look. "You need to rest yourself."

"I'm fine, nothing that a few good nights of sleep will fix once we're back at Hobson's Point. I've been cutting into my downtime to work on my spiral, that's all," Verdan said reassuringly. "_Hyn_. There, much better." Verdan perked up as the refreshing energy of the spell dispelled his physical and mental fatigue. He'd need to rest properly later, but he had patients to work on.

When they arrived, Tim was awake and in pain, Verdan moving to his side and giving him a small burst of healing to take the edge off.

"Verdan, did we get everyone?" Tim asked, grimacing as he shifted on the makeshift bed.

"Yes, everyone is safe, don't worry. You did well," Verdan said reassuringly, patting Tim on his good shoulder as he did.

"The wolf?" Tim asked, trying to crane his neck to look around.

"Is fine, don't worry, the Fwyn are watching it," Verdan said, nodding over to where the wolf was still asleep. Tim woke before it, despite the greater physical injury, but that was due to the abyssal energy lingering in the wolf. It would be some time before it was truly on the path to recovery.

"Alright, let me just close my eyes for a few minutes, then I'll be good to go," Tim said, letting them settle him back down as his eyelids drooped shut.

"How is he?" Gwen whispered, following Verdan as he stepped away from the sleeping guard.

"He lost a lot of blood before I got to him, but he's replaced most of it now. With that extra little bit of healing, he'll be on his feet within the hour. Healing spells tend to encourage sleep as the body focuses energy on repairing itself, so don't worry about how he drifted off." Verdan explained, while moving over to the injured Fwyn.

The Fwyn were awake and resting on their dirt beds; their wounds were now little more than scars. They were fine to travel; it would just be the ones rescued from the cages who needed a little longer. Thankfully, as they Fwyn hadn't had a collar like the wolf, the corruptive energy in them was clearing out at a much higher pace. They were recovering nicely without further intervention from Verdan.

Another hour, and a touch more healing from Verdan, had everyone ready for travel, and he saw no reason to put it off. Even the wolf was up and about, though it was staying close to Tim and eyeing the rest of them warily.

Elliot had recovered quickly from his condition—surprisingly quickly, actually. Verdan couldn't help but wonder if the large man was a Sorcerer of some kind as well; that might explain his fast healing.

"Ready to leave?" Verdan asked Gruthka, coming over to where the Fwyn was organising his folk.

"As ready as we will be; some of my people have been here for weeks. It will take time for them to recover, but they're fit for travel." Gruthka grimaced and shrugged in an oddly human motion. "There's nothing more we can do for them right now."

"I'll do another round of infusing the worst with a cleansing concept tomorrow. Hopefully, that will help," Verdan offered, and Gruthka inclined his head in thanks.

With everyone ready, they set off out of the ruins, heading first to the makeshift fort that had been set up previously. While it hadn't been as key a defensive emplacement as Verdan had hoped, that was mainly due to the lack of support the Darjee had brought.

Someone must have made these bone charms for them, so they clearly had some magical contacts, but Verdan hadn't seen any here. One possibility was that the Darjee were trading with some other group that created the bone charms, which was why they weren't in the hunting group. Alternatively, it could be a question of status, with the magic users being much higher in the ranks of the Darjee than regular hunters.

Still, from what Kai had told him originally, no one was aware of the magical capabilities of these Darjee. He'd have to speak with him further about the bone charms, find out if they were something new or not. It wasn't a priority for the moment, though.

Verdan's musings didn't keep him from watching their surroundings carefully as they moved through the ruins. They hadn't seen any further signs of Darjee, but that didn't mean anything.

Thankfully, they exited the ruins without issue, their enlarged group moving out past the fort and into the wilderness. From here, it was down to Gruthka and the Fwyn to guide them back to Gwen's family home.

Kai made his way over to Verdan once they were a few hours out from the ruins without any sign of Darjee pursuit.

"So, what are your plans now? Are we heading straight for Hobson's Point?" Kai asked, glancing over at Verdan with a questioning expression.

"Yes, I think so. Everything I ordered must be close to arriving by now, if not there already. Besides, after buying that property, I do want to spend some time there," Verdan said with a shrug. This jaunt out from the city had already been so much more than he had planned for. He was fine now, but he knew he'd be dreaming of the war tonight. The screams of the Darjee had been hard to hear.

No, what Verdan needed now was some time away from everything. They could settle into their new home, and he could focus on his alchemy. The loggers could get back to work, and in turn, the glassblowers could make him some glassware for his new lab. It would all come together nicely.

"Very well. Do you intend to be adventuring like this often? If so, I will look into hiring additional guards to watch over the estate in our absence."

"No, no need for that at all. I will be settling in and leaving the rest of this to the professionals. Next time I'll just hire some adventurers to go out and deal with it." Verdan told Kai firmly. He had no intent to do this again any time soon.

Kai grunted noncommittally and said no more, giving Verdan a long look before dropping back to speak to Gwen.

Ignoring Kai's lack of faith in his ability to remain in the city, Verdan started to consider his plans for his first alchemy project. Alchemy had long been the province of Witches and not something that Wizards had dabbled in. It would be a breath of fresh air to do some experimenting and see what he could achieve.

They followed the same rough path back the way they had come, the different groups keeping to themselves as they traveled. They had been lucky not to take any losses, but a fair number of them were nursing various injuries.

They had a thirty-minute stop after around three hours of travel, pausing so that Verdan could cast a few minor healing spells and help things along. The injured Fwyn were all but completely healed; their connection with the earth helped them heal quickly, even without Verdan's help.

Tim was also making good progress, though his brother was hovering over him protectively. Tom hadn't taken the news of his brother being injured very well. Verdan doubted that the two of them spent that much time apart, let alone got into trouble without the other.

The wolf was also hovering around Tim and was Verdan's hardest patient. He knew he'd need a more stable setting to look at removing the collar safely, but every time he saw the cursed thing, he wanted to remove it then and there.

The sun was dipping below the horizon when they stopped for the healing top-up. Thankfully, it took only a few minutes for Verdan to work through his patients, so they were able to push on afterwards. Conscious of the dimming light, Verdan conjured several pale lights to help guide the way for the non-Fwyn, knowing that the small creatures didn't need any help.

Between creating the fort, fighting the Darjee, and the day's travel, the Fwyn were too tired to create a temporary shelter when they stopped for the day. Instead, they raised an area of compacted loam for everyone to sleep on, saving the rest of their energy in case they were called on during the night.

Verdan meditated for an hour or two after the watches were set, and everyone tried to get some sleep. He split his time between adding to his spiral and actively circulating it to speed up his recovery.

With all the healing and combat spells, Verdan was running low on Aether, far too low for his liking. Normally, Verdan liked to maintain a healthy reserve of Aether, but his recovery rate was still so slow. Thankfully, he was almost ready to complete his second spiral and start working on his third. He just needed another hour or two of meditation to get it finished.

The change of watch told Verdan that the time he'd allocated for his meditation had passed, and he reluctantly stopped working on his spiral. Part of him wanted to infuse himself with some Aether and just keep going, but he knew that putting off his sleep would do more harm than good at this point.

Sighing heavily, Verdan stretched out on the soft ground and let his eyes rest on the stars above. The weariness Verdan had been fighting off quickly caught up with him, making his eyelids turn heavy and pulling him down into sleep.

_**_

Verdan woke twice during the night, drenched in sweat and with an offensive word of power on the tip of his tongue. Each time it took him several minutes to calm down enough to go back to sleep, leaving him weary and only slightly rested by the time morning came round.

"*Hyn*," Verdan muttered, tapping his leg and sending a burst of refreshing Aether through his system. The Aether burnt away the fogginess in Verdan's thoughts, waking him up properly and leaving him ready for action.

The Fwyn gathered together as their small camp woke up, clustering into small groups and sharing what looked like mushrooms and roots they had foraged the day before.

Tim was up and moving already, which was a good sign that the extra healing yesterday had done what Verdan intended. Superficial damage wasn't really Verdan's concern, or what he'd been taught when treating wounded combatants. Whether apprentice or archmage, every Wizard knew basic healing spells and first aid and knew the priority was to keep the subject alive. Cosmetic healing could come later; being able to get the wounded moving and out of danger was far more important.

Verdan took a moment to consider his Aether reserves before giving Tim an additional minor heal, focusing on improving his natural healing once more.

"Thanks, Verdan," Tim said, absently patting the wolf lying by his side. "I don't think I'd have made it without your magic."

"Not a problem. You are only out here because of me, after all," Verdan said with a slight smile, noting how the wolf was watching him with a cautious look in its eyes.

"And we're only here at all because of you," Tim said, a serious expression settling on his face as he looked up at Verdan. "Tom and I owe you our lives. We won't forget that."

"Just doing what anyone would in my position," Verdan said, uncomfortably shifting at the praise.

"Uh-huh," Tim said, giving Verdan a pointed look before sighing and gesturing to the collar on the wolf. "This fine lady seems to be intent on hanging around with us. Anything you can do about this collar? I've seen blood leaking from it a few times; it can't be good for her." Tim told him with a grimace and a concerned look at the wolf.

"Not yet. Though, if she goes with us back to Hobson's Point, maybe I can. You are right; nothing about that collar is good for her." Verdan told him with a frustrated wave of his hand. It irked him that there was so little he could do about it right now, but he couldn't change that.

"We'll see. I won't make her do anything, but she saved me from that Darjee, so if I can help her, I will," Tim said, a touch of resolve firming his voice as the wolf rested her head on his knee.

"Let's talk about it more when we get back to Hobson's Point. Nothing to be done until then, anyway," Verdan said, waiting for Tim to nod before leaving him to his thoughts.

Verdan gave the wolf a last glance as he walked away, meeting its blue-eyed gaze as it watched him leave, head still on Tim's knee. Seeing it like this made Verdan consider just why the wolf had been captured by the Darjee and imprisoned alongside the Fwyn and Elliot. The other question was why it was wearing that nasty collar and what the collar actually did because it certainly did something.

Verdan considered talking to Tim about it, but there wasn't really much to discuss before they got back to Hobson's Point. He was sure that Tim had considered the implications of the fact that the Darjee had captured it.

"Verdan, do you have a moment?" Gruthka called out in Low Imperial, walking out from one of the small clusters of Fwyn toward Verdan.

"Of course," Verdan said, pausing to let the Fwyn catch up with him. He'd been going over to talk to Tom about his display of magic, but that could wait. "What do you need?"

"I wanted to thank you again for your aid. You've been every bit the Wizard described in the stories of my people," Gruthka said, giving Verdan a respectful bow. The Fwyn opened his mouth to continue but paused and looked up at Verdan with uncertainty in his wide eyes.

"Is there something else?" Verdan asked softly, seeing now the reluctance in the Fwyn's body language.

"Yes, but please, take no offense at what I am about to say," Gruthka said, eyes still on Verdan as he measured the Wizard's reaction.

"I will do my best," Verdan temporised, wanting to give the Fwyn the chance to speak.

"My people will be leaving us today. I will remain to guide you back to Gwen's home, but the rest will leave."

Verdan frowned, unsure of what part of that he should have been offended by. Gruthka was clearly waiting for a response, so Verdan ran the words back through his mind and nodded slightly as he realized what Gruthka was actually saying.

"You don't want us to know where you live, do you?" Verdan said, knowing he'd guessed right when Gruthka cringed slightly.

"There is too much bad blood between us and the humans for a single action to wash away. Your status as a Wizard will help bypass that, but the sachka would be feared by all who saw him." Gruthka said, using the Fwyn term for Sorcerers with a look of distaste.

"I understand, but I would like a way to find you if I need to," Verdan said eventually, not wanting to lose contact with the Fwyn altogether. He could create an Aether construct with a message tied to it and send that, but that would be problematic. Messages sent over long distances had a homing function built-in, but the Aether cost was prohibitive for anyone with Verdan's current gathering spiral.

Verdan heaved an internal sigh as he considered yet another thing he would have been able to do, but not anymore. It would take such a long time for him to rebuild himself to where he had been during the war.

"If you visit Gwen's home, I will come to find you," Gruthka said after a few moments of thought. "A few Fwyn live nearby that could pass me a message, but please don't tell the other humans."

"You honour me with your trust and those of the other Fwyn," Verdan said, touched by the offering.

"You've earned it," Gurthka said simply as he gestured to the group he'd come from. "The Fwyn who would get in touch with you are those that you've helped rescue. Dru, in particular, will be living nearby with his newly-rescued uncle. Their family will gladly pass word should you arrive."

"I see no problem there, and I will try to come back sometime soon to make sure the Darjee are no longer an issue. You needn't stay to guide us to Gwen's home, either; we can make our way from here," Verdan said, not wanting to impose on Gruthka if his people were all leaving.

"Thank you, Wizard Verdan," Gruthka said formally, bowing as he spoke. "With that agreed, we will be on our way. It would be best if we returned to our homes as soon as possible."

Verdan smiled and shifted uncomfortably as Gruthka rose from his bow and made his way back to his people. The other Fwyn were seemingly ready to go, and in only a few moments, the Fwyn were all on their feet and heading off into the surrounding woods.

"Is everything okay?" Gwen called out, rising to her feet with a frown as she saw all the Fwyn leaving them. Kai looked equally concerned, but relaxed after a glance at Verdan.

"Everything is fine. The Fwyn are heading the rest of the way back themselves. We'll head for Hobson's Point instead. At this speed, I think we should be there by tomorrow afternoon," Verdan said, making a mental allowance for a slightly slower pace due to Tim's wounds.

"We should start now then," Kai said, climbing to his feet and shouldering his spear with a final glance at the departing Fwyn.

"I'm ready when you are," Tim said, waving away his brother's help as he got to his feet, the silver-furred wolf pressed up against his leg in support.

"I don't know the way to my cabin from here—not confidently, anyway," Gwen said, looking at the area around them with a slight frown.

"I was thinking of a more-direct landmark to use," Verdan said, pointing at the distant mountains that sheltered Hobson's Point. "If we head south towards the mountains, we'll come across familiar terrain eventually."

No one had any particular objection to that plan, so the seven of them started walking south, Kai leading the way, while Elliot and Tim followed at a slower pace. Elliot had recovered well from the effects of the Darjee bone charms and was back to his full strength. The big man kept his pace down to what was comfortable for Tim as they spoke about Hobson's Point and what sort of things could be found there.

Gwen was walking just behind Tim and Elliot, her hand stroking the sleek feathers of her familiar as it sat on her shoulder. Verdan wanted to discuss how she was feeling now that she'd had a chance to use her magic more, but he had other priorities right now.

"Tom, how are you feeling?" Verdan asked as he dropped to the rear of their group to walk with the quiet man.

"I'm fine," Tom said with a shrug. "I'll be happy once we're back, though."

"I will as well," Verdan said with a longing thought of the bed that was waiting for him. "How do you feel about what happened back there, with the powers you used?" Verdan cut straight to the heart of the matter, not wanting to dance around the issue.

"It's strange. I'm not sure how it happened; it just did. You always hear stories of folk being able to wield sorcery in dangerous situations, but I never expected to be one of them," he replied, a frown forming on his face as he spoke.

"Do you think you could do it again?" Verdan asked, cocking his head to one side in thought. The way that Sorcerers used Aether was increasingly odd to him.

"Maybe?" Tom said, his frown developing further as he sighed in frustration. "I don't really know. I asked Kai about it, and he said to meditate on the meaning of stone, but I don't know what that means." Tom looked over to Verdan with a hopeful expression, but this was well outside of Verdan's

experience.

"Kai knows best about these things, but let me know if anything else occurs to you. Alright?" Verdan said, reassured by Tom's nod of assent.

What sort of magic would flare up when the user was in danger but then subside again? Kai seemed to have full control, so why wouldn't Tom? For that matter, why tell Tom to meditate on the meaning of stone?

So many questions, so few answers. The next thing on Verdan's list was to talk to Kai about all this, that was for certain. For now, however, Verdan would devote a portion of his attention to working on his spiral, keeping just enough awareness to watch where he was walking. The Darjee had picked this area clean, so it should be a safe enough use of time.

TWENTY-THREE

THE REST of the day passed by slowly, and they took turns on night watch that evening. Rising early the following morning, they set off at the same steady pace, eager to reach Hobson's Point.

Having made good progress in expanding his spiral and recovering his Aether the day before, Verdan took the opportunity to question Kai on the situation with Tom.

The Sorcerer glanced back as Verdan joined him, nodding slightly before turning back to the direction they were going.

"I wanted to talk to you about what happened with Tom," Verdan said, as he came level with the Sorcerer.

"I thought you would at some point. I've been thinking of how to explain it to you, given your lack of knowledge about sorcery," Kai said, keeping his voice soft and pitched low to prevent them from being overheard.

"Thank you, I appreciate it," Verdan said with an internal sigh of relief. He'd been hoping that Kai would be able to explain this.

"Not a problem, though I would like to have the same conversation about your magic at some point. About those words I hear you use," Kai said, his voice trailing off as he shook his head. "Not that it matters right now; we are discussing sorcery. You should know that around one in ten humans has the potential for sorcery in their blood. Of course, that includes both the supremely-talented and those with barely any ability at all. Every sect has its own way of cultivating the Essence they favor and awakening their candidates to become Sorcerers. Their success varies from sect to sect, but I have witnessed at most two-thirds of the candidates becoming Sorcerers." Kai explained, a hint of displeasure entering his voice as he mentioned the sects.

"I see, but that doesn't describe Tom's situation." Verdan said with a frown.

"True, people like Tom are known as wildlings. They are Sorcerers who have awakened without the aid of a sect. The trigger to awaken them can be anything; I once met a wildling who had awakened their fire Essence when dancing at a feast. No one truly understands the process, and sects tend to dislike wildlings because of it." Kai made a second grimace of distaste as he mentioned the sects.

"A matter of control?" Verdan guessed, thinking of how Kai had described these sects so far. He doubted any of them would appreciate there existing a way to achieve power without joining them first.

Verdan remembered arcane societies that had established academies devoted to training the best Wizards they could and sneered at those from sponsored apprenticeships. The sects seemed to carry a matching level of arrogance, though Verdan would try to keep an open mind.

"I believe so, but I am far from being on good terms with any of the sects. It doesn't help that wildlings often have a more-intuitive understanding of their element. They struggle to master new elements, however, which is part of why the sects look down on them." Kai explained, the majority of his attention remaining on their surroundings.

"I see," Verdan said, his brow furrowing as he considered this new information. "Have we discussed additional elements before? I thought you were restricted from how you described it, but it sounds like you can change that?"

"Yes, it's one of the more spiritual aspects of sorcery. In order to cultivate an element, we must have a connection with an aspect of it. The aspect we have determines the form of our power. I have a strong link with the speed and agility of fire when unleashed, which has made me a Fire Enhancer. Tom seems to have something linked to the concept of stone, and I told him to meditate on that and see where his thoughts lead."

"So, what you're saying is that the concept that you resonate with, for lack of a better term, actually impacts the ways in which you can use your 'Essential Essence?'" Verdan asked, trying to get his head around the odd rules that Sorcerers seemed to work by.

Kai simply nodded in reply, and Verdan's brow furrowed even further as he tried to make sense of that. Using a concept to shape the Aether made sense. It seemed an odd way to do it, to fix in on just one broad concept, but he could understand it. Sort of.

The problem Verdan had was that, apparently, the concept they had influenced the ways they could manipulate the energy. That just didn't fit in with Verdan's understanding of Aether.

Everything that Verdan had been taught, and the way he was able to use such a variety of spells, was based on the flexibility of what could be achieved with Aether.

That being said, it did make sense that some concepts would work better than others with some groups of effects. He could see how a fire-based agility concept would make a poor fireball, but at the same time, something more like a whip or a seeking bolt of fire would be a good match.

Verdan sighed in frustration, but he couldn't help but smile at the same time. This whole different approach to magic was fascinating to him; he just wished it made more sense. He'd try and talk Kai into some tests once they were back at Hobson's Point.

"This is an important time for Tom. He needs to grab hold of whatever concept he has linked to. If he doesn't, he won't be able to cultivate more Essence, and he won't become a Sorcerer." Kai said, glancing back at Tom as he spoke.

"I see. Is there anything we can do to help?" Verdan asked, concerned that Tom might lose his grip on whatever concept he had found. Gaining power like this would be life-changing for Tom. Verdan didn't want him to miss out on that.

"Traditionally, no, there isn't," Kai told him, but Verdan saw a slight tenseness around Kai's shoulders as the Sorcerer glanced his way.

"And non-traditionally?" Verdan prompted after a moment of silence.

"Well, I've noticed something," Kai said, pausing as he visibly searched for the right word. "A resonance, like you said before. I've noticed one when you use some of those words for your spells. One, in particular, *thanr*, has the biggest effect on me. An equivalent one for Tom might make it easier for him to grasp his concept," Kai said, the word of power coming out of his mouth with a flat texture to it that made Kai grimace.

"I wouldn't use those words unless you have to. They have an inherent weight to them," Verdan said in warning. Fortunately, Kai had mispronounced the word, but it was worth telling him now.

"I've never tried to say it aloud before. How can you use those words so easily?" Kai asked, looking over at Verdan with fresh respect in his eyes.

"Be glad you said it wrong," Verdan said with a laugh, remembering his own experiences learning the words of power. "The closer you are to the true pronunciation, the harder it is to say. Those words are not meant for mortals to utter. Then there's the cost of using them as a concept, it's hard to say the least. If you ever hear me use four words or more in a row, expect something big to happen."

"Ah, that does explain a few things," Kai nodded with the look of someone who had just understood a mystery that had been bothering them.

"Let me test something," Verdan said, realizing he could do this part without any equipment. "Thanr. Did that resonate with you?" Verdan spoke the word of power without any Aether infusing it.

"No, it didn't," Kai said, cocking his head to one side in curiosity.

"I see. *Thanr*, what about now?" Verdan asked, conjuring a slight flame on the end of one finger. It used only the smallest amount of Aether and was the weakest fire spell concept he held.

"Yes, I felt that," Kai muttered, a little distractedly.

"Interesting. What about these? *Liff. Tyn. Garec.*" Verdan spoke the words one after another, first momentarily changing the direction of the wind behind them, then pulling a loose piece of stone to his hand from the ground before causing it to break down into sand. He made sure to not let Kai see the stone or sand, and the wind change didn't touch them.

"No...maybe...I'm not sure," Kai said, lifting a hand to feel the movement of the wind around them, ignoring the hand behind Verdan's back that held the sand.

"What you felt there was the concept of flow. I used it to change the movement of the wind," Verdan said as a way of explanation. Glancing behind him, he saw Tom looking around with a puzzled expression; it looked like he might have sensed one of those as well. Interesting indeed.

"The wind?" Kai said softly, shaking his head after a moment. "I've never had even a thought of a concept to do with the wind, are you sure?"

"I have no idea. Your way of doing all this is strange to me. Maybe you should do some meditation yourself," Verdan said, not wanting to prejudice Kai into any assumptions. If this process was the same as creating a spell concept, then it was always best to do it yourself. Something you built from the ground-up was smoother and more complete than a foreign concept that someone else created. Verdan had learned that long ago the hard way.

"Maybe," Kai said softly, lost in thought for a moment before shaking himself out of it. "I will have to think about this."

"Of course, I'll leave you to your thoughts," Verdan said, slowing his pace to let the Sorcerer take the lead once more.

That had been an interesting conversation. Verdan felt like he was starting to understand more of how sorcery worked. He'd been wrong in assuming it was a bastardized version of Wizardry; that much was clear. Some of the core principles did carry over, like the use of concepts and the manipulation of Aether, but it was different enough to be its own thing. It was almost closer to the natural magic the Fwyn used than to Wizardry. That couldn't be the case, though, as humans didn't have natural magic. Verdan had read numerous reports on projects trying to replicate natural magic within humans, all of which had failed. In the end, that line of research had been banned due to how invasive the experiments were getting.

Verdan allowed himself a satisfied smile as he considered the amount of research that lay before him. This was a project he could truly dive into, a whole new type of Aether magic.

As far as anyone in the Grym Imperium had been able to determine, despite numerous experiments, there were four main sources of magical energy.

Aether was the first and most common; it was used by Witches, Wizards, Sorcerers and naturally magical creatures. Abyssal energy was the next most-common, to Verdan's everlasting disgust. Abyssal energy, or Corruption as many called it, was used by the spawn of the abyss and their mortal worshippers like the Cyth, and also apparently the Darjee.

Next was Exeon, the Celestial energy, which was used by gods and creatures of the divine. While Gwen's familiar might use Aether to empower her, the creation of the familiar would have been through Exeon.

The final source of energy, known as Parada, was the most mystical and the hardest to quantify. Many researchers tried and failed to make it perform as reliably as Aether, eventually leading to it being all but ignored by mainstream Wizardry.

For a short time, Verdan had wondered if part of sorcery was to do with Parada, but it was clear that it used Aether as its main fuel; Verdan could see the movements of the energy himself.

Even thinking about Parada made Verdan wonder if it was still in use in this new world. Aether usage had become strange and unrecognizable, it would be amusing if the opposite had happened with Parada.

Verdan mused to himself about what sort of strange schools of magic Parada could have birthed. It almost made him want to try his hand at researching and quantifying it; but no, he had enough on his plate at the moment as it was.

Sorcery and alchemy were both full-time pursuits by themselves. All being well, they should be enough to keep Verdan busy and keep his mind occupied. At least, for a little while anyway, and by then, he might have even started to come to terms with this new life.

Verdan couldn't help but quirk his lips into a melancholy smile as he thought of his old friends and comrades, many of whom would have loved to be in his position right now. This was a whole new frontier of magic as far as he was concerned, the sort of opportunity they'd have all dreamed about, one that the war had taken away from them.

_-**-_

They started to see more signs of life in the woods around them as they journeyed back to Hobson's Point, the long walk back slowly passing them by until the mountains stretched up before them.

The clearing at the base of the switchbacks soon came into view, and Verdan quickened his pace as he led the way back up to the pass they had come through. It was early evening now, but the moon was bright, and Verdan was willing to use a spell to light their way if it meant sleeping inside the city rather than roughing it outside for another night.

The others seemed to have the same opinion, or at least they voiced no objection when Verdan suggested it, and in short order, he had an orb of white light atop his staff and was moving through the pass at a decent pace.

It had taken them a whole afternoon to get through initially, but they were heading back at a much faster pace. Even Tim was moving quicker now, the worst of his injuries healed by Verdan's ministrations.

The bright moon covered the rocky pass in a soft light that meshed well with the spell that Verdan had cast, and they moved forward with purpose as they rushed to reach the end.

Soon enough, the flickering lights of torches atop the gates leading into Hobson's Point came into view. There was a distant flicker of movement as the guards saw Verdan's light, but thankfully they didn't shoot at them.

"State your business!" A deep voice called out as Verdan, and the others came close to the gates. A few new figures had arrived atop the gate; Verdan realized the guards must have woken their commander.

"We are returning from dealing with the issue that was restricting the loggers to the city. We've traveled all day to sleep in a bed once more. Let us in." Verdan called back, too tired to argue more than he needed to.

"Come forward slowly. We're opening up," the voice shouted back after a short delay.

True to their word, the gates opened slightly a minute later, revealing a pair of armed guards. One of the pair peered at Verdan and the others as they approached before relaxing and calling something back over their shoulder.

The two guards stepped to one side, letting them pass through the gates, where a stocky man with a thick beard was waiting for them.

"I apologize for the brash treatment, Master Sorcerer. We needed to confirm your identity," the man said, his voice surprisingly deep, even for his large frame.

"Not a problem, I understand completely," Verdan said, waving away the apology as he dispelled his light. There was no need for the additional light source now they were back in the city. "My name is Verdan Blacke. These are my companions."

"Thank you, Sorcerer Blacke," the big man said with a short bow, eyeing the tip of Verdan's staff warily. "My name is Lieutenant Silver. I have command of the watch and our defenses for the pass."

"A pleasure to meet you, Lieutenant. I'm sure we'll be dealing with each other in the future," Verdan said, suppressing a yawn as he started to turn away.

"Your pardon, Sorcerer Blacke, but could you tell me more about what you found out there? You said you dealt with the issue plaguing the loggers?"

"Yes, we did, but it's a long enough story that I have no desire to go into it right now. Why don't you come by tomorrow afternoon, and I will update you?" Verdan stifled another yawn as he spoke. He was almost tempted to banish his fatigue, but then he'd struggle to sleep for a few hours.

"I apologize, Sorcerer Blacke, but the watch is run independently of the sects in Hobson's Point. I answer to my Captain, not to you," the lieutenant said in a voice tight with tension.

"What?" Verdan said, looking back in surprise at the other man, that hadn't been at all the reaction he was expecting. "Why wouldn't you answer to your Captain first?"

The lieutenant looked as confused as Verdan and glanced uncertainly between their faces before shaking his head and walking away with an annoyed frown.

"What just happened?" Verdan asked aloud, looking to Kai for instruction.

"It's common for sects to control the guards of the city they are based in, putting Sorcerers in all the key command positions and often using the normal guards as little more than fodder. He thought you were trying to muscle in by ordering him to report to you, and then mistook your confusion for mockery." Kai explained quietly.

"Why am I not surprised?" Verdan muttered, rubbing his face with his free hand.

"You are unfamiliar with the way sects work?" Elliot questioned, a look of surprise on his face.

"I'm from somewhere very different, where none of this was a problem," Verdan said with a heavy sigh. "There are no Sorcerers either, which is why Kai has been explaining how all this works for me."

"I see. It must be an interesting place indeed," Elliot said with a thoughtful expression.

Verdan wasn't completely sure that he should have told Elliot that; after all, he'd already said about how they spoke Low Imperial and that he was a Wizard. He was too tired to be able to judge all this properly.

The lieutenant was long gone now, so Verdan started back towards their new home. He doubted he was going to make any good decisions when this tired.

Fortunately, the way back to the estate was relatively simple. They'd been gone for a surprisingly long time; Verdan hadn't really been keeping track, but it must have been at least a week, maybe closer to two.

The buildings stood dark and empty when they arrived, the group breaking up as everyone went to their respective rooms. Fortunately, the floor on which Tim and Tom slept had an empty room, so Verdan sent Elliot with the brothers before heading to his own room.

When Verdan finally made it to his bed, he didn't bother to do more than take his boots off, throw his robe to one side, and prop his staff against the wall before climbing in and falling into a deep sleep.

_**_

Verdan woke up what felt like only a few hours later, the new day's light waking him as it crossed his face. While he felt better than he had the night before, he still didn't feel refreshed. He probably needed several good nights of sleep if he was going to start feeling awake in the mornings.

"Hyn," Verdan murmured absently, tapping his chest and sending a pulse of Aether into himself to banish the last of his drowsiness. As always, the magic had an immediate effect, letting Verdan blink away his tiredness and look at the warm sunlight coming through the window with fresh eyes.

Getting ready for the day, Verdan realized his clothes were in somewhat of a state, and he wasn't much better. *"Glanae,"* he commanded, a second burst of Aether cleaning both him and the clothes he was wearing, leaving a slight pile of dirt on the floor.

A simple cleaning spell like that to freshen up in the morning was one of the many advantages of being a Wizard. A personal concept was vital for many spells, but the cleaning spell was one of the first that every Wizard learned. They learnt it before they knew about personal concepts, before they could even cast a simple light spell.

Verdan smiled to himself as he remembered when he had questioned why it was the first spell that all apprentices learned, when other spells were technically easier to perform. His teacher had told him that it was a tradition, an ancient one even by Wizarding standards. Apparently, it was simply down to the tendency for apprentices to get so caught up in their studies that they neglected their personal hygiene.

It was such a silly reason for such an ancient tradition that it had always stuck with Verdan, and he'd looked forward to teaching it to an apprentice himself one day.

Verdan's smile dimmed as he considered how unlikely such an event was now. He wasn't even remotely qualified to be teaching people about Wizardry.

Pushing it all out of his mind for the moment, Verdan grabbed his staff and headed downstairs. Now that he was refreshed and mentally aware, he replayed their arrival in the city last night in his mind and winced a little.

Old habits of working closely with imperial guardsmen had come to the fore there. He'd have to be careful to make sure that Lieutenant Silver and the others realized that Verdan was on their side.

Verdan had a few thoughts on how to achieve that, but he put it to one side for now as he followed his nose to the kitchen. Unsurprisingly, Kai was already awake and preparing breakfast. Interestingly, the only other person present was Elliot, who was perched on one of the seats at the table, bacon sandwich in hand.

"Good morning," Elliot rumbled, taking a hefty bite out of his sandwich and narrowing his eyes in satisfaction.

"Good morning. I'm sorry we couldn't take more time to situate you last night," Verdan said, taking a seat at the table. He was conscious that he basically dumped Elliot onto the brothers and went to bed—not exactly a great first night in the city.

"Not a problem. Kai has been more than welcoming this morning," Elliot said, gesturing to the sandwich in his hand.

"So I see. Is that fresh bread?" Verdan said, addressing the last to Kai, who was in the process of plating something for Verdan.

"It is. Bob came over with a basket of provisions from the Plucky Wanderer just after dawn; someone must have told him we'd come back." Kai said, coming over to hand Verdan an omelet.

"Huh, that was nice of him," Verdan murmured, his attention already on his food.

"He said that he's had more business since we stayed there. I think the better-quality food brought in more patrons."

Verdan nodded silently, appreciating the gift from the tavern owner. It was also a good reminder for him that he needed to go speak with Samuel, the representative of the local workers. So much to do and so little time.

After finishing his breakfast, Verdan headed outside and glanced at the sun's position; it must be around mid-morning.

"Morning, Boss," Tim called out from his left, where he was leaning against the wall of the building, while the wolf lay at his feet.

"Morning, how're you feeling?" Verdan asked, walking over as he spoke.

"Back to normal, thanks to you," Tim said with a warm smile. "It feels odd to be back in the city again, though."

"It's been a hectic few weeks, hasn't it?" Verdan said, smiling slightly as he considered just how much different those weeks had been for the two of them.

"That it has. I feel like we've barely had time to breathe between getting back and heading out again. I'm glad we went, though, or those Darjee would have kept preying on the Fwyn," Tim said with a scowl on his face as he thought of the Darjee. The wolf picked up on his mood and sat up to rest its head on his thigh.

Seeing the wolf move brought Verdan's gaze to the collar on its neck, reminding him of yet another task he needed to find time for. It was an important one at that; Verdan wanted to get that collar off the wolf as soon as possible, but he needed a workspace for that, which meant he needed to check in with Tobias to see if the alchemy equipment had arrived yet.

"True, we did a lot of good out there," Verdan said, giving Tim a reassuring smile and patting him on the arm. "What matters now, though, is getting enough rest and taking the time to recover from it all fully." Verdan told him, knowing how hard it was to bounce back from those kinds of situations. Just how close they came to being sacrificed by the Cyth would leave scars, let alone almost dying to the Darjee.

"I know you're right," Tim said, dropping a hand down to pat the wolf on the head. "It's just that I can't help but think about what else is going on outside the city—how many people are in danger of dying, and no one is helping them."

"We do what we can, Tim," Verdan started to say, but the other man scoffed and rose from his leaning position.

"We both know that's not true. What you've done since you got here is more than anyone else in the city has managed in a long time. Thinking back on how little I accomplished disgusts me. If you hadn't rescued us from the Cyth, I'd have died having made no impact on anything. I refuse to let that happen," Tim said, passion filling his voice as he spoke.

Verdan heard the echoes of so many of his old friends in Tim's words; they'd all once believed the same thing. Part of him wanted to reassure Tim that he would do what he could, but the futility of it all made him keep his silence. No one even remembered how they'd worked to make the Imperium a better place. When he'd graduated, Verdan and his friends had volunteered to be assigned to the guard beyond what was required. They'd believed that it was their responsibility to work with the guardsmen to keep people safe. Yet, despite all their efforts, in the end, the war undid it all.

"Listen, Tim," Verdan started to say before pausing, uncertain of how to continue.

"No, it's okay, Boss. It's nothing on you; you've only helped people since you got here. I just wish there were more Sorcerers with your attitude around," Tim said, rubbing his face and heading for the door to go inside. "I'm going to get something to eat. Shout me if you need anything."

Verdan watched Tim and the wolf head inside before sighing heavily and rubbing his face. He could already tell this was going to be an abyss of a day.

CHAPTER

TWENTY-FOUR

Verdan headed out into the area surrounding the estate in search of Samuel, noting once more the dilapidated state of the buildings near his new home. He could almost see the issues caused by the city's failing economy.

"Master Verdan, it's good to see you back safe and sound," a voice called out from a side alley as Verdan walked along. He glanced over and saw Samuel come his way, a welcoming expression on his face. "I hope you have good news for us."

"I do. The issue was caused by creatures being driven south by Darjee hunting parties. I've dealt with some of the creatures and the Darjee themselves, so things should start to return to normal in due course."

"I've got volunteers ready to go as we speak; I'll give them the word and get a few parties down there this afternoon. Get one of your lads to give me a list of what you need making; we'll get it done for you," Samuel said with a broad grin as he grabbed Verdan's hand and gave it a firm shake.

"Make sure they know it's not going to be completely safe," Verdan warned, not wanting to see Samuel's people rush into danger. That whole area was going to be up for grabs for predators now. Who knew quite how it would play out?

"Oh, don't worry about that. My boys can take care of themselves. Our problem was how frequent those attacks were—they were causing too many injuries, and not enough work was happening. Saying that, I might see if some of the glassblowers fancy coming out to stand guard; not like they can do much until we get them the fuel they need anyway." Samuel waved away Verdan's concerns before finishing with a thoughtful expression.

"Well, you have that in hand. I'll leave you to it," Verdan said, satisfied that Samuel had everything settled. He'd send one of the brothers over with a list of what he needed at some point in the next few days. The lack of fuel for industry almost meant a lack of fuel to heat homes, and Verdan had no intention of demanding all the fresh wood be used for his orders.

"Thank you again, Master Verdan. We all owe you one," Samuel said as Verdan smiled in thanks and headed back the way he'd come.

All these thanks for just doing what anyone would in his situation made Verdan uneasy. He'd head to the workshop next and see if any of his deliveries had arrived yet.

Verdan's hopes of getting some time away from people were dashed when he saw a pair of young men waiting outside the workshop on the Crea estate. Neither of them looked armed or particularly tense, so Verdan headed their way with only a little reluctance.

"Good morning, can I help you?" Verdan asked as he approached.

"Morning, Master Verdan," the one on the right said, the honorific making Verdan frown slightly. He didn't remember anyone being this formal with him when he left; why was it becoming an issue now?

"Mr. Brock sent us over to see if you needed anything and to say that your supplies are due any time now. Today was the earliest they could get here." The man continued, oblivious to Verdan's irritation.

"Ah, good, thank you. I don't need anything for now, but please let me know when the goods arrive," Verdan said, a little disappointed that the alchemy gear hadn't arrived yet. He'd hoped that he'd be able to start setting things up today, but that wasn't going to happen now.

"No problem, he's told us to stop by daily, so we'll update you tomorrow." The two young men gave him something approaching a bow and scurried off, no doubt reporting back to Tobias on what he'd said.

With the alchemy side of things postponed, Verdan pondered his list of things before deciding where to start. A lot of what he wanted to do would require experimentation, so it would be best to begin with what needed the least setup.

Heading back to where he'd left Kai and Elliot, Verdan found the two of them still conversing at the table.

"Boss," Kai nodded to Verdan as he walked inside, Elliot turning and giving Verdan a brief smile before looking back to what was left of his breakfast. Surprisingly, Elliot seemed to be a particularly slow eater, which was odd given his size and apparent appetite— not at all what Verdan had expected.

"Kai, could you go find Tom and meet me outside the lab complex? I want to do some tests on you both. If that's okay?" Verdan said,

turning the statement into a question at the last minute as he realized that Kai might have his own plans.

"Not a problem. I think he's still upstairs. We'll meet you there,"
Kai said, rising to his feet and heading off straight away.

"Tests?" Elliot queried, turning back to Verdan once more.

"My magic works differently from theirs, and I'm trying to understand the nature of what they can do. Mostly for my own interest,
of course," Verdan said, taking Kai's seat so that Elliot wouldn't
need to twist to see him.

Elliot's green eyes held an odd gleam as he studied Verdan, eventually nodding his understanding. "I see. I'd noticed the differences
myself. You called yourself a Wizard, and you stated that you were
from somewhere far away. You are a man of mystery. I would like
to learn more about where you come from; a land without
Sorcerers must be odd indeed."

"It's very different, as you can no doubt imagine," Verdan said,
being careful with his words. There was a keen intelligence hidden
in Elliot's gaze, one that Verdan didn't want to come afoul of. "If I
may ask, do you have some form of magic yourself?"

"What makes you ask that?" Elliot said, one bushy brow rising
slightly at Verdan's question.

"You were kept in one of those cages, the same as the Fwyn. They
seemed designed to contain magic-users, from what I could tell,"
Verdan explained his reasoning, watching Elliot carefully. There
was something about the big man that intrigued Verdan, something more than what he could see on the surface. Verdan was
tempted to examine him more closely with his Aether senses. He'd
have to see if he could talk Elliot into agreeing to it.

"I see, but by that standard, what of the wolf that young Tim has with him?" Elliot asked, leaning back in his chair with a soft smile. "Are you of the opinion that it has some form of magic as well?"

"I'm undecided on the wolf, but it does strike me as odd that it was being kept in the same cages, yes."

"I see. Well, I can assure you that I am no Sorcerer—will that suffice?" Elliot said, the slight smile on his face widening as he watched Verdan's expression. The Wizard was fully aware that Elliot had worded that statement very specifically, and the smile on Elliot's face told him that he knew that Verdan knew.

"It will do for now," Verdan said in a dry tone, giving Elliot a pointed look before moving the conversation along. "So, tell me, what's your plan now that we're back?"

"Truthfully, I'm not completely certain," Elliot said with a soft shrug, leaning forward to rest his elbows on the table and his chin on one fist as he frowned in thought. "I would like to stay here— for now anyway. All of this is very interesting, and I would like to watch it unfurl. My brother and sister will no doubt be here soon, as well. I missed our meeting when the Darjee caught me, so they will seek me out."

"You're welcome to wait here until they arrive. That isn't a problem," Verdan said, feeling responsible for Elliot's welfare. Once the big man was back with his family, Verdan's responsibility was over, but for now, he felt obliged to give him somewhere to stay.

"I appreciate that. Thank you, Verdan," Elliot said, giving Verdan a broad smile. "However, I can only accept your aid if you allow me to assist you in your work. I'm sure there is something I can do to assist."

"By all means, please do. What sort of work are you skilled with?" Verdan asked, intrigued by what possibilities Elliot might bring to the table.

"Well, I'm particularly strong, as you might imagine, but my preference would be anything related to creating or crafting. I've dabbled in countless trades and crafts; I'm sure I can pick up whatever you need me to."

"Crafting?" Verdan echoed, sitting forward in his chair with interest. "Like alchemy?"

"Sadly, no, it's not something I've been directly involved in. The closest I've ever gotten to it is making bespoke equipment for actual alchemists, sometimes glass, sometimes metal."

Verdan's initial disappointment at not getting a trained alchemist he could call on was immediately remedied by Elliot's follow-up. This was exactly what he needed right now.

"That's perfect, actually. Rest today and finish healing up, but if you could find a local foreman named Samuel, he can direct you to whoever will be making the glassware I ordered and when they're going to start. Working with them to get things ready for me would be incredibly helpful."

"Consider it done! I need a new project anyway, so this will do nicely," Elliot said as he got to his feet. "For now, however, I'm going to poke around the city and see what I find. I'll see you later." Elliot gave him an absent wave and strolled out of the room, leaving Verdan to his thoughts.

Verdan had been worrying about the glassware side of things; after all, he had no real information on the workers here in Hobson's Point or the quality of their work. Knowing that Elliot was on the case was somewhat of a relief. Verdan had the impression that the other man was competent at his work. Hopefully, Elliot would live up to that.

Heading over to the alchemy complex as he considered some of the potential custom orders for Elliot, Verdan found Tom and Kai waiting for him at the front entrance.

Both men eyed Verdan with curiosity as he approached them, clearly interested in what he had in mind for their work today.

"Let's head inside, away from prying eyes," Verdan said, opening the door to the main building and stepping inside. He doubted there was anyone watching them right now, but he'd caused quite a few ripples recently; it was best to start taking precautions now.

"So, what do you want us to do?" Kai asked as he and Tom stepped in after Verdan and shut the door behind them.

"First, let's start with some questions. Tom, how are you doing with your newly-developed magic?" Verdan asked as he grabbed a nearby chair for himself. The building as a whole was low on furniture, but this had once been the reception room for the building, so it had a few left over.

"Not so well," Tom said glumly, sitting heavily on a chair himself while Kai leant against the wall. "I've been trying to meditate on stone, but it's not going anywhere."

"Show me," Verdan said, keeping his tone and expression neutral.

Tom sighed, held out a fist and closed his eyes as his face scrunched up with effort. Verdan was already watching the Aether around them, so he immediately felt a small disturbance around Tom, too weak to be noticeable without looking for it.

Looking again with his physical eyes, Verdan saw that gray stone had covered Tom's fist and a portion of his wrist, but that was all.

"That's all I can do," Tom said, red-faced and breathing heavily as he looked at his stone-covered fist. With Tom's concentration removed, the stone began to slough away from his fist, disappearing completely in a few seconds.

"That's not a lot in comparison to last time. Have you practiced much?" Verdan asked, tapping his lips in thought.

"I've tried, but it doesn't feel right," Tom said, grimacing in frustration and looking away from Verdan.

"The initial awakening of a wildling is usually quite substantial, but it takes them time to work back to that point for regular use," Kai offered as an explanation.

"Interesting. Do you remember activating or using this power when it first happened?" Verdan asked, making some mental notes to look into later.

"No, not really, it just happened," Tom said with a shrug.

"Okay, now can you feel this—garec? Or do you feel this—drea? If both, which was stronger?" Verdan asked, using the words for rock and earth, respectively.

"Both of them, but the first more, a lot more. I remember hearing you use it before; it reminds me of when those Fwyn were using their magic. It was like a pressure in my chest, but it's different now."

"Different how?" Verdan pressed, intrigued by what Tom was saying.

"The pressure is gone. It just made something inside me tingle, that's all," Tom said, furrowing his brow as he rubbed his chest.

"Interesting," Verdan said simply, leaning back in his chair as he considered why it had changed.

The pressure that Tom had felt might have been a build-up of Aether inside him that was somehow manipulated by Verdan's use of a word of power. If so, that would also explain the resonance that Kai felt when he used the relevant words.

When a Wizard brought their Aether into them, it was guided into their spiral and then compressed at their core. The whole process was done under firm mental control from the Wizard, to the extent that outside forces would need to wrest control from the Wizard first to effect the Aether.

Rising from his chair and pacing the room, Verdan considered the implications of that thought. This resonance that both Kai and Tom felt implied that they had no internal control over their Aether and, more interestingly, that the Aether was aspected.

Aspected Aether was elemental in nature, but those elements were myriad. In fact, now he was considering it, that did match what Kai had told him so far; it was just difficult to believe.

Natural magic-users like the Fwyn or those spiders they'd fought used aspected Aether; they naturally converted it when they absorbed it from their surroundings. For a human to do the same thing was amazing. There were clear limitations, of course, but it was still fascinating.

Even more interesting was the variety on display. Creatures like the Fwyn might have a few different aspects that they used, but that was across their entire species. Verdan had met only a handful of Sorcerers, and each one was different.

Verdan whirled back to the others with a slightly mad gleam in his eye, his growing smile making both of them shift uncomfortably.

"Describe the whole process to me, start to finish. Take your time; we can be here all day." Verdan resumed his pacing as soon as Tom began to speak, his eyes closed and mind focused on what Tom was saying.

_**_

The rest of the interview with Tom and Kai was somewhat informative for Verdan, but not to the degree he'd hoped for. On the one hand, he'd confirmed that they used breathing exercises and meditation to draw in Aether, or Essence as they called it, and aspect it to their particular flavor.

On the other hand, that brought Verdan no closer to understanding the process, which was frustrating.

"Is that all you need, boss?" Tom asked hopefully, shaking some dust from his hand where he'd been trying to create a stone gauntlet.

"Yes, that should do," Verdan said, somewhat reluctantly. Kai and Tom both sighed in relief and started to leave at a quick pace. "For now, that is."

Verdan chuckled to himself as the two Sorcerers all but fled the building. He wasn't so blind to think that everyone enjoyed research and experimentation, which made him appreciate their actions all the more.

He had a lot to think about now, but it was just approaching noon, so there was plenty of time left in the day for other business. The question was what to work on next. He needed to talk with Gwen at some point, but before that, he should go speak to Lieutenant Silver. They'd gotten off on the wrong foot last night, and Verdan didn't want to let things sit like this for too long.

The longer he waited before clearing up the misunderstanding, the more chance it wouldn't work, and he'd have made an enemy of a vital community member.

Mind made up, Verdan stopped at the house to let people know where he was going. Tom and Kai were discussing guard arrangements to watch over the estate when Verdan walked in.

"I'm heading to speak with Lieutenant Silver. I was hoping one of you would want to come along. I don't want to cause any more misunderstandings," Verdan said, still a little irritated about the issue from the night before.

Tom and Kai shared a silent look before Kai nodded and got to his feet. "I'll come with you. I have quite a bit of experience dealing with city guards."

"Good, let's go," Verdan turned around and headed back out at a fast walk, starting to retrace his steps from the night before, Kai hurrying to catch up with him.

"You seem more bothered by this than I had expected," Kai said, giving Verdan a curious look as they headed for the gate. "It was only a small misunderstanding. They'll figure out that you don't work in the same way as the sects eventually."

"'Eventually' isn't good enough," Verdan said, a touch of anger coloring his voice as the base of his staff beat out a firm rhythm on the ground. "I'm sorry, Kai, you didn't deserve that." Verdan slowed his walk and tried to get his emotions under control.

"No need to apologize," Kai said, waving the outburst away without a second thought. "This is the first time I've seen you like this, though. Is everything okay?"

"Yes, I'm fine," Verdan said shortly, grimacing as he realized he'd been a bit too short with Kai then. "It's difficult to explain."

"Is it because they assumed you would act like the sects and simply try to take over? Or is it because you were tempted to do so?" Kai asked softly, keeping his attention on Verdan.

"Am I so transparent?" Verdan asked, chuckling a little as he let go of the shame he'd felt at the thought. The temptation had been there on the walk back to the house, the thought that the guard were clearly not capable of managing on their own, so he should take charge.

"I don't know any sects that don't run the guard for their cities. Whether their motives are good or bad, they end up taking control in the end," Kai told him with an expressive shrug.

"I don't want to do it; as tempting as it is, it feels wrong," Verdan said slowly, realizing that the anger he'd felt at Kai's words had mainly been directed at himself. "In my homeland, I worked with the guards on a regular basis. I will see if I can have a similar relationship with them here."

"Perhaps," Kai said with another shrug. "The people of Hobson's Point have had some bad experiences with Sorcerers over the years. They'll be slow to trust any newcomers, especially strong ones."

"Sorcerers have a lot to answer for," Verdan said, shaking his head with a heartfelt sigh. He could almost feel the uphill battle that he was going to be constantly fighting to be considered different to them.

"They do. It's part of why I've linked myself to you. I can only do so much on my own," Kai said wearily, his heavy tone making Verdan look over in surprise.

"You've done a lot since we met. Don't underestimate yourself," Verdan admonished.

"Indeed I have, but alongside your own actions," Kai said, a hint of a sad smile on his face. "My attempt on my own ended up with my capture by the Cyth."

Verdan started to argue further to try and make Kai understand how much skill he wielded. He might not have Verdan's versatility, but the fire Sorcerer was a powerful combatant and deadly with his spear. Before Verdan could make his arguments, he realized they were at the gate they'd entered the night before.

None of the guards on duty looked familiar, but that was to be expected. Verdan hadn't expected to find Lieutenant Silver here. This was simply the best place to start.

"Excuse me. I was looking for Lieutenant Silver. Do you know where he is?" Verdan asked, walking up to a nearby guard. The man turned to regard Verdan as he approached, his eyes widening in recognition.

"He's off-duty right now, but he'll be meeting with the Commander later today at headquarters, Master Sorcerer." The guard answered promptly, obviously happy to be answering such an easy question and directing Verdan elsewhere.

"Please, just call me Verdan," Verdan said, restraining a sigh at the confused look on the guard's face.

"I know where the guard headquarters are. We can head down later today," Kai offered in a soft voice.

"Works for me," Verdan said before turning back to the guard. "Thank you for your help."

"Not at all, Sorcerer Verdan," the guard said, stumbling over Verdan's name.

Verdan gritted his teeth and smiled at the guard, ignoring the glint of amusement in Kai's eyes.

Verdan and Kai returned to the manor, Kai heading off to spar with Tim and cultivate his essence, while Verdan settled down to work on his gathering spiral.

A few hours of work let Verdan finally finish compressing his second spiral so that it was a cord of tightly-wound Aether that was itself curled around the first spiral.

With two completed, Verdan moved straight onto his third. The third spiral was when Wizards began to have enough Aether to work more-powerful spells. Not to the extent of the empowered fireballs that Verdan liked to use, but more like the blades of wind he often employed.

Thankfully, the more a Wizard used a concept and intent, the more solidified it became in his mind. A solid, strong concept meant high Aether efficiency, to the extent that Verdan was using spells that no other Wizard with a similar gathering spiral could manage.

Still, he was a long, long way from the thirty-four spirals he'd had when he'd been cursed. Thirty-six was the traditional threshold for a senior Wizard; he'd been so close.

Thankfully, the space where the Aether was housed in Verdan's core was still of the right size for thirty-four spirals. He could sit and actively draw in Aether for days and not hit his limit. He'd eventually have to work on increasing the size of his reserves, but he'd need to actually reach that limit first, which would take time.

A knock at the door broke Verdan from his meditation, and he looked up to see Kai standing in the doorway. Verdan updated his mental image for his spiral and set it to his subconscious again as he rose and quirked a brow at Kai, wondering what he wanted.

"It's coming up to late afternoon. I was checking when you wanted to go and visit the guard headquarters?" Kai asked, leaning against the doorway as he spoke.

"Now will do fine. I'll meet you downstairs in a few minutes," Verdan said, waving for Kai to head down.

Getting his things together, Verdan cleared his mind and shook off his thoughts of days gone by. While he didn't want to forget his old life, he didn't want to ignore his new life, either.

Heading downstairs, Verdan found Kai waiting outside the entrance to the manor, spear resting on his shoulder and a thoughtful expression on his face.

"After you," Verdan said, gesturing for Kai to lead the way. "Is something bothering you?"

"I've been thinking about what you were saying earlier. The idea of working alongside the guard is one I've had before, and I've done my best to do it, but it never worked properly." Kai said, speaking at a measured pace as he considered his words.

"Why didn't it work?" Verdan asked with interest.

"There's always a situation beyond their capability," Kai said as he led Vedan through the city. "If a few Sorcerers are supporting the local guard, it's not so bad, but there's never many. The greater the threat, the less the guard can do, and the more the Sorcerers take charge until they are running the whole thing."

"I see, and the sects taking in all the Sorcerers means that there are likely none in the guard, to begin with," Verdan said, Kai nodding in confirmation at his assumption. "Interesting. I will have to consider if there's anything I can do to assist."

"Here we are, the headquarters in Hobson's Point," Kai said, cutting off their conversation as they came up to a large building in the center of the city. Several guards were on watch outside, with a two-guard patrol leaving and heading off into the city as Verdan and Kai approached.

"Do you know the name of the person in charge?" Verdan asked as they headed for the entrance.

"No, I've not interacted with this guard very much. We probably should have brought one of the brothers with us," Kai said with a grimace of annoyance.

"Yes, actually, that would have been a very good idea," Verdan said, a little disappointed in himself for not thinking of that earlier. He wasn't on top form today, and that needed to stop. Verdan couldn't afford to be distracted right now, not when he was still establishing himself.

"Good afternoon, can we help you?" One of the guards outside the entrance to the building asked as they approached. The man eyed them both warily, his gaze lingering on Kai's spear and Verdan's staff.

"Yes, I was looking to speak with Lieutenant Silver. I understand he's here for a meeting?" Verdan kept it simple, not wanting to send any mixed messages.

"I'll see if he's available for you. In the meantime, if you don't mind waiting over there?" The guard asked them, waving to a bench set against the wall of the building. Once he was sure they were following his directions, the guard called over one of his colleagues and sent them inside with a message.

"Well, this should be interesting," Kai commented as they took a seat at the indicated bench.

Verdan nodded, noting how the guards were positioned and the seemingly-regular patrols they had. This was an organized system, and that boded well for cooperation between Verdan and the guard.

CHAPTER
TWENTY-FIVE

A FEW MINUTES passed as Verdan and Kai waited outside, idly discussing some of the areas around Hobson's Point that Kai had visited. Sadly, it seemed that the majority of the northern section of the continent had been abandoned. Verdan remembered Kai mentioning something along those lines before, but hearing how few settlements there were nearby really drove it home.

"Excuse me, Master Sorcerers, the Commander will see you now." A grizzled-looking guard came over to address them. Of all the guards they'd dealt with, this man looked the wariest of them, making Verdan wonder just what he'd had to deal with in the past. Surely Sorcerers weren't bad enough that simply speaking to them was a potential problem.

"Please, lead the way," Verdan said politely, rising to his feet and gesturing for the guard to go first. As the man turned away, Verdan gave Kai a look and mouthed the word 'Commander', but the Sorcerer shrugged and shook his head.

Intrigued by who they were meeting with, Verdan followed after the older guard, nodding to the original one he'd spoken to as they went past. The guard cautiously returned the nod but kept his focus on the job at hand, which was reassuring.

The more Verdan saw of the guards in the city, the happier he was with them individually. That just made him more confused about the state of play, though. Verdan didn't understand how professional and well-trained guards like this could let the surrounding countryside fall into ruin.

Verdan would be shocked if there were enough farms producing food for the city in the area by this time next year. He knew first-hand what Cyth would do with half a chance, let alone if they were running rampant like this.

The interior of the guard headquarters was part-administration, part-housing, and part-armory from what Verdan could see, as they made their way inside and up to a higher floor.

The guard knocked on a plain-looking door halfway down one corridor, pausing briefly before opening it and letting Verdan and Kai inside. Looking around, Verdan found himself inside an office with a large central table that had three men sitting around it.

A relatively small, bald man on the far side met Verdan's gaze without issue. There was a confidence there that was born of self-assurance, and Verdan took an immediate liking to the man.

At the end of the table to Verdan's left sat Lieutenant Silver, who was maintaining a carefully neutral expression. Opposite him at the far right of the table was another new face, but one that bore a lot more suspicion and not a little anger.

"Thank you, guardsman, we'll be fine from here," the bald man said, rising from his chair as he gestured for Kai and Verdan to sit opposite him. "Please, take a seat."

"Thank you," Verdan said, taking the offered seat while Kai remained where he was leaning against the wall next to the door. "Thank you for seeing me as well."

"Not at all. We're always welcoming to Sorcerers staying in Hobson's Point," the bald man said, his eyes flicking from Verdan to Kai and back.

"As long as they don't interfere in guard business," the angry-looking man on Verdan's right interjected, leaning forward to glare at Verdan with a hint of a sneer on his face.

"I apologize. I didn't realize that I'd been intruding?" Verdan said, raising a brow at the man who'd spoken. That was a lot of aggression from someone that Verdan hadn't met before.

"Intruding?" The man spat, his eyes narrowing angrily. "You've swanned into our city, taken control of a valuable estate, and started ordering about the local workers like you own the city. We won't put up with your kind here!"

"My kind?" Verdan asked, arching an eyebrow questioningly at the increasingly red-faced man.

"A Sorcerer who thinks they are better than us, that you can just take what you want without consequence. Don't think we've not noticed how you've poached two previous members of the guard and that you have a Witch working for you!"

Verdan felt Kai stiffen behind him at the mention of Gwen, but the bald man cleared his throat and drew the attention of the room back to him. "Lieutenant Michaels, if you can't maintain the necessary composure, I will ask you to leave." Michaels sneered at Verdan once more but kept his silence.

"I might not feel as strongly as my colleague, but I am also concerned," Lieutenant Silver said into the silence. "Hobson's Point has managed well enough without Sorcerer interference. We don't need a sect moving in and causing chaos."

"You are under a few misapprehensions here," Verdan said slowly, organizing in his mind the points he wanted to make. "The first thing to address is that I am not a Sorcerer, nor do I represent a sect. I am a Wizard first and foremost, similar in some regards to a Sorcerer, but very different at the same time."

"A Wizard?" The bald man asked with a touch of curiosity in his tone. "I haven't heard that term before."

"Lies already. What more proof do you need that he's working against us, Commander!" Michaels shouted, rising to his feet to point at Verdan.

"Enough!" The Commander snapped, not raising his voice but making it crack with authority as he silenced Michaels. "You are dismissed, Lieutenant."

Michaels opened his mouth to argue but thought better of it and instead stormed out of the room, glaring at Verdan and Kai as he went.

"I apologize for that. Lieutenant Michaels was out of order. While some of his concerns regarding your actions are warranted, there is no need for that kind of display," the bald man said with a frown as he glanced at the door that Michaels had stormed out through.

"I look forward to proving him wrong; I have only the best intentions for Hobson's Point," Verdan said, keeping his anger at the way Michaels had spoken to him firmly quashed.

"I certainly hope so. As you may have gathered, I am Commander Griffon, the overall leader of the city guard here. Lieutenants Michaels and Silver are my right and left hands, respectively. Lieutenant Michaels commands the eastern approach while Lieutenant Silver watches over the mountain pass."

"I see. Without wanting to cause offense, what about the land outside of the city?" Verdan asked in a neutral tone, not wanting to provoke the other men.

"We send out patrols, but there's little we can do. Most of the protection falls to adventurers now. The towns and villages hire them to patrol the area or drive off specific beasts." Griffon said with a scowl, clearly unhappy with the situation.

"Is it a question of manpower?" Verdan asked, probing for the reason they were unable to act.

"It's a question of capability," Silver said, gesturing to Kai as he continued. "My men are well-trained and ready to fight, but they are at a severe disadvantage. Sorcerers like your friend here can meet the creatures on their own terms, but if we tried that, the casualties would be severe."

"Is that why the logging camp to the north was left abandoned?"

"One reason, yes, though we were considering an expedition alongside some adventurers to resolve that. I believe you've taken care of it, however?" Griffon explained, arching a brow in Verdan's direction.

"To an extent, yes," Verdan said, launching into a quick summary of the issues they'd encountered, leaving out the Fwyn as much as he could and focusing on the Darjee side of things.

"That is concerning," Griffon said eventually, leaning back in his chair with a thoughtful expression. "I've heard of the Darjee before, but I've never encountered them myself. What are your thoughts, Lieutenant?"

"I believe we should focus on our more immediate concerns," Silver said after some thought. "The Darjee will be back, but we have time to prepare. For now, the other, more-local concerns are the priority, in my opinion. Particularly the most-recent situation."

"What situation is that?" Verdan asked.

"There's an elemental bear harassing a nearby village," Griffon said, gesturing to the east. "We've put out a request for someone to kill it, but so far, nothing. This particular variant has a layer of rock armor, so mundane weaponry is poorly suited to it. Magical weapons are rare this far north, so we're stuck waiting until someone with the right means decides to help." Griffon explained, giving Verdan a meaningful look that made it clear what he wanted.

Verdan sat in thought for a few moments as he considered the implications of what Commander Griffon had said. Verdan had assumed that the guard would have some form of magical countermeasure to monsters, but it seemed that instead, they just threw bodies at the problem. Such a hideous waste of life.

Still, with no Sorcerers, no Witches, and apparently no clerics or templars, Verdan could see how Griffon would have few options. He did mention magical weapons, and that they were rare, so some knowledge of enchantment might have survived, which was good. Still, enchanters were rare and hard to work with during the height of the empire, never mind now.

Thankfully, Verdan had some options to help them with, both in the short- and long-term. He'd need to look into an alchemical solution as well, but that could wait for when he had his equipment.

"I may be able to assist with this," Verdan said, breaking his silence as he considered the options he had. While he did want to help, he didn't want to intervene directly; that would only lead to the kind of dependency that none of them wanted.

"Excellent, I will organise a squad to lead you out to the village..." Commander Griffon started to say before pausing as Verdan raised a hand and shook his head.

"Actually, I have something else in mind. How familiar are you with temporary enchantments?" Verdan asked, pausing to take in the blank expressions on their faces before continuing. "A temporary enchantment is one that replicates what an enchanter can achieve with sigils, but through an Aether construct. The effect will last until the construct has run out of power, which will happen when the enchantment is triggered as well as passively over time. Does that make sense?"

"Not all of it, but I think I understood parts of that," Griffon said, his eyes narrowing in thought. "What you're saying is you could temporarily enchant the weapons of some of my guards?"

"Equipment in general, to be specific. Weapons are the most-common for temporary enhancements, however. I will need to work on the process and methodology, but the concept is doable." Verdan explained, part of his mind drifting back to when he used to do this for the guardsmen he worked with. Not even the Imperium could afford enchanted weapons for all its defenders, so Wizards like Verdan helped where they could.

"That would change everything," Lieutenant Silver said, eyes wide as he looked over at his commander.

"Yes, it would," Griffon muttered, looking down for a few seconds before nodding to himself and looking at Verdan once more. "We would need to see an example, first of all. If you can deliver what you've promised with this, that would go a long way to proving your good intent."

"I'll go one step further than that," Verdan said, the talk of the elemental bear preying on his mind. "Give me three types of weapons, preferably two melee and one ranged. I'll enchant them to better pierce and penetrate, and then you send that squad you mentioned after the bear with those weapons. Kai and Tom will go with the squad as support, allowing you to field test the weapons but ensuring that the problem is dealt with."

"What cost will this carry for us?" Griffon asked with a hint of resignation in his tone. No doubt he thought Verdan was going to fleece him for every coin he had for this. After just explaining how they needed exactly this kind of help, it wasn't like Griffon could turn down the offer either.

"Initially, nothing," Verdan said, spreading his hands as he spoke. "Consider this a gesture of goodwill on my part. In the future, I will ask for compensation for my expenditure of time and Aether, but I will be reasonable. I will also not spend all my time enchanting for you. I have my own projects to work on."

"That is very generous of you," Griffon said, his brows rising in surprise as he took in what Verdan was offering.

"I'm used to a more-cooperative relationship with the guard than what seems to be the norm around here," Verdan said with a slight shrug, not wanting to be celebrated for what he considered the bare essential level of support they deserved.

"I know you've said you're from somewhere far away, but I must admit that I struggle to imagine just how different such a place is if the city guard is supported like this," Griffon said, shaking his head slightly in disbelief. "Just how far did you travel to get here?"

"Too far," Verdan said succinctly, unable to help the sadness that coloured his tone.

"I have a question," Silver said, somewhat hesitantly. "You said that these will only be temporary enchantments. How do we know when they are about to expire?"

"That's a good point," Verdan said, musing on the issue with interest. Under normal circumstances, a Wizard would be there to watch the Aether levels, but that was obviously not going to work here. It was a relatively simple job to do, but it would require the ability to sense Aether first and foremost.

Two potential ideas occurred to Verdan. The first was showing Kai how to do it, an easy solution. The problem then was that the guard would forever hound Kai to join their patrols. In good conscience, Verdan couldn't do that to him.

The second idea was more work for Verdan, but in the long run, it might even be better. Just over one in five of the population should be Aether-sensitive, according to an old Imperium study, anyway. Under Imperial law, anyone with sensitivity was given the chance to become a Wizard, and around half of those sensitives were able to do so.

Those Aether-sensitive people should still exist now; they just lacked the support to become anything more. Verdan had no intention of training new Wizards, but some sensitivity training to keep track of enchantment strengths was something else.

"So," Verdan said, speaking slowly as he got his thoughts in order. "Thinking of the people under your command, are there any that are able to sense Sorcerers or their activity?"

The two guard officers exchanged a look and shook their heads, both looking equally confused by Verdan's apparent tangent.

"Right, let's go even more fundamental than that. Someone give me something you can carry in one hand," Verdan said, holding a hand out as he mulled over spell constructs and words of power.

"Here, will this work?" Lieutenant Silver asked, offering a short dagger hilt-first to Verdan.

"Yes, perfect," Verdan said, taking the dagger and laying it on top of the table. He remembered some vague notes on sensitivity training tools; this would be a bastardized version of that principle. "*Grym liff.*"

IMPERIAL WIZARD

IMPERIAL WIZARD
IMPERIAL WIZARD
IMPERIAL WIZARD
IMPERIAL WIZARD

"What was that?" Silver asked, cocking his head to one side in confusion as he stared at the dagger on the table.

"I've created a weak flow of Aether within the dagger—not enough to achieve anything, but enough to be felt. Here, hold the dagger. Good. Now, focus on the hilt in your hand, extend your sense of touch outside of your skin, and feel the ebb and flow of magic throughout the blade. Do you feel it?" Verdan instructed, watching with interest as Silver followed his instructions.

"No, nothing," Silver said after a few moments. Commander Griffon tried as well, to a similar outcome.

"No matter. Take that dagger and give your people the same test I gave you. If they do feel it, send them my way with the weapons; they will be your means of detecting if they need charging."

"Fascinating," Griffon muttered, turning the dagger over in his hand as he eyed it with a mix of suspicion and fascination.

"Please send over the equipment and soldiers tomorrow. I can't promise they will be ready by the end of the day, but I can start work with all due haste," Verdan instructed. It felt good to be of service again, though part of him was tempted to go out there and kill that bear himself.

"Very well. Thank you for your time, Wizard Verdan. You've given us much to think about," Griffon said, rising to his feet with a slight smile.

"Excellent. You know where I live if you have any questions," Verdan said, taking the dismissal for what it was and rising to his feet as well. That wasn't how he'd expected this meeting to go, but it was probably better overall.

CHAPTER

TWENTY-SIX

VERDAN BID the Commander and Lieutenant goodbye and stepped out of Griffon's office to find the same guard who'd brought them in waiting for them.

"This way, please," the guard said, motioning for them to follow as he retraced his steps and took them back to the entrance.

Verdan spotted Lieutenant Michaels lingering at the end of the corridor as they left. The Lieutenant saw them from the corner of his eye and turned to give Verdan a baleful look as they passed by.

Verdan wasn't clear on what he'd done to anger the other man, but something was clearly eating at him. It didn't seem to be anger at Sorcerers in general, or he would have directed some of that anger at Kai. Not that it mattered right now; either Michaels would get past it, or he wouldn't. There wasn't anything Verdan could do about it.

Kai waited until they were out of the building and heading back to the estate before asking the question that Verdan had been expecting. "Verdan, would you be able to enchant my spear in the same way?"

"Yes and no," Verdan said, holding up a hand to forestall any questions. "Yes, I could do it, but no, I won't. Giving you the same style of temporary enchantment I have in mind would be a waste. I have a few ideas for what to make for you and other Sorcerers, but I need to do a few tests first. In fact, I can probably find my way back from here on my own." Verdan reached into his pouch and pulled out a handful of silver. "Take these and head to the market. Get me a few copies of what everyone has to practice on. They don't need to be particularly well-made, but the quality of the materials needs to be there. Does that make sense?"

"It does," Kai said, his eyes bright and eager as he took the coins and headed off without further ado.

Verdan chuckled to himself and shook his head. Fighters like Kai were always the same; any suggestion of an upgrade to their weapon had their full attention. He wasn't sure how he would handle the enchantment for Kai's spear, but it seemed a waste to use his Aether to power it when Kai could provide the power himself.

Verdan hummed happily to himself as he walked back toward his estate along the causeway. He couldn't remember any examples of enchantments designed to use someone else's Aether—after all, what would be the point?

Any Wizard could make their own construct-based enchantment, which would no doubt be far more efficient than what Verdan was going to do for Kai. However, poor efficiency was better than nothing, and it was made all the sweeter by being something new and different.

It was a shame the alchemy equipment hadn't arrived yet, but experimenting with enchantment would be more than enough to keep him occupied for now.

_**_

To Verdan's surprise, he found Tobias and his butler, Brent, waiting with Tim and his wolf at the entrance to the Crea manor. Tim must have been the only one present when they arrived, and the ex-guard looked at Verdan with evident relief when he arrived. No doubt Tim was unused to hosting one of the most influential men in the city.

"Ah, Verdan, good to see you again," Tobias called out when he saw Verdan approaching them.

"Tobias, good to see you," Verdan said, hoping that this wasn't a sign of things going wrong. "Please, come inside."

"Thank you," Tobias said with a broad smile as he followed Verdan inside. The gaunt businessman still looked pale to an unhealthy degree, but it was nowhere near as bad as when Verdan had first met him.

"What can I do for you, Tobias?" Verdan asked as they settled themselves in the sitting room, Brent and Tim standing watch outside.

"Actually, Verdan, it's more a question of what I can do for you," Tobias said, his pale blue eyes twinkling as he crossed his legs and leaned back in the chair he'd chosen. "I was hoping to hear how your expedition went, and offer my expertise in acquiring some staff for the estate. I can't help but notice that you seem to lack any professional help for the domestic side of things."

"I hadn't considered that," Verdan said, cocking his head to one side as he considered Tobias's words. "How many staff would you recommend?"

"That depends entirely on what you need. Are you going to have helpers in the workshop, for instance, or just some help here in the manor?" Tobias questioned, his lips curving into a smile at Verdan's uncertain expression. "That doesn't include the need for guards and the like as well, though I think you needn't worry about that for the time being."

"Oh?" Verdan made a questioning noise, unsure of what Tobias was referring to.

"The people in this part of the city are a tightly-knit community, one that you seem to have won over quite nicely. Samuel is very influential, and he speaks highly of you. No one here would try anything, so you only need to worry about outsiders trying their luck."

"I see," Verdan said shortly. He hadn't realized Samuel had quite that much pull in the local area, but his being able to organize both the loggers and the glass workers made sense now. He'd have to speak with him again and see if he knew of anyone seeking work. Local men and women would make good guards once trained. "Leave the guard situation for now. I will address that myself, and the same for any helpers in the workshop. What do you recommend for the manor?"

"A housekeeper and a chef, which would form the foundation of the future staff you will no doubt have."

"Very well, and do you have any candidates?" Verdan asked, deciding to go with Tobias's proposition for now. Things could always be changed later, but it would be good to have some more organization.

"I do, actually; a husband and wife who worked for an old friend of mine. He passed away a few years ago, and they've been doing odd jobs here and there ever since. I could probably get them here today if you'd like to meet them?"

"Yes, that would work well with my schedule," Verdan said, considering the other tasks he had on his list. "What would their pay be?"

"I will handle that," Tobias said with a throwaway gesture. "Consider it my thanks for getting the logging camp cleared out. Once the lumber shipments start coming in again, I'll have more business coming through my warehouses, after all."

"Most appreciated," Verdan said, inclining his head to the other man in thanks. He didn't like being beholden to anyone, but Tobias's reasoning for his generosity made sense.

"My pleasure," Tobias said, a touch of humor in his voice. "Now, tell me about this expedition. I can't help but notice the wolf that young Tim has acquired, as well as the additional member of your group. I'm sure it must have been quite the trip!"

_**_

Tobias proved a most-appreciative audience for Verdan's recounting of their trip, though he left out any mention of the Fwyn, as he was unsure how Tobias would react. Right now, Tobias was a key part of Verdan's growing presence in Hobson's Point. Verdan didn't want to damage that by challenging too many preconceptions at once. It was enough that he was making them re-evaluate Witches, for now.

Kai had arrived with the spare weapons for testing while Tobias had been listening to Verdan. Seeing that Verdan was busy, the Sorcerer had placed them within one of the rooms in the workshop. Once Tobias left to gather the husband and wife he was recommending to Verdan, the Wizard took the chance to accompany Kai to where he had stashed the weapons.

Kai had managed to acquire three of each weapon type their group used for Verdan: swords for Tim, maces for Tom, and spears for

Kai. They were all laid out on a table for Verdan, and all seemed to be made of reasonable quality materials. It was hard to tell; Verdan was no blacksmith, but they all looked good enough for what he needed.

"This is perfect, thank you, Kai," Verdan said, picking up a sword first of all. Tim didn't have any power as far as Verdan was aware, so they were a good place to start. There was a chance that Verdan would damage the weapon through this process, so he wanted to start with the least-important ones.

"Do you need me for anything with this?" Kai asked, gesturing to the weapons on display.

"Maybe," Verdan said, drumming his fingers on the sword as he considered how this would all work. "If you could wait for the first one or two, then we'll know for certain."

Kai grunted his assent and leaned against the wall, watching with interest as Verdan pulled over a chair and sat with the sword across his legs.

Closing his eyes, Verdan sank deep into a meditative state, letting his mind freely wrap itself around the problem.

An Aether construct was all about storing an amount of Aether, with a set concept that included drawing on that storage. If Verdan removed that reserve of Aether, what he was left with was a concept and the framework that bound it.

The problem then was what concept to use. A cutting concept would be fairly universal, but the efficiency of using aspected Aether to achieve it would be variable. If Verdan was using a specific example of an element to cut, he could make it work—like using high-pressure water, for instance. But, he couldn't provide specific concepts and intents and still have the construct interact with any exterior Aether source. After a moment of consideration,

Verdan decided it was worth a try anyway, to see if the premise was sound, if nothing else.

With his action decided, Verdan considered what words of power to use. The right choice would make all the difference here. If possible, he wanted to keep it to two and rely on a clear concept for the strength of the construct.

"*Hyn liff*," Verdan intoned, providing as clear a concept as he could of what he wanted. The words were the same as those he'd used for the dagger he'd altered for the guard commander, but the concept was markedly different. If all went well, any exterior Aether fed into the blade would now be channeled into a cutting concept, enhancing the blade's edge.

Opening his eyes, Verdan examined the sword in his lap, noting the slight sheen that the metal now held. This was a clear sign that the Aether had taken hold within the material.

"Kai, here, can you sense anything?" Verdan asked, passing the blade over to the Sorcerer.

"Yes, but it feels like unaspected Essence before we draw it in. Is this what your Aether is?" Kai asked, his eyes on the blade as he ran a hand along its length.

"Yes, or rather, Essence is Aether, just aspected. That doesn't matter right now, though—try and feed in your Essence," Verdan said, deciding that it was going to be too much work to try and correct the terminology for everyone. Going forward, he'd refer to Aether for the energy in general and Essence for when it had been aspected by a Sorcerer. That would help keep confusion to a minimum.

"This feels strange. Normally only augmentors can add their Essence to items," Kai said, a frown furrowing his brow as he concentrated on what he was doing. "Wait, I think I figured it out.

You have to feed a strand in and then run the Essence through that."

"Whatever works for you," Verdan said, shrugging slightly. The terminology and method used didn't matter as long as the Essence went in.

"There—I have it," Kai said, exhaling heavily as he looked up from the sword, smiling victoriously at Verdan. "I never expected to be able to put my Essence in a weapon like this!"

"Very good," Verdan said, rising to his feet and walking over to look at the sword. There was a slight discolouration to the blade's sheen now, a discolouration that was steadily growing as the sword began to turn a dull red.

"Damn!" Kai yelped, dropping the sword and shaking his hands as if burnt.

"*Ast!*" Verdan barked, throwing a hand out to form a shield around the now-glowing blade. There was a palpable aura of heat around the sword now; the glow had become yellow-white and was steadily brightening.

"Out! Away from it!" Verdan said, pulling Kai into the corridor while maintaining the shield around the sword.

Another few seconds went past before the sword began to cool down, but the intense temperature had distorted its proportions. What had once been a reasonably well-forged sword was now misshapen and useless.

"Well, that was interesting," Verdan muttered, releasing the shield and nudging the damaged sword with the end of his staff. That hadn't been what he was expecting at all. This was going to require some thought.

TWENTY-SEVEN

VERDAN TAPPED a finger against his lips as he watched the second test sword peak at a bright red color before it started to cool. His initial idea had been that the amount of Essence that Kai had poured into the blade had overpowered Verdan's construct. However, with the results from this test, that didn't seem to be the case.

The second test had used a lot less Essence from Kai but had the same unfortunate result. While it could be that Kai needed to use even less Essence, Verdan doubted that was the case. It was more likely that there was another aspect to this that he hadn't considered yet.

Perhaps the issue was the use of Essence rather than Aether; that was the only other thing that jumped out at him. The problem Verdan had with that was that Essence was Aether, just aspected to a specific elemental concept.

"Tell me again how you cultivate your Essence," Verdan said, knocking the damaged sword off to one side with his staff before heading back to his chair.

"We meditate and draw in the world's energy from our surroundings. Though, that is what you call Aether, right?" Kai said, pausing to look over at Verdan for confirmation before continuing. "Right. So we draw in the Aether and regulate the flow by breathing exercises. As we draw it in, we focus on the concept that resonates with us, and the Aether is converted to Essence to be stored in our core."

"The Aether is converted to Essence," Verdan repeated, looking up at the ceiling for inspiration as he considered what Kai was saying. 'Conversion' was the key word here. Aspecting Aether to create Essence must have a more significant impact than Verdan had anticipated.

Thinking back on what Kai had said, Verdan's mind lingered on the description of how a Sorcerer focused on the concept they held while cultivating. That sounded almost like how Verdan held a concept in his mind to cast a spell.

Creating the Aether construct a third time, Verdan made a change for this one. He used the Aether to form channels within the blade, giving access to Kai's Essence but not trying to impart a concept to it. If Verdan were to add his Aether, it would do nothing, but he was confident that Kai's Essence would do something different.

"Kai, run your Essence through the blade, as before. However, this time, I want you to focus on the blade being wreathed in flames, like something an augmenter would do," Verdan instructed, eyes glittering with anticipation.

Kai nodded and took the blade, his eyes gaining a faraway look as he fed his Essence into it. The whole process was much smoother now on their third attempt than it had been at first, and it took Kai only a brief moment of concentration.

Kai had barely begun the process when fire began to lick out of the metal itself, enshrouding the top third of the blade with yellow flames. Kai dropped the sword immediately, mistaking it for the same issue as before.

The flames continued to writhe around the sword for a moment before the remaining Essence within was consumed, and it returned to its normal state. The blade itself was cool to the touch and completely unaffected by the fire, just as it should be.

"How?" Kai murmured, looking down at the sword with wide eyes.

"Your Essence must have an inherent concept attached to it. When it was entering the sword, the competing concepts were fighting each other, and the result was the sword itself being heated. You could form your own temporary enchantment by guiding the concept as you did." Verdan explained with a broad smile, rather pleased with himself.

"But, this is something only an augmenter should be able to do!" Kai half-objected.

"I'm not as confident with how Essence works now that it's demonstrably different, but I think you could learn to do this without me with some training. For now, I can put these temporary enchantments on, and it will work," Verdan said with a gesture to the sword. "The Aether will be used every time you channel Essence into the construct, and it will require a steady flow of Essence, but not a bad result, really."

"Not a bad result," Kai echoed, shaking his head in disbelief. "How many times could I use that construct of yours before it failed?"

"Let me see," Verdan said, examining the construct with his Aether senses. The integrity of the construct was good. There were a few areas where the Aether had been worn away but nowhere near enough to impact functionality. "It's hard to say. We'll need to examine it over time and compare the loss of integrity to usage."

"Right, of course," Kai said, giving Verdan a long look before shaking his head. "You do realize how many enemies you'll make with this, right?"

"Why would this make me any enemies?" Verdan cocked his head to one side, confused by the statement.

"A potential new way of doing things that allows non-augmenters to do something like this?" Kai shook his head and rubbed his face. "The sects won't like it, not one bit."

"Well, it's a good thing that there aren't any sects up here, then," Verdan said, bridling at the thought of someone limiting the research he could do for such a pathetic reason. "Besides, only I can make these, so the impact will be minor, for the moment."

Kai didn't say anything, but the look in his eyes told Verdan that the reality of the situation might not be so straightforward.

"Look, I'm not curtailing my work just because some idiots might take offense," Verdan said, his tone growing heated as he raged at the stupidity of humanity. "I might be academic by choice, but that doesn't mean I won't fight for what I believe in." A moment passed in silence before Kai inclined his head in acknowledgement, and Verdan sighed heavily as his anger faded. That was a bit much of a response on his part, but it cut right down to old wounds.

"Boss?" A faint call came from outside the room, interrupting them before Verdan could say anything further.

"I'll take a look," Kai said, grabbing his spear as he went to leave the room. Pausing at the door, Kai looked back at Verdan with a resolute expression, "For what it's worth, I feel the same. I'll back you up all the way."

Verdan sighed to himself as he heard Kai walk away. As much as what he'd said was true, he also didn't want that kind of conflict. Verdan was tired—tired of the unnecessary fighting, of the doubt and the politics of it all.

The fight against the Darjee with the Fwyn had been almost a relief for him. The good and bad had been clear to see, there were no moral shades of grey, and he'd had good support from his allies. Even so, Tim had almost died in the process, and Verdan didn't want any more blood on his hands.

Shaking himself out of it, Verdan put the test swords to one side and headed out to see what was going on.

Verdan caught up with Kai at the entrance to the workshop, where he was talking with Tim.

"What's going on?" Verdan asked as he walked over to them. Tim glanced at Kai for permission before turning to Verdan and answering his question.

"There's a couple at the gate for you, Mr. and Mrs. Barbeau. They said that Mr Brock had sent them your way. I got one of the local lads to watch them while I came to find you."

"Good work, Tim," Verdan said, glad that Tim hadn't just let them wander in or left them unsupervised. "Bring them over to the manor and give your assistant this." Verdan passed Tim a few copper darns for the man he'd conscripted and sent him on his way.

"Who are they?" Kai asked as the two of them started toward the manor.

"Tobias said he was sending a prospective housekeeper and chef my way. This sounds like it might be them," Verdan said, unsure of who else might be trying to visit him.

Kai waited with Verdan at the entrance to the manor as Tim brought over their visitors, his wolf companion walking along at his side. Some of her silver fur was stained dark red around her neck, reminding Verdan that he had to look at helping her sooner rather than later.

Putting that aside, for now, Verdan stepped forward to welcome Mr. and Mrs. Barbeau. Mrs Barbeau was a middle-aged woman with some streaks of gray running through her dark hair. She smiled warmly at Verdan, and seemed to exude a motherly aura.

Her husband, by contrast, looked to be a few years younger despite his short, gray hair. Like Tobias, Mr. Barbeau had a gaunt physique, but he didn't look as unhealthy as Tobias had when Verdan had first met him.

"Welcome. My name is Verdan Blacke. I'm the new owner here," Verdan said as they drew near.

'"A pleasure to meet you, Mr. Blacke. My name is Adrienne, and this is my husband, Henry." Adrienne gave him something approaching a curtsy, and Henry bowed silently. "Mr. Brock sent us to discuss an opening in your household. if you have time?"

"Ah, please, none of that. Call me Verdan, and, of course, please come inside," Verdan said, opening the manor's front door and waving everyone in.

"Boss, I don't want to impose, but Sylvie's collar is cutting her a fair bit. Can you take a look?" Tim asked softly once the Barbeau's had gone inside with Kai.

"Sylvie?" Verdan queried, a smile tugging at his face despite the situation as he gave Tim a judgemental look.

"What, she's silver, and I can't just call her 'wolf,' can I?" Tim crossed his arms defensively, blushing a little. Silvie whined softly and rubbed her head on Tim's knee, making him smile and absently muss her head.

"Of course, that would be silly," Verdan murmured, masking his amusement as he crouched down and tried to get a look at the wolf's collar.

Understanding his intent, Sylvie sat down and turned her head away, exposing the collar and the bloody flesh around it. From what Verdan could tell, the collar prevented the flesh from ever fully healing around it, causing it to remain as a partially-open wound. The risk of infection was high, let alone the pain and discomfort.

"*Iacha*," Verdan rested a hand on Sylvie's head, sending a burst of positive energy into her. Verdan did his best to direct it to heal the wolf physically, but the vile corruption in the collar worked against the Aether as soon as it entered her.

Having healed the wolf several times now, Verdan was becoming more familiar with the corruption within the collar and how it acted against him. He estimated that it was reducing the efficacy of his Aether to a mere third of what it would normally accomplish.

The flesh around the collar was somewhat healed, but that was all. It was enough to hopefully reduce the pain the wolf was in, but nowhere near as much as Verdan wanted.

The more Verdan interacted with this form of corruption, the more frustrating he found it. Cyth corruption would have just fought directly against his Aether, letting him break it down directly. The collar, however, acted to suppress any Aether entering the wolf but didn't stop it from acting. It was far more subtle and more effective.

"Thank you," Tim said, a sad smile touching his face as he looked at the freshly-healed flesh. "She doesn't let it stop her, but I can tell it hurts her."

"I'm reluctant to do this, but I can't wait any longer while she's suffering. Head into the city, see if you can get a sleeping draught and a surgical kit. We'll try and sort everything today."

"Got it, thanks, Boss," Tim said, straightening under Verdan's touch. "Come on, Sylvie, let's go grab everything."

Verdan watched Tom walk away, Sylvie at his heels, and ran a hand through his hair; he hated feeling so helpless. The coming operation was risky, but he dared not involve anyone else, not with this strange corruption contained in it.

"Verdan?" Kai asked from behind him, reminding Verdan that he had other things to deal with.

"I'll be right in," Verdan said over his shoulder, taking a moment to compose himself before following Kai into the manor's sitting room.

_**_

"So, Tobias told me that you and your husband used to work for a friend of his, is that right?" Verdan asked, taking a seat opposite Adrienne.

"Yes, that's right, it was Mr. Brock's cousin. She was a touch eccentric, but that means we're used to odd happenings around the house, which Mr. Brock said would be the case for you." Adrienne gave him a warm smile as she spoke, her husband bobbing his head in agreement.

"Yes, well, that will likely be the case," Verdan said honestly. At this point, things were already quite strange, and it would only get more so over time. "So, why do you want to work here, knowing that?"

"Henry and I like to support new things being done, not just keeping things the same. By that, I mean that we like working for an active employer and doing what we can to help them. People underestimate the worth of having a well-run household, but I can confidently say that it makes everything easier." Adrienne lifted her chin as she spoke, challenging Verdan to gainsay her.

Henry tapped a finger on the armrest of his chair, getting Adrienne's attention, before flicking his long fingers through a series of shapes.

"Ah, yes, Henry says that he also makes a fantastic mushroom and steak pastry," Adrienne said, smiling lovingly at her husband before looking over at Verdan. The confusion on his face must have been clear as Adrienne chuckled and reached over to pat Henry's hand. "My husband is mute. It's why we always work as a pair. His skill in the kitchen is top-notch, however."

"I hope you don't mind me asking, but is it a physical issue?" Verdan asked gently, not wanting to give offense.

"We don't know; he was born this way. We communicate well enough with hand signs, though. By now, I know the way he thinks," Adrienne said, squeezing Henry's hand as they shared a warm smile.

"Well, Tobias has said he'll be paying you for the time being, so I see no reason not to give you a chance. You're welcome to start whenever is convenient for you," Verdan said, enjoying the broad smiles on their faces.

"Would tomorrow work for you?" Adrienne asked after a glance at her husband.

"Perfect," Verdan said, starting to rise from his chair before pausing as he thought of a problem. "Where do you live at the moment? Is it far away?"

"On the other side of the city, but Mr. Brock put us in touch with a man named Samuel. He said there's an empty house we can move into that's just a minute or two away."

"Never mind then," Verdan said with a wry smile. It seemed that all the details had already been taken care of.

"We'll start moving our things across now, and then be here bright and early tomorrow," Adrienne said, pausing as her husband signed something. "Ah, do you have any preference for your breakfasts?

"I'm a big fan of bacon and egg sandwiches in the morning, but I'm open to trying new things as long as there's enough for everyone," Verdan said before turning to Kai. "See if Samuel has some people he can send to help them move their things over, please." Verdan tossed Kai a pair of silver darns that the Sorcerer caught with a nod.

"Thank you, Verdan," Adrienne said, hesitating over using his first name for a moment.

"Not a problem," Verdan said, happy to help them and the local workers at the same time. "I look forward to your cooking tomorrow." Verdan addressed the last to Henry directly, making the other man smile and nod in response.

Seeing them out the door, Verdan headed back to his workshop. He was going to meditate and work on his gathering spiral for an hour or two and then maybe work on that enchantment some more. If he could improve the resilience of the construct to the foreign Essence, it would last longer and be more efficient for Kai.

_**_

Tim found Verdan in his workshop a few hours later, a small cloth sack in one hand and a leather case in the other.

"I've found everything I can, Boss," Tim said, hoisting both his burdens onto the table next to the sword Verdan had been working on.

"One moment, let me tidy up," Verdan said, holding a hand up for Tim to wait as he organized his work. "Right, show me what you have."

"I didn't find a sleeping draught, there aren't any alchemists in the city anymore, and the herbalist I found doesn't know the recipe to make them. They did have the ingredients that the Crea family used to order for them, though, which were these," Tim said, pushing the small satchel over to Verdan.

Opening it up, Verdan found a bundle of purple leaves and a corked flask of clear liquid. Pulling out the leaves, he noticed that they had a gradient of color, starting as a light lilac in the center and ending at a deep violet at the edge.

"I don't recognise these. What are they?" Verdan asked, carefully sniffing the leaves and noting their slightly sweet smell.

"Dusk Valarias—not that I know what that is—and the bottle is full of moonwater she made," Tim said, somewhat nervously. "She didn't know the potion's recipe or if anything else was needed, but this was what they bought from her."

"Moonwater, of course it is," Verdan muttered with a sigh, eyeing the clear liquid in the bottle with mixed feelings. Moonwater was made by leaving an open container out in the light of a full moon, which caused it to be purified and become a great medium for medicines.

Moonwater was a great example of Parada, the most mystical and frustrating of the energy types. Just putting a bowl of water out in the moonlight did nothing, but if you did it through a ritual with the intent to purify it with the light of the moon, you got moonwater. It was maddening; it made no sense for the intent to come before the energy. One study had even shown that the ritual itself didn't matter, just that one was done, and it was taken seriously.

Exactly why it was being used for a sleeping potion mystified Verdan, and he was confident that they were missing at least one ingredient. If the moonwater replaced the distilled water he was used to; it was likely that the dusk valarias were the primary ingredient. That still left an adjuvant or something to draw the effect of the plant into the potion.

"She didn't know any part of the recipe, or what else was used?" Verdan asked, just to be sure.

"No, sorry, Boss. She said that the Crea did it all themselves; she just provided the herbs and things she gathered. She had a surgical kit; her husband was a doctor." Tim patted the leather case as he spoke, reaching down to unlatch it and show Verdan the contents. Everything Verdan expected of a non-magical kit was there; he'd be able to at least make a good attempt at removing a lot of the collar with this.

Verdan paused as something Tim said registered with him, and he frowned. "The Crea? As in the family that owned this estate?"

"Yeah, they were the last alchemists in the city. The rest headed south where the money is," Tim said with a shrug.

"Well, it looks like I know my next stop then. I'll finish up here first, but come find me at the guest house in a few hours if you've not heard from me first, okay?" Verdan said absently as he clipped the kit closed and moved the two bundles off to one side.

"Sure thing, Boss, thanks again for this," Tim said, his easy smile unphased by the missing ingredient or their lack of a recipe.

Verdan wasn't sure what he'd done to deserve such faith, but he was damned if he was going to let Tim down on this.

"Don't worry, we'll sort something out," Verdan said, putting on an assured front for Tim's sake.

_**_

The guest house of the estate was the old servants quarters at the rear of the workshop. It was a decent-sized building, designed to house a number of people, but was now solely occupied by Natalia Crea, the last surviving member of her family.

When Verdan first came to look at acquiring the estate, one of the conditions that Tobias had told him of was that the new owner be an alchemist. Verdan was hoping that this desire to see the alchemy carried on meant that Natalia still had some of her family's knowledge stored away. It was a slim hope, but it was all Verdan had to go on.

Coming to a halt at the front door, Verdan gathered his thoughts for a moment before knocking. This was going to be a delicate conversation.

A few moments passed before Natalia opened the door, her reaction at his presence hidden by the same black lace veil that she had worn when he last saw her.

"Wizard Blacke, to what do I owe the pleasure?" Natalia asked, her husky voice sounding somewhat strained as she touched the tops of the elbow-length gloves she wore to seemingly reassure herself they were there.

"I need a favor. If you have a few moments?" Verdan asked, mentally crossing his fingers that she wouldn't just reject the idea out of hand.

"I can listen, but I make no promises," Natalia said, stepping to one side and gesturing to the hall behind her. "Please, come inside."

"Thank you," Verdan stepped inside and propped his staff against the wall before following Natalia through to a room not too dissimilar to the sitting room in the mansion.

"So, what favor have you come to ask?" Natalia asked as she sat on one of the chairs. While she wasn't dressed to match the veil and gloves, instead wearing a simple dress, Verdan couldn't help but admire her elegance and poise. His arrival must have been a complete surprise, but she acted as if this was all expected.

"It's a somewhat delicate situation, but I hope you'll be able to help," Verdan said, taking a seat opposite her as he gathered his thoughts. "You may have seen Tim and his wolf, Sylvie, around the estate. We rescued Sylvie from the Darjee when we went north, but they put a horrific collar on her. I have some modest healing skills, but the corruption within the collar is actively working against my magic."

"I see, but I'm not sure how I can help with this." Natalia said as Verdan paused.

"I aim to remove the worst of the collar from her surgically. Hopefully, that will weaken its resistance; I was hoping for your aid in creating a sleeping potion to keep her unconscious through the procedure. Tim acquired some ingredients from a herbalist that used to supply to your family, but we're missing something, and I need equipment and a recipe. Can you help us?"

"You're asking for a lot. I've tried to put alchemy behind me," Natalia said after a few moments of silence. "Why now, why this urgency? Can you not order the recipe and wait for your own equipment?"

"She's waited long enough for some relief, only my reluctance to go this far has been stopping me. Now I'm doing it, I can't in good conscience make her wait."

"You talk about the wolf like it's intelligent," Natalia remarked in a questioning tone.

"She's no ordinary creature, that's for certain," Verdan said, sighing as he ran a hand through his hair. "Yet another reason to resolve things now. She's too intelligent to leave like this."

"Very well," Natalia said, taking a deep breath and squaring her shoulders before continuing. "I will help you prepare, but don't expect me to aid in the creation of the potion. That will be entirely down to you."

"Thank you," Verdan said earnestly, "I will make the potion in one of the rooms I've set up in the workshop. I just need the recipe and some equipment."

"Good. Now, what ingredients do you already have, and how strong does the potion need to be?"

"I have moonwater and dusk valarias, but I'm short one ingredient. I believe it would be something to draw out the properties of the plant, but I leave the specifics to you."

"Hmm," Natalia remained silent for a moment before nodding to herself. "I know the recipe you are looking for. The remaining ingredient is shadow Dryd, which needs to be mixed into the moonwater alongside the dusk valarias, but only once the leaves are ground. I have a small collection of Dryd in storage. Some shadow Dryd won't be a problem."

"What is 'shadow Dryd'?" Verdan asked, eager to learn from someone with practical knowledge.

"You're unfamiliar with Elemental Dryd?" Natalia said, cocking her head to one side with interest when Verdan shook his head. "I remember you saying you were a novice, but this is beyond what I expected."

"The small amount I have done is likely very different to your own methods, though I'm willing to learn."

"Very well. Elemental Dryd is the result of refining the organs of various magical creatures. The process is somewhat esoteric and varies from alchemist to alchemist, but my family were experts at harvesting fire and acid Dryd." Natalia rose and gestured for Verdan to follow as she led him back out of the room. Her pride in her family was evident in her voice, but so was the underlying melancholy.

"Fascinating. So does the process change depending on the type of Dryd you're trying to create?"

"Yes, and by the type of creature at that. There are a number of factors, including the strength of the Essence in the creature," Natalia said, a hint of passion entering her voice as she explained.

"Would you be willing to teach me some of this process?" Verdan asked, regretting the question the moment he spoke. He could visibly see the tension flow through Natalia's body, and she tugged anxiously on her gloves before shaking her head.

"I've left that behind me. It's no longer who I am," Natalia said quietly, stopping outside a hefty-looking door and pushing it open. "The Dryd is on one of the shelves, you'll need only a small container, and even that will make several potions."

"Thank you," Verdan said, cursing himself as he stepped into the storage room and sought out the Dryd that she had mentioned. He'd known that she was scarred, both mentally and likely physically, by her past. Jumping straight to her teaching him had been a big mistake; he'd been too eager by far.

Looking around the room, Verdan saw that it contained a well-organized and precisely-labeled selection of equipment and ingredients. As Natalia had said, there was a whole shelf dedicated to various containers of Dryd, showcasing a variety of aspects. Given her statement on their expertise, it wasn't a surprise that the majority of the Dryd was fire or acid aspected, with one or two singular containers being more specific variants on those themes, like lava or corrosion.

Seeing those more specific aspects made Verdan think of how Tom's earth magic was very stone-focused; perhaps it carried over to Sorcerers as well. If so, that presented a whole range of interesting ideas, as there were countless sub-sections to an element. After all, a sub-section was all about intent and specific circumstances, so what the term 'lava' meant for one person wasn't going to be exactly the same as someone else. Close enough for grouping, yes, but not exactly the same.

Grabbing the Dryd container and an empty box, Verdan loaded up with a few empty vials, a mortar and pestle, and a few odds and ends he might need. Satisfied he had everything, he headed back into the corridor, closing the door behind him.

Her veil hid Natalia's expression, but Verdan could tell from the way she held herself that she was still uncomfortable.

"Thank you for this. Is there anything I can do to repay you?" Verdan asked, gesturing to the box he held with his chin.

"Perhaps, I will need to think about it," Natalia said hesitantly, her voice soft and uncertain.

"When you have decided, please seek me out. I am at your service," Verdan straightened and gave her a half-bow. He owed her for this, and it was a good excuse to spend more time with her.

Since waking up in this new world, Natalia was the first person he'd met who seemed to share his passion for learning and knowledge. When she had been explaining about Dryd, it had almost been like he was speaking with a different woman altogether. He wouldn't pester her, but if she came to him for something, it would be a good chance to talk through some more questions he had about alchemy.

"Thank you, Wizard Blacke," Natalia said somewhat stiffly. "I wish you success with your operation."

"Thank you," Verdan said, inclining his head once more before heading back toward the front of the building. He didn't want to overstay his welcome, and he could sense his presence was becoming a bit too much for her.

Verdan got the last few instructions on amounts and the process as they walked to the door. He was confident he could replicate the fairly straightforward recipe now. Satisfied with what he had learned, Verdan left the guest house and started back toward the workshop. There was a lot to do and little time to do it in.

_**_

"Moonwater here, ground dusk valarias here, and shadow Dryd to one side," Verdan muttered to himself as he arranged the ingredients on the workbench in front of him. He'd already ground half of the leaves of the dusk valarias, the sweet smell of the leaves becoming far more prevalent as he worked.

Moving the moonwater to a larger container, Verdan added the ground leaves and a few pinches of shadow Dryd. The Dryd was a gray, coarse, sand-like substance with an odd texture to it. As he added it to the mixture, the Dryd dissolved almost instantly into the moonwater.

Natalia's instructions were to add the Dryd until the dissolving process slowed, which would indicate that there was enough for the number of dusk valarias that he had used.

Watching carefully with his Aether senses, Verdan added more Dryd to the mixture. Interestingly, Verdan was able to watch as Aether spread out from the crushed leaves to infuse the surrounding moonwater. There was insufficient strength in just the leaves to infuse the whole flask, but the shadow Essence from the Dryd was changing when it encountered the Aether from the leaves, propagating it across the whole flask.

Fascinating. This was an extremely interesting interaction between Aether and Essence. The Aether from the leaves had an inherent intent, a property of the plant itself, whereas the Essence coming from the Dryd was aspected but had no accompanying intent that Verdan could sense. The two then combined to provide both intent and aspect for the new potion.

Verdan's eyes went wide as he realized why there were so many forms of Dryd in Natalia's storage room. Not all aspects would suit the intent of the potion; it would make no sense for a fire aspect to work to put a creature to sleep, for instance.

Adding a last pinch of Dryd, Verdan watched as the last part of the moonwater became infused with the intent of the dusk valarias. Now he knew that the Dryd was providing the raw power for the potion. He didn't need to judge the amount by the rate at which it dissolved; he could do it by eye.

Verdan smiled happily as he considered how much Dryd he would save compared to the average alchemist. From what Natalia had said about the amount to use, he was only using two-thirds of the recommended amount. Anything further would add more

Essence to the mix, but it wouldn't improve the actual effect of the potion.

Corking the flask he'd mixed everything into, Verdan looked at the mixture with pride. His first foray into alchemy was a success and had yielded quite a few interesting results, not the least of which was the use of moonwater. Previously, Verdan would have used Aether-purified water as the base for a potion, but the ease with which the Essence and Aether spread through the moonwater was impressive.

Drumming his fingers on the table, Verdan considered what to do next. There were a few things he could set his hand to, but nothing as urgent as the surgery.

No, it was time to do what he could.

CHAPTER
TWENTY-EIGHT

"WE'RE HERE, Boss. Where do you want her?" Tim asked as he came in, Sylvie padding into the room behind him.

"Up on here, please, Sylvie," Verdan said, addressing the wolf directly, much to Tim's surprise. He'd prepared a workbench for the procedure, using his magic to scour it clean earlier.

Sylvie leapt up onto the workbench with surprising grace, sitting down where Verdan had pointed without complaint.

"Good, now, drink this, please," Verdan said, placing a bowl in front of Sylvie and pouring in the sleeping potion. The wolf obediently started to lap up the potion, confirming Verdan's suspicions on how much it could understand.

Tim didn't say anything, but Verdan could see a thoughtful expression on his face. Perhaps he was realizing what Sylvie could understand as well. Looking back to the wolf, Verdan watched carefully to ensure that she drank the whole potion, nodding to himself in satisfaction once she was done.

Natalia had told him that the potion was fast-acting, but it was still a relief to see it impact Sylvie almost immediately. At first, the wolf began to look sluggish, but in short order, that progressed to her falling asleep on the table.

Waving for Tim to be patient, Verdan gave it another few minutes for the potion to take full effect before gently shaking Sylvie. Thankfully, the silver-furred wolf didn't even twitch; she was well and truly out of it.

"Okay, grab the kit. It's time to get to work," Verdan said, taking a deep, steadying breath as Tim grabbed the surgical kit and laid it out next to the unconscious wolf.

Taking a pair of clippers, Verdan started to remove the fur around the collar, rolling her over partway through to get to the other side. A lot of her fur had been damaged by the collar, so it wasn't as bad as it might have been.

With the surrounding fur removed, Verdan studied the collar in more detail, noting three parts to its structure. There was the collar itself, the fragments of bone that were woven through the collar and her skin, and the longer piton-like hooks that went deep into Sylvie's flesh.

With nowhere obvious to begin, Verdan started with one of the long filament pieces of bone. Pushing the leather of the collar down to expose the bone, Verdan attempted to cut through it with the clippers.

The sharp iron tools had performed well against her fur, but they weren't enough to get through the bone. It was clear that the heavy corruption running through this foul thing was protecting it from outside interference.

"*Torr*," Verdan said aloud, putting a basic Aether construct onto the clippers that would enhance their cutting ability and feed from his Aether directly.

Reaching down, Verdan exposed the piece of bone once more and tried to cut it with the clippers. Immediately he felt resistance, as something pushed back against the Aether, but the effect was far less than when he had been healing Sylvie.

The snap of the bone cracking between the blades of the clippers was a welcome sound, and Verdan placed the clippers to one side before carefully grasping the thin piece of bone with some forceps and drawing the two pieces out. The blood-covered bone felt slick and greasy in Verdan's hands, and he was quick to drop the disgusting thing into a nearby box. He'd put all the pieces in there and burn the whole thing later.

With a single, small piece of the collar removed without issue, Verdan felt a bit of tension leave him. He'd been concerned that there would be more protection on the collar, but it seemed totally focused on the creature wearing it.

Picking up the clippers once more, Verdan ensured they were brimming with Aether before cutting as many bone strands as he could. Tim followed along behind him, pulling the fragments free using the forceps and dropping them into the box.

Considering that this must be quite far outside Tim's zone of comfort, his hand was steady, and he was focused entirely on the task. Verdan was impressed. Competency was a rare beast. It was always nice to see.

Slowly, they worked across the whole collar, removing a disturbing amount of bone in the process. Periodically, Verdan would pause and give Sylvie a small healing pulse, just enough to accelerate her natural healing slightly.

Once the threads of bone were removed, the collar was only held in place by the four pitons of bone that went deep into her neck. Cutting around the pitons, Verdan pulled away the leather of the collar, forcibly keeping his thoughts away from just what sort of leather it was.

Dismissing the construct on the collar, Verdan took a scalpel from the kit and applied a similar construct to it, magically enhancing its ability to cut. Once done, Verdan turned his attention to the final portion of the collar, the pitons.

The pitons came an inch or so out of the wolf's flesh but were thick enough to give the impression of their size. Grasping the end of one of them, Verdan gave it an experimental tug, but it was caught on something within her.

Verdan had suspected that they were kept in place somehow, but he'd wanted to check before going in with the scalpel; the less damage they did here, the better.

Cutting in and around the first piton, Verdan quickly found the issue; there were barbed protrusions around the outside of the bone. There was no way this was a natural shape, which meant they were there by design, a sickening display of magic that made him glad they'd killed all the Darjee they found.

The whole thing was around four inches long, one on the outside and three deep into Sylvie's neck, but thankfully the barbed protrusions were in the middle, so Verdan didn't have to cut all the way down.

Throwing the foul piton into the box, Verdan gave Sylvie a dose of healing before moving on to the next one. She'd lost a lot of blood through this, but he could see the wounds closing on her neck as his healing accelerated her natural rate. In fact, now that he thought about it, her wounds were healing at a rate far higher than he'd expected from the Aether he'd used. Considering that there was still some corruption produced in the collar's remnants, that was particularly impressive.

Filing the information away for the moment, Verdan turned back to the task at hand and began to remove the other pitons. Each one required several cuts around it for Verdan to peel the flesh back far enough that the barbs would come free without ripping great wounds in Sylvie's flesh.

One of the tenets of healing magic was that less trauma meant faster healing. It was easy to seal two pieces of flesh together after they'd been sliced apart; repairing a jagged gash from ripping something free, not so much.

It was the bloodiest, messiest part of the operation, but soon enough, they were done. The last blood-soaked piece of barbed bone was tossed into the box, and Verdan was free to focus on healing Sylvie.

The corruption within the wolf was still strong; the collar's removal weakened it, but it was still powerful enough to drastically reduce his Aether's efficacy.

Much like with Gwen's recovery, it would take Sylvie a few days to fully cleanse herself, maybe longer. This form of corruption wasn't one that Verdan was familiar with; he was basing his judgment on Cyth corruption. Regardless, Sylvie had held up well, and the job was done; now she just needed to rest.

"Is that it, are we done?" Tim asked, bloodied forceps still at hand in case he needed to do anything further.

"Yes, all done. It's down to her now, but we've got rid of that foul thing," Verdan said, his lip curling as he looked down at the box.

"Thanks, Boss. I realise how much this all took and how much magic you used on her," Tim said, gesturing at the blood-soaked fur around Sylvie's neck. "What I'm saying is, I owe you for this, and I won't forget it."

"No, no, you owe me nothing," Verdan said with a shake of his head. "I'd do this for anyone or anything I found with such a horrific collar. No one deserves this."

"That's as may be," Tim said, his jaw firming and his brow furrowing as a stubborn look came over him. "But I still owe you one, and you'll not talk me out of it."

"I won't argue with you, even if you're wrong," Verdan said, a ghost of a smile on his lips as he did some final checks and channeled a bit more Aether into Sylvie, ensuring that she wasn't bleeding anywhere. "There, she's good to go. I'm going to dispose of the refuse, take her back to the mansion, and clean her up a bit. She's going to be groggy and sore when she wakes."

"Sure thing, Boss," Tim said, his attention fully on Sylvie now that Verdan had declared that he was done. There was something in Tim's eyes that looked a bit off, a sort of worry that Verdan wasn't expecting with how well that had all gone.

"What's wrong? You look concerned?" Verdan asked softly.

"Do you think she'll stay now that she's all healed up?" Tim asked, his voice little more than a whisper as he softly stroked the silver fur on her side. "I've never had a companion like this before. She's already become such a big part of my day, of my life. It's always been me and Tom, never anyone else."

"You wouldn't try to make her stay if she wanted to go?" Verdan asked, curious about what Tim would say.

"No, that wouldn't feel right at all," Tim said, frowning to himself as he muttered his answer. "She's not a pet. Sylvie's too smart for that; you saw her before. It's almost like she can understand us.

Sometimes I think she's just as mentally there as any other person, but I don't know if I'm imagining it."

"I don't think you are," Verdan said, mentally kicking himself as he realized how little contact modern-day humans had with non-human sapients. "The Darjee captured her, and they hunt sapient creatures. That alone would be enough for me to agree. Beyond that, she acts like no wolf or dog I've ever known, beyond her desire to follow you around."

"I never thought of that," Tim said, face pale as he looked down at his companion in a whole new light. "So, if she isn't a wolf, what is she?"

"Who knows? For all we know, she actually is a wolf, just one that's a breed apart," Verdan explained with a shrug; it made no real difference what she was at the end of the day.

"I was hoping you'd ease my mind, Boss, not make things even more complicated," Tim said, rubbing his temples with his eyes shut.

"Well, the potion will have been somewhat countered by the corruption, so I would expect Sylvie to transition to a normal sleep in a few hours. Take that time to think about everything and set the tone for your relationship now that she's free. If she does understand us, perhaps simply asking her what she wants is the way to go. Why make it more complicated?"

"Yeah, I suppose it is that simple," Tim said with a laugh, shaking his head at himself. "Sorry, Boss, I'm getting all worked up over nothing here."

"No need for that. I've seen my share of weird and wonderful things. It's nice to put that knowledge to use every now and then," Verdan said with a warm smile, patting Tim on the shoulder as he started to gather up the various pieces of equipment they'd used and run a cleaning spell over them. "Now, help me clean up."

_**_

Verdan started the next day with a quick energy spell to perk him up. He'd ended up staying later at the workshop than expected after the surgery, but he was satisfied with both his progress on the third spiral and the improvements to the construct for Kai's spear. He'd used up two of the spares they had in the meantime, but he was confident enough now to work on Kai's actual spear.

Once that was done, he'd need to test with Tom to see if the same construct would work, or if they'd need to make any changes to the design for his weapon. Verdan was quietly confident in his construct, but thorough testing was the key to success.

Heading down to the kitchen, Verdan found both Kai and Henry already present. For a change, Kai wasn't the one making breakfast and was instead sitting with a crumb-covered plate in front of him.

Henry perked up as Verdan walked in and arched a surprisingly expressive eyebrow at him with a grin. Seeing he had Verdan's attention, Henry tapped what looked like a fresh loaf of bread and then a ceramic container filled with eggs before making a questioning motion.

"The eggs, please. Do you have any mushrooms?" Verdan asked, taking a seat and watching with interest as their mute chef got to work.

Kai was a reasonable cook and was a deft hand at prepping food, but Henry was on a different level altogether, moving with impressive speed and precision.

It wasn't that the chef was fast or rushing through the process. It was that he knew precisely what he was doing and acted with purpose in every motion. Verdan had always found that there was something soothing about watching an expert at work. Their grace and effortless skill never failed to impress.

In no time at all, Verdan had a mushroom omelet in front of him, seasoned and cooked to perfection.

"Thank you, Henry," Verdan said, satisfied that he'd made the right choice with the Barbeaus.

"The weapons and their prospective wielders will be here today," Kai said, a touch of a smile on his face as Verdan set about devouring his delicious breakfast.

"I've had a few ideas for how to quickly find the ones we need. We should be able to cut down their numbers quickly," Verdan said, reluctantly pausing between bites to respond to Kai.

"So, you're testing for Aether sensitivity, right?" Kai asked with a thoughtful expression, his fingers idly drumming on his spear.

"Yes, why?" Verdan asked, intrigued by where Kai was going with this.

"Tim and Tom have been approached by a few people looking for work as guards. Some of them have decent experience. There just isn't a lot of call for trained fighters at the moment. If I get them here tonight, could you run through the same tests with them, see who passes?"

"Why not? I can see a few more guards being useful," Verdan said with a shrug. He was a little concerned about the money side of things, but he still had a reasonable amount left to use. Of course, he also had a steady source of income from the city guard on the horizon, which would help. Something about using the money earned from equipping the city guard to pay the wages of his own private guards amused Verdan to no end.

"Excellent, I'll send the brothers out to round up some people," Kai said, heading out of the room at a quick trot.

Something about Kai's speedy exit made Verdan feel that he'd been conned there, somehow. Maybe there was an ulterior motive that Kai had for increasing the number of guards?

Shrugging, Verdan went back to his breakfast. He trusted Kai to not screw him over too badly. It was probably something simple, like Kai wanting other people to do guard duty so he didn't have to.

Finishing up his food, Verdan headed outside to see Adrienne directing a trio of guardsmen on where to deposit a handcart with a few cloth-wrapped bundles. Given that some of the bundles looked to be almost six-foot-long, Verdan was fairly confident that those were the weapons he was waiting for.

"Good morning, Verdan. These fine gentlemen have a delivery for you. They were just telling me that they would carry everything to where you needed, isn't that right?" Adrienne turned her sunny smile on the three guardsmen, who gave a somewhat reluctant nod.

"Good morning, Adrienne. Over by the entrance to the workshop will be fine, thank you," Verdan said, gesturing to the big building as he struggled to keep a straight face.

"Did my Henry see to your breakfast already?" Adrienne asked, half-watching the guardsmen as they pushed the handcart over to the workshop.

"He has, and it was just as delicious as advertised," Verdan said, knowing what she was fishing for.

"Excellent! You could do with a bit more weight on you. Those lovely boys of yours have already told me that you spend far too much time meditating. A balanced diet is important," Adrienne said, her tone giving Verdan flashbacks to his visits home to see his mother.

Some things never changed.

"I'm sure that now Henry is here, that won't be a problem," Verdan said, being careful to promise nothing that she could hold over his head later. His work on his gathering spiral was far too important to ignore.

Adrienne's eyes narrowed, and she started to say something when she noticed that the guardsmen were about to unload the weapons and take their handcart. "No need for that, gentlemen. We'll need that to move them around, you see. I'm sure you understand."

One of the guardsmen started to argue, but they soon gave up when the other two swiftly abandoned him.

"How did you know we were going to be moving these around a lot?" Verdan asked as the two of them walked over to the handcart.

"Oh, I had no idea. I just thought we could do with a free hand-cart," Adrienne said with a cheeky grin that made Verdan chuckle. He had a feeling that she was going to keep him on his toes.

"Well, once I've taken these inside, it's all yours," Verdan said, shaking his head at her antics.

"Actually, I do have a question. If you have a moment?" Adrienne's tone went serious, so Verdan stopped and gave her his full attention, motioning for her to continue. "Well, I wanted to know what our budget was for the household. Have you set some funds aside for us?"

"Ah, yes, a good point. Here, this should cover us in the short-term," Verdan said, producing a dozen silver darns for her. He had to provide for six people and a wolf at the moment, so no doubt the food bill was going to go through the roof.

"Excellent. Would you like to review my purchases at the end of
the week?"

"No, no need for that. Give me a summary at the end of the month
and let me know when you need more funds. Other than that, I
trust you to manage the day-to-day expenses." Verdan had full
confidence in Adrienne; Tobias hadn't steered him wrong yet,
after all.

"Thank you, Verdan," Adrienne said, her warm smile back in full
force. "I expect for a household of six..."

"Seven, actually," Verdan interrupted, holding a hand up to apologize as he did so. "Please tell your husband to prepare meals for
Sylvie as well. Tim's wolf." Verdan explained, clarifying who he
meant when he saw the blank expression on Adrienne's face.
"She's in recovery at the moment and will need plenty of food."

"Yes, of course, the wolf," Adrienne said, coughing into her hand
before continuing. "So, food and household costs for seven. That
will likely come to around a silver to a silver-and-a-half per day. I'll
do what I can to keep us to the lower side of that, but expect a
monthly cost of around thirty-five to forty-five silver."

"I see," Verdan said thoughtfully. He knew he had a poor idea of
the relative value of things with the darn currency system, but that
sounded about right. The dozen silver darn he'd given her would
last them a week or so from the sound of it, which was fine by him.
"Very good, keep me updated."

Adrienne left him to go inform her husband that he was now
cooking for a wolf as well, something Verdan should probably have
mentioned previously. He'd have a word with Henry later to ensure
that it was more than just slop in a bowl as well.

Verdan seemed to be the only one who was picking up on the intelligence of the wolf, how it wasn't trained but just responded to the

things that Tim said. Perhaps intelligent creatures were more common these days, and that was why no one was remarking on it.

It didn't really matter; the creature was doing no harm as far as Verdan was aware, and he still owed it a full healing. The least Verdan could do in the meantime was make sure she got some decent meals.

_**_

Verdan carted the weapons from the guard into his workshop and took stock of what he'd been sent. Commander Griffon had followed his instructions and given Verdan three groups of weapons to work with.

He had four crossbows, four spears, and four swords, all of decent make and design and all fairly well-used. They had been looked after and kept in good shape, but the signs of use were there. Verdan supposed that it only made sense for them to send him used weapons rather than newer ones, in case he damaged them somehow.

Laying the spears out on a table, Verdan considered the construct to attach to them. He hadn't been completely honest with the commander; he wasn't just going to put a Pierce construct on them. A necessary piece of fiction, as Verdan had no intent for anyone to know what words he did or didn't know.

It had always annoyed Verdan that he couldn't use the word for Pierce, but it just didn't resonate with him, and he'd never developed a good concept for it. What he did have, however, was an excellent concept for Break. Maybe it wasn't quite as good for getting through armor as Pierce would be, but the guard would never know that.

"*Hyn. Durst.*" Verdan spoke, keeping the two words separate as he meshed the concepts into the construct he was weaving. Using a concept about breaking things was difficult, but Verdan quite liked the end result. A strike from this spear now would be effective against all manner of protections, both mundane and magical.

"*Hyn. Torr.*" Verdan moved on to the swords next, sticking with the tried-and-tested cutting enhancement.

"*Hyn. Grym.*" Verdan gave the crossbows a power enhancement, which was the best he could think of right. A Break enchantment like the one on the spears wouldn't work, as it was the bolts hitting the creature and not the crossbow itself. Hopefully, raw power would make up the difference.

Working mechanically through the weapons, Verdan kept a weather eye on his Aether reserves as he expended a week's worth of power. Doing so many enchantments back-to-back left Verdan feeling somewhat light-headed, and he took a few minutes to sit down and catch his breath afterwards.

Verdan hated expending large amounts of Aether, but he had the reserves to use and, if he were being honest with himself, he still felt guilty about his lousy first impression on the city guard. Hopefully, providing the weapons today would help improve their opinion of him.

Sighing, Verdan ran a hand through his hair as he stacked the weapons on the table and closed the door behind him. "*Gward,*" Verdan whispered as the door closed, placing a ward on it that would alert him if the room was disturbed.

While the Aether constructs on the weapons were temporary, they still warranted additional security. The last thing Verdan needed was someone breaking in, stealing the weapons, and selling them off.

Massaging his temples to relieve his headache, Verdan made his way down to the room where he'd left the weapons that Kai had brought him. Initially, he'd intended to use the weapons from Commander Griffon to test the potential sensitives being sent to them. However, with Kai bringing in some additional people, that wouldn't work.

Instead, Verdan dragged in a second table and laid all the weapons out. Everything was there, from the one with the successful enchantment for Kai down to the misshapen swords. Working through them, Verdan made sure that half the weapons had Aether constructs in them, and half didn't.

Of the half that did, he created a gradient, from a weak construct that would fail after a single hit all the way up to one that was veritably burning with Aether. Verdan wanted to know if these people were sensitive to Aether, but he also wanted to know how good their sense for it was.

Verdan's headache escalated with each further use of Aether, but he grit his teeth and ignored it. Better to get it done now while he was already struggling, than to come back to it another time and have the same issue. Besides, he'd not really pushed himself recently, preferring to conserve Aether and use his most-efficient spells.

An important lesson to learn for any Wizard was that Aetherburn, the headache that developed from high usage, only got worse the more you used it, but that sometimes you had to work through it. The shorter the time frame, the more of a toll it took, but you could also build a tolerance to it.

Verdan's tolerance seemed to have faded to a mere shadow of what it once was, and it was going to be painful to get it back to where he needed it.

Verdan paused as he laid out the last weapon in the jumbled order he'd put together. The throbbing headache from his Aetherburn was making it hard to really focus, but he considered his own attitude for a moment.

His instinctive reaction to getting Aetherburn for the first time since he'd woken up was to throw himself into possibly one of the most painful training regimes he'd ever experienced. He'd already been through the training once before. Did he really need to subject himself to that again?

The war was over. It was hard to remember that sometimes. Verdan kept expecting someone to run into the room and declare that they were being attacked or that something had gone wrong. Yes, there were still monsters, still creatures of darkness and agents of corruption, but he'd already decided that it wasn't his responsibility to try and protect everyone. So why was he trying to prepare himself for Aetherburn, for battle magic?

Verdan looked blankly down at the damaged sword in front of him, wondering just what he was doing. The potential research, learning, and experimentation were what had driven him at first, but he felt as though he was slipping away from that as time went on. The whole expedition to free the logging camp from monsters had somehow snowballed into a rescue mission.

Verdan didn't regret his actions—he couldn't—but he worried that he was falling into old habits. He was a researcher, not an Aether-damned war Wizard.

Frustrated with himself, Verdan went back to the manor. He'd spend some time meditating and working on his spiral. Focusing on that would ease his Aetherburn and soothe his mind.

_**_

"Verdan, the city guard are here for some form of test," Adrienne's voice brought Verdan out of his meditative state sometime later. He wasn't sure how long he'd been working on his spiral, but, thankfully, his Aetherburn was gone now.

"I'll be down in a minute," Verdan called back, taking a moment to finalize the changes to his spiral and mentally get himself in order before heading downstairs.

There were just over a dozen guardsmen waiting patiently in the courtyard between the workshop and the manor. Kai, Tom, and Tim were out gathering their own testees, but, to Verdan's surprise, Elliot was watching over the new arrivals.

The big man loomed over even the tallest guard there, his muscular frame putting all of them to shame as he stood near the manor's entrance with his arms folded.

"Elliot," Verdan said as he stepped outside, his staff in hand. It always pays to be prepared in strange situations like this.

"Verdan. Kai asked me to watch over the estate while he was away," Elliot said, a twinkle in his eyes belying his stern posture.

"Thank you. You didn't need to, though," Verdan said, not wanting Elliot to feel obliged to do something he didn't want to.

"You opened your home to me," Elliot said simply, with a shrug of his large shoulders. "The least I can do is offer my time in its protection."

Verdan considered Elliot's words before nodding. It wasn't like he was going to try to argue with him.

"Good morning, everyone. Who is in charge here?" Verdan called out as he looked over the group of guardsmen.

"That would be me, Wizard Blacke," a familiar voice called out as the group shifted somewhat and Lieutenant Silver stepped into view.

"Oh—I thought you didn't feel anything when I tested you?" Verdan asked, curious as to why the Lieutenant was here.

"I'm not sure. I didn't feel it at first, but I spent a few minutes carrying the rock, and when I let go, it felt like something was missing." Silver explained with a hint of frustration.

"Interesting. You might have a slight amount of Aether sensitivity then," Verdan said as he gestured for Silver to follow him to the workshop. "We'll run you through the test first and see how it goes."

"Very well. Lead the way," Silver said, gesturing for the guardsmen to accompany them as they stepped inside.

"This way then, please," Verdan said, guiding the group up to the room he'd prepared in advance. There were too many to go into the room directly, so he told them to organize themselves before heading inside. It would take several minutes for each test, so the sooner they started, the better.

"So, how do we do this?" Silver asked as he followed Verdan in. The lieutenant eyed the arrangement of weapons with a curious expression, his eyes flicking over to Verdan for guidance.

"Simply order them correctly, with those that have the least energy at the top left and those with the most energy at the bottom right," Verdan said, taking a seat with his staff across his thighs. He was intrigued by how this would go.

Lieutenant Silver didn't waste time thinking about the task; instead, he got straight into it by reaching out and grabbing the closest weapons. Based on whatever he was sensing, he then ordered those two and moved to the next set.

Verdan watched with interest as the guard officer slowly moved the weapons into something approaching the right order. The ones without Aether altogether seemed to confuse him somewhat, but Verdan put that down to a lack of confidence in what he was sensing.

Still, there were a few mistakes in the lieutenant's order, but the general progression was correct. Not a bad effort for someone who hadn't been able to sense Aether at all initially.

"There, that's the best I can do without guessing," Silver said, stepping back from the weapons and frowning at them, seemingly unsatisfied with his performance.

"Are you sure?" Verdan asked, verbally poking the other man to see how convinced he was in what he'd done.

"Yes. That's as good as I can do," Silver said, his frown disappearing as he answered in a firm tone.

"Very well, jumble them up, please, then send in the next person," Verdan said, mentally tallying Silver to the list of people he'd work with. The man was brusque, but he'd only gotten three wrong in the end, which was enough for what Verdan needed.

Silver gave Verdan a look before returning the weapons to their original order, though Verdan wasn't sure if that was intentional or not. If it was, then that was the kind of precision that would serve Silver well when he worked with Aether.

Sadly, the next two to take the test performed to a far less satisfactory degree, getting at least half of the weapons in the wrong order. Still, Verdan would trust them to know if Aether was present, just not how much.

The third person was a complete failure. They actually put an empty weapon at the end for the most Aether, saying that it felt the most full of energy as they did.

In the end, ten of the people tested had enough sensitivity to be suitable for what the guard needed. Four of those, including Lieutenant Silver, were sufficiently advanced that they would be able to track the usage of the Aether in the weapons. Once they had enough experience with that, they would be able to tell how many more times the weapons could be used before the constructs failed.

The more self-sufficient that Verdan could make the guardsmen, the better. Though, he did still need to look into a way to either allow the construct to be charged with Essence. That, or to find some way to manage the expenditure of his Aether. Otherwise, the guard was going to bleed Verdan dry with requests for enchanted weapons.

Still, that was a problem for another day. It was time to get some work on his spiral done before Kai's group came to have their testing done.

CHAPTER
TWENTY-NINE

KAI BROUGHT ALMOST twenty people to be tested, of whom only three had sufficient sensitivity to manage the enchanted weapons. Taking Kai's advice, Verdan hired six of them at a modest wage, one that was all but covered by the sale of the enchantments back to the guard.

It was a little frustrating that the first money Verdan earned wasn't even enough to cover his expenditure, but it was a good trade. Those enchantments had cost him a good portion of Aether and a few hours of trouble, but he'd gotten six guards for a month in exchange.

While Verdan appreciated his warm welcome from the locals, it was still best to be prepared. The value of what could be stolen from him was only going up, and that would be a hard temptation for desperate people to resist.

Two days after the testing, the squad of guardsmen assembled. They were led by Lieutenant Silver, who had one of the swords that Verdan had enchanted. There were the ten that Verdan had signed off as having sufficient sensitivity, but two of the others had also joined them. While they lacked the sensitivity of the others, those two would still be able to tell if the enchantment had power or not, which was something.

"We're ready to head out," Silver stated, the group waiting just outside of the Crea estate's grounds. "The bear attacked a farm just a few days ago. It's a menace that needs to be dealt with."

"I agree, which is why Kai and Tom are coming with you," Verdan said, gesturing to the two Sorcerers, who were approaching them with their travel packs already shouldered. "That being said, take this as well." Verdan produced a crossbow bolt and passed it over to the Lieutenant, who looked at it curiously.

"What is this?" the Lieutenant asked, no doubt able to sense the Aether within it.

"It's a standard bolt, but with a single-use enchantment that will break whatever it hits. If you struggle with the bear, shoot it with that, and hope for the best. No charge or debt incurred; just make sure to deal with the beast." Verdan explained, adding that it was freely given when he saw the indecision on Silver's face. Verdan needed this joint venture to be successful, so an extra enchantment for free wasn't a problem.

He'd made a construct for the bolt the day before, as further prac- tice to refine his methodology on a more-expendable level. Verdan had no interest in enchanting arrows and bolts by the dozen, but the odd one here and there would be fine. It also helped that it took a fraction of the Aether while still having a strong effect.

"Thank you, I'll make sure we don't waste it," Silver said, exam- ining the bolt for another moment before passing it to one of the nearby guards with a crossbow. "Keep this separate or mark it somehow. I don't want it being used by accident."

"Verdan, Lieutenant," Kai called out as he reached them, Tom a few steps behind him with an uncertain expression. "We're ready to go when you are."

"Then let's be about it. The more time we waste, the more chance of another attack," Silver declared, motioning for the guards to start heading down the road.

"Good luck," Verdan said as the Lieutenant and the two Sorcerers set off to join the group. He'd done what he could to help and prepare them. It was down to them to see things through now.

Glancing at the sky, Verdan saw that they were a few hours short of noon; plenty of time for him to get some more work done on his spiral. There wasn't much else for him to do right now, after all.

The alchemy supplies were still outstanding, and everyone else was already busy. Gwen was spending a lot of her time reading and practicing her magic, Tim was training extensively with the sword, and Elliot was off doing crafty things.

Verdan shook his head at himself. He was always complaining about how he wanted peace and quiet, but the moment he got some, he didn't know what to do with himself.

_**_

Verdan spent the rest of the day building his spiral and Aether reserves, ending the session at two-thirds of the way to completing his third spiral. He'd made good progress recently, which would hopefully continue over the next few days.

"Excuse me, Verdan, a messenger came for you a few minutes ago," Adrienne said, coming into the kitchen as Verdan finished his breakfast. Pausing to kiss her husband on the cheek, Adrienne took Verdan's dishes for him with a smile. "He said he was from Mr. Brock and his employer would visit you around lunchtime. He wants to discuss a shipment with you?"

"Ah, I see," Verdan said with a slight sigh. A meeting with Tobias likely meant there was a problem with the shipment. It was a few days late by this point, so that wasn't that surprising, but it was still frustrating. "Not a problem. I will be meditating upstairs when he arrives."

Thanking Henry for the delicious breakfast, Verdan returned to his room and settled into his familiar meditative pose.

"*Hyn*," Verdan muttered, tapping his knee and sending a pulse of positive Aether through him, temporarily reinvigorating mind and body alike.

Feeling far more settled, Verdan sank into his meditation, working on wrapping the flowing strands of Aether within him into ever tighter and more compressed spirals around the existing prime spiral.

Weave after weave of Aether was bound into the correct pattern, flowing all the way down into the core of Verdan's reserve. With each successive spiral completed, the process became harder and more mentally taxing. The effort of finishing a layer now was nothing compared to what Verdan remembered from the past.

Time flew swiftly by, and Verdan made reasonable progress before Adrienne came to tell him that Tobias had arrived.

"Verdan, good to see you," Tobias said, rising from his chair in the manor's living room, a mug of something steaming in his hand.

"Tobias, a pleasure," Verdan said, shaking the gaunt man's hand before waving for him to take a seat. As always, Brent lingered in the background, and Verdan acknowledged him with a nod before leaning his staff to one side and sitting down. "So, tell me, what's happened?"

"A guard patrol found the convoy that was bringing your supplies, amongst other things. It's about four or five hours' travel south-east of here. Their description of it makes me think that someone or something raided the convoy. I've spent all morning arranging for a sizable force to head down and retrieve it. I have a meeting with Commander Griffon shortly to see what aid his men can provide. I know you are a powerful magic-user. Can you help?" Tobias implored, a worried look in his eyes.

"I will come to the meeting with you to see what Commander Griffon says. It might be that you don't need me for this," Verdan said, uncomfortable at the idea of heading back out again so soon. He hadn't even settled from the last excursion.

"Thank you," Tobias said, a hint of tension leaving his posture as he exhaled. "Just consider it. That's all I ask."

"You're quite worried," Verdan stated as he got to his feet. "Was the caravan worth that much?"

Tobias had sipped his drink and was just putting it back down when Verdan spoke, the merchant turning to look at Verdan with a hard expression. "The goods are meaningless; I have the money to replace all of them if needed. The dozen or more good men and women who were working that caravan are my concern."

"I'm sorry, that was a thoughtless comment from me," Verdan said, holding his hands up in apology. "Do we know how many people were in the caravan?"

"No, I'm sorry, I shouldn't have snapped," Tobias said, shaking his head as he got to his feet and motioned for Verdan to lead the way outside. "The team went over empty-handed but with a list of materials for you and other buyers. They will have hired people and equipment for the journey back, but I don't know how much. We could be looking at as little as ten in total, or a score of caravan hands on top of the six we sent."

"I understand," Verdan said, his gut clenching as he realized just how many people had gone missing. Knowing that anyone had been hurt trying to get his goods back here was bad enough. Putting numbers to it made it all so much worse.

Verdan couldn't help but feel guilty about the whole situation. Tobias wouldn't have sent anyone on this journey if he hadn't turned up and needed the supplies. Logically, Verdan knew he wasn't actually to blame, but that didn't help the weight he felt settling on his shoulders.

Two of the new-hire guards were outside, so Verdan sent them with a message for Tim and Gwen to meet him at the estate in two hours, along with the rest of the guards. Verdan didn't want to be the first person people turned to for help, but that didn't mean he would leave those people to die.

They had no idea of how long it had been since the caravan was attacked or if prisoners had been taken, but Verdan owed it to Tobias and his people to check. If Kai was here, Verdan would trust him to be enough to resolve the situation, but he wasn't. In fact, with Silver and that squad of guardsmen after the bear, who knew how much manpower the city guard could spare?

On that concerning thought, Verdan followed Tobias and Brock out of the estate and toward the guard headquarters. Verdan wasn't sure what he was expecting from this meeting, but Tobias clearly wanted his presence.

The guards at the headquarters informed them the Commander was waiting for them with another group and escorted them inside. A hint of concern appeared on Tobias's face as they followed the guard, making Verdan wonder who this other group was.

"Sir, Mr. Brock, his bodyguard, and Wizard Blacke are here to see you," the guardsmen announced at a partially-opened door, holding a hand up to stop them from coming any closer. Verdan noted the correct term being used for him with pleasure. That was a step in the right direction.

"Ah, good. Send them in, please," the Commander called out, the guardsman lowering his hand and pushing the door fully open for them.

Commander Griffon was in a different, larger office this time and was seated at the head of a good-sized oval table. On the right-hand side of the table was Lieutenant Michaels, a well-dressed man that Verdan didn't know, and another individual in robes.

Looking over the two newcomers, Verdan found his eyes drifting to the second as he noted the dark green and black patterning on his robes. Stretching out his Aether sense, Verdan could sense that this robed individual was a Sorcerer. He didn't know what aspects the Sorcerer used, but the subtle tension that appeared in both Tobias and Brock when they saw him told Verdan all he needed to know.

"Mr Brent, thank you for joining us, and you, Wizard Blacke," Commander Griffon said, giving both of them a respectful nod.

"Not a problem, Commander. I've already given Wizard Blacke an initial overview of the situation." Tobias said in a formal tone. "Though, I would ask why my esteemed colleague and a member of the Weeping Death are with us?" Tobias's voice carried an acid touch as he looked at the well-dressed man, making Verdan wonder just what he was walking into.

"Actually, I'm here because Disciple Garveth here approached me about reports they've had of growing issues in the area. The Weeping Death have a small cloister a few days from here, and are growing concerned. As the most prominent property owner within the city, I felt it was my civic duty to ensure he was heard." The merchant said with a smug smile that put Verdan on guard immediately. The tone of voice and the smugness together were never a good sign in the kind of slimy merchant that this man reminded him of.

"A discussion that we will now proceed with, Mr Feveraux. Please, Mr Brock, Wizard Blacke, take a seat," Commander Griffon said, something in his voice telling Verdan that he was relieved they were here for this.

Following Tobias to the table and taking a seat, Verdan eyed the Sorcerer warily, the other man giving him just as much attention. The Sorcerer was a thin, wiry-looking man with dark, hooded eyes and a guarded expression.

"Good, now that we're all here, Disciple Garveth, please could you pass on your message?" Griffon said in a stilted tone, his face inscrutable, but his body language was overflowing with tension.

"Very well," the Sorcerer said, rising to his feet and smoothing out his robes with an absent motion of one hand. "Elder Budaev of the Northern Glade Cloister has seen the rise in attacks on innocent, hardworking mortals like yourselves in recent months." Garveth paused, his eyes flicking to Verdan, who did his best to not look disgusted at the use of 'mortals'.

"Accordingly, my Elder has decided that the time has come for action. Either Hobson's Point will act to protect its people, or he will be forced to intervene. For the good of the populace, the Weeping Death Sect shall take up ownership of the city of Hobson's Point." Garveth said, his tone even and uncaring as he delivered his ultimatum.

"Please relay to your Elder that such action is neither needed nor welcomed. We are an independent city, and we will remain that way," Griffon said, his lack of surprise making Verdan wonder how much of this he had expected in advance. "Hobson's Point will deal with the local threats directly, whatever they may be."

"A bold statement," Garveth said, raising a brow at the guard commander's veiled threat. "Lieutenant Michaels tells me that there's an elemental bear in the area that has been threatening locals. Such a creature is beyond mortal means." Garveth all but sneered at Griffon, his disdain written across his face.

"Then you will be surprised to learn that we are hunting the beast at this very moment. Do not underestimate us," Griffon said in a cold tone, a touch of anger creeping into his expression.

"You, this is your doing, isn't it?" Garveth all but spat, turning to glare at Verdan with murder in his eyes. "I don't know what sect thinks it can meddle here, but the Weeping Death will have this city. Meddle again, and we will put you down like the dog you are." The disciple abandoned all pretense to civility as he focused on Verdan, ignoring the effect his words were having on the room.

"I see," Verdan said calmly, his anger burning cold in his chest as he looked at the personification of everything he hated about this new era. "I will give you the opportunity to walk away, but speak to me like that again, or treat these people in that way, and it will be the last thing you do. I will not tolerate such abuse of power." Verdan rose to his feet in a measured motion, staring directly into Garveth's eyes as he drew his line in the sand. Part of his mind was screaming that this was nothing to do with him, but he couldn't turn a blind eye.

It would be easy to let the oaths that bound him slip away, to lighten the responsibility on his shoulders and ignore this. Verdan just couldn't do it. He couldn't betray the memory of the Imperium, of what he'd fought for. Somehow, magic users had become tyrants, not protectors. But in this city, Verdan would stand for what he believed in.

"Elder Budaev will hear of this,' Garveth snarled, but Verdan could see the fear in his eyes as he backed down from Verdan's challenge.

Garveth might not be a Wizard, but he could likely sense the huge amount of Aether that Verdan was holding onto right now. One wrong move and an empowered wind blast would have crushed him against the wall.

"Such high-handed behavior—what else can be expected from an ally of yours?" Feveraux sneered, glossing over the open desire to take the city that Disciple Garveth had stated. "I hope you all see this 'Wizard' for what he is: a manipulator trying to steal the city for himself." Feveraux stormed out of the room with an affronted sniff, leaving behind a tense silence as Lieutenant Michaels rose to his feet and whispered something to the Commander.

"No, we're sticking with it," Griffon said aloud, shaking his head at Michaels's suggestion. "Go escort our esteemed guests from the building and double the patrols in the city until further notice."

"Yes, Commander," Michaels said stiffly, coming to attention before leaving the room.

"Well, that wasn't quite the outcome I was hoping for," Tobias said once the door shut behind Michaels. Griffon grunted a reply. His eyes closed as he frowned in thought.

"I'm sorry if my presence aggravated the Sorcerer. I didn't mean to make things harder for you," Verdan said, feeling a little guilty over how that had all ended.

"No, this isn't the first overture they've made to take control of the city, though they've never been this brazen before," Griffon said, opening his eyes once more as he got up from his chair and began to pace the room. "Garveth made a mistake mentioning the bear as well. Suddenly the timing of its appearance is incredibly suspicious, as well as how the first sighting was when it attacked a farmstead. These are huge creatures, but they rarely leave their territory."

"You think that the Weeping Death brought it to the area as a pretext for this takeover?" Tobias asked, tapping one long finger against his chin.

"I think so, yes," Griffon said, nodding sadly at the look of horror on Verdan's face. "Though that leaves us with one question, Verdan. How do you think our new weaponry will fare on the hunt?"

CHAPTER

THIRTY

KAI BOUNCED his spear against his shoulder as he strode along the road, his eyes peeled for any sign of their quarry. The village was just over a day's walk from Hobson's Point, and Lieutenant Silver had called an early stop last night so they would enter the creature's potential territory during the day. Fifteen people and a cart full of supplies being pulled by a donkey was a tempting target, after all.

Thankfully, there had been no attacks or delays on their trip so far. Under normal circumstances, Kai would consider that a good thing, because it meant that the guard were patrolling as they should and keeping the land safe. Knowing that this wasn't the case in this area, Kai was conscious that it could indicate something dangerous was denning nearby.

This particular village, Willowbrook, and its surroundings had been attacked several times by the elemental bear over the last few weeks, according to Lieutenant Silver. With multiple attacks in the area, the beast must have found a lair rather than be passing through. Putting those two observations together made Kai concerned; the last thing he wanted was an impromptu encounter with the creature.

Their first destination was the village itself, to see what the locals knew about the current situation and to prepare accordingly before beginning their hunt.

"Jenkins, how close are we?" the Lieutenant asked, his voice pitched to reach the guard leading them forward. Jenkins was from a small farm just outside Willowbrook, so he knew the way there like the back of his hand.

"Not long, Sir," Jenkins called back, not taking his eyes from watching their surroundings. "We just need to pass over the creek, and then it's over the hill, and we're there."

"Good. Once we arrive, take a few others and lead a patrol of the area, Jenkins. Try and ascertain if there are any local threats we need to be concerned about beyond our target."

"Yes, Sir," Jenkins said, his shoulders straightening in pride at the lieutenant singling him out to lead a patrol.

The group continued steadily through the light woodland that was so common in the area, coming to a dried-up creek a few minutes later. Jenkins frowned at the dry creek bed but shook his head and continued onward.

Kai and Tom were in the middle of the formation they had been maintaining, so Kai had been taking the chance to help Tom with activating his mace. Verdan had made sure they both had Sorcerer-friendly enchantments on their weapons, and Kai was still experimenting with his own.

Tom still struggled to use his Essence; he could manage a few small things consistently now, but nothing on a larger scale. Thankfully, channeling his Essence into the weapon was relatively straightforward, so Tom was using that as Essence control practice.

If all went well, then Kai and Tom wouldn't be involved with the fight against the elemental bear at all, but Kai had been on far too many hunts to trust in that. These guardsmen were unused to fighting back against such creatures from anything short of a highly-fortified position, after all.

With their new weapons, they would likely prevail even if it all went wrong. At the very least, Kai expected them to drive the beast off by wounding it. How many of them would live through the fight was less certain, but that was why Kai and Tom were here.

A distant howl came to Kai's ears on the breeze, echoed by a series of other howls a moment later. Kai's pulse quickened as he heard the distinct gravelly undertone to the howls. Those were no ordinary wolves.

"Jenkins, which way to the village?" Kai snapped, his blood pumping already as he readied himself for a fight.

"That way, right on the other side of Oaktop, it's too steep for the wagon is all," Jenkins said, gesturing to a fairly substantial hill that the path meandered around.

"What's wrong, Disciple Kai?" Silver asked, a concerned look on his face as his hand fell to the sword belted at his side.

Kai had managed to stop Silver from calling him 'Master Sorcerer,' but the Lieutenant refused to drop the honorific altogether, despite Kai's lack of a sect.

Kai was saved from an explanation by another chorus of howls, this time a little clearer and definitely coming from the far side of the hill. The rumbling undertone was clear for them all to hear, and more than one guard went pale as they heard it.

"Ash wolves, damn it! Peters, Auger, Baras, Laar, get up that hill and give the Sorcerers covering fire. Auger, you have command. The rest of you, let's move it!" Silver barked out orders, sending four of the crossbow-wielding guards running for the hill, with Kai and Tom in close pursuit.

Only the spear-wielders had their enchanted weapons to hand; the rest were in the wagon for safe-keeping. Silver's reasoning was that spears would be the most crucial against the bear, so they would be ready if the group was attacked. If anything else came, however, the rest of the guards would deal with it, saving their enchantments for when they mattered.

Ash wolves were fast and incredibly vicious, so if they were attacking Willowbrook, there was no time for the guards to swap weapons. Still, a crossbow bolt would take one of the beasts down if they could hit it, though that wouldn't be easy.

"Tom, protect the guards on the hill. I'll go for the wolves," Kai called out, igniting a portion of his Essence as he sprinted for the hill. Energetic fire flowed through Kai's limbs as he raced out ahead of the others, powering up the hill in great bounds.

Oaktop had a steep slope on one side and a gentle descent on the other, giving Kai a clear view of the situation once he vaulted over a boulder and finally crested the hill.

Willowbrook was only a few hundred feet away from the base of the hill Kai stood on, its north and eastern sides bounded by a small river. Walls should have completely encircled the village, but Kai could see where something big had torn through the gateway on the western side. The gates and a good portion of the wooden palisade in that area were splintered and torn.

Focusing on the damage, Kai could see where the villagers had started repairs and put a makeshift barricade in place to cover the exposed areas. Under normal circumstances, closing the gates would be enough to ensure that the wolves wouldn't get through. However, with only a rudimentary barricade holding them back, it was a much more dangerous situation.

Glancing back, Kai saw that Tom and the crossbowmen were making steady progress, while the rest of the guards were hurrying the donkey along as best they could.

Distant yells were coming from the village, and Kai looked back to see a dozen ash wolves lope out of some woods to the northwest of the village. An array of arrows and projectiles issued forth from the village's defenders, driving the wolves back but not managing to injure any of them.

The threat of injury might drive off ordinary wolves, but ash wolves were incredibly aggressive in the right situation, such as when they thought their prey was cornered or weakened.

Seeing how this would end in advance, Kai started sprinting down the slope toward the village, calling on every iota of the speed he could muster from his Essence as he went. There was no time to wait for the others, not if he wanted to save the villagers.

The wolves had drawn back somewhat, but this time they didn't fall back to the woods, instead spreading out and sinking down low as they stalked toward the village.

A volley came from the village again, this time with a pair of arrows hitting one of the approaching wolves. The creature yelped in pain and backed away, but the other wolves ignored it, pushing on at a quicker pace toward the village.

Two of the closest wolves saw Kai moving quickly toward them and broke off from the group, loping toward him as they split up, moving to come in from either side.

The village defenders were attacking as quickly as they could, but the two wolves that broke off to chase Kai had spurred the rest on, and they were racing toward the barricade.

Angling toward the closer of the two wolves, Kai raced straight toward it as he shifted his grip toward the rear of his spear. Closing with his target at speed, Kai thrust out as it pounced at him, twisting his hip and shoulder to project his spear as far as it would go. Uncomfortably hot blood washed over Kai as he tore open the creature from sternum to gut.

A croaking gurgle from behind was all the warning Kai needed to throw himself to one side, a gust of pressurized, superheated ash blasting through the space he'd just been standing.

Rolling up out of his dodge, Kai closed with the other wolf, keeping it off-balance with fast jabs of his spear until an opening presented itself, and he drove it home for a killing blow.

Pulling his spear free, Kai continued toward the village at a run. Ash wolves were a nightmare for non-Sorcerers, but when you were fast enough to keep up with them, they became dangerous, not lethal.

Flickering orange flames were licking up from the barricade when Kai arrived. Multiple blasts of hot ash must have kindled flames among the untreated areas of wood. Seven wolves were still attacking the village, the others having been wounded and driven off by the villagers.

The ash wolves were half again the size of a normal wolf, but they lacked enhanced strength, so they could only rip the barricade apart so fast. For every moment that they did, the villagers were hitting them with spears and arrows, then hiding when one of the wolves unleashed their ashen breath. A scream of pain from inside the barricade told Kai that not everyone had been able to find sufficient cover from the blast.

Maybe if the villagers didn't have to hide, they would kill the wolves in time, but right now, the wolves would be among them before they could manage unless they could get a distraction.

Drawing heavily on his Essence and feeding it into the flames in his core, Kai felt fresh energy flood his body as he rushed the closest wolves. The first one was too busy biting at a spear that was coming from between the axles of a sideways cart to notice him until Kai's spear burst through its chest in a spray of blood that sizzled against the wooden barricade.

A nearby wolf let out a menacing growl as it let out the tell-tale croaking gurgle and roared out its ashen breath. Taking cover behind the dead wolf, Kai avoided the worst of the blast, with only the heat really impacting him. As a fire Sorcerer actively burning Essence, it would take more than a little spike in heat to hurt him.

Bursting out from where he'd sheltered, Kai hurled his spear ahead of him, impaling the wolf who'd attacked him before it could recover from using its breath.

In his periphery, Kai saw a figure racing out from the barricade, moving fast as they attacked one of the wolves nearby.

Between Kai, the newcomer, and the archers inside the village, the remaining wolves were picked off before they could escape or cause any further issues. Kai was covered in the wolves' warm blood as he faced down the man who'd joined him outside the gate.

Thick, shoulder-length black hair, dark brown eyes, a stern expression, and a partially-burnt tunic gave the man a near-feral look. A look that was only complimented by his broad shoulders and impressive presence.

"Thank you for your aid," Kai said, keeping one eye on the other man as he wiped his spear clean. He didn't release his Essence quite yet; there was a wild look in the other man's dark eyes that he wasn't sure about.

"There were too many for me to fight alone. You're faster than I am, currently," the man said in a deep, throaty voice, giving Kai a half-smile that was just short of threatening.

"I see. My name is Kai. Are you a local?" Kai asked, holding a hand out toward the other man. There was a thick layer of tension in the air, but it seemed to defuse as Kai shifted to a more relaxed stance.

"Blane, and no," the man answered, sheathing the two short swords he held to shake Kai's hand. "I'm looking for my little sister. She said she was heading through this area when we last spoke. Have you seen her? She's a little shorter than me, with long hair. Her name is Tara."

"No, sorry, I haven't met anyone like that, but I've recently been further north. We've only been back in this area for a short time," Kai said slowly, thinking back on the people he'd seen recently. None of them matched that description, though it was a bit lacking in details.

"Another failure," Blane muttered, looking out into the woods surrounding Willowbrook as he sighed heavily. "I'll head for the city next; maybe she's there."

"Are you heading there now?" Kai asked, letting his Essence die down as he relaxed a little. There was something strange about Blane; he didn't feel like a Sorcerer, or a Wizard for that matter, but there was something to him. Kai had seen a lot of things, but whatever Blane was, it was something new.

"Maybe," Blane said, grimacing slightly as he looked at the villagers taking down part of the barricade and putting out the smoldering flames. "I don't want to abandon these people to their situation. I've only been here a day or so, and I can tell they've been having problems for a while. I am no Sorcerer, but I can still make a difference." Blane shuddered in distaste as he mentioned Sorcerers, a more-blatant reaction than most people would allow themselves. Kai couldn't argue the sentiment, but Blane clearly felt safe from reprisal, which was interesting.

Tom and the crossbowmen joined them before Kai could respond, the guards sweeping the area for threats before moving to help the villagers with Tom.

The surviving ash wolves had long since fled, but Kai was watching the woods all the same, just in case.

"Come, let's lend a hand. Then I'll introduce you to Tella, the village head," Blane said, moving to help with the aftermath of the battle.

Kai watched the odd man walk away with a guarded expression. He wished he was more familiar with sensing external energy, like Verdan. For now, he'd settle for keeping a wary eye on the other man.

-**=

Kai and the others worked with Blane and the locals to extinguish the small, smoldering flames, treat wounds, and generally clean things up from the ash wolf attack.

Lieutenant Silver and the rest of the guards arrived not long after the villagers had finished cleaning up from the battle. Almost a dozen had burns, but thankfully they hadn't lost anyone to the attack. One unfortunate man had caught the edge of an ashen breath and had lost a lot of the skin on his forearm, but the makeshift barricade had blocked the worst of it.

Once Silver had arrived, someone went off to fetch the village head, Tella. Tella was a stern-looking woman who immediately took charge of the villagers in the area, directing them and putting specific people into groups based on their tasks.

Wherever Tella stepped, the chaotic scramble to recover from the attack became organized as they were given purpose. It was impressive.

"Lieutenant Silver, it's been a while," Tella called out as she approached them. "Bobby, go ahead and grab some folks to get those corpses processed. Someone might pay for their parts, and we can't turn down the meat." Tella gestured to a burly man off to one side, who grunted and tapped a few others on the shoulder before moving toward the ash wolf bodies.

Kai noted the headwoman's words with interest. Maybe that was something Verdan would want. Enchanters valued monster parts as they made prime materials for use, but there were so few out there that most of what was harvested was used for more mundane purposes.

Verdan had already displayed knowledge of enchantment, not to mention his ability to make Kai able to enhance his weapon. So, perhaps these would be worth acquiring for him. Alchemy was more plant-based, as far as Kai knew, but Verdan had ordered those hearts, so who knew. Kai was learning not to make assumptions about what Verdan could or couldn't do.

"Headwoman Tella, I wish I was back in better circumstances," Silver said, giving the woman a respectful half-bow that she waved away with a scowl.

"None of that, the blood between us may be thin, but it's there all the same," Tella said, looking over the guards that Silver had brought, as well as Tom and Kai. Seeing the two of them, she frowned, taking in their lack of guard attire and the blood that covered Kai. "Sorcerers?"

"Yes, but they are working with us and are reliable—you can trust them," Silver said, giving Kai a warning look.

"Huh, strange times we live in, that's for sure," Tella said, her brow furrowing as she gave Kai and Tom a second, more appraising look. Her gaze lingered for several seconds before she turned back to Silver and cocked her head in his direction. "So, you have my thanks for your aid with the wolves, but what brings you out here? With supplies, no less." She gestured to the wagon that accompanied them.

"We're here to hunt the elemental bear, to stop it from doing any more damage," Silver declared, his words rippling out through the surrounding villagers as they stopped what they were doing to look at him in disbelief. The stoic guard officer squared his shoulders under the weight of their stares, not giving an inch.

"Hunt the bear," Tella repeated flatly, shaking her head at them. "A creature that did that." She paused for effect as she pointed to the damaged palisade wall around the gates. "It wasn't even trying that hard to get inside; if it had really tried, we'd all be dead. If you go provoking it, maybe next time we won't be so lucky."

The atmosphere was tense as the villagers looked at Silver with grim expressions, many of them nodding along with Tella's words.

"Maybe we should discuss this somewhere more private. There are aspects to this that you don't know," Kai offered, drawing some of the attention to himself.

"Very well, come with me," Tella said after a long pause, turning on her heel to head back into the village. "The rest of you, get back to it!"

Kai gave Tom a nudge and then set off after the headwoman as the villagers got back to their work. Silver gave a few instructions to his guards before joining them.

Willowbrook was a reasonably large village, filling the area between the river and the hill with a tightly packed but well-organized mass of buildings. Tella's house was somewhat in the middle of it all, and was both her home and the site of all official business for the village.

"Please, come in, take a seat," Tella said, waving for them to enter and guiding them through to an office of sorts. There were only two chairs, and Tom was already moving to lean against the doorway, so Kai reluctantly took the one next to Silver. It would have been rude not to, no matter how little he wished to.

"Good, now, what warrants this secrecy?" Tella asked, her gaze resting on Kai.

"Lieutenant Silver and his men are equipped with special weaponry that can hurt the creature. Perhaps even enough that they can kill it without Tom or myself helping," Kai explained, choosing his words carefully to try and maintain some secrecy about what they had. So far, only the guard knew exactly what they had. Kai hadn't explained the test to the mercenaries and ex-guards he'd brought to Verdan, so they would have suspicions but nothing else. The longer they kept this under wraps, the better.

"Special weaponry?" Tella echoed, looking over to the Lieutenant this time.

"Yes, which we'll need to keep secret from your people. I'm sure you understand," Silver said, holding Tella's gaze with his own.

"If you fail, a lot of my people are going to die," Tella said softly, tension building in her posture. "Are you sure you can take it down?"

"With what Verdan gave us, I think the same as Disciple Kai. We have a good chance without their help. With their help, I am certain we can bring the beast down," Silver said firmly.

"Don't make me regret this," Tella said after a few moments of thought. "I'll back you and yours. The hunters might know where it lairs. Ask for Callum. He's in charge these days." Tella got up and crossed to a cabinet as she spoke, pulling out a small flask of something and taking a hefty swig of the contents.

"Thank you, Tella," Silver said, rising to his feet and giving the headwoman a formal nod.

"You can thank me by killing the beast. It's caused too much death already," Tella said, taking a second swig from the flask. "Now, get gone; I've work to do."

"Of course," Silver said, leading the way as the three of them left the building. "I'm going to organize a patrol and see what we can do to help the villagers. See if you can find that hunter she mentioned.Find out what he knows."

"Will do," Kai said, giving Silver a half-wave as he headed back toward the damaged gates.

Tom and Kai spent the next half-hour finding the head hunter, who was gathering a group of a dozen others to head out of the village when they caught up with him. Callum was an older, dark-haired, slender man with an innate stillness to his movement that was almost disconcerting. He didn't twitch, fidget ,or shift around; every movement was deliberate and purposeful.

"Can I help you?" Callum asked as the two Sorcerers approached, his eyes flicking between the two of them before settling on Kai.

"We're here with the guard. Tella said you might know how to find the elemental bear, where its lair might be. Can you help?" Kai asked, cutting straight to the chase.

The hunters that had gathered around Callum went still at Kai's words, all of them turning to look at their leader with a mix of fear and hope.

"Maybe. we've tried to stay out of its way more than we've tried to find out where it's denning. I can tell you that it's west of here, that's for sure, but the actual location, I don't know," Callum told them, showing none of the reaction his subordinates did.

"Would some of you be willing to help us look?" Tom asked, speaking up for the first time since they'd reached the village.

The silence hung for a few long moments before a tall, young-looking woman with long dark hair raised a hand and stepped forward slightly.

"I saw it not too many days ago when I found the lost traveler and guided him back here," the woman said, her voice little more than a whisper. "I'll guide you back there and help you hunt it."

"Enough, Clara, I will go with them, but you're staying away from that beast," Callum said in a tone that brooked no dissent. The head hunter stepped over to the younger woman as he spoke and Kai noted the strong family resemblance between them.

"No, Dad, I'm going. After what it did, someone needs to make sure it's hunted down," Clara said, a surprising amount of venom in her whisper-quiet voice.

"There's too much of your mother in you," Callum said, a sad smile touching his face as he reached out to tuck a loose strand of hair behind her ear. "We'll both go, then. Someone needs to watch your back. Ole, you're in charge of the hunters until I'm back, understood?"

"Yes, Callum," a grizzled-looking older man said, squaring his shoulders and giving a few other hunters pointed looks.

"Good. Now, when are we heading out?" Callum asked, turning to face Kai once more. Like when they first arrived, Kai was impressed by how utterly still the head hunter remained when he wasn't actively doing something, a useful skill indeed.

"I'm unsure; we need to speak with Lieutenant Silver. It's his command," Kai said with a subtle shrug, happy to put such decisions on the guard officer.

"Then let's go. Ole, take everyone else east to see what game you can find," Callum said, giving Ole his parting orders as he started toward the gate, Clara hurrying after him.

Kai started after the two hunters before pausing as he noticed that Tom wasn't keeping pace with them. Going back, Kai waited until the other hunters had left before nudging Tom. "What's wrong?"

Tom started at the touch, giving Kai an apologetic look before shrugging. When Kai raised a brow in his direction, Tom shifted his weight a few times before finally replying.

"It's just all becoming real. We're going after an elemental bear, a creature that Sorcerers only go after in groups." Tom told him, shaking his head in disbelief as he spoke.

"You don't have to go," Kai said neutrally, not wanting to push Tom into a situation he wasn't ready for. The ex-guard hadn't long been a Sorcerer. Giving him more time to adjust wasn't a problem. It would change their emergency plans, but that wasn't a huge problem.

"No, no," Tom said, shaking his head and holding a hand up to stop Kai. "That's not it; I'm just not sure how much use I'll be. I can't even control my power."

"You'll learn, don't worry," Kai said confidently. Tom had been putting the work in; it was only a matter of time. "Look, we're only here if things go wrong. Until then, you just need to watch my back. We look out for each other, alright?"

"Yeah, I can do that," Tom said, the big man taking in a deep breath before nodding to himself as he exhaled. "Yeah, I can do that.

Nothing will get to you while I'm here." Tom promised solemnly, his eyes serious as he met Kai's gaze.

"I know, Tom, I know," Kai said, giving the big man a warm smile as he patted him on the shoulder. Kai remembered how Tom had ripped through the Darjee at the ruins; he had no doubts in his ability. "Come on, let's see what the good Lieutenant has planned."

_**_

"So, you think you know where the bear might be denning?" Lieutenant Silver asked, keeping his voice pitched low so that only those in the small gathering could hear. Kai and Tom stood together to one side, while Silver spoke with Callum and his daughter, Clara. Silver had also brought in his impromptu second-in-command, Jenkins, for the conversation. Kai might have seen a happier guard at some time in his travels, but he wasn't sure when.

"Yes, I saw it myself, as well as quite a few fresh tracks only a few days ago when I found Blane," Clara said, her voice still little more than a projected whisper.

At the mention of Blane, Kai glanced over to where the odd man was helping some of the villagers hoist a new log into position at the palisade. He still wasn't sure what to make of Blane, and the fact that he'd been near the elemental bear just made that even more prevalent in Kai's mind.

"....should we head out to find it?" Callum was asking as Kai brought his attention back to the conversation.

"I'm not sure. This isn't something to rush into," Silver said, a thoughtful expression on his face as he looked at the position of the sun in the sky.

"The place I saw it is an hour or two from here; we'd have time to go after it today if you want," Clara said, a mixture of longing and bloodlust in her voice. For her to want the creature dead that badly, it must have killed someone she knew.

"Or, we can scout the same area, just the two of us," Callum interjected with a glower at his daughter. "Lieutenant Silver and the others can settle in and rest. We'll all be better coming at this hunt fresh and rested."

"I agree," Kai offered, sharing a nod with the older hunter. Callum had the look of a man who'd fought some of the nastier things out there, which was experience they sorely needed. "We don't want to be fighting this creature tired; that's a good way to get people killed."

Clara gave Kai a fulminating look, but her displeasure didn't faze him at all; he'd had worse glares in his time. Kai was more concerned with keeping everyone alive and killing the bear than he was about making friends.

"Very well, tomorrow it is. Jenkins, take that patrol we mentioned earlier and make sure that the area is secure. Callum, if you could scout the area Clara has in mind and report back this evening, that would be ideal. With some luck, you'll be able to confirm if it's there or not, so we can start with purpose tomorrow. If not, well, we'll deal with that in the morning."

"Aye, that works for me," Callum said, giving the barest hint of a nod as he spoke.

With an initial plan to follow, the group broke up as they all went their own way. Callum must have made another attempt to convince Clara to leave it to him as Kai heard her scoff and all but storm out through the village gates, head held high.

Kai wasn't the only one watching the spectacle; he could see Blane watching from off to one side. From the way Blane's eyes followed the young huntress, Kai could guess his intentions. Looking back at the departing figure, Kai could see what Blane admired. Clara had an attractive figure, and Kai had a thing for fierce women as well.

Thinking about fierce women brought a certain blue-eyed Witch to mind, and Kai smiled fondly. He would never have dreamed of looking upon a Witch with anything less than suspicion even a year ago, but he wasn't the kind to lie to himself. At first, Kai had been able to ignore her beauty and her captivating gaze, but that had all changed the night of the storm.

Kai had awoken when she'd raced upstairs to disrobe, and he'd seen firsthand how she faced down the fury of the storm to master her power. She had been in no danger, but he'd seen the determination in the way she held herself, the ironclad will to succeed.

Kai's smile turned bittersweet as he dreamt of what may be, what he knew he could never have. Kai's road was one of death and ruin; he deserved nothing less and would be damned before hurting anyone else.

Dragging his mind out of the familiar spiral of darkness, Kai focused on the here and now. There was a job to be done.

"The hunters help you on your mission," Blane said, the odd man walking over to stand near Kai, his dark brown eyes hooded in shadow as he caught Kai's gaze.

"That they are," Kai said, pausing for a moment as he considered the fighting prowess Blane had shown. Another fighter, especially one who had tangled with monsters before, would be welcome on the hunt. Considering his words, Kai looked away and spoke in a casual tone. "Both today and tomorrow, when we seek the beast itself."

"They'll be fighting?" Blane asked with concern, a worried expression playing across his face.

"You think her father can stop her?" Kai retorted, looking back at Blane to catch the man's grimace. "It's life or death for everyone here."

"What would you have me do? I can't abandon Tara," Blane said in frustration, glaring at Kai.

"How long have you been looking? Will a few days make a difference?" Kai asked, gesturing to the village around them. "A few days here will make a big difference to these people."

Blane grunted noncommittally, but Kai could tell his words had hit home. He just needed a little more to bring him round.

"My employer has many contacts within the city. If you help us with the bear, I will do everything I can to help you search the city for your sister," Kai said, facing Blane directly now.

"Your oath on it, a proper oath, not one to be twisted by words," Blane said, his voice intent as he squared off to Kai. "I will help you track and kill the beast, and you will help me find Tara." A blade was in Blane's hand, hilt toward Kai. Blane's gaze was intent as he stared at Kai, his jaw set in a stubborn manner.

Realising what the other man wanted, Kai took the blade and cut the top of his wrist. "I swear by my Essence; I will keep to the Oath." Kai's words were heavy as they left his mouth, his heart beating unnaturally loud in his ears as his blood trickled down his hand.

"I too swear, by the blood of my people, that I shall keep to the Oath," Blane spoke, his words carrying a matching weight to them as he kept his eyes on Kai.

It had been a long time since Kai had taken a blood oath, but it was just as uncomfortable now as it had been then. Swearing on your Essence was an extreme measure, one viewed as archaic and barbaric by most sects. Kai was bound now to the words and spirit of the Oath.

If Kai ever knowingly broke the Oath, his Essence would turn on him, wounding him and severely weakening his power as a Sorcerer. He wouldn't die, but it would be incredibly painful.

"Perhaps some Sorcerers are still worth a damn," Blane said, looking at Kai with a touch of respect in his eyes. An absent wipe of his hand removed the blood from his wrist, revealing a freshly healed cut. "Call on me when the time comes to leave. I will do my part."

Kai stood mute as Blane inclined his head and walked away. He'd known that he could sense foreign energy in Blane, but that was a long way from watching him heal a cut in a matter of seconds. Just what was he dealing with?

"Was that a blood oath?" Tom whispered, giving Kai a wide-eyed look from where he stood a few feet away. Tom had stayed quiet enough that Kai had forgotten he was there, leaving him in an uncomfortable position.

"It was, but I would urge you to forget about such things. A blood oath can do damage beyond anything you could imagine. I've seen it," Kai said, thinking back to some of the darkest days in his old sect.

"I believe you; I've heard the stories," Tom said fervently, eyeing the cut on Kai's wrist warily.

"Good. Now, we've gained another ally for our hunt, but I want to know more about the attacks here. There must be a reason why the bear didn't do more damage." Kai gestured to the intact village around them as he spoke.

"You make it sound like destroying the palisade should have been easy for it," Tom said, looking at Kai with a curious expression.

"Because it should. Elemental bears are shrouded in their element but can also conjure and fight with it. We know that the one we are hunting is an earth-based creature, so it could have undermined the wall and toppled it in only a short space of time. Not to mention that a creature like that could rip out chunks of the ground and throw them, but I see no evidence of that here." Kai explained, looking around as he spoke for any impact marks on the village's interior. As far as he could tell, the damage had only been done to the exterior of the village, which was odd.

Looking for a way to help, Tom went to assist a logging team going to the nearby wood to gather the large logs needed for the palisade. With the ash wolves driven off, they would likely have a short window of opportunity where the nearby area was devoid of any potential threats.

While Tom worked, Kai spent some time speaking with the villagers about the attack on Willowbrook. From what he gathered, this was indeed an elemental bear attack; their descriptions were too apt for it to be anything else.

The bear had been causing a number of problems for the area as a whole, but it had only struck the village itself once, causing the damage he could see at the gate. When Kai questioned how they drove it off, he was told that the rocky exterior of the bear was damaged on its front left shoulder, giving them an area to target.

Exactly what kind of damage they were talking about, or how severe it was, Kai didn't know, but it did potentially explain how they drove it off. Kai wasn't completely convinced, but there was no conflicting information to make him think that anyone was lying or misleading him.

Perhaps the bear had already been wounded, and the villagers managed to reopen the wound, causing it to retreat?

It still didn't explain the lack of damage to the area, but Kai didn't know what else to do. This wasn't his strength.

There were still a few hours of daylight left when Kai gave up on his investigation, so he decided to take the time to work on his cultivation. On the way back from the fight with the Darjee, Verdan had demonstrated that Kai might be linked to air as well as fire. Since then, there had always been more pressing things to do, more urgent matters to take care of. Right now, however, he had hours to himself and no responsibility until tomorrow.

Kai left messages with a few villagers for Tom and Lieutenant Silver, letting them know where he was going, before heading out of the village and back up the hill, Oaktop.

Settling himself on the highest point he could, Kai closed his eyes and started to cycle his breaths, breathing deep and filling himself with what he now knew was Aether.

Considering the element of air, Kai immediately thought of the wind. The flowing freedom it represented. When he was younger, Kai had often sat atop buildings, enjoying the wind playing across his face as he struggled with his cultivation exercises.

Thinking back to that time, Kai gripped onto everything he loved about the wind and used it as a focus through which he fed the Aether he was drawing in from around him.

There was nothing, no sense of Essence filling his soul, no sense of fresh energy flowing through him. A whisper of disappointment raced through him as Kai realized it wasn't working. Still, he had nothing else to do this evening; he may as well stick with it.

Time passed steadily as Kai maintained his focus, despite the lack of any immediate result. He remembered the guided meditation that he'd had to perform to first unlock his fire Essence when he was still a candidate for the sect; this wasn't too dissimilar.

Of course, the majority of the time Kai had spent as a candidate had been used in learning how to meditate, and in the most-basic breathing techniques of the sect. Those that were able to awaken their Essence within the timeframe of the training course were taken on, the rest were sworn to secrecy and either discarded or hired as servants.

Kai finished his meditation when the sun began to dip below the horizon, feeling a strange sense of pressure in his chest for a moment as he stood to head back. The sensation swiftly faded, however, so Kai put it down to a twinged muscle. He would ensure his morning routine carried more stretches than usual to compensate.

Reminiscing about his time as a candidate had put Kai in a melancholy mood. It was only one step from remembering those times to remembering his sister, and that was a wound that was far from healed.

Steeling his mind and focusing on the task at hand, Kai started back to the village. They would be hunting the bear on the morrow, and he needed his rest.

CHAPTER

THIRTY-ONE

VERDAN RETURNED to his estate after the meeting with Commander Griffon, Tobias, and the others. The guard commander had promised a half-dozen guards for their rescue expedition, but that was all he could do. With Lieutenant Silver and his squad away hunting the bear, Griffon was reluctant to commit forces elsewhere.

Verdan understood why. The Weeping Death was playing a long-term manipulative game with them all. Even knowing that it still went against the grain for Verdan. His sense of responsibility for the fate of those bringing the goods to Hobson's Point would be enough for him to aid Tobias, but his growing dislike for the Weeping Death didn't hurt either.

"Boss," one of Verdan's new guards greeted him as he approached. The man was standing watch at the entrance to the estate and gave Verdan only a brief glance before returning to his vigil. If nothing else, these new hires were professionals through and through, something that Verdan could appreciate.

"Who's here at the moment?" Verdan asked, curious to see what the guard knew.

"Tim and his wolf are out back training with the Witch. The big guy is in the mansion with some of the others. Henry is putting out lunch for us all," the guard said, nodding absently towards the mansion.

"You have a problem with Gwen?" Verdan asked, keeping his tone curious, not accusing.

"Not personally, but she's a Witch," the guard replied, shifting uncomfortably under Verdan's gaze.

"Will it be a problem?" Verdan asked, quirking a brow at the other man.

"No, no, of course not. We were told that there was a Witch here upfront. Some of the others are a little warier than I am, but as long as she keeps it under control, I can work with her." The guard shrugged a little, spreading his palms open.

"Do they really have such a bad reputation?" Verdan asked after a moment, pleased that his new hires weren't going to be an issue but still concerned.

"There's a reason most of them live out on their own. A lot of them are helpful people, alchemists and the like that are really useful. They just can't live in a large settlement."

Verdan thanked the guard and made his way toward the mansion, finally putting together what bothered him about the bias toward Witches. They were viewed as dangerous and wild, but that didn't seem to extend to prejudice in most cases. The fear of the people he'd first rescued when he woke up made more sense now; they were trapped in a small room with a potentially deadly magic-user. In that situation, of course, they would panic.

Verdan realized now that while Witches were a problem, everyone seemed aware that it wasn't intentional. Maybe if there weren't Sorcerers out there abusing their power, it would be different. Right now, however, Witches were treated as more of a natural disaster—people simply avoided them to stay safe.

One thing that Verdan wanted was to integrate Witches back into society as best he could. Interactions like the one he'd just had reassured him that such integration was possible. It wouldn't be easy, but Verdan was confident they could do it.

The kitchen of the mansion was quite busy when Verdan stepped inside. Elliot and the other five guards that Verdan had hired were clustered around the big table that dominated the room. Each person had a plate full of food, and Henry looked on from the business end of the room with a satisfied smile.

"Verdan, how was your meeting?" Elliot asked as he delicately sliced a sausage into portions with a knife and fork that looked tiny in his big hands.

"Productive, though somewhat concerning. We're putting together a rescue force to go after a caravan hit by some Cyth, if you're interested in coming?" Verdan asked Elliot, unsure of what the big man would decide. Verdan had very much gotten the impression that Elliot wasn't a fighter, but a noble cause inspired all sorts of behavior from people.

"I would be more of a detriment; I wage my war against such things with what I make, not directly," Elliot said, a sad smile touching his face for a moment. "A shame that Cullan or Branwen aren't here; my siblings would join you without question." There was a hint of tension in Elliot's frame as he spoke, with an almost apprehensive posture that was ill at odds with Elliot's normal confidence.

"We all act in our own ways. You'll see no pressure from me," Verdan said, smiling as Elliot openly relaxed at his words. "As for the rest of you," Verdan said, turning to the five guards as he continued speaking. "I won't force you to join the rescue, but volunteers will be greatly appreciated."

"Will we get hazard pay?" An older guard asked, a network of scars around his mouth giving him a slight slur.

"Five silvers each, though I want at least two of you to stay behind to watch the estate," Verdan said after a quick consideration. There was a certainty of battle here, and he did need the extra blades on their side, so hazard pay seemed reasonable.

Four of the five guards immediately stated their acceptance, the fifth having a coughing fit as he tried to speak up around a mouthful of food. The others laughed at his struggles, and the unfortunate guard could only glare as he tried to clear his throat.

"The expedition leaves first thing tomorrow, with an expectation to arrive by late morning and track the Cyth back to their home immediately. Get some rest and come to the workshop in the morning. I'll be equipping you with some enhanced weaponry." Verdan told them, watching with amusement as the four chosen guards perked up and the unlucky fifth slumped in his chair.

"You can rely on us, Boss," the same guard spoke up again, half of his face stretching into a broad grin.

Taking his leave, Verdan set off for the rear of the workshop, where the old servant quarters were. He could hear the distant crack and rumble of lightning and thunder magic, so it was safe to say that Gwen was still nearby.

Coming into view of the impromptu area, Verdan could see that Tim and Gwen were training while Sylvie lay a short distance away and watched. The way the wolf tracked the two of them as they trained seemed to have intent behind it, but perhaps Verdan was reading too much into it.

Regardless, he was glad to see that she was resting and giving her wounds time to heal properly.

Verdan had the rest of the day to get things done, and he needed at least a few hours to put temporary enchantments on the weapons for the guard and then actively meditate to recover the expended Aether.

Turning to the matter at hand, Verdan paid attention to the training going on in front of him. It was a simple exercise, if a little more dangerous than Verdan would have expected.

Tim and Gwen were running a basic scenario again and again. Tim would head a short distance away and then charge in, dodging blasts of lightning that Gwen sent his way as he went. Gwen hadn't mastered defensive magic yet, but she swapped over to a different aspect of storms as Tim closed in, buffeting him with strong gusts of wind and rain.

Tim reacted to the change with practiced ease, making Verdan wonder just how much time these two had spent training together. It was good to see and was precisely what they needed right now.

There was an art to fighting back against magic-users when you had no magic yourself. It was mainly around reading the intent and correctly predicting your opponent's actions, key skills for any warrior.

"Hey, Boss, didn't see you there," Tim called out as they finished their latest bout, ending with Tim touching Gwen with his blade.

"Looks like you've been having a good training session. How has it been going?" Verdan asked, walking over to them as he spoke.

"Pretty well," Tim said with a half-shrug. "I'm getting better at dodging, and Gwen is getting better at control. There were a few accidents at first, but we got past that."

"I'm much better than I was," Gwen added proudly, giving Verdan an almost defiant look as she lifted her chin and squared her shoulders.

"Really?" Verdan said, a smile tugging at the corner of his mouth as he moved so that there was a clear line between him and Gwen. "Show me. *Ast.*" Verdan conjured a half-dome shield to protect him, gesturing for Gwen to go ahead.

"Okay, okay, okay," Gwen muttered to herself, taking a deep breath as she turned to Verdan and threw a hand out. Crackling arcs of blue-white energy coursed down her arm, momentarily building in her palm before blasting out at Verdan's shield.

Verdan felt the impact of the blast on his shield and immediately fed more Aether into it, keeping it stable despite the strong impact. Gwen hadn't been lying; she really had been practicing.

There were two metrics to measuring the strength of a Witch, from what Verdan remembered; their efficiency with what they drew in and the raw amount of what they could draw.

Gwen had drawn enough Aether from the surroundings to power a decent mid-range spell, but her efficiency wasn't great. The actual strength of the impact was above that of the blades of air that Verdan favored, but she used a lot more to get that strength. Still, in a short battle, she would be able to hold her own, and Witches could recover quickly.

"Very good, you're improving nicely," Verdan said, dismissing his shield absently as he continued toward the two of them. "How do you feel about putting that practice to good use?"

"Are we heading out?" Tim asked, perking up a little at Verdan's words, while Gwen bit her lip and frowned.

"I am, and you are welcome to come with me, but you're equally welcome to stay here if you don't feel up to it," Verdan said gently, talking mostly to Gwen but including Tim in the offer to not go.

"I'm in. What're we doing?" Tim said, almost buzzing with energy as he bounced on his heels.

"I'll brief everyone later on. We're heading out first thing tomorrow, so get your things ready and rest up," Verdan said to Tim, motioning with his head for Tim to head back to the mansion.

"What about you, Gwen?" Verdan said in a soft voice, looking back at the Witch to see if she had made a decision.

"I'll think about it. I'm not sure if I'm ready," Gwen said, looking down at her palms as she clenched her hands into fists with a crackle of sparks. "I've gained a lot of strength, but my control is only just enough to make sure that Tim is safe when we practice. If I came with you, I'd be more of a problem than anything."

"I see. I remember feeling like that when I first learned large-scale battle magic, the kind that could kill your own people as easily as the enemy if your control slipped for even a moment," Verdan said, his eyes dark as he recalled a more desperate time. He empathized with Gwen, and that made him giving her the option to stay back even more important. He'd never had that choice, and he'd made a few mistakes that weighed heavily on his soul.

"That's hard to imagine; your magic seems so tightly controlled," Gwen said with a shake of her head, gesturing to the arm he'd used to project the shield a few moments earlier.

"Yes, but it wasn't always that way. Power will come with time, but the control you have to work for."

"I understand, thanks," Gwen said, nodding her head a few times thoughtfully as he kept her eyes on her closed fists.

"When this is done, I'll see if I can help you with some exercises I learned. In the meantime, though, I have an errand to run," Verdan said, excusing himself from the distracted Witch and making his way toward the workshop. He would have some time before Tim returned; he may as well use that to start adding some temporary enchantments to the spare weapons Kai had bought him.

_**_

Verdan spent the rest of the evening meditating, and alternating between working on his spiral and actively speeding up the rate at which he drew in Aether. In times like these, it was equally important to both lay the foundation for the future and gather as much Aether as he could for the upcoming fight.

"*Hyn*," Verdan tapped himself with an energy spell after catching a few precious hours of sleep. Like burning flame through dry timber, the Aether tore through Verdan's mind and body, wiping away his fatigue and exhaustion.

Verdan descended from his room in the mansion to find Henry already making breakfast in the kitchen, releasing delicious smells into the rest of the building. The draw of breakfast had brought a few of the others to the table in the kitchen. Verdan's gaze was immediately drawn to Tim, who sat at the end, Sylvie curled at his feet.

"Morning, Boss," Tim called out, the others echoing the sentiment a moment later.

"Morning, how's Sylvie today?" Verdan asked, sitting next to Tim and casting his gaze across the resting wolf. Her neck was a mess of partially-healed cuts and wounds, but she seemed to be doing well enough physically. Verdan had left Tim to look after her the evening before, while spent his time meditating to recoup what he used during the surgery.

"Tired, but she's okay. I talked with her, well, at her," Tim paused and struggled with his words for a moment before shaking his head and focusing back on Verdan. "Doesn't matter. The point is, I explained the situation, and she's decided to stay."

"Excellent, I'm glad to hear it," Verdan said, smiling at the two of them as he reached down to touch Sylvie. "*Iacha*."

Sylvie looked up at him curiously as Verdan channeled positive Aether into her, gauging as he did the effect of the corruption that was lingering in her system. It seemed to be reducing nicely; he estimated a full recovery in a couple of days.

"Verdan, Mr. Brock and his people are outside. He asked if you could come on out as soon as you can," Adrienne said, stepping into the kitchen and giving them all a motherly smile. She signed something to her husband, who chuckled and walked over to kiss her on the cheek before returning to the stove and adding more bacon.

"Very well, I'm coming now," Verdan called back before turning to look at the others at the table and motioning at their food. "Eat up and get ready. We leave within the hour."

"Yes, Boss," Tim and the guards chorused back as Verdan got up and started to head outside, pausing only for a moment when Henry pressed a breakfast sandwich into his hand.

Outside the mansion, the courtyard had become the gathering point for quite the group of people. There were half-a-dozen guards in their official capacity, several empty carts hitched to donkeys, and two dozen armed and armored mercenaries. At least, Verdan assumed that was what they were, given that there was no consistency among them in what they wore or how they were armed.

Tobias and Brent were also present, with Brent watching their surroundings while Tobias arranged for various supplies to be loaded onto the empty carts and last-minute preparations to be made.

Verdan made sure that Tobias knew he was awake before heading into the workshop and gathering the weaponry on which he'd placed the temporary enchantments. Kai's decision to expand Verdan's guard and do more Aether sensitivity testing was already paying dividends.

Altogether there were around thirty people in this expedition, but Verdan knew that a lot of the pressure would be on him when they found the Cyth that had raided the caravan. The normal Cyth Lai were corrupted by their worship but gained little power from it, unlike the magic-wielding Cyth Baynes. Aether forbid if they encountered anything stronger than that, like a Cyth Scerrd, or a Horror.

At least Verdan could rely on his guards, and on Tim for that matter, to provide solid support. Their weapons would help equalize the field in case multiple stronger Cyth were present. They wouldn't counter the strong Cyth directly, but it would give the non-casters a few advantages of their own.

As he considered what to do in such situations, Verdan looked at a familiar dark-haired Witch as she emerged from the mansion to join the group. Their eyes locked across the courtyard, and Verdan gave her a respectful nod. It was not easy to knowingly enter a fight when you were in her situation. Still, the large raven on her shoulder was living proof that her control would be all she could hope for soon enough.

Gwen's decision to join them eased Verdan's mind considerably. A storm Witch was a powerful ally, even a partially-competent one like Gwen. If nothing else, he wouldn't be the only source of magic defending the mercenaries.

Eventually, all was in order, and they were underway. The clamor of their passage as they wound through the streets of Hobson's Point drew more than one passerby's attention, and Verdan saw the faintest flickers of hope and fear in the eyes of those that watched.

Hobson's Point had been plagued by desertion, with people heading south to avoid the tribulations of living at the northernmost edge of civilization. The whole place was only a few bad monster attacks away from falling to pieces, which meant a well-funded and well-armed expedition like theirs was potentially a tipping point.

If they failed here, it might very well be the last straw for the city's attempts to fight back against encroaching threats.

There was no way Verdan would allow this mission to fail. He would put everything he had on the line before he let innocent people be left in the clutches of a Cyth raiding party.

Tobias and Verdan led the expedition from the front,with Brent, Gwen, and Tim a close second, while Sylvie padded ahead of them. In truth, Verdan was somewhat surprised that Tobias was joining them on the expedition; it was good to see that he was taking this just as personally as Verdan.

One of the city guards that had joined them was familiar with where the caravan had been attacked and took charge of getting them there, which would take several hours.

This close to Hobson's Point, there were unlikely to be any monsters or problems, but Verdan kept a weather eye out as they traveled. There were undercurrents at play here. Commander Griffon was confident that the Weeping Death was manipulating events, and Verdan wasn't in mind to disagree.

The road from Hobson's Point to Dresk went almost directly east, cutting through several small areas of woodland before reaching what the locals referred to as the Imperial Line. Apparently, a main highway ran the length of the continent, a relic of an earlier age.

The Grym Imperium had constructed roads throughout the continent, some of which were quite grand in design, but nothing that matched what they were describing.

Sadly, their destination was a few hours short of the line, which in itself was interesting. It was hard to tell without seeing it all on a map, but it sounded as though the caravan was attacked halfway between the Imperial Line and Hobson's Point. A coincidence, perhaps, but with their other concerns in mind, perhaps not.

Once they passed the halfway mark to their destination, Verdan created an Aether construct and bound it to his staff, creating a sixty-foot radius ward that stretched around them. The ward would scan the surroundings once every minute, and if it detected any Cyth, it would notify him.

Once a minute gave the Cyth plenty of time to close in, but it was still a layer of security, and Verdan didn't want to commit too much Aether just yet. For now, he'd rely mainly on the sharp eyes of the men and women that Tobias had hired.

Their surroundings began to grow more heavily wooded, some areas becoming thick with trees that stood old and proud alongside the road. The whole area had a sense of quiet antiquity that Verdan appreciated greatly.

"Sirs, the site is just up ahead, on this side of the ford," the guard said, his fingers tightening on the spear he held. "We didn't see any

Cyth presence when we were last here, but perhaps we should be cautious."

"I'll leave this to you, Verdan. What do you think?" Tobias said, stepping back and looking at Verdan expectantly.

"I'll head forward with Tim, two of my guards, and two of your hirelings, Tobias. We'll scout the site, and I'll try to detect any Cyth nearby. If it's clear, I'll send your men back to bring the rest of you in," Verdan said, part of his mind accessing the ward he'd created and altering it to ping the surroundings twice as often, just in case.

"I'll come as well. I know what it should look like, so I can tell if it's been disturbed," the city guard said, trying in vain to control the relief on his face when Tobias had handed control over this part to Verdan.

"My people are at your disposal," Tobias said with a gesture for two of the nearby mercenaries to approach. "You'll be scouting ahead with Verdan. Make sure to follow his orders."

The two mercenaries nodded and gave Verdan a once-over, tensing a little as they took in his lack of armor and weaponry, but relaxing at the staff he was carrying.

Their reaction intrigued Verdan; he couldn't imagine that a staff would have the same use for a Sorcerer as for a Wizard. For him, it provided an easy object to attach Aether constructs to, like the ward he'd just created. Still, they seemed to recognise him as a magic user, or perhaps they thought he was some form of quarter-staff-wielding mystical fighter. Personally, Verdan hoped it was the latter. He'd loved stories of staff-wielding heroes who could access mystical energies as a child.

Lips twitching with a hidden smile, Verdan motioned for Tim to pick two guards and approach. The five of them were close enough to have heard what they were going into, and the four guards immediately had a whispered argument over who was best equipped to go.

"Verdan, why aren't I coming with you?" Gwen asked quietly as the guards argued.

"If I'm gone, the rest of the expedition is vulnerable to some of the stronger Cyth. I need you here to make sure someone can stand up to any Cyth that might attack," Verdan said, holding a hand up to forestall her argument. "I know full well that it's unlikely to happen, but it's about planning for the worst-case scenarios."

Gwen looked as though she might argue further but grimaced and gave him a short nod. One hand reached up to absently stroke the feathers of her raven as she joined him in watching the debating guards.

The argument had gone on long enough by that point, so Verdan cleared his throat meaningfully, prompting it to end rather abruptly. After a final few whispered insults, Tim and two of the guards came to join them, completing their scouting group.

Tobias went to speak with the rest of the expedition, bringing everyone to a halt and setting perimeter guards while they waited. In the few moments they had before they set off, Verdan turned to the two of his guards who had come with Tim.

"I'm sorry, we've not had much of a chance to speak yet. Could you tell me your names?" Verdan grimaced internally; he should know their names by now, but so much had been happening recently that he just hadn't had the chance.

"No problem, Boss, you're a busy man. The name's Pawel. Pleased to meet ya," the first guard said, holding a hand out for Verdan to shake. Pawel was about five-and-a-half feet tall, with a slender frame, but he moved with the kind of controlled grace that spoke of years of training. Pawel had a sword sheathed on his belt and a shield on his arm, but Verdan noticed daggers tucked into his belt as well.

"And I'm Pania," the other guard said, reaching out to shake Verdan's hand next. "Pawel and I are the only ones with daggers and the know-how to use them. Barb moves better in the country, but we're better sneaks, if you follow my drift." Pania winked at him with a smirk as she produced a throwing knife in one hand as a demonstration. Pania was a little taller than Pawel but shared the same build and graceful movement, likely from the sneaking she mentioned.

"I see; I'll leave the sneaking to you then. I'm better at direct fighting, really," Verdan said with a shrug. He'd never really tried to be that stealthy; others specialized in that sort of thing, but his skills were more focused elsewhere.

"You got it, Boss," Pania said, her smirk gaining a malicious edge as she nudged Pawel and started off in the direction they'd been heading. "We'll scout forward, but not too far. We'll shout if we find anything."

"Sounds good—the rest of you, with me," Verdan said, motioning for the guard to lead the way and the others to follow him as they started down the path the guard had pointed out.

Pania and Pawel had already disappeared into the woods on either side of the rough path they were using, so Verdan manually triggered an Aether pulse of his construct, reassuring him that there were no Cyth within sixty feet.

One of the weaknesses of such a spell was that the Cyth could have been sixty-one feet away when the pulse went out and could even now be charging Verdan to try and kill him, unnoticed by the construct.

Situations like that were exactly why Wizards tended to form a retinue that traveled with them. Verdan was confident that with Tim and Sylvie watching his back, there was no chance that anything was going to sneak up on him.

True to the guard's words, the remnants of the caravan were only a few hundred feet away, and Verdan could immediately sense the lingering corruption in the air.

"There was a Cyth Bayne here, maybe two of them," Verdan muttered in a dark tone as he surveyed the scene. The caravan had been hit right on the road, with multiple scorch marks around the broken carts and on nearby trees to show where corrupt magics had bombarded them.

Blood and gore had been spilt around the wreckage, but there were no bodies to see, only drag marks where their attackers had taken them.

"Why does this feel worse than the Darjee?" Tim asked, more to himself than anything, as he walked beside Verdan, helping check the wreckage.

"Wait for a moment," Verdan said, holding up a hand to motion for Tim to hold that thought. "*Canfo.*" Verdan sent out a larger pulse of Aether, extending it up to several hundred feet from where he stood, looking for any Cyth nearby.

If there were Bayne involved, then this became a whole lot more dangerous for everyone. Normal Cyth activity told Verdan that a Bayne would only join a raid like this if at least one or two more were at their camp. That meant he was potentially fighting up to four or five of them, and that was if they didn't have anything else. Thankfully, the pulse picked up no Cyth, so Verdan was able to relax a little for the moment.

"It feels worse because the Darjee are slavers and horrid creatures, but they are a prosaic kind of evil. The uneasy feeling you have now is from the Cyth Bayne that the raiders had with them; it must have thrown around quite a bit of magic to leave this much ambient corruption. Without anyone doing something, the vegetation here will grow sick and wither."

"Can you stop it?" Tim asked, looking at some of the blackened scorch marks on the trees with a level of empathy that Verdan found surprising, until he realized that Tim had actually seen two cases of corruption: first, the state of Gwen when Verdan rescued them, and then, more recently, with Sylvie's collar.

"Yes, but I won't at this point," Verdan said, shaking his head as Tim turned with a questioning look on his face. Motioning for Tim to wait, Verdan turned to the two mercenaries that Tobias had sent them. "Both of you, head back and give the all-clear, but tell Tobias that we need to move quickly."

The two men moved off at a jog, leaving Tim and Verdan alone among the wreckage. Pawel and Pania were no longer sneaking through the undergrowth but were instead studying the tracks that the Cyth raiding group had left behind.

"Why won't you heal them?" Tim asked softly, picking up on Verdan's unease.

"There's going to be maybe as many as half-a-dozen magic users in the Cyth camp. They're not at my level, but they're not weak enough that I can walk all over them, and I only have Gwen as my backup," Verdan said, his voice little more than a whisper. He wanted to make sure that Tim went into this with his eyes open.

"Are you saying we shouldn't go?" Tim asked, his brow furrowing as he looked at the devastation around them with fresh eyes.

"I'm saying that I need to save my Aether; who knows how bad this will be? As much as I want to save the trees here, realistically, they can wait." Verdan explained, gesturing to the mostly-healthy plant life around them.

"Boss, Pawel has gone to track the Cyth a short way and see if there's an issue, but they're leaving a fairly clear trail; should be no problem following them home," Pania called out as she joined them, her eyes flicking between their worried expressions. "Everything okay?"

"Yes, just be aware that there will definitely be Cyth magic-users at their camp. Make sure you use the weapons I enhanced for you," Verdan said, gesturing to the sword at Pania's hip.

"Got it, Boss. I'll go make sure Pawel's okay and that he doesn't go too far," Pania said, giving them a rough salute before setting off into the woods.

"So, what now?" Tim asked.

"Now, we wait for Tobias, and then we track these bastards down and wipe them out, all of them."

CHAPTER
THIRTY-TWO

DAWN BROKE OVER WILLOWBROOK, but Kai and the others were already awake and getting themselves ready for their hunt. An elemental bear was no simple prey; they needed to go into this with the right mindset and as much preparation as possible.

Callum and Clara had managed to locate an area rife with caves where they believed the bear was denning, which was all that Lieutenant Silver had been waiting on. Their plan, such as it was, was to move straight toward the area and try to find tracks leading to one specific cave. If they couldn't, they'd set an ambush for the beast and prepare the area as best they could.

With so many unknowns to consider, it wasn't a bad plan, so Kai offered no objections as Silver organized them and gave their marching orders. With Blane and the two hunters joining them, they numbered eighteen now, a good number considering what they would be fighting.

According to Callum, the area they'd found was a heavily-wooded valley an hour's walk from Willowbrook. A nearby stream fed into a large pool in the middle of the basin, providing an easy water source for those living within the caves that riddled the valley walls.

If the bear was indeed denning in the valley, it was no wonder it had attacked the village; such a creature would claim miles of land as its territory, easily covering Willowbrook.

The group was quiet as they moved through the hilly woodlands of the area. There was an air of tension among them that Kai couldn't fault; better that they went into this cautiously. The weapons that Verdan had supplied would even the fight, but he doubted they'd get out of this without casualties.

"We're about a mile from the valley entrance now, and the caves run along the full length of it. We should start to move more carefully," Callum said, giving a pointed look to Silver and his guards. The guards were doing their best not to make too much noise, but Kai could see their lack of experience showing.

"I agree. Let's take it slow and steady. Callum, would you and your daughter scout ahead for us?" Silver said, motioning for the other guards to match his pace.

"Of course. We'll see what's up ahead and if there are any fresh tracks," Callum said, glancing over to his daughter before the two slipped away into the undergrowth.

"Blane and I will take the front, Tom. Stick with the lieutenant," Kai said, nodding to Blane as he jogged forward to be a good twenty feet ahead of the guards. Kai was no expert, but he'd spent enough time out in the wilderness to move quietly, unlike Silver and his people.

Truthfully, Blane was more on the level of Callum and Clara with how easily he moved through the undergrowth, but Kai wanted to keep the odd man close by, just in case.

Kai thought longingly of the armor that had been taken by the Cyth when they'd captured him; he had some leather to protect him, but that would do little against the claws of a bear. Perhaps once they were back, he'd look at getting Verdan to enchant his current armor, or buy something better for himself.

Bringing his attention back to the task at hand, Kai kept his eyes on their surroundings as they moved toward the entrance to the valley. This area was rife with thick forest and had more than its share of hills, making it difficult for them to see more than a short distance around them.

"Callum is coming back," Blane muttered after a few minutes, his nostrils flaring slightly.

"What do you mean?" Kai asked, glancing in confusion at Blane, who merely gestured to where the hunter was emerging from a thicket of trees.

"Disciple Kai, Blane," Callum greeted them in a whispered tone as he moved closer, keeping low to the ground as he moved.

"Just Kai is fine," Kai said softly, silently cursing the strange formality that Silver had developed with him. "What's wrong?"

"We've come across a fresh trail leading back to the valley. It's large enough to be our quarry, and the tracks look correct. There's certainly nothing else around here that leaves ones like that. Clara is tracking it now, but I will lead you to it," Callum explained, motioning for Silver and the others to join them as the guards caught up.

Callum reiterated the situation to Silver, who gave Kai a questioning look, but the Sorcerer spread his hands and gestured for Silver to take charge.

Technically speaking, Kai and Tom were here to offer support in case things went badly, not to take control of what was happening.

In some ways, this could be considered a training exercise for the city guards.

Realizing that Kai was taking a back seat to the operation, Silver instructed Callum to guide them forward, and they soon found themselves at the trail.

Damaged trees, flattened bushes, and large, shallow pawprints were all classic signs of an earth-aspect Elemental Bear. Their connection with the ground was so strong that they left only a slight imprint, despite their weight and size, but that connection did nothing to protect the vegetation around them.

These particular tracks looked shallow, even for an earth-aspect bear, but Kai had only seen a few examples in the past, the last of which was in a mountainous area with little soil. Without more to go on, it was hard to say if the tracks were unusually shallow, or if the difference in soil and terrain was what he was noticing.

Deciding not to say anything for now, Kai moved on with the group as they followed the trail down into the valley, where Clara was waiting for them.

"Clara, what did you find?" Callum asked as his daughter joined them.

"The tracks lead up to a pair of caves that share a single path; the tracks get difficult, though," Clara said, gesturing off to the east at the side of the valley.

"How so?" Silver asked, raising a brow at the younger hunter.

"There are few trees there, so I couldn't get too close without losing cover, but the tracks start overlapping, and with how shallow they are, they're easy to muddle up." Clara gave the lieutenant a shrug, one hand idly playing with her arrows as she spoke.

"I see. Is it still in there?" Silver asked, tapping the side of his thigh in thought.

"Looks to be, there's the path coming in and one going to the pool, but that's it."

"The trail goes to the pool, then here?" Kai asked, frowning a little, as he was sure that wasn't what she had said first.

"No, one goes to the cave, and another goes to the pool and back. I think it went back and came out again for a drink," Clara said with another shrug and a throwaway gesture, clearly not finding it important.

The explanation didn't sit quite right with Kai, but he couldn't put his finger on why, and he'd already decided it wasn't his place to lead, so he didn't push it further. There were a lot of things that he would have looked at more or done differently, but nothing that would endanger anyone. His role here was only to act if mistakes endangered the group. Simple mistakes or oversights would be a learning experience.

"So, we will set an ambush for the creature as it emerges from the lair. Are there any good vantage points nearby?" Silver was asking as Kai focused back on the conversation.

"I think so. This particular cave is quite low, so there are plenty of others that look down on it."

"Right, let's move quickly then. The two of you lead us to the cave and point it out, then head up with the crossbowmen. Auger, you're in command but listen to their advice, understand?" Silver said, taking swift action now that the moment was upon them.

"Yes, Sir," one of the guards with the crossbows said, the others with a similar armament moving to gather around him.

"No problem, let's go. It might not stay in there for too long," Clara said, all but bouncing on her toes impatiently as she waited for them to organize themselves. It was a stark contrast to the absolute stillness of her father, which Kai chalked up to a lack of experience on her part.

"Agreed, let's move," Silver said, motioning for them to follow the hunters as Clara immediately set off back toward the cave.

This plan felt rushed to Kai, and he glanced at Blane, who was also frowning slightly at Silver. It was one thing to follow the creature here. It was another to set an impromptu ambush on its doorstep and simply hope that it didn't come out before they were ready. Kai would have preferred the ambush to be further from the cave. Perhaps on its path to the water or out of the valley.

Still, they did have a few more advantages than usual, so perhaps an aggressive tactic was the right move on Silver's part. They'd soon find out, one way or another.

Kai kept his spear at the ready and his eyes open as the group closed in on the caves that the trail led to. The valley's center was thick with old trees and had a good amount of cover for them as they moved. The sides, where the caves were, had far less to conceal them.

Clara pointed out the two caves in question, which were at the top of a steep incline that led partway up the valley wall.

"Okay, you go find your positions, but don't shoot at it until it's at the base of the ramp. We don't want to have to go in the cave after it," Silver said, sending the hunters on their way as he started assigning ambush spots.

As the backup in this situation, Kai, Tom, and Blane were given a flanking position, where they could see everything that was happening and respond as needed.

The lieutenant split his men into two groups and gave them positions flanking one of the trails. Silver was banking on the fact that if the bear had already been out once today, it would likely only emerge again to go to the water. A reasonable assumption, and one that might pay off for them.

If not, they would still be in a position to strike, but the guards would all be coming at it from one direction, which was less than ideal.

Watching some of the higher areas, Kai saw flickers of movement as the hunters and crossbow-armed guards settled in. They were as ready as they were going to be.

"When do you think it will come out?" Tom asked quietly, pitching his voice so that it just reached Kai. The three of them were in a thicket of trees, spread out enough that they had their own sections.

"It could be in two minutes, could be two hours; nothing for it but to settle in and wait," Kai said, not moving his focus from the two caves.

Blane didn't comment, but from the way he settled himself against a tree, Kai could tell that the strange man was expecting quite a long wait.

Tom started to work on his Essence control, but Kai shut that down immediately. He had no idea if an elemental bear could sense Essence usage, but after seeing how Verdan could sense and examine Aether and Essence, Kai was taking no chances.

As they waited, Kai's mind drifted to some of the things they'd seen and the odd pieces of information that were still niggling at him. There was something he hadn't seen, something he hadn't put together yet, and he hated that feeling.

Reviewing everything in his mind, Kai felt certain that the key assumptions were correct. This was an elemental bear, it was earth-aspected, and it was denning nearby. The descriptions from the villagers, the tracks, and the trail they'd followed proved all that.

Beyond that, he was less certain on the fact that it had been wounded, and that was how the villagers had driven it off, but nothing else made sense there. An adult elemental bear could destroy a village without even seeing them as a threat.

Movement caught Kai's eye, breaking his chain of thought as something moved in the shadows at the entrance to the smaller of the two caves. Something big.

Tension filled the air as the creature stepped out into the sun; Kai could almost feel the attention of all the hunting party focus on it. The bear slowly emerged from the cave, shaking itself as it started to descend the path down to the tree line.

The bear was covered in rocky protrusions that moved like fur when it walked, and Kai could see how its steps seemed to impact the whole area around it, spreading the weight out enough to leave only a slight central imprint. It was hard to judge from this distance, but he'd put it around seven or eight feet at the shoulder and twelve feet long, big by any standard.

As it continued closer, Kai caught sight of a patch across its left shoulder where the rocky protrusions had broken away, revealing the skin beneath. Instead of the healthy, healed skin Kai expected, the bear's shoulder was covered by a large, angry wound that looked incredibly painful. That must be the weak spot the villagers aimed for, but it didn't look like a bite or claw injury.

Kai frowned as the creature started down the path. It was big, but it wasn't that big, not for an elemental bear. If he didn't know better, he'd have said it wasn't fully grown.

The horrible realization of what was about to happen hit Kai like a bucket of ice water. The bear hadn't used any elemental attacks against the village because it couldn't. It wasn't fully mature. They needed to call off the ambush; if they attacked this bear, people were going to die.

"Tom, stay here, don't attack unless it does. Blane, get up to the archers and tell them to abort," Kai hissed to the other two. "It's not fully grown. The mother will be somewhere nearby."

Blane and Tom both paled at Kai's words, and they looked back in disbelief at the huge creature. Without the time to convince them, Kai slipped back from his tree and started toward Lieutenant Silver as Blane went for the archers.

Elemental bears were incredibly territorial, which had made Kai wonder why it was out here, but they were also particularly vengeful. If something had wounded the cub, the mother would have chased down the attacker and killed it, taking the territory for herself. That wound on the young bear was too old for something Willowcreek had done, which meant that something had happened to it elsewhere, and the bears had come here in response.

Kai shivered as he realized that Willowcreek had driven the bear off by shooting its injury, but clearly not with enough force to wound it further. If they had, that village would no longer exist; the mother would have ripped it apart.

Hurrying as quickly as he dared through the trees, Kai closed in on the lieutenant's position. He was almost to them when a voice rang out into the silence.

"This is for my mother, you overgrown piece of shit," Clara yelled at the beast, making it swing around toward the sound.

Skidding to a halt and looking over at the cub with a sick feeling, Kai watched as a single arrow shot down into the wound on the bear's shoulder, ripping open the slightly-healed wound. The bear reared back from the attack, roaring in anger and pain.

Immediately, the rest of the ambush started to unfurl, with bolts from the enchanted crossbows slamming into it and shattering small pieces of its armor. At the same time, Silver and his guards rose to come at the bear from both sides. They were out of position, but not too badly.

Kai saw all of that but ignored it, trusting that they had it under control. Instead, he ignited his Essence and went straight for the larger of the two caves.

He could be wrong. He prayed that he was wrong. If it was just this bear, the guard would be able to handle it with no issue. Its lack of elemental abilities would spell its death.

Kai blazed past the angry bear without pausing, absently noting that Blane and Tom were moving in to support the guard.

As Kai reached the halfway point up the ramp to the caves, an ear-splitting crack temporarily silenced the roaring of the bear behind him. Kai felt a swell of power within the cave and brought his spear up defensively, right as the entrance to the cave exploded outwards in a spray of shattered rock.

_**_

Kai dove to the ground as the spray of fast-moving rock whipped over his head, half flying toward those around the bear and the other half toward the range fighters up above. Kai could feel the power controlling those fragments of rock, and he thanked his ancestors that he'd managed to dodge.

A bass bellow of rage ripped through the air as the dust from the explosion settled, revealing a second elemental bear. Unlike the cub, this one stood easily ten to eleven feet tall and at least fifteen feet long. It all but filled what was left of the mouth of the cave with its bulk.

Kai risked a glance behind him and saw that the cub was trying to flee, but the spear-wielders had it surrounded, and it was being brought down. They just needed time.

The ground shook as the second bear came storming out of the cave, its head swinging down toward Kai as its huge jaws opened to bite him in half.

Hot, fetid breath washed over Kai as he slipped by the bear's jaws, bringing his spear up and striking at the bear's neck as he moved away. Rocky armor covered the majority of its neck, causing the tip of Kai's spear to skitter off, leaving only a faint mark where he had struck.

The bear started to follow him, but a cry of pain from its cub drew it back to the other fight, and it started down toward the others. Cries of alarm from the guards and barked orders from Silver let Kai know they were preparing to meet the creature. If they were facing just the one adult bear, it wouldn't be a problem, but splitting their focus between two was a bad idea, not to mention that injuring the cub further would drive the mother into a rage.

Gripping his spear tight, Kai poured Essence into it, not the gentle trickle that he had done during their tests, but as much as he could give it. Now was not the time for reserves.

Flames erupted from the head of his spear almost immediately. Tongues of dancing yellow licked over the metal before becoming deeper and darker, shrinking in on the spearhead as it began to glow with the heat. The dull red color slowly strengthened as Kai flanked the bear, coming at it from behind.

Taking his spear in both hands, Kai burst into a sprint and kicked off, putting everything he had into a single thrust of his spear, right at its armored legs. The tip of the spear was now glowing brightly, and the heat emanating from it enveloped Kai, pushing at the resistance his Essence gave him.

This was the first time he'd used the enchantment Verdan had given him, and it didn't fail to impress. The blazing spearhead hit the rocky armor of the elemental bear and pierced straight through, leaving behind flickers of flame and heating the surrounding rock and flesh as it went deep into the lower leg of the bear.

The creature instinctively bucked to one side, throwing Kai into the wall of the cave and winding him as the air was expelled from his chest. His spear was still in hand, but Kai was momentarily stunned by the impact, giving the enraged bear enough time to close with the guards.

Three guards were valiantly standing in its way, buying their comrades the time they needed to finish the other creature, which was even now falling beneath the attacks from above and the enchanted weapons the guardsmen were using.

The mother bear bore down on the three guards with the brutal power of an avalanche, and though Kai had gotten up and was moving again, there was no way he could get there in time.

The bear was barely ten feet from the lowered spears of the guards and was showing no sign of stopping when Tom sprinted through their line and planted himself in its way.

As Tom hunkered behind his shield, Kai saw smooth gray stone form around both shield and man, connecting him to the ground below and protecting him. The stone grew rapidly but was nowhere near thick enough to stop the massive impetus of the bear as it slammed into him.

Cracking stone, cries of pain, and a roar of surprise blurred together as the bear plowed into Tom, ripping him from the ground and flinging him through the air to crash into a nearby tree with a bone-jarring thud.

At the same time, the bear's charge was arrested just enough to knock it off balance and fling its upper body to one side, changing the charge into a half-roll that crushed two of the guardsmen. All three enchanted spears sank into the bear as it hit the guardsmen, the Aether within them combined with the force of impact forcing them through its armor and drawing blood as they plunged into it.

Tom had fallen to a heap at the base of the tree, leaving Kai to jump onto the bear before it could stand. He had spotted an area on its side where the flesh was freshly healed, and it's armor was weak. Angling for that spot, Kai thrust his spear down as hard as he could, spraying blood out onto him as he pulled his spear out and ripped the wound open.

The bear shook and threw itself back, sending Kai tumbling to the ground as it barreled into the group around its cub, sending several guards flying as it cleared the area.

The smaller bear began to rise slowly to its feet, blood covering a good portion of its body from where the enchanted blades had struck it. Taking stock, Kai winced as he saw that the two guards hit by the rolling bear were lying unmoving on the ground, and so was Tom. Some of the others were favoring legs or had obvious injuries, but they still had the numbers to do this.

The tense moment was broken by an arrow flashing in from the high ground where the ranged fighters were set up. The bigger bear moved to intercept the shot a fraction of a moment too late, and it pierced the younger one's throat through a section where the armour had been cut away.

The bear gurgled as it tried and failed to breathe, sending its mother beyond the rage it had already been in. One paw went down and pushed into the ground, scooping up rock and earth that it hurled at the archer who had killed its child. The main ball of earth and stone was joined by dozens of smaller ones, as the bear channeled a terrifying amount of power into the attack.

Kai had a brief glimpse of Clara standing at the edge of the bluff the archers were on, a triumphant expression on her face before the barrage struck. Rock cracked and broke under the sheer force of the impact, causing the entire bluff to collapse and come tumbling down onto their position.

Kai heard the screams of those caught in the falling earth but could spare no time for them now. He had to finish the bear before it could take them all down. Its armor was sundered in multiple places, and it was bleeding heavily, but somehow it was still on its feet.

Burning more Essence, Kai restored the flame on his spear and pushed strength into his battered body. Silver and his people were harassing the creature up close, just as they'd discussed, but a swipe of the huge creature's paw crippled one of them, its claws shearing through armor and bone alike as it ripped a leg clean off.

Blane rushed past the dying guard and inside the bear's reach, out of Kai's sight. In response to whatever he did, the bear reared back instinctively, but its left leg gave out from where Kai had hurt it earlier.

Darting in, Kai put his weight behind a thrust into its right knee, the flaming blade of his spear penetrating deep into its flesh just above the joint. Kai must have hit something important as that leg immediately gave out, sending the bear off-balance to land on the ground face-first.

There was no artistry in what came next—no technique, no skill. Every human left alive around the beast simply swarmed it, going for any soft targets they could. The bear lashed out with tooth and claw, throwing some of them aside and wounding others, but it wasn't enough.

Silver braved the bear's jaws and was the one to deliver the finishing blow. The lieutenant waited until it snapped at someone else and then leapt forward, driving his blade into an existing wound on the side of its neck. The arterial spray of blood spelled the end for the heavily-wounded bear, and it slumped, its strength finally fading.

There was a moment of stillness as they watched the creature die, the sound of the survivors' heavy breathing echoing loudly around them.

"Clara?" Callum's voice reached them from where the hunter stood at the shattered remnants of the bluff they'd sheltered behind. The man was staring down at the rubble that had been piled on the valley floor with a distraught expression.

"Jenkins, check the wounded, see who can be saved. You two— with me," Silver barked, limping toward the rubble with a determined set to his shoulders. The two guards that Silver had pointed to hurried after him, along with Blane.

Jenkins and the other guard still standing were moving among the fallen, checking who could be saved and who was already gone, but Kai had his eyes on one in particular.

The bear had thrown Tom into a tree with enough force to dent the trunk where the Sorcerer had impacted it, but his stone armor had been in place. That was all that had saved Tom's life.

With years of practice, Kai checked Tom over for injuries, noting the huge swelling down his side with professional eyes. His new friend would live, but he'd feel like he wished he hadn't for a while. Kai estimated that Tom had broken an arm and cracked or outright broken quite a few ribs, but just how many, he wasn't sure.

Kai was reluctant to move Tom too much, in case of a concussion or head injury, but he was satisfied that there were no life-threatening injuries at the moment.

Kai headed over to where Silver and the others were digging through the rubble. Driving his spear butt-first into the ground, Kai moved in to help. His Essence was still burning, so Kai was able to shift some of the larger rocks, exposing the broken bodies trapped within.

Callum fell to his knees as Kai revealed Clara's body, the old hunter crying silently as he stared down at his daughter.

"I'm sorry," Kai whispered, squeezing the other man's shoulder as long-buried emotions stirred within his chest. Min had been about Clara's age when Kai had lost her.

"It killed her mother when it attacked the village, and now it's taken her, too. I told her not to take that last shot, to wait until they were both fighting again, but she didn't listen," Callum's voice was barely more than a whisper as he reached out with one trembling hand to touch his daughter's face.

"Let's get her out of there," Kai said, the weight of the dead settling onto his shoulders with a familiar pain. Maybe this wouldn't have happened if he'd noticed the signs and understood what they meant. If he'd been the support that they had really needed.

Working together, they unearthed the three bodies within the rubble, Clara and two of the crossbow-wielding guards. Kai remembered their names from the day before—Laar and Baras.

Two of the spear-wielding guards had been crushed under the bear's bulk, and one of the swordsmen had bled to death after his leg had been ripped off. That meant that six of them had died taking down both bears. A third of everyone who had come here.

The survivors were bloodied and battered, and Kai knew that he was no exception; it would all hit him as soon as he stopped burning Essence. But first, he wanted to take a closer look at the wound on the younger bear.

The creature was covered in wounds from the fight, but the festering injury on its shoulder was something else entirely. Now that he was closer, Kai could see that the problem came from a puncture wound in the center. Taking his belt knife, Kai dug into the wound and pulled free a corroded and almost-destroyed arrowhead. An oily and unpleasant Essence had been in the arrowhead, though it was all but expended now. He doubted this was from where it was shot at the village; they had no one that could use Essence in this way.

Remembering the wound on the mother, Kai's frown deepened, reflecting the unease in his mind. Elemental bears were known for tracking down those that hurt their cubs and forcefully claiming their territory as their own. The mother had used two large bursts of power, but there had been little altering of the landscape or regrowing her armor.

If she'd also been shot by an arrow like this, she would have been able to shrug it off faster than the cub, but at a cost to her Essence stores.

It was all guesswork, really, but Kai was starting to build an image in his mind of how this might have happened, and he didn't like it one bit.

Cleaning his knife and retrieving his spear, Kai started towards the caves, to see what territory the bear had claimed for itself.

CHAPTER

THIRTY-THREE

"What have you found?" Blane asked, coming up to Kai as he paused at the entrance to the two caves.

"What do you mean?" Kai asked, glancing at Blane out of the corner of his eye. If they hadn't just fought together, he might suspect the odd man with his strange energy of being part of this, whatever it was. As it was, he was willing to give Blane the benefit of the doubt.

"Your body language has changed. You became a lot tenser when you examined the wound on the cub," Blane said evenly, resting a hand on his sheathed sword.

"I found this," Kai said after a brief moment of thought, passing Blane the remnant of the arrowhead. "I think someone attacked the cub, and then the mother chased them down and killed them, taking their territory for herself."

"The caves?" Blane asked as he inspected the arrowhead for a moment before shrugging slightly and passing it back to Kai.

"The caves," Kai confirmed with a nod of his head. Deciding to start with the larger cave, he began to step forward before hesitating and looking over to Blane. "I'm sorry about Clara."

"We barely knew each other. I had hoped to return after finding my sister and try to change that," Blane said softly. "I regret that I'll never have that chance."

"Well, let's see who took that chance away from you," Kai said, circulating his Essence and channeling enough to his spear to ignite the tip, illuminating their surroundings.

The initial section of the cave was normal and lacked any defining features beyond a large depression where the bear had been sleeping. Further in, however, Kai found what looked like an area of storage, with crates and barrels lining the walls of the cave. Just beyond that were what used to be living quarters.

Once, there would have been what was, in essence, a small home here, with several bunks, an enchanted lantern for light and all the amenities of living in one place for some time. Now, however, there were great swathes of rock that had been damaged, piles of rubble, and shattered furniture everywhere.

It was easy enough to see what it had once been; the bear hadn't bothered with destroying the surroundings once it had killed whoever had wronged it.

"What was this?" Blane asked, frowning as he picked up a piece of a table and examined it in the dim light from Kai's spear.

"An outpost or a cache, but an active one from the look of it. Though, why would anyone stationed here be attacking an elemental bear cub?" Kai examined the remnants of the enchanted lantern, but it was too damaged to be rescued. Not wanting to keep using his Essence, Kai went back to the intact storage section and found a few mundane lanterns, lighting them with his spear.

With the better quality of light, the two of them split their search, with Blane checking what could be scavenged from the intact stores while Kai investigated the damaged area. Ideally, he wanted to try and find some form of clue to the identity of the people who'd been here, but it seemed the bear had devoured its victims, and there wasn't much else to be found.

The lack of identifying marks on the barrels and crates was telling. Kai was leaning toward this being an outpost for a sect, or something similar. What he didn't understand, though, was how the bear was involved.

The assumption that these Sorcerers, whoever they were, had attacked the bear cub seemed a sound one, but Kai lacked the information to really understand what they were doing here.

"Kai, I've found some healing supplies. I'll take them out to the Lieutenant now. Have you found anything?" Blane said, holding up a bundle of what looked like mundane healing equipment.

"No, and I don't think I will," Kai said, shaking his head a little with a grimace. "Let's head back and see how the others are doing. We'll need to report this to Silver, if nothing else."

Blane nodded and gathered a few more things before they both made their way back out of the cave. The guards had spent the time dressing wounds and moving the fallen to one side. Thankfully, Tom had woken up while they were gone, though he looked groggy and out-of-sorts.

"Lieutenant, I need to speak with you," Kai called out, sharing a look with Blane as the other man went to pass out the additional medical supplies.

"Disciple Kai," Silver said, acknowledging Kai with a nod as he came over. "I saw that you went to check the caves. What did you find?"

"Nothing good," Kai said grimly, motioning toward the smaller bear. "I'm sure you noticed the wound on the cub. I believe that a group was stationed here and attacked the cub for some reason. The mother then pursued them, killed them, and took the caves for herself, which is why they abruptly appeared in the area around Willowcreek."

"Stationed here?" Silver queried, raising a brow questioningly.

"Yes. Inside the cave, there are provisions and what looks like the remnants of an outpost." Kai explained.

"Remnants?"

"The bear," Kai said flatly, Silver breathing out heavily as he turned to look at their fallen.

"So. Someone caused all this," Silver said, more to himself than anything. Kai left him to process that for a moment, waiting until the Lieutenant gave a crisp nod and turned back to him. "We'll move out as soon as we can. We need to make sure that Commander Griffon is informed."

"I agree, but what about your wounded?" Kai asked, gesturing to the guards, who were a little worse for wear.

"We'll keep the pace slow; no one is unable to walk, and Willowbrook isn't far. If need be, we can leave the wounded and the supplies with them while the rest of us head back."

"You seem eager to return," Kai said, a little surprised by how quickly Silver was talking of leaving his people in the village.

"I don't like any of this. We've had problems with a few sects trying to push in recently. The Commander knows more, but he needs this information as soon as possible."

"I can take it to him," Blane said, walking over to join them from where he'd been passing out the supplies. Kai could have sworn

Blane had been outside of earshot, but the other man had already demonstrated that he had keen senses.

"You can trust him," Kai said, nodding to Blane as he gave his support.

"Very well, let's work on the message for you to take," Silver said, settling in to run through the message that Blane was to pass on to Commander Griffon.

While the two of them were occupied, Kai moved over to Tom and knelt down next to his companion. Tom was sat up against a tree but looked punch-drunk at best.

"Hey, how're you feeling?" Kai asked, reaching out to lay a hand on Tom's shoulder.

"Like I just got hit by an avalanche. Everything hurts," Tom said, slurring a few words here and there.

"I know, that was a big hit you took," Kai said, shaking his head in disbelief as he remembered how Tom had taken the full charge of the bear. "Try and move your Essence around your body. It's not as good as what Verdan does, but it'll help."

"Got it, sure," Tom said, his voice trailing off as he slumped back against the tree, utterly exhausted.

"You'll be fine," Kai said, patting the semi-lucid Sorcerer on the shoulder as he went to go patrol the area. The last thing they needed was something trying to pick off survivors as easy prey.

_**_

Blane set off back to Hobson's Point before Kai finished his patrol, which had been blessedly uneventful. In that time, Silver had organized what remained of their expedition, and buried their fallen. It was a grim task, but one that had to be seen to. Several of their weapons had expended their magical power, but Silver made sure to gather them all up. While Verdan might be able to make more, they still represented a powerful boon for the Hobson Point guards.

Kai took all this in as he returned, noting as he did that Tom looked much improved. Cycling his Essence had brought some color back to his face, and he seemed to be breathing easier. There was nothing else for them to do here. It was time for them to set off back to Willowbrook.

The journey back out of the valley was a lot harder than on the way in. Everyone was physically capable of walking, but some of the more wounded guards struggled with the hike.

Kai did what he could to support the injured and help them get past obstacles, but he'd taken a bit of a beating himself, and it was hindering his ability to help. Still, he did what he could, and though their progress was slow, they were getting there.

Callum kept ahead of the group as they traveled, the hunter mourning silently for his daughter and in no mood for any discourse with them. There was an unspoken decision to leave him to grieve by himself. At the end of the day, they barely knew Callum, and Kai couldn't help but feel that anything more than the condolence they'd given would feel insincere.

When they did reach Willowbrook, Callum disappeared through the gates without a backward glance, leaving them to speak with Tella. The headwoman had clearly been alerted that they were arriving, as she was waiting at the gates with helpers to care for the wounded.

"Is it dead?" Tella asked Silver in a worried tone, taking in the wounds and the missing comrades.

"Yes. Both of them. The one that attacked you was merely a cub," Silver said in an exhausted tone. The lieutenant was physically one of the healthiest of the group, but Kai could see the emotional pain in his eyes. Duty was keeping him upright and on mission, but he was suffering.

"I'm sorry for your loss," Tella said, reaching out to rest a hand on Silver's arm. "I have to ask, but I saw Callum come in alone...."

"Clara didn't make it," Kai confirmed on Silver's behalf. "She killed the cub but drew the mother's ire."

"I shouldn't have let her go with you; I knew she was hurting from her mother's death," Tella whispered, more to herself than anything. "May the ancestors watch over her soul. May they watch over all of them." Tella squeezed Silver's arm before motioning for them to follow her into the village.

"I know we sent Blane on ahead, but I still don't feel comfortable lingering here. This new information about the bear and how it arrived concerns me greatly." Silver said quietly, glancing over to Kai as they followed a short distance behind Tella.

"I agree. I suggest giving them an hour of rest with some food and water. If we set off before noon, we should be back by early evening, even at our slower pace. The travel will hurt their recovery, though."

"It can't be helped; I'm not leaving them here unsupported," Silver said with a shake of his head.

"Ah, Sir, sorry to interrupt, but I have a thought," Jenkins said, approaching the two of them with a wince as he held his side.

"Go on, Jenkins. What is it?" Silver turned a questioning look on his subordinate, who tried to straighten under Silver's gaze but ended up wincing and hunching a little.

"Well, sir, it's the wagon we came up with. All those supplies were for us if we needed to act as a detached garrison of sorts. If we're heading back, why not give them to the village, and we can cycle the wounded through riding on the cart to give everyone some rest?"

"That's not a bad plan at all," Kai said, nodding at Jenkins before looking at Silver. "What do you think?"

"I agree. Well done, Jenkins," Silver said, his subordinate beaming at the praise. "Get everyone some food and somewhere to rest. I'll speak with Tella; we leave in an hour."

_**_

The villagers were thankful for the supplies; they'd been hunting less than usual to avoid the bear, so their reserves of food were running low. The volume of supplies they could leave with them wasn't enough to make up for that, but the people of Willowbrook welcomed it nevertheless.

With their wounds cleaned and rebound, the remnants of the expedition looked better as they set off back to Hobson's Point. Three people could ride comfortably in the cart at a time, but those spaces were reserved for those who struggled the most with traveling.

It was slow going, and they ended up having to take a few breaks to swap the people in the cart, but as the sun dwindled down in the sky, they saw Hobson's Point.

The guards on duty greeted their returning comrades happily, congratulating them on their victory. Despite their losses, it was a historic moment, and a proof of concept for Verdan's weapons.

"We'll escort you back first," Silver said, directing them toward the Crea estate as they entered the city.

"Thank you, I wouldn't want Tom to be walking much further in his state," Kai said softly, eyeing the earth Sorcerer with concern.

Tom had recovered somewhat, but he was struggling to breathe at times and was currently riding in the cart.

"This is the first time we've been able to push back on the problems in the area with any real success, and we owe that to the two of you. I won't forget that," Silver said, inclining his head respectfully.

Kai turned his attention to the city as they moved toward the estate. He'd felt a little odd since they entered, but now the hair on the back of his neck had stood up, and he was feeling an itch on his back. Kai had long since learned to trust his instincts, and they told him they were being watched.

That was to be expected when a group like them went through the city, but Kai was sensing something beyond that. There was malicious intent involved here.

Kai had been slowly drawing in Aether and converting it to Essence from the moment they finished the fight with the bears, but he hadn't recovered all that he had expended. He had enough for a few short fights if needed, but another big or intensive one might be a problem.

A few minutes later, the first sign of something amiss came when an oncoming wagon suffered a broken wheel and its cargo scattered around it. There was room for people to walk through, but not for their cart.

Conscious of watching eyes, Kai kept his expression distant as Silver took them down an alternative path. The alternate path toward the estate led them onto a disused street which ran through an abandoned neighborhood.

To Kai's utter lack of surprise, two figures stepped out to block their way when they were halfway through the new street.

"Weeping Death," Silver growled as the two figures revealed themselves. They wore black and green robes, and both moved with the
confidence of someone who knew they were the most powerful
person present.

The two Sorcerers moved a little closer, and Kai studied them in
more detail. Both of them were short and lithe, wearing close-cut
robes that eschewed the traditional flowing style. The woman on
the left held a long blade which was partially coated in something
dark in one hand, and a flask of some sort in the other. Her
companion, however, carried only a wand, leaving his other hand
free.

The coated weapon wasn't a surprise, given the sect name that
Silver had announced. Kai had heard of the Weeping Death in the
past; it was one of the smaller sects that specialized in poisons and
assassinating other Sorcerers. What members of such a sect were
doing here was beyond him, but that was a question for later.

Kai was confident he could take one of them in his current state,
but he had no chance against both of them. All they would need to
do would be for one of them to keep him engaged while the other
dealt with Silver and his guards. Then, when he had no allies left,
they could overpower him.

Kai knew he could kill one of them and escape if he abandoned the
guards, but that wasn't going to happen.

"Oh no, what a shame! We seem to have come upon the city's
valiant heroes as they return," the male Sorcerer said in a sneering
tone.

"And with their 'Wizard' friend out of the city as well! What a dire
coincidence," the woman added with a tone of exaggerated
sadness.

"Well, best we put them out of their misery," the man said with a shrug as he spread his hands. The two of them were walking steadily closer as they spoke. They would attack soon.

"Attack us, and you're crossing a line. The sect will be barred from Hobson's Point, and the pair of you will be arrested." Silver barked out, readying his weapon as his guards formed up around him.

Kai felt Tom move to his side, but he knew this kind of fight was well outside of Tom's league; he lacked the experience for it, even if he were completely healthy.

"Oh my, how adorable," the woman exclaimed with a high-pitched giggle. "As though you mortals could do more than annoy us."

As much as Kai would like to disagree, the wand and flask the other Sorcerers were carrying meant he was dealing with a projector and a manipulator, respectively. That gave both of them some ranged capability and synergy with each other. Depending on their strength, they could even take Kai down before he could reach them. He doubted that, though, or they wouldn't be closing in like this.

"We have more capability than you know. Another step forwards will be taken as intent to attack," Silver said firmly, motioning for the crossbow-wielding guards to ready themselves.

"Oh, please, do show me," the man said, stepping forward and raising his empty hand to conjure a half-dome shield of roiling green liquid that seemed to coalesce out of the air.

"Fire!" Silver barked, the two remaining crossbowmen, Peters and Auger, shooting on his command. Both bolts struck the liquid shield and immediately began shriveling and falling apart, all but disintegrating by the time the bolts crossed through the shield.

"My turn," the man said with an evil smile, flicking his wand out as he unleashed a trio of green liquid projectiles toward them.

"Stay back," Kai barked as he leapt forward, igniting his Essence and channeling it into his spear as he moved. The spear's tip ignited into bright yellow flames as Kai spun it in a circle, intercepting each of the missiles with the burning spearhead.

The liquid in the missiles splashed and sizzled on impact with Kai's spear, but the flames devoured most of it as the two opposing Essences clashed. The liquid that survived the flames splashed around the spear, some hitting Kai and burning his skin where it landed, making him hiss in pain.

As the caustic liquid was created from Essence, Kai's own cycling fire Essence protected him somewhat. Thankfully, the projectiles had little Essence infused into them, making them easy to resist. For Silver and the others, however, they would have been much worse.

"Auger, use it," Silver all but growled from behind Kai, but the Sorcerer dared not take his eyes off his two opponents.

"I thought he was an enhancer?" The woman questioned, looking somewhat concerned about Kai's presence for the first time since they arrived.

"He's definitely an enhancer; it must be the spear. We'll be well rewarded for claiming it!"

"You can try," Kai said, settling into a defensive stance and giving them both a challenging look.

The two Weeping Death Sorcerers sneered in response and blurred into action, racing straight toward Kai and the others. Despite their words, the woman kept slightly behind the man so that she could take advantage of his shield.

Kai readied himself to try and engage the man first and try to split them up. A Sorcerer would die to a crossbow bolt like any other. He just needed to get the guards an opportunity.

"Block this, you bastard." Auger's voice barely registered for Kai, but he heard the thrum of a crossbow firing and felt the air shift as another bolt flew past him toward the shielded Sorcerer.

"Pathetic," the male Sorcerer sneered, lifting his wand to fire another wave of projectiles back at them.

The bolt struck the outer edge of the liquid shield, but instead of disintegrating, it seemed to glow slightly as it slipped straight through. The Sorcerer barely even had time to realize that his protection had failed him before the bolt sunk into his upper chest, right below his throat. Whatever power had allowed the bolt to pass through the shield gave it enough force to penetrate his body down to its fletchings.

"No!" The woman screamed out as a spray of blood hit her, and her companion hit the ground. "You bastards, you'll pay for this!" Clenching her fist and shattering the flask in her hand, the surviving Sorcerer raced at Kai as a dark liquid coated her hand.

Kai knew she was a manipulator, and the chances were that her element was poison-based. Being cut by her blade or getting touched by her other hand would be painful for him, and lethal for the others.

"Stay back. I'll deal with her," Kai said calmly, moving forward to meet the other Sorcerer as he expended more Essence to speed himself up. As a Sorcerer, she was faster than the average person, but she wasn't an enhancer like Kai.

With the advantage of strength, speed, and reach, the fight against her was one-sided from the start. The poison Sorcerer would throw portions of the liquid she held to try and catch him unawares, but Kai dodged the attacks with ease.

Her solo fighting style was rudimentary at best, and she'd brought only a single flask of poison. Arrogance would be her downfall.

His first attack to slip by her guard took her in the left shoulder, the burning blade of his spear slicing through the flesh and muscle with ease. The second took her right hand, sending it to the floor with the blade still in hand.

In a panic, she threw all the remaining poison she had at him in a loose spray, stopping him from dodging it all. Droplets struck his bare skin and warred with his Essence, but in such a low concentration, the attack did little more than inconvenience him.

In return, Kai's third strike landed square in her chest, piercing through to her heart and cremating it in a flash of Essence. While she'd been a poor duelist, Kai knew better than to leave an enemy alive.

Kicking the body free to withdraw his spear, Kai looked around the street for any other attackers. From what he had seen of these two, he doubted there would be, but it was wise to be thorough in these situations.

"Are we clear?" Kai called out, keeping his eyes open as he moved back to the rest of the group.

"Looks that way. Jenkins, get those bodies in the cart and cover them," Silver ordered.

"What is the Weeping Death doing here, and why did they mention Verdan?" Kai asked as he came over to the Lieutenant.

"They've been trying to take over the city recently, but I don't know how Wizard Verdan is involved. Perhaps something happened after we left?"

"Let's get moving. I want to check in on the estate," Kai said, a knot forming in his gut as he worried if the others were in danger. This felt like an impromptu ambush, but if this sect was trying to work against them, people like Gwen and Tim were valid targets as well.

Gwen was growing in power, but she was no match for a trained Sorcerer, not yet.

Hurrying onward, they joined the more populated streets of Hobson's Point once more and reached the estate within a few minutes. One of the guards that Kai had helped get a job was standing watch in a relaxed pose, which was a good sign.

From the guard, they were able to get the summary of the rescue force that Tobias Brock had put together. That at least explained the comment on Verdan being out of the city.

Silver and the guards went back to their headquarters with the bodies. Kai doubted there was a second ambush waiting, but he warned them to stick to the busy streets anyway.

A quick check around the estate reassured Kai that everything was in order, which wasn't surprising. Like most Sorcerers, the Weeping Death would likely focus on what they believed were threats, chief of which would be Kai and Verdan, with Tom a distant third.

Kai considered heading out after Verdan and the others, but it had been long enough that one way or another, the matter was resolved. All Kai could do now was watch the estate and ensure that everything remained safe and secure until Verdan came back.

THIRTY-FOUR

THE REST of the rescue expedition joined Verdan and the others at the ambush site in short order. Pawel and Pania were still absent while they tracked the path the Cyth had taken, but Verdan expected them to return soon.

"Okay, load up the supplies," Tobias called out as he entered the area, wasting no time in getting people moving. Verdan doubted his encouragement was necessary, as everyone seemed to understand that time was critical and moved to load the abandoned goods onto the empty carts as swiftly as possible.

Verdan kept watch while the others worked, ensuring that nothing crept up on them via regular pulses with his ward. Thankfully, Pawel and Pania returned while the third cart was being loaded up, declaring that they'd found the trail the Cyth had left.

"Verdan, do you have a moment?" Tobias asked, coming over to speak quietly with Verdan. "I'll only get in the way if I come any further. I think this is the point where we split up. I'll head back with Brent and the city guards. Everyone else has been instructed to follow your commands, so that won't be a problem."

"I was going to suggest the same thing if you didn't. This mission is looking to be more dangerous than we'd anticipated," Verdan said equally softly. "You go back. I'll make sure that we bring back everyone we can."

"We owe it to them to try, but don't go getting yourself killed, you hear me?" Tobias had a look of genuine concern on his face as he spoke.

"Don't worry, I've done this before," Verdan said reassuringly, patting the merchant on the shoulder and gesturing to the loaded carts. "We need to get moving. Every moment counts."

"Right, yes, of course it does," Tobias said, the gaunt man turning to walk away before pausing and looking back. "Good luck, Verdan."

Nodding in response, Verdan watched as Tobias walked away and gathered the group that would be returning with him. Without them, there were thirty-two people, a wolf, and a raven on this mission. That was just enough to count as a good-sized raiding group in Verdan's mind.

The problem was that Verdan had growing concerns about the size of the Cyth camp they were going after, but it was far too late for second thoughts now. It was either push on or abandon those who were taken. There was no going back for more people; it had already been longer than Verdan would like as it was.

"Pawel, Pania, lead the way. Let's get moving," Verdan called out as the carts set off back to the city. He'd meant what he'd said to Tobias; every moment counted and he intended to make the most of them.

The Cyth were a race that had been completely twisted by the dark powers they worshiped; they had no need for captives. Anyone taken by the Cyth had only blood-soaked altars, a dagger to the throat, or corruption to look forward to.

One of the worst memories Verdan had was from when he took part in destroying a large camp of Cyth, and they found the mass graves from the years of raiding and butchery. The sheer number of people that had died at the hands of those foul creatures had cemented Verdan's hatred of them, and they were just as evil now as they were back then.

Watching everyone prepare to move out was a sobering experience for Verdan. Tobias's hirelings lacked the true discipline of the guardsmen that Verdan remembered, but they would do for now. Tim was progressing nicely, and the four guards that Verdan had brought were showing their skill, but he'd still have traded most of them for a good squad of Imperial guards.

Shaking off his morose feelings, Verdan focused on the here and now and led the group into the woods under Pania's direction.

The tracks they'd found were going south, toward a particularly thick section of forest that the locals were familiar with. Apparently, the area used to be rife with logging camps, thanks to an odd quirk that caused the local vegetation to grow much faster than normal. However, the thick greenery attracted plenty of wildlife, which in turn attracted monsters and stronger beasts.

Without Sorcerers to back them up, the locals had given up the area, rather than continue to fight a losing battle, a typical story in the slow death of Hobson's Point. The guard force they had now was a fraction of its former glory, so even the patrols didn't go that far anymore. It seemed that in the absence of the loggers, the Cyth had moved into the area as well.

There were a few things that might cause the plants to grow faster, but none of them were particularly useful in their current endeavor. Putting it aside, Verdan mentally marked the area as one to come back to in the future for further study.

For now, they had more important things to focus on.

_**_

An hour or two of hiking through the woods brought them to the border of the heavily-forested area and the first sign of the Cyth's presence.

It wasn't something that the others would note, except for Gwen, but Verdan could feel the sickly corruption in the flora around him.

"On your guard—we're in Cyth territory now," Verdan said calmly but authoritatively.

Whispered relays of his order spread through the group as weapons were drawn. A thick layer of tension hung over the group, one that only grew as they continued forward and the signs of corruption began to build.

Cyth corruption drained the life from that which it infected, slowly at first but faster over time as the Cyth grew in power. This life drain killed the smallest things first, as they lacked the reserves of energy and strength to resist.

For a forest like this, that was shown by the patchy areas of grass and moss. Even areas that should be covered with growth were threadbare, to the extent that it was noticeable even to those who weren't looking for it. The lack of low-lying vegetation gave the area a strange appearance, and Verdan could see it affecting some of the others.

It was a small thing, but anyone looking at it would realize that it was unnatural, which bothered some more than others. Thankfully, Verdan was long since immune to such an effect due to repeated exposure.

"This is horrible," Gwen said in little more than a whisper as she looked at the barren areas with wide eyes.

"This is the Cyth. They corrupt and destroy the world around them piece by piece. They are a plague upon life and should be rooted out and destroyed wherever they are found," Verdan growled, gripping his staff tight as he picked up the pace.

Over the next few minutes, all traces of grass disappeared, and the larger plants and bushes started to thin out. Verdan saw no sign of fresh growth either. All the plants here were old and established, with roots that had the vitality to survive the corruption.

"I can feel its pain, how it suffers from their presence," Gwen said, one hand holding her stomach and the other resting on her raven.

"Hold up," Verdan called out just loud enough to reach the nearest members of the group. He wasn't detecting any Cyth with the ward he'd created, but too much noise was still a bad idea.

Gwen was pale and uncomfortable-looking as she frowned down at the ground. Verdan hadn't expected her to react this strongly to the corruption, even with how established it was.

"What is it, Gwen?" Tim asked as he came over to rest a hand on her back with a worried expression.

"I can feel something; it's familiar somehow, but it's in so much pain. What's happening?" Gwen turned to look at Verdan with a confused and somewhat nauseous expression.

"You said it felt familiar. In what way?" Verdan asked, his brow furrowing in thought.

"I don't know. There's just too much."

"When did it start? Can you tell which direction it's coming from?" Verdan asked, wracking his mind for what might be the cause of Gwen's pain.

"When we entered the thicker forest. At first, I thought it was the corruption, but it's been getting stronger. I can feel that it's coming from that way," Gwen said, pointing deeper into the forest.

The path they were taking had been skirting the exterior of the thickly-forested area and was now heading further inward, but Gwen was pointing directly toward what Verdan assumed was the core of the forest.

"A fast-growing forest, one filled with pain because of the corruption, it might be a spirit. Gwen, listen to me. You need to ask it not to share its pain. It should listen to you." Verdan said, concerned with how pale Gwen was looking.

"Okay," Gwen murmured, a look of tension overtaking her face as she focused on something internally.

A few tense moments passed before Gwen sighed in relief, and her whole body seemed to relax.

"Okay, it's stopped sharing the pain. I can still feel some of it, but not as much," Gwen said, slumping down to sit on the floor with a heavy exhalation. "What in the goddess's name just happened?"

"I think this is an older forest than we realized, one that's developed a spirit, much like the glade of your family's home. This one is strong, though, very strong. Perhaps even as old as the one that watched over the glade, which may mean that it can control Aether. The wellspring of vitality that it represents may have drawn the Cyth here to begin with." Verdan explained, wishing, not for the first time, that he could communicate with spirits directly.

"Why am I the only one it's done this to?" Gwen asked with a touch of bitterness as she saw that everyone else was unaffected.

"Spirits will only communicate with beings that are heavily tied to nature, like Witches. You're already outside my area of expertise by being able to talk back to it," Verdan said with a slight twinge of envy. The steps he trod as a Wizard had been walked a thousand times before, and he knew it. He missed that feeling of exploring new ideas and concepts.

"I can still feel it, though it's distant now," Gwen said, her gaze vague as she focused on something only she could sense. "It's asking for help."

"That's why we're here, though I hadn't expected to run into a powerful spirit as well," Verdan said, focusing back on the current issue and holding out a hand to help Gwen back to her feet. "Can you keep it under control?"

"Yeah, I've got it," Gwen said, taking a deep breath as she composed herself. "It's been in pain for so long. It was desperate for someone to help. It knows now that we're going to destroy the source of the corruption."

"Good, now, let's see about relieving it of its pain," Verdan said, signaling for the group to move out once more.

Verdan kept a weather eye on Gwen as they carried on, but she seemed to have everything under control now. He was concerned with how the spirit had been able to affect her by communicating its suffering. It meant that the spirit was strong but that the corruption level was very high.

The gradient they'd been following was still increasing as well. At this point, the only vegetation growing was old, strong trees. Anything smaller had gone, and nothing new was making it through, leaving large gaps in the canopy.

While the growing lack of cover was a problem, it also let them see more of their surroundings, showing just how much of the area had been sucked dry by the Cyth corruption.

Verdan was looking at one particular tree that was in the process of finally losing the battle against corruption when his ward pinged. The Aether construct informed him of two groups of Cyth, one ahead and on the left and the other mirroring on the right. Fifteen of them altogether.

"*Disir bel*," Verdan called out, gesturing to first one area and then the other with his staff. With each gesture, a fist-sized ball of light shot out from his staff toward the area he'd indicated, hovering in place above where the ward had detected the Cyth. "Ambush!"

To their credit, the mercenaries reacted quickly to Verdan's call— just not quite quickly enough.

The early afternoon light was bright, but dark clouds lingered overhead, giving just enough dimness for the Cyth to have hidden in two parts of a long, winding gully.

The Cyth boiled out of their hiding places as soon as Verdan's light shone over them, abandoning their position without a second thought. A quick look with his Aether senses told Verdan that only Cyth Lai were present, the most common of Cyth types.

Each Cyth was a horrible blending of beast and humanoid, some of them more one than the other, but all of them bearing crude weapons and a deep thirst for the blood of their enemies.

Verdan's group was quite spread out in an attempt to catch more signs of any Cyth as they passed, but that meant his ward only extended a short distance past some of the mercenaries.

The first casualty of their mission came as a cloven-hoofed Cyth with rippling muscles hurled its rusty ax as it charged out of hiding, the weapon catching an unsuspecting mercenary in the chest.

The surrounding humans flocked together as they put up a united front against the Cyth, the rest of the group racing forward to support them.

Verdan conjured small areas of shielding at a distance, turning aside lethal blows and throwing off the aim of the Cyth. He could have done more, but he dared not expend the Aether.

Outnumbered and outmatched, the Cyth hurled themselves at the humans with no regard for their safety, causing them to be cut down one by one until no more stood and fought.

With his small shields preventing lethal blows, only one more of the mercenaries was killed. Several were clawed or bore small wounds, but nothing too serious or debilitating.

The unfortunate woman who was killed had had her throat ripped out by a more canine Cyth; Verdan just hadn't been able to get a good angle on the tussle. The longer-range shield he'd been using was limited by what he could see, which was problematic in a chaotic fight.

Really, they'd been lucky that Verdan had stopped as much as he had. Hopefully, that luck would last.

CHAPTER
THIRTY-FIVE

Verdan kept the rest of his group close after the ambush; he dared not use more Aether to try and detect the Cyth, so proximity was their best solution.

The fact that the Cyth had been lying in ambush for them concerned him, and he had a few troubling theories about that, but he knew little for sure.

They were close now, though. Only the oldest trees remained, and Verdan saw the first signs of transformation on a few of them. The corruption from the Abyssal energy would slowly change any life-form strong enough to resist it, just one of the many ways the new Cyth were born.

Those too weak to be converted were sacrificed on the bloody altars of the Cyth, while others became Cyth Lai, Cyth Bayne or, if they were powerful enough, Cyth Scerrd.

Trees and other forms of plant life that survived long enough also went through a change, becoming wyrch. No matter the original form, a wyrch lost all leaves, flowers and fruit, becoming denser

IMPERIAL WIZARD

and with hardened bark. The Cyth would water the wyrch with blood, causing them to grow rapidly before being harvested.

A building of wyrchwood meant that the Cyth had been present for some time and were organized enough to cultivate the Abyssal trees. Verdan had only seen it a few times, but it was difficult to forget.

Even knowing that it was coming, when they finally came within sight of the Cyth camp, it was like a punch to Verdan's gut.

Twisted, gnarled, and knotted wyrchwood rose up in the distance, glistening in the light from the slight sheen of blood that never faded. The Cyth camp was made up of half-a-dozen different buildings that encircled one central, much larger building. The Cyth had no need of walls or defenses, relying on their weaker members to protect the camp.

Tearing his eyes from the glistening buildings, Verdan ran his eyes over the multitude of Cyth present and steeled himself for a long and painful battle. There were easily a hundred Cyth Lai in the camp, which didn't include any raiding parties or patrols.

They showed no sign of being aware of the humans approaching, but Verdan felt a shiver run down his spine and coalesce into ice in his gut. Something was watching them.

"Form up, gird yourselves for the fight. They are strong, but they fight alone. Fight together, and we can get through this," Verdan called out, projecting as much confidence as he could as he moved toward the front of the group.

"That's a lot of Cyth. Are you sure we can do this?" Gwen asked nervously as she stepped into place behind Verdan, pitching her voice so only he could hear.

"Truthfully, there could be twice as many, and it wouldn't matter. What will make a difference is what they have beyond these. Think how much damage you could do if you threw a volley of lightning blasts at them."

"I hadn't thought of it like that," Gwen said after a moment of thought, a touch of confidence in her voice once more.

"Don't worry, Gwen, between me, Sylvie and the others, we'll keep them off you. The two of you just need to take care of those nasty magic ones," Tim said as he stepped up next to Verdan, Sylvie growling her assent as she bared her teeth at the distant Cyth.

Flickers of darkness among the Cyth were followed by a chorus of howls, brays, and inhuman sounds as a large group of Cyth flooded out of the camp. Verdan guessed at them outnumbering the smaller human force two to one, a mistake on the Cyth's part.

If they'd all attacked at once, he wouldn't have been able to deal with everything at once, no matter what he said to Gwen. This way, they had a chance to whittle down the Cyth before the big fight.

They were a long way from the camp, but that just gave them all plenty of time to take in the unruly force heading toward them. Verdan could almost taste the tension in the air. He would need to ensure his first few actions were obvious enough to bolster the confidence of Tobias's hirelings.

Tim and his small group of guards had taken up position in front of where Verdan had placed himself, their presence seeming to encourage the surrounding fighters. Perhaps they saw the presence of Verdan's guards as a sign that he would be paying closer attention to them. A fair assumption.

A flicker of energy from the direction of the approaching Cyth came moments before a streaking ball of dark energy shot out on a parabolic arc toward them. There was enough power in the attack that Verdan could see dark green streaks of energy within the mass.

"Gwen, this one is yours," Verdan said, gesturing calmly toward the swelling ball of dark green and black energy that was sailing up into the sky.

"Ceravwen, I hope you're watching over me," Gwen said in a whisper as she raised a hand and unleashed a bolt of lightning at the oncoming ball of Abyssal energy.

Unlike Verdan's spells, Gwen's connection with the goddess gave her magic the slightest touch of Exeon, celestial energy. As the antithesis of Abyssal energy, it made it perfect for countering the Cyth.

The roar of lightning and blinding after-image of Gwen's spell faded to reveal an empty sky. She'd annihilated the Cyth attack with her own.

"Now the fun begins," Verdan said, looking over to give Gwen an encouraging smile, one that didn't quite touch his eyes.

Seemingly enraged by the failure of their attack, the hidden leader of the group sent the Cyth Lai into a jog, one that slowly increased in speed as the Cyth neared them.

"*Hoer niwlla,*" Verdan called out loudly, making sure that all the surrounding fighters could hear him as he thumped the base of his staff into the ground and made a throwing motion.

Icy mist flowed out and up from Verdan, passing harmlessly over his allies' heads before gravity dragged it down to the ground like a waterfall of freezing fog. The effect would spread out and blunt the Cyth charge, as well as sap their strength with its magical cold.

A few tense moments passed as Verdan finished forming the fogbank, expending a decent amount of Aether to ensure that it was potent enough. The temperature inside the fog would be considerably below freezing, with the water in the air turning into tiny particles of ice.

"*Rew liff*," Verdan said, stepping out past his protectors and pointing to one end of the fog before drawing his finger across to the other side. Moisture coalesced out of the air to form a thick layer of ice, running the distance of the fog. The ice wasn't that thick, but was wide enough to stretch slightly inside the fog.

Direct damage and combat spells were all well and good, but sometimes a lighter touch would give better results.

The fog rippled in several places as half-a-dozen shards of abyssal energy came blasting through. Some went too high, some too low or off to one side, and Verdan conjured a shield to block the single one that was on-target.

The mercenary the shard had been flying toward had raised their shield but gave Verdan a thankful nod as they saw the blue Aether protecting them.

Verdan returned the gesture but was quick to look back to the fog as dozens of shapes burst through it. The Cyth were moving slower than before, and many had frost covering parts of their body.

The first wave out of the fog immediately slipped on the ice that Verdan had created, breaking up the coherence of their charge as many were trampled or knocked others over.

"*Rew durst!*" Verdan cried out, clenching his fist then explosively opening it as all the ice he'd created shattered in a spray of ice shards. A dozen or more Cyth that had fallen over were killed immediately, their bodies riddled with shards of ice. The rest were peppered with razor-sharp ice, drawing blood and causing even more chaos among them.

To top it off, Gwen started unleashing small blasts of wind, knocking the Cyth over and into each over. The wind did disperse the fog somewhat, but it had served its purpose.

Fresh Cyth came racing out of the fog, shaking off the cold as they bore down on the humans with bloodthirsty howls.

Verdan began to throw out the blasts of pressurised air that he was fond of, but he'd barely killed three Cyth when he felt the two Baynes accompanying the force emerge from the fog.

The Baynes looked like their brethren, but were larger and festooned with abyssal iconography and symbols. Both creatures immediately focused on Verdan as they caught sight of him, unleashing a barrage of low-powered missiles.

"*Ast*," Verdan lifted a hand as he formed a blue half-dome shield in front of him and raised his staff to point at one of the Bayne. "*Thanr laif!*"

Flames rippled down Verdan's staff as he used it to focus his spell, unleashing a concentrated beam of fire at the target. The Cyth had raised its own shield of dark green and black energy, and it was able to hold out against Verdan's attack, but not against the lightning bolt that Gwen followed up with.

Grunting under the strain of both attacking and defending at the same time, Verdan grinned as the Cyth Bayne was blasted off its feet and sent spinning to the ground.

The other Bayne unleashed a second barrage, this time sending half of its missiles out at the mundane troops that the rest of the Cyth were fighting.

"*Garec bel*," Verdan spat, ripping several chunks of rock from the ground and throwing them at the Bayne. The Abyssal shield was good enough against energy like his fire, but a physical boulder would shatter it much more easily.

Earth magic wasn't Verdan's forte, though, and though it was satisfying to watch the third chunk of rock crush the Bayne's head, it had cost more Aether than he wanted to spend.

The cracking of lightning from behind him was deafening, but it reassured Verdan that Gwen was laying into the rest of the Cyth. Following suit, he launched a multitude of air blades into those still standing, using only a fraction of the Aether he'd spent on the earth magic.

While Verdan had focused on the casters, the rest of the battle had been going well for the humans. Tim had made the center of their defensive line his own, his sword dripping Cyth blood as he cut down the creatures with swift motions of his blade. The four guards that had accompanied Verdan were equally centric to the defense, their enchanted blades reaping a heavy toll.

The magical frost, followed by the ice and the explosion, had weakened a good number of the Cyth, and the rest struggled to break into the human formation. The exchange with the two Cyth Baynes had taken mere moments, allowing Verdan and Gwen to shift their focus to helping the rest of their group before too much damage was done.

Sylvie and Tim worked together to finish the last few Cyth. Sylvie would harry and bite at their legs, distracting them and giving Tim the opportunity to lop off limbs and heads.

Tim had thrown himself into training his swordplay since they returned from the fight against the Darjee, and it showed.

"Check the wounded. Anyone with an injury that won't allow them to fight, gather over here," Verdan called out as the final Cyth hit the ground. The last vestige of the fog was concealing them from the Cyth camp, but that wouldn't last long.

Four or five people presented themselves with nasty wounds from where the Cyth had gotten up close and personal. Giving each one a small healing spell, Verdan detailed them to the rear of the formation until they were healed enough to fight.

"Three dead, and a dozen more with small injuries," Verdan muttered, watching as the dead were dragged back from the battle and left separate from the fallen Cyth. He'd forgotten that they lacked any magical healing for the fighters, an oversight on his part.

Verdan's resolve to carry on wavered; they'd destroyed a good portion of the Cyth, but there were many more yet to come. Two Cyth Baynes had been sent, which meant that there were probably several more, and the chance of a Cyth Scerrd was high.

Verdan could win against that, but he couldn't shield his allies in the process. A lot of the mercenaries would die, that much was certain, and that weighed on him, but it was the thought of taking Gwen and Tim in there that gave him pause. Verdan had lost everyone he knew and cared for, and the thought of losing any of his new friends was like a vice around his heart.

Losing one of his new companions hadn't really seemed a possibility until now. He'd lost too many friends to the Cyth in the past as it was. Even just thinking that brought the weight of it all crashing down onto him.

"Are you okay, Verdan?" Gwen asked, appearing next to him with a concerned expression.

"I'm fine," Verdan said, hating the shaky tone in his voice. Closing his eyes, Verdan gripped both hands around his staff to hide the tremors building in them.

"What's wrong? Were you hurt?" Gwen asked, reaching out to grab his arm as she looked him over for injuries.

"It's just brought back some memories," Verdan said, struggling with the sudden weight that felt like it was crushing him. His heart was tight and pounding, his mind drifting down a path that would do him no good despite his best efforts.

He'd kept away from the thought of just how many people he'd lost, of how many that he'd had to abandon without any explanation, racing to finish his spell before the curse broke him. The knowledge that he'd never seen any of them again was a crushing weight that sapped his strength and left him weak. This was exactly why he was keeping his sleep to a minimum; he couldn't afford to deal with this right now, and their faces haunted his dreams.

"*Hyn*," Verdan muttered, releasing the Aether into himself and banishing the tiredness and pain. Taking a deep breath, he settled himself and got his mind back on track. "There, that's better." Verdan straightened and exhaled heavily, locking away the grief once more as he did.

"What did you just do?" Gwen asked, her concerned expression replaced by a thoughtful frown.

"Energized myself," Verdan said with a throwaway gesture. "Don't worry about it. I'm fine."

"You didn't look fine a few seconds ago," Gwen said, folding her arms as she narrowed her eyes. "What about if that happens again while we're in a fight?"

"It won't. I'm fine," Verdan stated flatly, stepping away from Gwen as he turned his freshly focused mind to the problem at hand. "Form up everyone. We're going in." Verdan pitched his voice to reach everyone, ignoring Gwen's protests as he focused on the Cyth.

Part of him knew that she was raising a valid concern, but if he stopped and actually thought about it all, he wouldn't be in any shape to do anything. No, the best solution was to power on; he could deal with the raw emotions once everyone was safe.

_**_

"Boss, they're moving," Tim announced with a gesture, bringing everyone's attention to where the Cyth seemed to be gathering.

With their earlier losses, they were only outnumbered two to one, but they'd already shown what they could do against such numbers. The real problem was going to be how many higher-order Cyth were present.

Strangely, the Cyth didn't charge out at them as they closed in. It wasn't normal Cyth behavior to be timid or cautious, and Verdan felt his hackles rising with each uncontested step they took.

They were maybe a hundred feet from the closest building of the Cyth camp when the first retaliation to their approach came. The Cyth Lai had pulled back to cluster around the main building, but two dozen started forward to intercept the approaching humans.

"Gwen, see if you can call down a lightning bolt, rather than conjure one yourself," Verdan instructed, noting that the sky had grown dark with ominous clouds. The darkest clouds were directly overhead, and it seemed to deepen in color before a forking bolt of lightning slammed down into the approaching Cyth. The impact sent many of them flying, killing several immediately and leaving the rest dazed and disoriented for a moment.

"Got it," Gwen cried out happily, raising a hand and drawing down another two blasts that tore into the surviving Cyth. Those that had survived the initial hit were blasted and fried by the following impacts, leaving only a scattered few Cyth alive.

Gwen swayed a little as she lowered her hand, so Verdan stepped in and quickly launched a series of air blades at the survivors, quickly cutting down the unarmoured Cyth.

The remaining Cyth started to spread out, leaving the bulk of their number at the main building but taking away the risk of Gwen annihilating all of them with a localized lightning strike.

Verdan's eyes narrowed as he observed the intelligent response to their attack, but he couldn't see the creature directing the Cyth Lai. With all the wyrchwood around, he couldn't sense any concentration of abyssal energy that might give away the position of a Cyth Bayne. They'd have to get closer for that.

The moment the first human stepped inside the Cyth camp, the full assault began. The scattered Cyth Lai started to rush in, while two more Cyth Bayne revealed themselves as they each launched a trio of abyssal darts directly at Verdan.

"*Ast!*" Verdan barked out, conjuring an Aether shield to catch the darts with one hand as he pointed his other hand at a nearby clump of Cyth lai. "*Thanr bel!*"

The ball of fire that Verdan launched grew in size and intensity as it flew before exploding violently on impact. However, Verdan didn't manage to see the damage he'd done, as a flare of sickening corruption from the main building sent a wave of nausea through him.

Staggering a little at the impact of the energy on his Aether senses, Verdan felt a growing sense of horror as he turned to see a tall, hairless creature with flowing horns step into the sun. A network of dark black veins laced with a putrescent green threaded their way across its flesh. It could only be a Cyth Scerrd, and a dangerous one at that.

The creature held a staff in one hand and leveled it in Verdan's direction with a keening call. The staff was made of what looked like a humanoid spinal column that had been fused together and elongated with additional bones. The skull atop the staff had eyes that glowed with abyssal energy, and twin blasts of it fired out at Verdan.

Verdan hunkered behind his half-dome shield, feeling the impact of the blasts as they dug at his Aether.

"Gwen!" Verdan shouted to grab the Witch's attention as she sent a blast of wind to knock several Cyth into each other. "Get the two Cyth Bayne. I need to focus on the Scerrd!"

"Got it!" Gwen called back in a strained voice, lightning sparking around her arms as she sent a blast of energy at the nearer of the two Cyth Bayne. The Cyth caster conjured a shield to protect it and returned fire with a salvo of fast-moving abyssal darts.

"Shit!" Verdan heard Gwen curse as she engaged in the duel, but his focus was solely on the Cyth Scerrd. All the plans that Verdan had thought out were useless now. The Scerrd was far too dangerous for him to do anything but focus on it completely.

Cyth were created by corrupting a host; if Verdan hadn't rescued her, Gwen would have become a Cyth Bayne like the ones she was fighting. Not just humans could be corrupted, however; beasts and other races were just as vulnerable, and the more energy the base creature could hold, the stronger the Cyth that was born from it.

Verdan had initially thought that the Cyth Scerrd heading the camp had once been a human, maybe a Sorcerer that had been captured, but the truth was far worse. The creature's eyes were pools of Abyssal energy, and despite its horns, Verdan recognised the base creature that it had been formed from. This Cyth Scerrd had once been one of the maevir, an ancient people steeped in magic and power.

Verdan had to tear his eyes away from the corrupt maevir and strengthen his shield as it launched another pair of Abyssal energy blasts at him. Each blast of energy was like a sledgehammer pounding onto his shield, but Verdan poured Aether into the spell to maintain it. Now wasn't the time to be frugal.

"*Thanr bel*," Verdan whipped a hand around and threw a ball of flame toward the creature, who raised its staff high and conjured an almost-opaque shield of energy. The spell struck the shield and exploded, the fire wrapping around the shield and burning the Cyth Scerrd.

The creature's visage twisted into a spiteful expression as it recoiled from the flames, and Verdan grinned as he followed up with a trio of air blades to keep the pressure on it. For all its power, the creature was inexperienced in fighting other casters. Its shield was too close to it and didn't have enough flank protection.

"*Durst!*" Verdan intoned, focusing his Aether and intent into a single piercing blast that was intended to shatter the Cyth's shield. It wasn't his finest concept, but he made up for his lack of finesse with a chunk of raw power.

Aether met Abyssal energy with a flash of light, the shield of energy rupturing in the face of his shield-breaker spell.

"*Thanr laif!*" Verdan unleashed a lance of concentrated flame at the Cyth Scerrd before it could recast its shield, drawing a howl of pain from the creature as the side of its body was bathed in flames.

Black and green Abyssal energy flowed out from the Scerrd's staff to coat its body, smothering the Aether fueling the flames and banishing them. The remaining abyssal energy gathered before the Cyth, shielding it from further assault.

Expecting the shield, Verdan turned his attention to the rest of the battle. The clash of steel, shouts of pain, and roars of rage were a constant now as the small knot of humans fought back against the Cyth.

A few mercenaries had fallen to the physically-powerful Cyth Lai, but with Verdan and Gwen keeping the attention of the enemy casters, the humans were steadily winning. All Verdan needed to do was make sure things stayed that way.

Gwen was using a barrier of wind to deflect the attacks of the two Cyth Bayne, but she was panting heavily, and her face was red as she gathered a crackling fistful of lightning and threw it at one of the two Bayne.

Gwen's attacks lacked the power to get past the defenses of the Bayne, but they couldn't afford to spend the power to breach the wall of wind she'd conjured. A stalemate of endurance.

"*Durst*," Verdan gestured to the closer of the Cyth Bayne as he hit it with a low-powered shield breaker, shattering what was left of its defenses. "*Aer!*" A pressurized blast of wind shrieked through the air to scythe into the Cyth, knocking it from its feet.

Verdan's senses tingled as the Scerrd released a hail of abyssal darts at the group as a whole, dozens of them firing out from it in a storm of corruption.

"*Grym ast!*" Verdan bellowed, throwing up a dome three times the size of what he usually used, catching as many darts as he could. Each one that hit the shield ate at Verdan's Aether, sapping his strength and leaving him with a throbbing pain in his head.

Wiping his face, Verdan saw the bright streak of red across the back of his hand. He was reaching his limit, but he wasn't there yet.

Gwen had also tried to block some of the attack, but even so, Verdan could see a few fallen humans with black veins and terrified expressions. The average person had no defense against corruption like this.

Looking back at the Cyth Scerrd, Verdan unleashed a barrage of his own, mixing blasts of air with balls of flame as he stuck to his most Aether-efficient spells.

The corrupted maevir's shield took it all without fail, a rictus grin of pain and malice spreading across the creature's face as it maintained the new and far more powerful shield. The amount of energy it would expend to maintain a strong shield was horrifying, but the creature did so without pause.

The bone staff was turned to Verdan once more as the Scerrd sent blast after blast of thick corruptive energy at him. Verdan hunkered down behind his shield, thankful that the Cyth Lai were ignoring him to focus on his companions; this duel was all he had the focus for.

"Movement in the trees!" One of the mercenaries shouted out, pointing to the far side of the Cyth camp. Sure enough, Verdan could see movement among the wyrch heading this way. Even from this distance, Verdan could see the horns and bestial forms of those approaching, likely a returning Cyth raiding party.

"There must be another fifty of them. What's the plan, Boss?" Tim asked with a grunt of effort as he beheaded a wounded Cyth he'd been fighting, the enchantments on his blade proving their worth yet again.

The Cyth Scerrd chose that moment to start to conjure a fresh barrage of Abyssal darts, all the while maintaining its powerful shield.

Verdan's mind went into overdrive as he fought through the growing Aether burn that he was feeling. The Cyth Scerrd mustn't have been taking them seriously initially, but the fire lance that

Verdan had hit it with had changed that, and it wasn't taking any chances now.

If it were only a normal Scerrd they were facing, Verdan would be able to defeat it, even in his current state. The beacon of corruption that stood opposite him, however, was drawing on a well of power that Verdan couldn't match and had a powerful magical item assisting it.

If he were alone, Verdan might be able to fight the thing to a stand-still, but needing to protect the others made victory an impossible outcome. His empowered shield had eaten up as much Aether as the big shield-breaker he'd used earlier. He had only a few more spells like that left in him.

The raiding party reinforcements changed things. Their chances of winning were all but gone. There were too few fighters still standing to engage a fresh Cyth raiding party.

Verdan needed to throw up another empowered shield if he wanted to protect everyone, but it was a costly spell, both in Aether and mental strain. Looking around him, Verdan saw that Gwen, Tim, Sylvie, and Verdan's personal guards were all relatively close by, so he steeled his soul and made a decision.

_**_

"*Ast*," Verdan all but whispered, conjuring only a slightly enlarged version of his shield that protected those next to him. "Everyone take cover!"

Those closest to Verdan ducked in behind the shield as a swarm of abyssal darts fell on them, a dozen or more hitting the shield Verdan had conjured and each one further sapping his Aether by a barely noticeable amount.

Anyone who made it within his shield was safe, but not everyone did. One mercenary, in particular, was struck across the arm on the way in. The foul corruption was already necrotising her skin by the time Verdan could turn his attention to her. The inherent Aether inside her was being subsumed and destroyed rapidly. Despite that, she was one of the lucky ones.

Four other mercenaries were caught in the open too far from Verdan's shield or any other shelter. Verdan recognised one of them as the man who'd pointed out the oncoming raiding party, though there was little left of him now. Three darts had struck him, two hitting him in the head and rotting away his flesh with disturbing speed.

Death by Abyssal corruption was an incredibly painful way to go, and the anguished screams of those that the darts had caught were like knives into Verdan's soul. Guilt tore at him as his overconfidence was thrown back in his face. He'd been too dismissive of the threat the Cyth posed, too sure in his ability to protect the others.

Getting a taste of his old power had gone to Verdan's head, and now they were all paying the price.

"We need to pull back," Verdan called out, putting action to words as he staggered away from the Cyth Scerrd, not taking his eyes off the creature as he held a spell at the ready.

"We can take them, Boss!" Tim argued angrily, even as he matched Verdan's retreat. None of the surviving members of the group were stupid enough to stray far from Gwen or Verdan at this point.

"No, we can't," Verdan said tiredly, his tone of voice causing the others to give him concerned looks. "I can't protect all of us, and there's too few left to fight the raiding party. Gwen's not in much better shape, either. *Aer.*" Verdan absently threw a curved blade of pressurized air at a Cyth trying to sneak up on them as they backpedaled, slicing its neck open before it could get close enough.

"Then what do we do—retreat back the way we came?" Tim exchanged a worried look with Pania as Verdan was forced to summon a new shield to block a more-concentrated abyssal dart that targeted them.

"I don't know," Verdan muttered hoarsely, his mind torn between the effort of maintaining his spells and the screams of the mercenaries that were being slowly withered away.

He'd chosen a smaller shield to preserve his Aether, to give them a better chance of getting out of this alive, but that made it no easier to live with.

"Verdan, I'm not sure how much longer I can keep this going," Gwen said, the strain in her eyes making Verdan curse himself. Not only had he been too confident in his abilities, but he'd also pushed Gwen to join them. Gwen wasn't ready for this; she was little more than a novice by Wizarding standards. A powerful novice, but inexperienced and lacking the instincts needed for a caster duel.

The conversation of his companions faded into the background as Verdan countered another round of Abyssal darts and blasts. He needed to do something big, something that could give them the time they needed to escape. This was all on him, and he needed to make it right.

Wiping the blood from his nose, Verdan reached over to grab Tim's shoulder and get his attention. "Tim, get everyone ready. I'm going to delay the Cyth, and then we're all going to run. Don't stop for anything."

Tim nodded, but his eye lingered on the smeared blood on Verdan's hand and around his nose. Verdan wished he had words of reassurance for his companion, but the throbbing headache from his Aether burn was making everything more difficult.

Turning back to the Cyth, Verdan saw the creature slam its staff into the ground, Abyssal energy coalescing around the skull to form a sphere of darkness that the Scerrd launched out toward them.

Like a dark imitation of the fireball spell that Verdan used, the abyssal sphere swelled in size and intensity as it flew through the air in a long parabolic arc. A trail of loose corruption followed it through the air, and Verdan grimaced as he felt the power behind the attack. This would need an empowered shield, and a strong one at that.

Verdan began to raise his staff and force the words of power out through his raw throat when Gwen stepped up next to him and caught his hand.

"I've got this," the Witch said, her voice firm despite her pale complexion.

Thunder rolled through the dark clouds above, and rain began to lash down at them. The cold droplets were strangely refreshing, but Verdan's eyes were on the large ball of Abyssal energy that was now plummeting toward them.

"Almost, almost," Gwen muttered, one hand coming up toward her raven, which was circling high above them. "There, got it."

Verdan's robes flapped around him as a blast of wind swept through the camp, one that only grew stronger as Gwen channeled her power. Verdan had to lean into the gale as it began to howl through the camp, directly into the Cyth Scerrd as it tried to follow after them.

Ordinary wind wouldn't be able to move something made of energy, but this wind was infused with Aether and Exeon. Verdan allowed himself a slight smile as he watched the sphere's trajectory shift until it eventually struck the ground a distance behind them.

The sphere erupted into a huge explosion of corrupt energy, leaving a shroud of darkness laced with dark green behind to linger around the impact site.

"Well done, you've bought us a few moments," Verdan said, clapping Gwen on the shoulder as the wind died down. Urging her forward with the others, Verdan glanced back at the Cyth with more concern than he'd shown.

All that was left of the original Cyth defenders was the final Cyth Bayne, the Cyth Scerrd and less than a dozen Cyth Lai. It wasn't a lot compared to what they'd first encountered, but it was enough.

Even now, the Cyth Scerrd was gathering the survivors and starting the chase. Verdan was struggling as it was; there was no way he could protect them from any attacks the Cyth threw at them while also fleeing as fast as he could.

No, this wasn't going to work. They were going to get run down before they could make it to the forest. There were less than twenty of them left, and though they still outnumbered the Cyth chasing them, Verdan dared not let anyone get too close to the corrupted maevir. The chances of him being able to shield against its attacks were lower the closer it got. Unlike Wizards, the Cyth casters needed no words of power to cast their spells, so they were always quicker off the mark.

The Scerrd sent a twisting dart of energy after them, forcing Verdan to stop and conjure a shield to block it, slowing the group down further. Interestingly though, the Scerrd didn't move to close the gap; it simply started gathering the energy for another attack.

For a moment, Verdan's heart sang with the hope that the Cyth was calling off the pursuit, but as soon as he began to move away, it started to follow.

No, this wasn't going to work. Verdan knew he needed an alternative, to somehow give them space enough to break away from the Scerrd. If they could hide away in the part of the forest that was healthy long enough to recover, he could work with Gwen to batter through the powerful shield it used.

For that to happen, though, they needed time. They needed rest. None of which would happen while the Cyth were stalking them. Verdan still had a few big spells left in him, even with the growing Aether burn, but he doubted it would be enough.

The temptation was there to throw everything into one final, intense spell, but if that failed, they were doomed. So far, the Scerrd's new shield had taken everything without issue. Verdan had a few tricks up his sleeve in raw firepower, but not enough to feel confident.

Verdan felt a swelling of energy from behind them and spun around to conjure a shield, catching almost all of the Abyssal darts flying their way. Dismissing the shield as soon as he could, Verdan heaved himself into a fast jog once more, his chest heaving from the exertion.

Another mercenary lay dying mere paces from Verdan, his skin already gray and losing color from the multiple darts that had hit him. One less person to come back to Hobson's Point, one more death to weigh on Verdan's conscience.

They just needed a bit of time, just enough to get away and put some distance between them and the Cyth. Just enough to give them a chance to recover and prepare.

Time. That was it. That was the key here. Verdan was trying to solve this problem like a war Wizard, like the person the war had made him into, but that wasn't who he was. Verdan was a scholar first and a fighter second.

"Tim, come here!" Verdan yelled, skidding to a stop and turning back to face the oncoming Cyth. "*Ast!*" Verdan created a half-dome shield in front of him, leaving a portion of his mind to support it as he focused everything else on the words he needed.

It had been a long time since Verdan had crafted a new spell on the fly, let alone one of this caliber, but old skills were rarely truly lost.

Four words, that was all he could manage. Anything more would strain him too far, both magically and physically. Verdan's throat was raw from the spells he'd cast, and he dared not push it too far. The Aether from a four-word spell might well cause an explosion if he mangled the words.

"Boss, what's wrong?" Tim panted, arriving next to Verdan with Sylvie a moment behind him. "We need to go!"

"No, no time. I need to stop them chasing us," Verdan said absently, his mind full of spells and meanings. "Stand behind me when I cast; I might need you to carry me." This spell was going to be a lot, and the Aether burn was going to be bad, really bad.

"I hope you know what you're doing, Boss," Tim said, stepping back behind Verdan with a worried expression, not that Verdan could blame him. Still, that didn't matter now; all that Verdan could focus on was the spell.

The Cyth were starting to throw attacks at him, sensing that he was doing something different. Verdan could spare no Aether for the shield, so he needed to work quickly.

Verdan exerted the self-control he'd spent years developing and dragged his focus to the wording. Four words.

Amsera, time's passage. *Gward*, a warding construct to maintain an effect. *Raf*, the essence of slowness. *Sia*, the act of shaping. Verdan kept each word, each intent, in mind as firmly as he could. There was only one shot at this.

"*Gward sia amsera raf*," Verdan all but choked out the spell, the final word tearing the insides of his throat as it left. Every ounce of Aether he had was funneled down into the construct he was creating, binding it to his staff as he raised it high and drove it into the ground.

Aether drained from Verdan in a torrent, pouring down into the staff until it seemed to shimmer blue with potency.

Locking eyes with the Cyth Scerrd as it started to coalesce another powerful sphere of corruption, Verdan twisted the staff symbolically, activating the construct bound to it and feeling the last of his Aether be sucked out into it.

Outwardly, there was no great sign of his spell, no shining light or crack of thunder. The staff still glowed a slight blue, but that was all. No, there was something else, a haze to the air beyond the staff that stretched out in a long cone, encompassing the Cyth pursuing them. Cyth that were now almost entirely frozen in place.

Interesting—he hadn't expected there to be a visible effect to the spell. Straightening from his half-crouch, Verdan felt light-headed as he turned to Tim, darkness eating away at the corners of his vision as something trickled out of his nose.

Wiping his face, Verdan looked at the dark blood smeared on his hand and then back to Tim. "I might have overdone it."

Tim said something, his eyes wide as he looked between Verdan, the staff and the Cyth. The dull roar in Verdan's ears drowned out whatever Tim was saying, however, and Verdan managed a single step toward him before falling into darkness.

THIRTY-SIX

"WHAT DID YOU JUST DO?" Tim asked, eyes wide with shock as Verdan rose from his crouched position and turned to face him.

The Wizard had a strangely unfocused look in his eyes, and he took barely a single step forward before his legs gave way and he tumbled forward.

"Damn it!" Tim cursed as he awkwardly caught the Wizard under the arms and supported him with his free hand, noting how surprisingly light Verdan was. A quick check confirmed that Verdan was still breathing, but his eyes were closed, and he didn't look like he was waking up anytime soon.

Footsteps announced the arrival of the rest of their group, who stared in confusion at the frozen Cyth. No, looking closer, Tim realized they weren't actually frozen.

Peering at the odd-looking Cyth with the skull staff, Tim saw that the creature was still moving, albeit incredibly slowly. That meant there was a time limit on whatever Verdan had done, a time limit until the Cyth were free and they were being hunted once more.

"We need to leave before that thing breaks free," one of the mercenaries said, their voice riddled with fear, not that Tim could blame them.

"But what about the people here? We need to see if anyone can be rescued," Pania argued hotly, pointing at the main building of the Cyth camp.

Tim remembered when he'd signed on as a guard for a merchant with his brother. The Cyth had ambushed them and taken them all back to their camp. The merchant had been taken for sacrifice early, and Tim had sat in that dark cellar waiting for his turn on the cold stone with the bloody knife.

Tim still had nightmares of his time there, of what would have happened if Verdan hadn't rescued them. He didn't have it in him to leave others to that fate if he could stop it.

"Pania is right. We can't leave them," Tim said simply, laying Verdan on the ground and fixing the others with a firm gaze.

"Well, what about this effect? Can we go in and slit the throats of those Cyth? That would solve the problem," Pawel pointed to the mostly frozen Cyth with one hand.

"No, I can't use Aether in the way that Verdan can, but I can feel that a whole area is under the effect of that spell, not just the creatures in it. We could break the spell if we disturb the staff or interfere too much." Gwen frowned as she focused on something none of them could see, her raven swooping down to land on her shoulder gracefully. "I can feel where it's limited to, and I can guide us around it."

"What about throwing things into it, they'll never see it coming," Pawel said, a malicious glint in his eye as he drew one of his daggers. "I've got a few of these to spare."

"What if introducing new things to the field causes it to break down faster, or break it altogether?" Gwen said, shaking her head emphatically. "We can't risk it. If that thing breaks free, we're all dead."

"I agree. Gwen, lead us around it," Tim said, wishing silently that Verdan was awake and they could use Pawel's plan.

"Are you seriously considering this absolute madness? We need to leave!" A mercenary cried out, looking at Tim as though he'd lost his mind.

"I'm not leaving without the captives," Tim declared, Sylvie growling approvingly as she nuzzled his leg.

"That raiding party will rip us apart, though," the mercenary said in a pleading tone. "They outnumber us three to one."

"I can deal with them. A few blasts of lightning will even the odds," Gwen said confidently, straightening up and lifting her chin as if to dare anyone to disagree.

For a moment, Tim thought the mercenaries might argue further or leave, but after a hushed argument between them, they settled on staying and helping.

Pawel and Pania volunteered to stay with Verdan, along with three of the mercenaries, the other six coming with Gwen, Tim, Ruan, and Barb.

Ruan was an older, bald man with a full beard and a scarred face. One particular scar had disfigured the right side of his face, giving him a slur and a fierce countenance. He was a tough man and a brave fighter, from what Tim had seen so far.

Barb was a tall, muscular woman with dark braided hair and a series of ritual scars that flowed down her cheeks and onto her arms. That kind of scarification was only seen in people from the far north, beyond the Grey Peaks, the mountain range that Hobson's Point was built up against.

Where Pawel and Pania were quick and deadly, Barb and Ruan were strong and tough, exactly what they were going to need to survive this.

"Ready when you are," Tim said, nodding to Gwen as they arranged themselves into who was doing what.

"Follow me, stay close," Gwen said, leading them in a wide arc around the area affected by Verdan's spell. In the time it had taken for them to get organized, the Cyth caught in the spell had moved ever so slightly further forward. If nothing else disturbed them, Tim reckoned they would have several hours before the Cyth broke free.

Gwen's path took them around one of the smaller buildings before cutting in toward where the central and largest of the Cyth buildings sat.

"We can't enter these two—the field overlaps with them—but the rest are untouched," Gwen explained, pointing out the building they went around and one other.

"Alright, Gwen, stay out here and rest while you can. Everyone else, teams of three, let's get in there, find everyone and get them out, understood?"

There was a chorus of answers as they split up and went to the different buildings, Tim taking the main one with Ruan, Barb, and Sylvie backing him up.

The entrance had no door or way of keeping them out, so they were able to walk straight in, finding themselves in a large chamber covered in the growths of the corrupted wood they saw outside and decorated with bones of all shapes and sizes.

"This place feels horrible," Tim muttered, shivering against the oily feeling of the air inside the building. "Spread out and see what you can find."

They each went in a different direction, Tim heading through another entrance into what was clearly a sacrificial room of some sort. A long table-like object dominated the room. It was made from the same corrupted wood as the building and had grooves along its length leading to a drain at one end.

The floor was stained a dark brown color, and the whole room reeked of death. Tim knew he would find no one alive here.

"Tim, Ruan, I've got something!" Barb shouted out, grabbing Tim's attention.

Barb had taken the furthest door from the entrance, which turned out to be a set of winding stairs leading down to a sealed door. Barb was trying to break it down with her shoulder when Tim and Ruan arrived.

"Let me through, I'll chop into it," Ruan said, drawing his ax and squeezing past Barb to line up with the door. Taking a steadying breath, Ruan braced himself and began to deliver a series of heavy blows to the door.

The corrupted wood held up well against Ruan's ax, but it wasn't immune to the heavy hits and slowly began to splinter beneath the assault. Tim watched impassively as Ruan continued making headway, his mind on the approaching Cyth raiding party. This was taking longer than he'd hoped.

"Keep going. I'm going to go check on what's happening outside," Tim said as he ascended the stairs and hurried back outside.

Gwen was sitting on the ground where they'd left her, eyes closed and breathing rhythmically. Three of the mercenaries stood around her, looking off toward the approaching Cyth.

The raiding party didn't look like it was moving too fast; they likely hadn't realized that the camp had been compromised, but that wouldn't last. Time was running out to get the captives released if they wanted to avoid a battle here.

Part of Tim couldn't help but wonder if there were actually any captives left at this point, but he refused to let that stop him.

Heading back inside, Tim hurried down to where Ruan was finishing off a hole in the door and holding a burning piece of wood through to look at the interior. Barb had made herself useful by gathering pieces of the wood that Ruan had cut free and binding them together to make makeshift torches.

"Should we really be burning that?" Tim asked, looking askance at the thick black smoke coming from the one in Ruan's hand.

"Better than being blind," Barb said with a laconic shrug.

"Hopefully," Tim muttered under his breath. "What can you see, Ruan?"

"Found them," Ruan said in a grim tone, dropping the burning wood and stamping it out before taking his ax to the door once more to widen the hole.

Once it was large enough, Ruan clambered through and took a fresh torch from Barb, holding it aloft so that they could see the captives.

A dozen forms lay bound at the rear of the room, propped up against the wall and unmoving. Tim was quick to climb in through the hole Ruan made and check on them.

Seven of the twelve were dead, and the last five were unconscious, their breathing labored.

"We need to get them out of here," Tim said, meeting the other's gaze with a grim expression. He remembered how Gwen had suffered from the bindings the Cyth had used. While none of these people were bound like that, the building itself might be enough to make them ill.

"How will we get them back to Hobson's Point?" Barb asked in a low tone, making Tim grimace and shake his head.

"No idea, but we can't leave them in here. Help me get them outside." Tim grabbed the first person and got them upright and into Barb's arms for her to carry upstairs.

Working together, the three of them got the surviving captives out of the building over the next few minutes, laying them in the sun outside.

Thankfully, once the survivors were clear of the Cyth building, they started to wake up. Tim had been more than a little worried about how he'd get them back to Hobson's Point alongside their unconscious Wizard, but hopefully, they'd be good to travel. It didn't matter how fast; they just needed to start moving.

"Tim, the Cyth have realized there's a problem!" Gwen shouted, pointing to the raiding party, which was now closing at a much faster rate.

"Right—you four, keep the survivors safe. Everyone else, to the front with Gwen," Tim instructed, leaving four of the six mercenaries with the survivors.

"Okay, here we go," Gwen muttered, her raven taking off from her shoulder with a series of loud caws. Closing her eyes, Gwen raised a hand to the clouds in the sky. They weren't as dark as before, but they seemed to start coming together overhead as Gwen channeled her power, darkening as they came.

The Cyth were maybe a few hundred feet from them when the first bolt struck, hitting the center of the group with sudden violence as thunder boomed and rolled around them.

The second bolt hit before the dirt from the first impact had even reached the floor, hitting a different part of the group this time.

The third bolt came down on a large, horned Cyth that towered over its companions, but a black shield with dark-green energy lacing through it appeared above the Cyth, stopping most of the blast. The shield was shattered, and the large Cyth scorched, but not to the degree of the other two bolts.

Gwen lowered her hand and shared a worried look with Tim. They hadn't considered that the raiding party might have a Cyth Bayne. That changed things, and not for the better.

_**_

The Cyth broke up into several groups in the aftermath of Gwen's attack, hurriedly spreading out to approach the camp from several directions at once.

Tim responded by sending the others to block the Cyth and ensure the wounded were protected. There was over a score of Cyth standing, less than before but still a threat.

Tim sent more of his companions away as the Cyth continued to leave and join the flanking attacks. They were too few to match the Cyth in numbers, but Tim trusted their ability to carry the day. He had to.

Eventually, it was just Tim and Gwen holding their original spot, with Sylvie waiting a step behind Tim and ready to assist. Thankfully, only two Cyth remained across from them, but they were the most dangerous of the lot.

The Cyth Bayne and the large horned Cyth that Gwen had singed earlier faced off against them, the Bayne standing protectively in front of its companion as it locked eyes with Gwen. The horned monster was easily seven feet tall, and its rippling musculature was covered in thick black fur and odd bony protrusions.

As the clamor let Tim know that battle had been joined elsewhere, their opponents started to approach, the caster throwing out a pair of Abyssal darts while the horned Cyth began to charge toward Tim.

"I'm not sure I have the strength to break through its shield with enough power to kill it, but I can keep it busy and stop it from attacking you," Gwen said, throwing out two low-powered gusts of wind that knocked the darts off course and into the ground.

It wasn't exactly what Tim had been hoping she'd say, but that was okay; he'd just have to manage. This was Tim's role; he understood that now. He was here to stand between his friends and their foes, giving them the time and space they needed to work.

It didn't matter that Gwen could blast the horned Cyth into oblivion, she needed to focus elsewhere, so Tim would handle it instead. He was her shield.

Something about that thought resonated with Tim, and he felt a surety of purpose that made him think of the day they rescued Sylvie. He'd been her shield then, just as he would for Gwen now.

Resolute and focused on his role with unusual clarity, Tim moved to meet the Cyth. The creature was carrying a club made of corrupted wood, much like its smaller brethren, but its club was twice the size and looked like it could cave Tim's head in with a glancing blow.

The horned Cyth brought the club around in a wide swing as it closed with Tim, making him skid to a halt and dodge aside to avoid it. Recovering his balance first, Tim slashed at the creature's knee, the enchanted blade cutting through the Cyth's thick skin with ease.

A blast of wind swept past them as Gwen continued her own fight, and Tim gave the Cyth some space as it jabbed the club at him angrily. It would be warier of him now, but it wouldn't last.

Tim's mind was racing as the Cyth steadied itself and closed with him once more; he could feel the enchantment on his blade failing. Tim couldn't sense the Aether directly, but he could feel the difference when he hit the creature. The enhancement was his biggest advantage right now, so he needed to be careful not to waste it on minor hits.

Tim's world narrowed to the thrum of the club cutting through the air as he dodged and dipped around the Cyth's attacks, biding his time. The creature was becoming wild in its attacks as it grew frustrated; soon, it would leave an opening he could use to end this.

A flicker of darkness from one side caught Tim's eye as the Bayne threw a single, oversized dart at him, one that tracked with his movements. Tim barely had time to panic when lightning obliterated the dart, partially blinding Tim.

Blinking madly and disoriented from the accompanying crack of thunder, Tim was disorientated and stunned for several precious moments. When his focus returned, it was just in time to see the Cyth's club coming down at him.

Barking a curse, Tim twisted to bring his shield around just in time to catch the club with a loud cracking sound that sent lances of agony through his body.

The sheer impact of the blow sent Tim flying, and he hit the ground hard, his arm sending spikes of raw pain into his mind as he gasped for breath. The boss of his shield was cracked, and his arm hurt to move; it was likely broken.

"I have little time, meu drassul, but I will not let this thing hurt you any further," a woman's voice came from behind Tim as he struggled to a sitting position. The voice was a throaty contralto, and definitely not one of the women he was traveling with.

The horned Cyth was bearing down on them, so Tim had no time and no focus to spare; he either got to his feet or died on his knees. Levering himself up, Tim felt the woman behind him grab his arms and help him up before stealing the long dagger he carried at his belt once Tim was on his feet.

Tim had no time to argue as the Cyth came in at them with a wild swing of its club, forcing him to throw himself back to avoid being crushed like a bug.

The woman who'd helped him up instead dove forwards into a smooth roll to avoid the club, rising gracefully within arms reach of the creature and flowing into a flurry of motion as she danced around the big Cyth.

Tim's dagger was like an extension of her arm as she flowed around the brutish creature, cutting with deadly grace as it tried to catch her. The dagger could barely penetrate the thick skin of the Cyth, but that was all she needed.

Long silver hair flowed freely behind her as she moved, giving an oddly ethereal quality as she steadily reduced the horned Cyth to a bloodied mess. With each new motion, Tim expected her to back off, to take a moment to recover, but she didn't. If anything, the pressure of her attack only rose as her victim's blood ran like water down her blade.

Tim was momentarily delayed as he realized that the woman was naked, and all she had was his dagger, but he quickly focused back on the situation at hand, pushing the rest off to be dealt with later.

With its attention on the woman, the Cyth didn't notice Tim's approach until his blade took it in the chest, sinking deep into the creature's flesh. The enchantment on Tim's blade failed halfway through the stab as it expended the last of its energy, but it was enough. The Cyth staggered forward and pitched to one side as it bled out, its bulk tearing the sword's handle from Tim's good hand as the Cyth collapsed to the ground.

Light flashed as Gwen continued her fight with the Bayne, but the strange woman who'd saved Tim turned on her heel and threw his dagger when Gwen's lightning shattered the Cyth's abyssal shield.

Flashing steel buried itself in the Bayne's eye, ending the fight with a finality that Tim could appreciate.

The woman turned back to Tim with a satisfied expression that slowly morphed into a wide smile as she walked toward him. She was liberally splattered with Cyth blood, and now that she'd finished fighting, there was a weight to her movements that spoke of deep exhaustion.

The woman flicked her hair back over her shoulder, drawing Tim's attention to her lithe form. Tim flushed and lifted his gaze, the words he was about to say dying in his throat as he caught her gaze.

Her amber eyes were the color of liquid gold, and her gaze had a warmth to it that Tim didn't expect. There was almost something familiar about the color, but Tim couldn't place it.

"Meu drassul, it's good to speak with you finally," the woman said, smiling tiredly as she wiped some black Cyth blood from her face.

"Who are you? Were you one of the captives?" Tim asked, his eyes drifting down to her neck as he realized that not all of the blood was from the Cyth. "You're hurt; how bad is it?" Tim pointed to the blood on her neck, noticing as he did that freshly healed scar tissue encircled her neck in a thick ring.

"It's fine. Some of the wounds from the collar have reopened, is all," the woman said, her voice thick with exhaustion as she seemed to slump in on herself. "I'm sorry, I would talk with you more, but I need to turn back. I knew I was too weak, but that creature would have hurt you badly, and I couldn't allow that." There was a fierce gleam in her eyes despite the weariness in her voice.

"I don't understand. Wait, the collar?" Tim asked, trying to process what she was saying and failing.

"I'm sorry, I have to turn back. I'll explain everything once I've been able to rest. Trust me, meu drassul," the woman gave him an oddly poignant smile as she stepped back, laughing softly as Tim averted his eyes from her naked form.

"Look, please just explain...." Tim started to say, his words trailing away as the woman's eyes glowed a bright amber and her form flowed from that of a woman to a wolf. A silver-furred wolf with amber eyes.

Tim stared in abject confusion at the wolf for a long moment, his mind refusing to accept what was clearly the truth. The wolf in front of him was Sylvie, which meant that the woman was Sylvie, and he'd been spending all his time with a shapeshifter.

In her wolf form once more, Sylvie began panting heavily and slumped down to lay on her side. Her eyes drooped shut as Tim watched; he wasn't sure if she'd passed out or fallen asleep, but she was still breathing, so she was okay. He hoped.

"Go, I'll watch her," Gwen said in a strained voice, coming over to give Tim a gentle push away. "The sooner we get moving, the better,"

Focusing on what he could control, Tim went to gather the others. Gwen was right, they needed to go. Questions could come later.

CHAPTER
THIRTY-SEVEN

VERDAN AWOKE to a splitting headache and the odd sensation of being dragged along on something. Heavy weights pressed down on his legs and stomach, and though the light was initially blinding, he blinked furiously and looked down to see a pale-looking man and Sylvie sprawled over him.

The three of them were in some sort of jury-rigged sled, and Verdan could see four people pulling them along at a steady pace with some rope.

"Hey, the Sorcerer's awake!" Someone called out from Verdan's left, making him twist around to see one of the mercenaries that Tobias had hired.

"Okay, everyone, take a few minutes to rest," Tim's voice rang out with quiet authority, the ex-guard coming into view a moment later.

Tim looked tired, and his left arm was in a sling made up of ripped-up tunic, but he seemed healthy enough despite that.

"Here, let's get you out of there," Tim said, relief evident in his voice as he gestured for the mercenary to help him and adjusted the other occupants of the sled until Verdan could clamber free.

"Thank you, Tim. What happened? I remember casting a spell. Did it work?" Verdan asked, thinking of the stasis field spell he'd cobbled together on the spot.

The thought of magic made Verdan turn his mind inward as he retasked his subconscious with the gathering spiral and judged how much Aether he had. The spiral would continue for up to a few days without input from him, though it would slow down over that time, so it was easy to get going once more.

With how much Aether he had left, Verdan estimated he'd likely been unconscious for more than a few hours but less than a full day.

"It did—well, I think so. The Cyth weren't frozen completely, but they were left moving incredibly slowly, enough that we were able to rescue the captives and defeat the raiding party before starting our escape. We're not far past the original ambush site now, and we should be back not long after nightfall." Tim gestured to the healthy forest around them and the late afternoon sun as he spoke. "I'm glad you're awake, though. I was getting worried."

"You did well getting everyone out. Did we lose anyone else?" Verdan asked the question that was burning in his mind, dreading the answer before he'd even finished speaking.

"Three of the mercenaries fell against the raiding party," Tim said softly, pitching his voice to reach just Verdan. "Beyond that, my arm was crushed, and some of the others have claw wounds, though nothing too bad. The worst are Sylvie and Fyle, one of the captives. They're both in the sled."

"What happened to them?" Verdan asked, looking back at the two unconscious forms in the sled, noting the odd hitch in Tim's voice as he said Sylvie's name.

"All the captives were in a bad way when we got there, but most of them bounced back when we got them out of the building. Fyle didn't." Tim's voice was somber, and he looked at the pale man with a guilty expression that Verdan knew well.

"This wasn't your fault, Tim," Verdan said, reaching out to squeeze Tim's shoulder reassuringly. Verdan wasn't in the best shape to be giving anyone advice or support right now. The lingering effects of the Aether burn had left his mind fuzzy at best. "Now, what happened to Sylvie?"

"Well, she was fighting, but she was different," Tim said hesitantly before grimacing and stopping to rub his face.

"Verdan, you're awake!" Gwen called out, interrupting Tim before he could explain further.

The Witch was approaching their group from the direction that they'd come from, Pawel and Pania accompanying her.

"Gwen, Pawel, Pania, I'm happy to see you're all unhurt," Verdan said, smiling and nodding at each of them in turn as they joined them. Gwen looked tired; she'd no doubt been pushing herself while Verdan was out of action. Hopefully, she could rest now.

"I think I speak for everyone when I say I'm even happier to see you awake. It's been a constant worry that the staff-wielding Cyth would chase us down, and I know I have no chance against a creature that powerful. We just scaled a nearby hill, and there's no sign of pursuit. I think we're free and clear." Gwen gestured back the way she'd come, to a sloping hill that Verdan could see a little ways away.

"Good to know. Let's not rest too long, though, just in case," Tim said before pausing and looking at Verdan. "If you think that's wise, Boss?"

"I do, let me gather my thoughts, and I can make this sled easier as well. In the meantime, let me see your arm," Verdan said, gesturing to Tim's injured arm.

"A big, horned Cyth hit me and shattered my shield," Tim explained as he gingerly removed the sling and showed Verdan his arm, wincing in pain as he did.

"I see. It looks like a number of small fractures, I don't want to apply too much healing in case it comes in wrong, but I can certainly speed it on its way. *Iacha*," Verdan explained, finishing with a minor healing spell to help with the swelling and accelerate Tim's natural healing.

Verdan went around and did the same for the other injured before finishing with the spell on the sled. The floating spell he'd used to leave his cave when he first woke up was enough to work with the right intent behind it. The Aether drain was more than Verdan wanted, but the base of the sled lifted slightly off the ground, making it much easier to pull.

His duty done for his companions, Verdan took a few minutes to collect his thoughts as they finished the rest break and got on the move once more. He felt restless. Thoughts of the Cyth Scerrd kept intruding into his mind, making him wonder how many more would die for his failure to kill the creature.

"*Hyn*," Verdan cast his energy replenishment spell on himself, the wave of Aether causing his muscles to relax and his mind to calm as he banished the tiredness and small aches. He should have done that as soon as he woke up; he already felt so much better, and the restlessness and intrusive thoughts were easier to manage.

_**_

The remainder of their journey back to Hobson's Point was thankfully uneventful, though Verdan had to recast his float spell on the sled twice more. It was a small price to pay for easing the burden of the others.

Verdan hadn't had the chance to talk further with Tim, but he'd swept Sylvie and Fyle with a specialized detect spell, finding traces of corruption in both of them. Fyle's was classic abyssal corruption, while Sylvie's was the strange Aether-devouring type that the Darjee had wielded.

Sylvie's corruption no longer had a source to renew it, but her weakened condition had worsened from when Verdan had last examined her. Perhaps there was some synergy with the abyssal corruption of the Cyth; he'd need to talk with Tim and see what had happened when she was fighting.

"There's someone coming out," Barb called out, breaking his train of thought and bringing his attention to the gates of the city.

"Impressive eyesight," Verdan said, brows raised in surprise as he struggled to make out the figures that they'd noticed.

"Thank you," she said simply, in the manner of someone who knew they were good at something and took the compliment for what it was.

As they drew closer, Verdan was relieved to see that it was Lieutenant Silver and a few of the city guards that were waiting for them.

"Lieutenant, good to see you. How was your hunt?" Verdan greeted the stern-faced guard, Gwen and Tim both inching close to hear what the Lieutenant had to say.

"Eventful. I lost some good men, but both the beasts are dead, and Willowbrook is safe. Sorcerer Kai and Tom both made it back, though the mother bear injured Tom. They're both at your estate currently. We thought it best to keep them in one place given certain....developments." Silver explained, shifting his weight slightly as he finished speaking

"Both creatures—there were actually two?" Verdan queried, wincing internally as he realized how bad the hunt must have gone.

"What about Kai, was he injured?" Gwen interjected, flushing a little as Verdan turned to cock an eyebrow in her direction but not looking away.

"Only superficially. We have much to thank him for," Silver said solemnly, a shadow of pain crossing his face for a moment before he turned back to Verdan. "Yes, there were two bears, but we would be best discussing that, and other new developments, in private. I can see some unfamiliar faces. How did your own expedition go?"

"That's perhaps best left for a private discussion as well," Verdan said slowly, his mind racing as he considered the things that Silver wasn't telling him.

"I see," Silver said, his eyes narrowing as he looked over the group. "Any of you who are in need of medical attention can wait at the gates. A doctor will be here soon. Those hired by Mr. Brock should head for the guard headquarters; your pay has been left there for you to collect. Everyone else, please follow me." Silver turned and headed back to the gates, his troops filing in behind him.

Verdan hesitated and looked at the rescued captives, not entirely comfortable with abandoning them to go and speak with Silver.

"If it suits you, Boss, me and Barb can look after these lot, make sure they get somewhere safe," Ruan said, his lisp a little more accentuated than normal.

"Thank you, Ruan. Find me if you need funds for anything, but take these for now. Make sure they're all fed and have somewhere to rest," Verdan said, relieved that someone was taking the responsibility for him.

Taking a moment to recast the spell on the sled, Verdan watched Ruan and Barb lead the rescued captives into the city. They'd lost a lot of the mercenaries that Tobias had hired, but they'd succeeded in bringing the captives home. That was something.

The Cyth Scerrd worried him considerably. The maevir were ageless and powerful; many of them were old before the very first Wizard even conceived a spell. For one of them to be corrupted by the Cyth had terrifying implications.

Verdan had heard tales of what a corrupted Wizard could achieve, of how they retained more of their intelligence, of their skill. Verdan had assumed that he wouldn't find anything so powerful, and that the worst he might find would be a corrupted Sorcerer. How wrong he'd been.

The thought of the vast amount of knowledge that creature might have sent chills down Verdan's spine. It might have lacked experience in how to fight effectively with its corrupt powers, but the sheer strength it had more than made up for it.

If the Cyth Scerrd had taken them seriously from the beginning, Verdan doubted that any of them would have gotten out alive. The shield it had conjured at the end had been an order of magnitude beyond what the Cyth Bayne were capable of.

They'd rescued the captives, but there would be another fight with the Cyth Scerrd, and Verdan needed to be ready.

CHAPTER
THIRTY-EIGHT

GWEN DIDN'T WAIT for Verdan once he'd gone in to debrief with Lieutenant Silver. Pawel and Pania had volunteered to stay while she, Ruan, and Barb went back to the estate.

It had been a trying few days, and Gwen was looking forward to getting back to somewhere familiar and safe.

She fully admitted to herself that part of her rush was to make sure that Kai was okay. She knew he hadn't been hurt, Silver had said as much, but it was still something she wanted to see first-hand.

The stoic Sorcerer had done a lot to support her, sometimes in the most subtle of ways. She still remembered fondly how he'd been on hand to help her during the storm where she'd gained her control; how he'd stayed up with her, simply talking, for hours afterwards. It was more support than she'd ever had before, and she'd quickly warmed to him.

She wasn't sure what they were, she didn't even know if she was right to even call them a "they". Something haunted Kai, kept him apart from everyone and kept him pushing forward. She'd worried that he'd put himself in front of the danger for everyone on this hunt, taking the brunt of the danger for himself.

Gwen's control allowed her to keep her Witch heritage a secret in the city, an open secret, but enough of one to keep judgment at bay. She'd seen anger, fear, and grief drive her family to spend years trying to master their gifts. She saw that same drive in Kai. She could only hope that it was taking him to a better place than where it took her family.

Thoughts of her family home brought her to the spirit there and, inevitably, back to the forest spirit that she'd connected with.

So much pain, so much raw anguish had poured into her from the spirit; it was a wonder that her mind hadn't snapped under the weight of it all. Those corrupted trees were a visible display of how the Cyth had been slowly destroying the forest. Though Gwen didn't know as much about the Cyth as Verdan, she could sense the way they were slowly withering it away.

It broke Gwen's heart to think of the suffering of the spirit; she only wished that she could help it somehow. Fighting the Cyth wasn't an option, not as she was now anyway.

Memories of lightning rose up in her mind, reminding her of the raw power at her fingertips. Verdan had once told her that weather Witches like her had the most raw power. It was time to really learn how to use that.

-**-

Elliot made sure to keep the door to the forge he was using closed when he was working, the heat would be stifling for a human, but it was nothing to him. He'd spent so long traveling that he'd forgotten how nice it was to have somewhere with a bed, and he didn't want to jeopardize that.

Some folks were fine with Elliot's people, but as they were reviled by most of the sects, such goodwill didn't go far in a city. Well, not a normal one anyway.

Hobson's Point was about as good a place for one of the idrisyr as he would ever find. The only magic-users were friendly and seemed good-hearted folk, eager to protect the city and its people.

Elliot idly reached into the fire with his bare hand and grasped the glowing orange hunk of metal that he was working with. Placing it on the anvil, Elliot took up his hammer and started to rhythmically pound down onto it, shaping the metal with each tremendous blow.

The hot metal was uncomfortably warm to the touch, but Elliot much preferred working with it in this way than any other. It was a reminder of the blood that ran in his veins, of the power of his people. Thinking of his people, Elliot turned his mind once again to his brother and sister.

Elliot had done some work for the locals and earned a bit of coin, which he'd used to send messages to some of the meeting points he had with his siblings. He didn't doubt that they were already searching for him, but he had no better way of getting in touch.

Cullan and Branwen would find him soon, Elliot had no doubt of that, and he knew his siblings well. Branwen would enjoy this new place, but Cullan would be quick to anger and quicker again to seek satisfaction for it. It wouldn't help that when they'd last spoken, it hadn't gone particularly well. Cullan would be in a bad mood from the start.

It had been a long time since Elliot forged for his brother, and sourcing this much good-quality metal in the city had been hard. Hopefully, it would be enough to mollify him.

In some ways, it was a shame that Kai and Tom had dealt with the bears; they would have made a good distraction for Elliot to sic his brother on.

Once the metal was cool enough, Elliot picked it up and placed it back in the flames. He had a lot to do, and he still needed a haft for it. Hopefully, it would be done before his brother found him.

_**_

Shen Garveth maintained a calm and uncaring demeanor as his agent reported the loss of two of their sect to the pitiful excuse of a man, Kai. To make matters worse, one of them had been killed by a city guard, a mortal.

Shen seethed as he rose to his feet and fetched paper and ink. This was an affront to the civilized world as a whole. Mortals should know their place—firmly under the boot of their betters.

The Great Elder understood this, which was why he'd assigned this mission to the Northern Glade Cloister, and Elder Budaev had given Shen the honour of orchestrating their opening moves.

Then, out of nowhere, this 'Wizard' arrived, and with him brought that degenerate Sorcerer and somehow found a Witch that could control her powers.

Verdan was interrupting their plans, and between him, the Witch, and the mortal-loving Kai, Shen and his remaining agents were at a disadvantage.

Shen dipped his quill into the inkpot, and the soft scratching of his quill echoed in the quiet room as he began to fill in his report. Patience was a virtue and a boon when planning the death of another. It was a tenet of their sect.

Shen would bide his time for now and report back to the Elder. No doubt Budaev would come to deal with this personally, and when he did, Shen would be there to watch.

A satisfied smile stretched across Shen's face as he sealed Verdan's fate with each line of his report.

_**_

The Purifier felt its senses return abruptly, the sudden influx of information disorienting it for a moment. The Wizard had been casting a spell of some sort, and then everything had become distorted. It could still feel the lingering effects of the raw energy that the Wizard used.

Carefully surveying the area, the Purifier saw no sign of the unclean ones. They must have fled when they realized the Pure were too numerous and too powerful.

It didn't matter; they had weakened the Host, but there were survivors for the Purifier to call on, and it knew where other Purifiers were hard at work, creating more of the Pure to grow the Host. Their losses would soon be recouped.

The surviving Pure moved to secure the area around their holy site, but the Purifier instead moved to the burnt piece of wood which had once been the Wizard's staff.

The Purifier remembered Wizards from the time before it was Purified. They were powerful magic users, and often became Purifiers themselves when they were brought into the Host.

Flickers of its previous life and glimpses of past memories gathered at the back of the Purifier's mind, but none of them were important. It knew much of the world, and it used that knowledge now to give the Host direction.

The Purifier's gaze rose to the distant forest, the part dense with the world's raw energy. When they finally broke through its defenses, the Purifier would personally refine every last drop and expand the Host to unseen heights.

Such a task would require more Purifiers to work alongside him and a great host to fend off the unclean ones. Such a working would take time. The Purifier had nothing but time, though, and it knew that the Host would win in the end.

The presence of the Wizard and the threat he represented prompted caution. For now, the Purifier would gather its Host and head east to where other Purifiers waited. It would return with a force much larger than this, and claim the forest to then drive them to even greater heights.

Not for the first time, the Purifier felt a pang of regret that its bonded mate from its past life had not been able to join him in the Light of the Host; her aid today would have been invaluable. He looked down at the bone staff in his hand and ran a finger down its length fondly; he was glad he'd been able to at least keep her with him this way.

About the Author

A part-time writer with a love of creating stories with heavy doses of magic and monsters. Native to the UK with a Welsh partner and two needy mastiffs, he has always loved mythology and the fascinating tales that are in every culture.

Follow me on amazon.

If you enjoyed this story please leave a review on Amazon and Goodreads. Reviews mean so much to authors.

For more stories like this one check out the following:

https://www.facebook.com/groups/LitRPG.books

https://www.facebook.com/groups/litrpgforum

https://www.facebook.com/groups/LitRPGReleases

https://www.reddit.com/r/litrpg/

ABOUT ROYAL GUARD PUBLISHING

Royal Guard Publishing was established in 2020 and is audiobook/ebook publisher ran by authors.

We primarily focus on LitRPG, GameLit, Progression Fantasy, Harem Lit and Cultivation Fantasy.

We hope to provide an escape and adventure for our listeners and readers.

We aim to provide a more authentic, transparent and personal experience for our authors.

https://royalguardpublishing.com/

https://www.facebook.com/RoyalGuard2020

Made in the USA
Monee, IL
26 September 2023

43420815R10282